Barbara,
Grateful for your support.
Keep the faith!

Ed Gen

Dear Mr. Hopkins,
Thank you for
supporting foxy.com
Jarzis!

CHINESE BROTHERS, AMERICAN SONS

An Historical Novel

Ed Shew

EARNSHAW BOOKS

Chinese Brothers, American Sons

By Ed Shew

ISBN-13: 978-988-8552-68-9

© 2020 Ed Shew

Images © John Shew

FICTION / Historical

EB129

All rights reserved. No part of this book may be reproduced in material form, by any means, whether graphic, electronic, mechanical or other, including photocopying or information storage, in whole or in part. May not be used to prepare other publications without written permission from the publisher except in the case of brief quotations embodied in critical articles or reviews. For information contact info@earnshawbooks.com

Published by Earnshaw Books Ltd. (Hong Kong)

Note

This is a work of historical fiction. Apart from the well-known people, events, and locales that figure in the narrative, all names, characters, places and incidents are embellishments based upon this author's research and imagination.

This book collects together information and commentary from hundreds of sources. I believe all materials used in any way are covered by fair usage rules, but if anyone wishes to query any passage, please contact me and we will review and if necessary change. All artwork (including the book cover) by my brother, John Shew.

- Ed Shew

*A man of humanity is one who,
in seeking to establish himself,
finds a foothold for others and who,
in desiring attaining himself,
helps others to attain.*

Confucius (551–479 BC)
a Chinese teacher and philosopher

Acknowledgments

Being an American of Chinese ancestry, I had heard a bit about the many Chinese migrants who toiled in perilous conditions to help construct America's first Transcontinental Railroad in the 1860s. But I wanted to find out more. I retired on June 30, 2011 and suddenly had the time, so I decided to write a book to keep busy. I began working on this book on July 1, 2011.

As I researched this railroad-building era, I learned more about the many Chinese who came over during the Gold Rush in the 1850s, and I decided to weave together a story, an historical novel, about two adventurous Chinese brothers who leave their families in China and come to America in 1854 in search of Gold Mountain. I wanted to create a vehicle to explore their hardships and the discrimination they faced, but also to explore their joys and sorrows, their relationship with each other, and their growing love for America even as they faced the constant pull to return to China, to the families they continued to support financially. I investigated what their hopes and dreams might have been, and took them from San Francisco through to the hammering-in of the Golden Spike, the completion of the Transcontinental Railroad in 1869. Throw in a few Chinese food references, some preaching from a Confucian pulpit and a dash of a love story and you have *Chinese Brothers, American Sons*.

As to the Chinese railroad workers, I am grateful to have the chance to give a voice to those whose labor on the Transcontinental Railroad helped to shape the physical and social landscape of the American West. But the story does not end there, as the epilogue reveals.

—Ed Shew, April 1, 2020

To My Wife, JoAnn

The Moon Represents My Heart

The role of the moon in Chinese culture is similar to that of the sun in Western culture, in terms of its importance and value. Western culture uses the sun to tell time, while Chinese use the moon, without which there would be no Lunar New Year. And time is of great importance to us all.

Many people are drawn to the moon's mystery and charm and it is not surprising that this celestial body is the theme of many songs, movies, operas, poems and plays. The moon is often associated with affairs of the heart, and in the classical Chinese tune "The Moon Represents My Heart," it represents deep and faithful love.

The moon also represents my heart. Take a look at the moon. On a moonless night, I cannot see the moon, and yet, I know it is there, somewhere, out there. The moon is changing all the time, from full-moon to half-moon to crescent moon to nothing. Then after several moonless nights, magically, the crescent moon returns and grows to a half-moon and finally becomes full again.

Crescent or full, the moon never fails to trigger in people a sense of infinite wonder. Couples who cannot be together physically can still enjoy the same night sky by watching the moon at the same time, and at that moment, or so it seems, they are together.

The moon mirrors my own feelings; my love is sometimes more obvious than other times.

To My Brother, John

The Chinese Peasant's Lament

Last sight of the village, looking back
I feel my heart cut in two.
I am one.
I am many.
On a watery path
From home to a new world. Why? To send money back.
To fight my family's hunger.
To make them proud.

The Empress does not care for the people.
The foreign Ghosts drain our wealth and power.
They won't leave.
So, I must. Disappearing into the clouds: What is our fate?

Wang Wei

Contents

Prologue. The Standing (mid-19th century — Sept 9, 1854)   1

1. The Coming (September 9, 1854)   11
2. The Arrival (November 9, 1854)   20
3. The Gold Mountain   31
4. The Inhumanity   50
5. The Chinese Food Culture   61
6. The Renewed Search for Gold Mountain   77
7. The Final Opportunity   97
8. The Streets of San Francisco (November 1859-spring 1864)   110
9. The Transcontinental Railroad (from sea to shining sea)   123
10. The Recruitment of the Chinese (February 1865)   135
11. Attacking the Sierra Nevada Mountains   142
12. The Summit Tunnel   151
13. The Strike (June 25, 1867)   172
14. The Summit Tunnel Is Broken (August 28, 1867)   191
15. The Forty-Mile Desert   207
16. The Arrival of Li Wu, Li Yu's son   217
17. The Chinese Strike Back   246
18. The Ten-Mile Day (April 28, 1869)   256
19. The Golden Spike (May 10, 1869)   269

Epilogue 1. The Time Machine   277
Epilogue 2. Back to the Future   289
Author's Note   291
Afterward   293
Bibliography   302

(left to right) Li Yu and Li Chang

Prologue

The Standing

ACCORDING TO an old Chinese proverb, "A journey of a thousand miles begins where you are standing." And so the story of the first wave of Chinese immigration to the United States began not in 19th century America but rather in China, the world that these migrants left behind.

In the mid-19th century, most Chinese, ninety-nine percent of them, lived as peasants in the countryside and served as the nation's raw muscle. Their costumes rarely varied; in south and central China the men wore baggy cotton trousers, sandals of leather or grass, and broad-brimmed, conical hats that protected their faces from the sun. Their lives followed an endless cycle dictated by the seasons. They pushed plows behind water buffalo that broke the soil, prepared the seed beds, and planted rice seedlings by hand in ankle-deep water. Stepping backward, they progressed from row to neat row; scythed the rice stalks at harvest, then threshed them over a hard-earth floor—in short, lives spent, generation after generation, in nonstop and backbreaking labor. This lifestyle developed an unbending spirit which later served them well in America.

The work was mind-numbing, but ingenuity was often evident, as when peasant farmers devised a complex system of irrigation that flooded or drained the fields. They built special equipment, water wheels and water mills that harnessed the forces of nature. In the countryside a peasant pedaled away on a treadmill field pump, as if putting in time on a modern stationary exercise bicycle. Foreigners who visited China in the mid-19th century marveled at the ingenuity of these machines, and at the remarkable economies they produced. Later, these same Chinese peasants adapted this technology to their mining efforts in America.

No group in China worked harder than the peasants. In the typical rural village, people slept on mats on dirt floors; their heads rested on bamboo pillows or wooden stools. They ate a spare but nutritious diet: rice and vegetables, supplemented by fish and fowl, which they cooked over a wok-shaped boiler. An armload of fuel warmed and fed a dozen people. Hardly anything was wasted; even their manure was used as fertilizer in the fields. In times of famine, people ate little more than a bit of rice to sustain them.

Most lived and died and gained little knowledge of life beyond their village. If a peasant traveled, usually only over a dirt road to a nearby market town to purchase or sell goods, he perhaps encountered countrymen bumping along on horseback, by wheelbarrow or on foot. A common sight during his journey was the baggage porter who accompanied a wealthier traveler or merchant with a long pole resting on his shoulders with luggage and measures of wealth dangling. This method of transporting possessions was also used by the Chinese in the gold mining American West and later in providing drinks to the Chinese builders of the Transcontinental Railroad.

Few peasants saw any member of the class who actually ruled their lives, as they mostly lived thousands of miles away. In mid-19th century China, the center of power was the capital city of Beijing—the heart of the empire, in the far north of the country — where a handful of bureaucrats and their civil servants could alter the destinies of its populace with a pen stroke.

Silent monuments to power were everywhere in Beijing. Surrounded by acres of marble, darkened by the shadow of three domes, the Temple of Heaven humbled visitors who looked upon it. But the Forbidden City intimidated even more. The ancient home to generations of emperors and constructed in the 15th century, this city within a city earned its place among the world's great architectural masterpieces.

The Forbidden City was a paradise on Earth. Dragons of marble, lions of bronze, gilded gargoyles carved into balustrades guarded a gigantic maze of palaces and pavilions, gardens and halls. A series of arches stretched from the edges of Beijing to this imperial labyrinth. Everything in this forbidden land, right down to the last courtyard, converged upon the imperial throne. The belief reflected was that the entire world sprang from the royal seat of China and its emperor was the son of heaven, the core of the universe.

The Great Wall of China, the longest structure on Earth, extended across northern China. The Wall - in fact, it is many walls — took many generations to build. Simply, its purpose was to protect China from foreign invasion. For more than 5,000 miles, the disparate lengths of wall wound their snake-like paths, east to west, over mountains and the Mongolian plateau — a massive effort, ultimately unsuccessful, to repel all outsiders.

Chinese rulers — the Ming dynasty — controlled the empire for 300 years, during which time the Great Wall helped keep out the northern invaders. But in 1644, the Manchus, nomads from Manchuria, fought their way through and conquered China.

To enforce their subjugation of the Han Chinese people, the Manchus (who named their reign the Qing dynasty; pronounced as 'ching') ruled that by law all Chinese men must shave the front of their heads and wear long, braided queues, as a sign of their humiliation. To shave off the queue was considered an act of treason.

But the most effective hammer in the Manchu toolbox was the imperial examination system, which used civil service tests as a means to social order and forced all aspiring officials to write essays on ancient Chinese literature and philosophy. Local, provincial and national exams — three tiers — determined entrance into and promotion through the Chinese civil service bureaucracy. While these tests created the illusion of meritocracy, the system was one in which power and prestige were achieved through lineage and not through individual hard work and depth of learning. Still, the examination process itself as well as its subject matter, converged with the Chinese respect for tradition and the Confucian emphasis on education. As can be expected, only certain groups took the tests. Women were entirely excluded. Elite families, with resources to hire tutors, prepared their sons for the examinations, which gave wealthy test-takers an enormous advantage over peasants' sons.

The examination system, in that era at least, had evil consequences in which the Chinese scholars constantly competed against each other for favor with the Manchu rulers. More significantly, the system served as a means of silencing the nation's most ambitious and talented young men. They memorized and mastered the Chinese classics when they might instead have questioned and challenged the system. And then they became agents of the oppressor group.

The very purpose of the hierarchy divorced the most talented from the masses from which they had sprung. Passing the first test transformed a young man into a local magistrate. Exempt from torture, he ascended into a world that severed him from the peasant life. Such men often ruled their districts like dictators. So absolute was his power that a Chinese man once told a Western observer, "I'd rather be a mayor in China than President of the United States."

The coveted places for officials at the center of the system in Beijing went to the select few who passed all the grades of tests. There, the Qing regime organized them further into nine grades, easily identified by garments of flowing silk robes emblazoned with the insignia of their office.

While Beijing emphasized respect for status above all, the people of Canton, the capital of the southern province of Kwangtung, looked out to the world beyond, across the ocean, and were usually more concerned with making money. The richest merchants in the city lived almost like royalty with mansions with inner courtyards and meticulous gardens, a world of carved mahogany furniture and stained-glass lanterns, of private libraries and art collections filled with gold and jade.

But just outside these mansions was terrible poverty. Indeed, the social distance between merchant and coolie, or unskilled laborer, in these coastal cities was almost as great as that between official and peasant in inland China. Nonetheless, the coastal region also supported a class of small entrepreneurs producing handicrafts, handling cargo, and fishing for a living in their floating villages of junks. In the province of Kwangtung, boatmen, peasants, and small merchants mixed in a way that rarely happened inland, providing a spark to the economy.

In the 19th century, China declined as a world power. In fact, China under the Manchus was humiliated by Western powers, newly empowered by the tools created by the Industrial Revolution. The Manchu ruling class created an elite welfare state for themselves, while most Chinese lived in filth, violence and poverty. While the population of China doubled from 1761 until 1846, the Qing dynasty mismanaged state funds and inevitably, overcrowding caused shortages of land, which led to higher rents for peasant farmers, and greater concentrations of wealth among landowners. The land did not produce enough food for the people of China.

Soon, people took matters into their own hands. Farmers chopped down entire forests on mountains near major rivers to create more arable land, stripping the terrain bare. The resulting soil erosion caused floods and in turn brought famine and epidemics. Tens of millions were killed. The foreign imperialists worsened the misery. The West tried to break into the enormous Chinese market, and it was British smugglers who found a way. They sold a dangerous and highly addictive drug called opium which cut a wide swath through every class—socialites seeking release from boredom to coolies wishing to ease the pain of heavy loads. Smoking opium through a pipe or sucking it in tablet form, heavy addicts fell into a near-comatose stupor; they gradually decayed into living skeletons. Demand spiraled and imports soared; the Qing dynasty was drained of its silver. Millions of Chinese wasted away.

The imperial government tried without success to stop the trade and in one case confiscated 20,000 chests of opium (a chest contained 130 to 160 pounds of opium) and dumped it in the sea. The British government's response was to launch a military attack. Provided with a long-awaited excuse to force China to open up, British forces invaded and crushed the Manchu-led forces.

In 1842, the imperial government signed the Treaty of Nanking under which a number of Chinese ports were opened to foreign trade. China agreed to pay massive indemnities and allowed the open importation of opium. The British established concessions at Amoy and Shanghai and turned the rocky island of Hong Kong into a colony. Britain, joined by France and other nations including the United States imposed a system of extraterritorial privilege, in which foreign nationals were not subject to Chinese law anywhere in the empire.

White foreigners swaggered through Chinese port cities like petty dictators. A young American bank teller boasted that if a Chinese man failed to make room for him on the street, he would strike him down with his cane: "Should I break his nose or kill him, the worst that can happen would be that he or his people would make a complaint to the Consul, who might impose the fine of a dollar for the misdemeanor, but I could always prove that I had just cause to beat him."

Unfair treaties with the West also inflicted destruction in the peasant countryside; the Qing government shifted the burden of the indemnities to the peasants by forcing them to pay increased taxes. Already slaves to the land and the landlords, living a hand-to-mouth existence, the peasants were thrown into even deeper debt. Many had to sell all their possessions— their plows, their oxen, even their own children—to pay down the debt. If they could not pay, rent collectors and local officials arrested them, beat them or threw them into jail. Caged like animals, left in filth, dying from disease, prisoners in Chinese jails were the living dead, purposefully forgotten by prison officials, left chained to decay into corpses.

Desperate, many Chinese finally turned to violence. The Taiping Rebellion which started in 1850 was led by a failed scholar Hong Xiuquan who one day on a street in Canton, heard a Christian preacher speak of Jesus Christ. He later fell into a fever and was visited by God who told him he was Jesus' younger brother and that he should found a heavenly kingdom on Earth and expel the Manchus from China. An impassioned speaker, he recruited tens of thousands of peasants and workers. The Taiping troops swept through the country, and while they were eventually crushed by the Manchu government with the help of the British, tens of millions of innocent country people died.

People yearned to escape, escape from famine, and war and the tax collector. But how? Nowhere was the urgency to leave greater than in the province of Kwangtung on the southern coast. With no food and no other options, many Chinese decided to leave China for the dream of Gold Mountain.

Gold Mountain was California. When gold was discovered there in 1848, a Chinese resident in California, one of the fifty Chinese there at the time, shared the news via letter with a friend in Canton. Soon the region hummed with excitement, and people talked of nothing else. If only they could reach Gold Mountain, perhaps all their problems would be solved.

Most people in Kwangtung province had only a dim concept of America. Almost no one had met anyone from America, or any foreigner at all. Their only perception of white people was often the rumors of blue-eyed barbarian missionaries kidnapping and eating Chinese children. But survival and a sense of adventure were stronger than the fear of the unknown.

The promise of gold ignited the imaginations of the poverty-stricken people of southern China. Hope soared among the poor. They decided they could briefly go to Gold Mountain, then return rich enough to ensure a new standard of living for themselves and their families. A handful of gold might be all that was needed to start anew, to purchase some land that would free them from the tyranny of rent, to build a house, to hire tutors for their children so they could pass the imperial examinations and become Mandarins. In short, to achieve the prosperity and status that was denied them solely by their birth as a peasant or "coolie."

Frantically, men in the region of Canton decided to leave.

ED SHEW

They borrowed money from friends and relatives, sold off their water buffalo, or signed with a responsible immigration broker, called a towkay, who paid for their passage in exchange for a share of their future earnings in America. While these brokers were clearly exploitative, they also provided some protection to men eager to migrate but who had no idea of how to protect themselves against the dangers ahead. During a Chinese man's sojourn in America, the broker usually made sure that mail, remittances, and news traveled to his family back home. For those eager men lacking the money, a credit-ticket system was in place. Chinese middlemen typically advanced $40 to $60 in gold, and in exchange the man assumed debt at an interest of about four to eight percent per month. It sometimes took up to five years to repay.

Knowing the young men who left for Gold Mountain might be gone for many months, if not years, the community knew it was important to bond each man to his home village. Most importantly, the purpose of his trip was to earn money to bring back home. Therefore, it was customary to marry him off to a local woman and to encourage him to father a child in the months or even weeks before he left. This step — the creation of a new family — had two purposes: an obligation for him to send back remittances, and a guarantee for him to preserve the ancestral bloodline.

On coming to America, the peasants of Kwangtung province and the city dwellers of Canton were not the passive and defenseless coolies they were often portrayed to be. They were not simpletons tricked by fast-talking labor contractors and "shanghaied" onto the ships against their will. They were mostly adventurers, young men mostly in their teens to mid-20s. And they came to Gold Mountain not in fear and servility, but with the courage and boldness that inspired immigrants from Europe.

CHINESE BROTHERS, AMERICAN SONS

Perhaps more so, for they came from twice as far away.

A Cantonese nursery rhyme of the era expressed the collective longings of entire families:

> Swallows and magpies, flying in glee:
> Greetings for the New Year.
> Daddy has gone to Gold Mountain to earn money.
> He will earn gold and silver, Ten thousand taels.
> When he returns,
> We will build a house and buy farmland.

That at least was the plan. Li Chang and Li Yu certainly had no intention of staying in America.

1

The Coming

Desperate for work, for the opportunity to get rich quick, and for the adventure of their lifetime, Li Chang convinced his young brother Li Yu to go to the new land of America. They left behind their mother Cheung Yee, and Li Yu left behind his new wife Sun Wei and their very soon-to-be born child.

"I am scared," Sun Wei said.

"Wife, don't worry," Li Yu reassured her as he packed. "I'm told the streets are all paved with gold. We will get rich in no time. We'll find the good life. We'll make our big dreams come true. I will send money home, and our family will starve no more."

Patting Sun Wei's growing tummy but avoiding eye contact, he said, "Take care of mother, and of little Li. I have my older brother to watch over me."

Sun Wei was a simple girl, in the beginning almost too shy to look him in the face. He respected her and believed that he loved her. He knew it might be the last time he would see her.

In the morning darkness and amidst driving rain, Li Chang and Li Yu bowed good-bye to their family and boarded an overcrowded ship with hundreds of others. Li Chang was the protective elder brother, aged twenty-six. Li Yu was younger by ten years.

CHINESE BROTHERS, AMERICAN SONS

The ship churned away backward with the wind driving the ocean's waves onto the splintering wharf. Sun Wei's eyes were on Li Yu, her face still and expressionless. The waters were now calm and still. She saw him reaching out his hand, but then he disappeared. All that was left of him was a memory, the memory of a love suddenly cut short. She stayed there, in the rain, scanning the horizon for his ship long after it had disappeared.

"Come back to me," she said.

On the ship, Li Yu's eyes were alive with enthusiasm, but also tinged with guilt.

The date was Saturday, September 9, 1854.

The Pacific Ocean crossing was grueling and hazardous. It took between four and eight weeks from Canton to San Francisco, depending upon weather conditions, sometimes longer if a ship was thrown far off course.

Disease spread quickly among the Chinese living in the close, unsanitary conditions on board the filthy and unventilated ship. Crowded conditions meant more revenue for the shipmaster. Every day the Chinese put corpses on the stairs and the sailors took them away and dumped them into the ocean.

"There will be no rest for their souls," Li Chang said. "They have to be buried in their home soil for that."

For almost the whole trip, Li Chang and Li Yu and their fellow Chinese passengers were locked below deck, a heavy grate put over the sweltering, airless hold. Li Yu fell asleep to the sounds of mice scratching and scurrying all around him.

Initially, the Chinese were fed hard, sour bread and slop consisting of the American sailors' leftovers mixed with salt water. It was lowered down in buckets as though they were pigs in a pen. But still the portions were so small that inevitably fights broke out among the starving Chinese. Eating was made even harder to stomach by the accompanying stink of body odor, human and animal waste and freight. By contrast, the American sailors up-top had potatoes, onions, flour, dried apples, and cranberries in addition to the usual staples of salt beef and pork, bread, rice, and pea soup.

Li Yu opened his eyes. Light filtered and flickered through the slats in the grate that covered the entrance to the ship's hold. The sunlight illuminated the dust particles floating through the air on the ever-swaying ship.

The gate's bar made the hold seem like a prison. Their fresh air was a whiff and stir when crewmen exchanged food buckets for the vomit and shit buckets.

"The Americans could have done a little bit better job washing out the vomit and shit buckets before filling them with food," Li Chang said.

Some men brought their own pigs, which slept under the bottom bunks. The bunks, for those that had them, looked like stacks of coffins in a death house but barely 17 inches above the one underneath—their noses brushed the bunks above. Others slept like cords of wood stacked across the floor.

"Here we are," said Li Chang with a forced smile, "migrating with our pigs our only family."

The aching loneliness that came from homesickness was worsened by the bruising falls and the tearing at their insides each time the ship rocked, tossed them off their bunks and knocked them against the hard sides of the hull.

For fun, the American sailors, their teeth tobacco-stained and their uniforms grimy with food and dirt, led a group of staggering Chinese on deck. The immense, moving sea was terrifying and disorientating. But the fresh air felt good.

Then Captain Henry Smithers said in broken Chinese, "Take your clothes off."

CHINESE BROTHERS, AMERICAN SONS

The sailors ripped the clothes off the ones who were too slow. They wiped their hands afterward as if they had touched filth. Then other sailors picked up a long serpent-like hose and aimed it at the Chinese. Li Yu barely took a deep breath before the blast of bitterly cold, salt water stung them and numbed their skin. At least it removed the smell of urine and excrement that had accumulated during their weeks at sea. The rest of the crew gathered around and made fun of them, pointing and laughing. The Chinese were hardly human to the crew.

But every day, Li Chang could hear American sailors getting flogged on deck.

Li Yu could write and he made some small money writing letters for the other passengers. Almost all of them were ill; the vomit buckets were overflowing.

The brothers met Wong Sun, who owned three fields, so his family had sold one to cover the costs for his trip. Wong Sun was coughing as he dictated a letter to his wife through Li Yu.

> I'm not going to get to Gold Mountain. But I can keep one small promise. I am enclosing with this letter a red scarf for your hair. I bought it in Canton. I cannot keep my other promises, but I'll make up for it in another life. We will meet again. I miss everything about home. I miss waking up every morning and listening to you start the fire in the stove. I miss tickling our daughter and hearing her laugh. I miss the wind rippling through the rice fields. I miss walking with you up to the cemetery to visit our oldest son.

"You're not going to die, a tough man like you," Li Yu said. "I'll write this letter, but you can give it to your wife yourself when you go home. Then you can both have a good laugh."

Li Yu saw that writing had its own power. It was like magic to an illiterate peasant like Wong Sun. Wong Sun said his oldest boy would be Li Yu's age if he had lived.

The comment spooked Li Yu. Various possible futures raced through his mind: walking the plank, drowning, growing old in jail, being thrown overboard in chains, being flogged to death, hung by the neck, his body returned to China. Because of fear he did not eat or feel hungry. His bowels felt loose and his bladder full, but he squeezed shut his asshole, not wanting to use the chamber pot. He slept and woke and slept again, and time seemed long and forever.

Li Chang encouraged his younger brother. "When we get to Gold Mountain, all will be better, you'll see. Try to eat, stay strong so we can find lots of gold and get rich and buy land back home."

After weeks at sea, they went topside again, the ocean occasionally flicking cold spit into their faces. Rocking and dozing, they felt the ocean's shifts. The peaked waves that looked like pine trees, the rolling waves, round like shrubs, the occasional icy mountain; and for stretches, green like grass.

"My hunger is all I can feel or think about," Li Yu said. "It's like a slithering snake around my head, sliding down my mouth into my stomach, out to my fingertips, then down my legs to my toes and back up to my brain. It never ends."

Li Chang didn't hear the scratching of mice or rats in the rafters and walls any more. They had all been eaten.

One dark, dreary day, while topside, Li Yu's somewhat gaunt face cracked a bright smile. His fellow Cantonese acted as if they had never seen a woman before in their lives. Amidst the whistles, humming and singing, Li Yu observed four young girls, about his age or younger. He had previously seen only men on the cramped, filthy ship. To his surprise, the girls were wearing clean, well-fitting clothes. Their faces were full, indicating they had not been starving.

One was about his height, with long black hair (not in a bun like the other girls), large eyes, and an oval face with high cheekbones. Her silky white skin stood out even more, as she wore a black cheongsam. With a bowed head, she glanced up and their eyes met. He instantly felt weak. She nodded and smiled shyly to him, and then she disappeared, with small steps, into a sailor's cabin on the other side of the ship.

Li Yu turned to Li Chang. "Why is she, why are they treated better than us?" he asked.

"They are young girls with marriage contracts to wealthy Americans or maybe sold as prostitutes to high-class brothels," Li Chang explained. "Who would pay a lot of money for a dirty, skinny woman?"

With Li Yu and most of the Chinese getting weaker every day, Li Chang finally approached Captain Smithers. He proposed that he cook food for the American sailors to improve their morale. In exchange, Li Chang requested the Chinese be given two daily meals of rice with bacon drippings and every other day to allow the Chinese to go on deck for two hours.

"You've already lost too much freight," Li Chang said through an interpreter.

"I don't care about losing you damned Chinese," Smithers shot back. "But I am wasting too much time flogging the crew over their dissatisfaction with the food. Go ahead, see if you can do better."

Smithers agreed to Li Chang's proposal and the fresh air and eating their familiar rice renewed the spirits of the Chinese. But Li Yu never got used to the movement of the ocean waves. To help pass time, he and Li Chang fished by tying pieces of rags to hooks and tossed the line over the ship's railing.

During the steel-cold nights, Li Yu tried to stay warm by drinking hot tea. Visions came to him, dreams of his wife, Sun Wei, being tortured. Devils cut her up into pieces, starting with her toes. He heard her scream; he heard her bones crack. He reminded himself it was an illusion. He had only known her for nine months before he left for Gold Mountain, but he missed her. He knew foremost that he needed to provide for her and their unborn child.

Then Li Yu dreamed of his own body being tortured. Devils poured molten bronze down his throat; demons beat him with clubs and iron chains. They mortar-and-pestled and packed him into a pill. After walking over mountains of knives and through fields of swords, he was killed. His head was chopped off, rolling into other people's nightmares. Gods and goddesses talked about him: "This man is too wicked to be reborn a man. Let him be born a woman."

Li Yu wondered if he had made a mistake setting off for Gold Mountain.

Even big brother Li Chang had his moments during the lonely nights on board the ship. Did he regret the decision? Leaving China was hard. Traditional Chinese revered their ancestors to a degree unheard of elsewhere; a primary obligation of family life was to tend the shrine of the family dead. "How can I honor my ancestors in America?" he asked himself. This duty tied Chinese to the place of their birth—that is, the place of their ancestors' death. Migration, especially across a wide ocean, prevented him from fulfilling this essential duty. But Li Chang was confident his reasons were compelling enough.

Also, he wondered how they would survive. Could he set aside very real fears and focus on the future? What would be in store? Would San Francisco be what he hoped or a disappointment? And the Americans, what would they be like? "Would Americans welcome the Chinese as the poster said or will they try to dupe me or worse, kill me? What kind of mess have I gotten Li Yu into?" Li Chang wondered.

One morning, when Li Yu woke up, he found his diary and writing brushes were gone. So was a string of a hundred cash that his mother had given him. He'd lost his links to home. And Li Chang was nowhere to be found. Li Yu had lost his family again.

He wanted to complain to the ship's clerk. But Chen Hu, also known as One-Eye, just told him to save his breath. "We are not even human to the clerk. They ship us here. They ship us there."

Li Yu curled up in a little ball and shut his eyes. The next thing he knew, One-Eye was shaking his shoulder. There was a bruise on his cheek. He had his brush and his diary. But the money was gone.

One-Eye said to write it off as a fee for a lesson. Li Yu asked him what the lesson was. "Don't trust anyone," One-Eye told him.

Li Chang shook his head disapprovingly. "No," he said. "The best way to find out if you can trust somebody is to trust them."

"Back in your village, the clan takes care of one another," One-Eye replied. "In America, it's every man for himself. And it's cheap at that price. Some pay with their lives." In the last week, Li Chang exchanged the writing of a half-dozen letters by Li Yu for a couple of the pigs still alive. He butchered the hogs. He fried pork chops and potatoes with onions for Captain Smithers and the American sailors. For good measure, he also fried some fish caught by Li Yu. Using the dried apples and cranberries, he made a bread pudding.

"No need to flog us anymore, Captain," one sailor said. "Can the Chinaman cook stay on after we get to San Francisco?"

On Thursday, November 9, 1854, the *Libertad* arrived in San Francisco after 61 days at sea with 180 Chinese aboard — one-fifth of all those who had set out from Canton, China. The rest had all died from fever or scurvy. The slightly-built Li Chang, a philosopher and peasant turned cook, and his younger brother, the now somewhat gaunt but still muscular Li Yu, a peasant and would-be writer and poet, were among the lucky ones to survive. Or were they?

Li Yu was now excited. "This is the land of opportunity!" he exclaimed as he stared out at the new world.

The Chinese had heard stories of glittering wealth — all they had to do was walk around and pick the nuggets of gold up from the ground.

As Li Chang and Li Yu were about to set foot on American soil, they heard a voice in clear English addressing them.

"You take care, y'hear," Captain Smithers said.

But there was no welcome to California, the land called Gum Shan or Gold Mountain. For the Chinese who survived the harsh trek across the Pacific, perhaps a greater threat came not from the severity of nature, but from the cruelty of fellow humans and the racism native to Gold Mountain.

Li Yu followed Li Chang as most of the Chinese scattered and headed for the gold fields.

"Stay close," Li Chang whispered.

2

The Arrival

At last freed from the hold of the ship, its lanterns pitching and swaying.

"Breathe in; breathe out," exclaimed Li Chang to Li Yu. Fresh air, free from the stale and stinking un-washed bodies pressed against them. The air, finally, reeked not of vomit and human waste. There was life and excitement in the shouting, joyful expectation of the rush to Gold Mountain.

Was there gold everywhere? On the streets, in the hills, mountains, rivers and valleys? Gold just waiting to be picked up? Li Yu was still full of hope.

"Gold will make us rich," Li Yu whispered to his brother. "So rich that no one, not even Old Man Yang, will dare speak against us when we go home."

Hugging himself inwardly, he pictured his pregnant wife's and his hoped-for son's faces when he gave his wife the gold that made him the richest man in the village. He could see the pride she had in him. And he held fast to this image, like a charm.

Li Chang recalled with fondness growing up in China, his parents, dirt-poor farmers. "Weed soup again today," was the cry. They were not even able to afford to eat the rice saved from the last crop. They had to use that for their taxes. So their mother Cheung Yee, gathered corn stalks, corn roots, dried sweet potato leaves and wild grasses from the fields and boiled them for soup. They were bitter and horrible, but mother said it fooled their bellies. Li Chang's didn't stay tricked for long, though. It grumbled and growled the moment he set his bowl down.

But he remarked to Li Yu, "If you put some ginger and green onions in the soup, it doesn't taste too bad."

A cook was born.

Somewhat weak from lack of nourishing food and exercise, Li Yu still felt as if the boat was pitching and rolling beneath his feet. But he walked briskly with his brother's aid, speeding past heaps of crated produce, sacks of flour and beans, and stacks of barrels. Above, he heard the screech of seagulls, and beyond the wharf, the clip clop of horses' hooves, the creak and rattle of wagons, voices deep and shrill. But he saw no further than his brother's back, for the same thick fog which shrouded Gold Mountain when they disembarked still enveloped them, its cold dampness penetrating, leaving a salty taste of tears. Li Yu swallowed his disappointment. He would see the mountains soon enough. Meanwhile, he looked for nuggets the men had said indented the street.

Beneath the sickly glow of street lamps, he saw horse droppings, rats feasting on piles of garbage, rags, and broken bottles. Metal glittered. A discarded can or gold? Stooping to grab it, Li Yu did not see the rock until it stung his cheek. Through the heavy mist, Li Yu made out white shadows, white boys hurling stones and mud. They yelled words he did not understand, but still felt.

What really bothered Li Yu was the mocking tone and high pitch by which they yelled "Chinese" at him—and the squinty faces they made using their fingers. It made him feel like less a person just because he was Chinese.

But with Li Chang's encouragement, Li Yu picked up the stones that landed nearest to him and flung them back at the boys as fast as they threw them. Years of hurling stones with his cousins out in the rice paddies of China made Li Yu's aim excellent, and the boys soon fled.

"Don't pick a fight every time someone calls you a name," Li Chang said to Li Yu. "But keep your head up, and be proud of who you are. Don't shoot a rude comment back at the person putting you down. Be the better person. Be strong and ignore it."

Pushing and shoving, they hurried themselves up the foul-smelling streets, most of them un-cobbled and un-guttered, past wagons pulled by draft horses and unwashed white men loafing on upturned barrels, until they reached a narrow street crowded with Chinese men. The scents of coal smoke, roast duck and ginger smelled like Canton, disguising the smell of open street sewers and reeking canals. Chinatown! The warm familiar smells and sounds soothed their confusion. They were in America, the Gold Mountain. And soon, just as soon as they had gathered enough gold, they would go home.

After a meal of all the rice and dried fish they could eat, Li Yu went exploring without Li Chang, who had disappeared.

Li Yu peered through a dusty, half-broken window in an alley. He looked down, and he saw a group of young Chinese girls. Most were too young to be called women. They were being herded down a flight of stairs into a large basement room with more young women and girls about the same age as Li Yu's wife in China.

"Those with contracts come over to this side," an old woman in black lacquer pants and jacket directed. "Those without go stand on the platform."

A girl named Wang Wei held out her papers.

"Oh my, she is the same girl on our ship, and she has the same given name as my wife," Li Yu said to himself, as the old woman took the papers. She pushed Wang Wei in the direction of the women without contracts.

"No, I belong over there," Wang Wei pleaded, trying to take back the papers.

The old woman snorted. "What a bumpkin you are! Those papers were just to get you into this country. Now don't argue, girl, you're one of the lucky ones." She pointed to the group of women with contracts. "Their fates have been decided, it's prostitution for them, but if you play your cards right, you may still get the bridal chair."

A shocked murmur rippled through the group of women. One of them took a piece of paper from an inner pocket. "I have a marriage contract," she said. "Not what you suggest."

"And me! And me!" the women around her echoed.

The old woman took the contract from the young woman. The paper crackled as she spread it open. "Read it!" she ordered.

The young woman's lips quivered. "I can't."

The old woman jangled the ring of keys at her waist. "Does anyone here read?"

The women looked hopefully at each other. Some shook their heads. Others were simply silent. None could read.

"Then I'll tell you what your contracts say." Without looking at any of the papers, the old woman continued, "For the sum of your passage money, you have promised the use of your bodies for prostitution."

"But the marriage broker gave my parents the passage money," the young woman persisted.

"You fool, that was a procurer, not a marriage broker!" She pointed to the thumb print at the bottom of the paper. "Is that your mark?"

Sobbing quietly, the young woman nodded.

CHINESE BROTHERS, AMERICAN SONS

"Well then, there's nothing more to be said, is there?" the old woman asked.

"Yes there is," a girl said boldly. "I put my mark on one of those contracts, and I knew what it was for." Her face reddened. "I had to," she added.

"So?" the old woman, hand on hips, prompted.

"The contract specifies the number of years, five in my case. So take heart sisters, our shame will not last forever," the girl said.

"What about sick days?" the old woman asked.

"What do you mean?" the girl asked.

"The contract states your monthly sick days will be counted against your time: two weeks for one sick day, another month for each additional sick day," the old woman said.

"But that means I'll never be free!" the girl said in anguish.

"Exactly," the old woman shot back. Like a stone dropped in a pond, the word started wave after wave of talk and tears. "Keep crying like that," the old woman shouted, "and by the time your owners come to get you, your eyes will be swollen like toads."

"What difference does it make?" a voice challenged.

"Depending on your looks, you can be placed in an elegant house and dressed in silks and jewels or in a chicken house," the old woman declared.

"Chicken house?" asked the girl.

"On your way here you must have seen the doors with the barred windows facing the alleys, but perhaps you did not hear the chickens inside, tapping and scratching the screens, trying to attract a man without bringing a cop. Cry, make yourself ugly, and you'll be one of those chickens," the old woman said stifling a laugh. The life of a Chinese prostitute was horrible; they were often mistreated by their owners and customers and most died of the harsh physical treatment within five years.

Slowly the sobs became muted sniffles and whimpers as stronger women hushed the weaker.

The old woman turned to Wang Wei's group. "Now get on the platform like I told you."

Silently, Wang Wei and the other women and girls obeyed. When they were all on the platform, the old woman spoke.

"This is where you'll stand tomorrow when the men come," she said. "There'll be merchants, miners, well-to-do peddlers, brothel owners, and they'll examine you for soundness and beauty. Do yourself up right, smile sweetly, and the bids will come in thick and fast from those looking for wives as well as those looking to fill a house. When the price is agreed on, the buyer will place the money in your hand, that will make the sale binding, but you will turn the money over to me. Do you understand?"

The women and girls nodded. A few murmured defeat. The old woman pointed to some buckets against the wall. "There's soap and water. Wash thoroughly. You will be stripped for auction."

"Stripped?" some of the women and young girls cried out. Most Chinese women were very private, never exposing themselves publicly and rarely naked even before their husbands.

"Women in the Gold Mountain are scarcer than hen's teeth and even a plain or ugly girl has value. But when a man has to pay for a woman, he likes to see exactly what he is buying," the old woman said. She grabbed a tight-lipped, thin, dark woman from the back of the group. The girl stared defiantly as the old woman ripped off her jacket and pointed out scars from a deep hatchet wound, puckered flesh in the shape of a hot iron. "Look carefully and be warned against any thought of disobedience or escape."

She threw the girl's jacket onto the floor. "It will be the chicken house for you, if you're lucky." She pulled the woman closest to her down from the platform and then herded them all toward the buckets of water. "Now get going, we've wasted time enough."

All around her, Wang Wei heard the sounds of the women and girls preparing themselves for auction. But she made no move to join them. She had been duped, she realized, by the soft-voiced madam, by the talk of freemen whose dreams were never to be hers. The Gold Mountain they had described, she realized, was not the America she would know. This, the dingy basement room, the blank faces of women and girls stripped of hope, the splintered boards beneath her feet, the auction block. This was her America.

Through a haze as chilling as the fog that had surrounded her at the wharf, Wang Wei was aware of a warm breath, an anxious nudging. It was the thin, dark girl the old woman had exposed as a warning.

"Didn't you hear what the old woman said? You're one of the lucky ones."

"Lucky. The madam in Canton said that, too," Wang Wei said.

Generally, the "fortunate" women were sold to well-to-do Chinese as concubines or mistresses. A small number were recruited to high-class establishments where they were patronized by a relatively stable client or clients. While they seemed to be well-treated, they could be sold at their master's will.

In the mining camps, conditions were more primitive and frightening than in urban brothels, and prostitutes faced a worse fate. These women were often called "Chiney ladies," "moon-eyed pinch foots," and "she-heathens" by their white customers. In the isolated mining areas, Chinese prostitutes were prone to being the victims of Chinese crime. They might be kidnapped by rival tongs – the criminal gangs who controlled Chinatown in

San Francisco. Some escaped by running away or by committing suicide.

"But it's true," the dark girl said. "There are women far worse off than you. Many are dead long even before the ship gets to Gold Mountain. But you made the journey with papers. You're thin, but beautiful and sound."

"What does that change except my price?" Wang Wei asked.

The girl took Wang Wei's hands in hers, held them tight and quieted their trembling. "You must learn as I have to let your mind take flight. If you don't feel, then nothing anyone does can hurt you."

Wang Wei looked up at the window and her eyes met Li Yu's. Li Yu felt something click, like a key turning in a lock.

Love at first sight? There was something there, something recognizably real, and he couldn't look away. He knew his heart would never be the same. Wang Wei smiled within her grief. She knew he didn't know what to do.

Li Yu tiptoed through the foul-smelling, dark alley to another broken window in back of the raised platform on which Wang Wei stood. He gingerly tapped on the glass and motioned her to come towards him. She put her fingertips of her right hand through the jagged glass, touching the fingertips of his left hand. Their anguished eyes met.

"Help me. I'm going to be sold tomorrow," she whispered.

But then Li Chang reappeared out of nowhere. Only five-foot or so but with muscular arms and strong as an ox, Li Chang twisted Li Yu's left arm behind his back and held him.

"Not now, later. Besides, you're married. Let it go. If it is meant to be, she will come to you," Li Chang said to his brother.

"I will find you, I will buy you back," Li Yu cried out, as he stuck his right hand through the broken glass for one last touch. But Wang Wei had already bowed her head in silence and turned

CHINESE BROTHERS, AMERICAN SONS

away, and the other girls now frantically pushed her aside... clamoring for attention.

As for the Li brothers, they would not see another woman for over six months.

San Francisco was a big stew of people. Every country in the world dumped someone into the pot. Two things worried Li Yu. Even if the Gold Mountain was pure gold, was there really enough gold for all the miners he saw? Almost all of them were armed with at least a pistol and knife, too. Why did they need so much protection? From what? Li Yu and his brother soon found out.

Li Chang, attempting to calm Li Yu's fears, reminded Li Yu, "We left China on September 9th and arrived in America on November 9th, and nine is a lucky number for us Chinese. It means longevity, happiness and good luck."

A Chinese clerk came by and offered Li Yu a job; he'd heard that Li Yu could write. So many Chinese came in every day that the Chinese Benevolent Association headquarters was buried in paperwork. Li Yu told him that he and his brother were here to mine for gold — the nuggets as big as melons. The clerk just sighed. "When you learn your lesson, and if you survive, there will be a job waiting for you," he said.

Li Yu had this funny feeling in his stomach again. "Why would anyone sit cooped up in a tiny office if there are such big nuggets to be scooped?" Maybe it wasn't as easy as they had heard.

Waiting to get some provisions, Li Yu bumped into a boy. Well, a young man like him, but with hair the color of fire. Through signs, they learned each other's names. It took a while to figure out his name, because his name was in reverse. In China, the family name was the most important thing, so they put the family name first and the given name second. Americans thought the opposite, because they put the given names first and their family names last. Strange. The boy's given name was Jimmy and his family name was Smits.

Sign language got them only so far, so then Smits took out what Li Yu thought was a stick. It ended in a point with some black stuff. He said it was a pencil. He was able to write on some paper without a brush and ink. Then through pictures and signs, Li Yu learned that Smits came from Ohio, many miles east of San Francisco and across many mountains and rivers.

Li Yu admired the pencil so much that Smits gave it to him. Li Yu tried not to take it, but Smits insisted. His new friend's heart was big. Li Yu wrote with the pencil. No more inkwells, no more ink sticks, and no more need to find water.

A group of white men just came over to them and hollered, "What's it like to be a Chink lover?"

"I don't know. What's it like being a redneck piece of shit?" Smits yelled.

"You are damned," a toothless white miner said.

"Alright then, we'll go to hell!" Smits shot back.

Li Yu did not understand why they were so mad at Smits. Smits explained they didn't like him being friendly to Chinese. In fact, many Americans didn't like foreigners. They wanted all foreigners to go home.

"But as long as there are enough Americans like Jimmy, don't be afraid, little brother," Li Chang said.

Secretly, Li Yu started writing, with his new pencil, a letter to Wang Wei (care of Chinese Benevolent Association, San Francisco):

Wang Wei,
    Our eyes met in that basement. I felt so helpless. My

brother pulled me away before I could help you. I will remember you. Will you remember me? I don't know where you are, but I hope this letter finds you very well. My brother and I are going to search for gold to make us rich. Last night I couldn't sleep at all. I can't stop thinking about you. I hope that somewhere you are thinking of me, too. There's nowhere in the world I'd rather be than to be with you. Sometime, somewhere, our paths will cross again. Remember to take a look at the moon. For it's written in the moonlight that we will be together.
Trust me.

Li Yu
c/o Chinese Benevolent Assn/San Francisco,
CA November 10, 1854

Li Yu gave the letter to the clerk. "Don't tell my brother," he whispered with some guilt. "Please help me find her. You're my only hope."

Before they headed optimistically to find Gold Mountain, Li Chang and Li Yu were told by the storekeeper that they needed warm coats and boots. When they asked the price, they were shocked. Li Chang said the coats cost too much. The clerk said they'd be sorry. Li Chang got the boots, at least, and their mining provisions.

3

The Gold Mountain

Li Chang and Li Yu shivered and coughed most of the time. "Our cotton clothes are meant for southern China," Li Chang admitted. "But at least, we have our boots."

Nevertheless, they began their search for gold. Like most of the Chinese who arrived in San Francisco, they headed for the gold fields where perhaps a fifth of the miners were from China. In the midst of a broken country, parched and dried by the hot sun, sparsely wooded with live oaks and straggling pines, was the valley of the American River, a still-bold mountain stream flowing out of the snowy mountains. The blue skies to the east gave a false sense of security.

Li Chang and Li Yu walked to the mining areas, since horses were reserved for the white miners. Sometimes long lines of Chinese on foot were seen on the road. Li Chang and Li Yu made their way through mountain passes, each carrying a huge load. They had an astonishing ability to balance heavy burdens — sacks of rice, tins of tea, two large rolls of blankets, two hogsheads, several mining tools, a wheelbarrow and a hand-rocker all swinging from each end of their back-poles. It was a mystery to the white miners how they managed to tote those weary loads so gracefully and not make a sound. But it came naturally to peasants from southern China.

In this valley was a flat gravel riverbed which in high water was an island, or was overflown. But at the time of their visit, it was simply a level gravel-bed. On its edges, men dug and filled buckets with the finer earth and gravel, which they carried to a machine made like a baby's cradle, open at the foot, and at the head a plate of sheet-iron or zinc, punctured full of holes.

The cradle was violently rocked back and forth by a handle, allowing muddy sand to pass out through a sieve at one end, leaving any gold behind. On the bottom were nailed cleats of wood. With this crude machine, four men could earn from $40 to $100 a day, averaging $16, or a gold ounce, per man per day.

Another item Li Chang and Li Yu saw was the "long tom," essentially a huge rocker, up to fifteen feet long, with water fed into it through a flume at the top. Later, sluice boxes — long wooden troughs with step-like slats or "riffle" bars — became a popular sight. Water ran through the sluice while river rock and sand were shoveled in at the top; the water rushed down, leaving particles of gold collected on the riffle bars.

The labor was backbreaking, frustrating and often unrewarding. In those early years, placer gold could be found in rivers and creeks where it was washed loose from deeper deposits and bedrock. Miners with pans scooped sand and gravel from the stream bed, swirled and flushed the water in a circular motion that left any heavy particles of gold at the bottom of the pan.

While the sun blazed down on the heads of Li Chang and Li Yu, each with a conical hat kept on their head by a silk chin strap, the water was bitter cold, and their hands were in the water and their clothes were wet all the time. But they had only just started the search for Gold Mountain — there were no complaints from them of soreness or coldness.

Ice had already formed on the edges of the creek. A nearby

Chinese miner said, "I cannot make my body go into the water again. 'One, two, three, go!' — but my body refuses. So, it just isn't worth it, anymore! We find a dollar or two in gold dust but spend more than that on rice. I'm giving up; it's useless." He walked over and tugged on his partner's shoulder and asked him if he was ready to go back to China. They were tired and hungry.

"You're tough guys, as we are," Li Chang told them. "Join us for some tea."

Li Chang and Li Yu made their camp on a small knoll, a little below the island, and from it they overlooked a busy scene. Now invigorated in body and spirit, those same Chinese miners nearby worked past sunset.

A dozen rough-hewn, wooden huts nearby served as stores and boarding houses. Food and supplies were scarce and prices exorbitant. Little stores selling flour, bacon, coffee, and the like opened and closed as the miners moved. Many things were a dollar a pound and a meal cost $3. Fortunes were made in these small businesses, usually owned by former miners. Eggs sold for a dollar apiece, butter for $6, a pair of boots for a $100. Anticipating the needs of miners for rugged wear, Levi Strauss made pants out of denim tent canvas and created an empire.

The Chinese-owned store was like other stores in the mining areas, containing a hodge podge of provisions and clothing, but everything in it was Chinese except the boots. These were the only articles of Western costume which the Chinese adopted, and most Chinese wore boots of an enormous size, on a scale commensurate with the ample size of their other garments.

Few of the Chinese miners paid for a bed; most, like the Li brothers, slept on the ground, with pine-leaves and blankets for bedding — without fear of cold or rain. Some slept in primitive tents, brush huts, abandoned cabins or shacks hastily slapped together from scrap lumber and flattened kerosene cans.

Li Chang and Li Yu observed that the Chinese gold miners, not surprisingly, tended to stay with their own kind, even if it meant that twenty to thirty men had to cram themselves into a space hardly large enough for a couple to breath.

In the gold camps, log cabins and tents clustered precariously on the steep slopes of rivers and ravines. Most of the towns were below the snow line, but the winters were wet, muddy and bitterly cold; snow flurries, ice and hail were not uncommon. Summers were dry, dusty and hot; temperatures often reached 100 degrees. Most miners worked and lived together in small companies, often made up of their traveling companions from home.

Without women, most miners were forced for the first time to perform all domestic chores for themselves: cooking, washing, housekeeping, and sewing repairs in their tattered clothing. Chinese men saw an opportunity in these economic activities deemed undesirable by white men. Setting up makeshift restaurants to sell hot cooked food, taking care of children, and doing laundry — all services that were traditionally considered women's work — these occupations created a stereotype of the Chinese as servile that would persist long into the future. Li Chang already envisioned his talent in cooking as a way to supplement, if necessary, their earnings from panning for gold.

The mining life, hard as it was, promised rewards. They were hoping that $200 or $300 could be amassed — enough by the standards of Kwangtung for a return home and a luxury retirement. Until that happy time, which mostly did not occur for any of the immigrants of any color, there were only the diversions of gambling, prostitution, and opium, and establishments offering these entertainments sprang up in the Chinatowns of San Francisco, Sacramento, Stockton, Maryville, and in the smaller mountainside encampments beneath roofs of canvas.

The next day, Li Chang and Li Yu crossed the American River to its north side and visited small camps of men in what were called the "dry diggings" or camps that had no water. The miners were "coyoting," digging small holes, or using flumes to bring in water from a distance to wash the dirt. Or they did "winnowing," in which sand and gravel were placed on a blanket, then tossed in the air and caught again, to separate gold from dirt.

Now a week had passed since they had arrived. They took a puppy they found, a chihuahua poodle mix, called him Rosco and ascended into the Sierra Mountains. Towards evening, they made camp and the next morning it was clear and cold. Li Chang and Li Yu never forgot that morning.

Li Yu, waking early, walked along the stream, and his eyes caught a glimpse of something shining in the bottom of a ditch with about a foot of water running in it. He reached his hand down and picked it up; it made his heart thump, for he was certain it was gold. The piece was about half the size of the shape of a pea. Then he saw another piece in the water. After taking it out, he sat down and began to think real hard. He thought it was gold, and yet it did not seem to be the right color. It seemed more like brass. Suddenly the idea flashed across his mind that it might be iron pyrites. He trembled to think of it! This question was answered soon. Putting one of the pieces on a hard river stone, he took another and hammered it. It was soft and didn't break. It therefore must be gold, but largely mixed with some other metal, very likely silver; for pure gold, he thought, had a brighter color.

When Li Yu returned to their camp for breakfast, he showed the two pieces to his brother Li Chang. Li Yu was so excited.

But was it really gold? Li Chang had heard that gold did not glitter, it shone. Sometimes it was bright; sometimes it was dull, but very seldom did it glitter. Was it fool's gold, which tends to be glittery in appearance because of its crystalline structure? Li Chang took the sample and turned it in his hand in the sunlight. If it was gold, the metal shone regularly as the specimen was turned. The specimen passed Li Chang's first test.

And there was the second test, hardness, which Li Yu performed down in the stream. He used the sharp edge of a knife and pressed in on the specimen in a place which was less visible, and an indentation was made into the metal with the blade of his knife.

"Yes, it is gold!" screamed Li Chang.

Li Chang and Li Yu went back to that same stream, and they kept a sharp lookout. And in the course of three or four days, they picked up about three ounces.

Li Yu wrote his first letter to Sun Wei, his wife, from Gold Mountain:

> We are eating well; soon we'll be sending money. Yes, it is a magical country. We are happy, not at all frightened. The Beautiful Nation is glorious, exactly the way we heard it to be. I'll be seeing you in no time. Today, we ate duck with buns and plum sauce.

Li Yu lied; they ate only rice and drank only hot tea. But Li Chang and Li Yu were happy. Li Chang learned the fine art of handling the pick and spade, and he taught his brother. Li Yu worked with his little pick, which he used about as well as a monkey. After working by stops and starts for some two hours, he threw out about a bushel of dirt without seeing any gold. Disheartened, he threw down his tools. They walked on and came up to where a dozen or so other Chinese were enjoying the rich sight of a few nuggets.

Li Chang, thus encouraged by the sight, swung his piglet to his back and told Li Yu, "Work harder! Gold Mountain will come to us."

It was now getting colder. Snow! When Li Yu first saw it, he thought, "Why are feathers falling from the sky?" Li Yu looked up at the flakes whirling by. They came from the heavens, cold and wet, a complete surprise. Li Chang had seen snowfalls in northern China, where he had done his cooking apprenticeship. Li Yu tried to catch them in his palms, but the little dots melted as soon as they touched his skin.

Li Chang sternly berated has brother. "What kind of Chinese wastes something to eat?" He tilted back his head and opened his mouth, looking like a little bird begging for food.

Li Yu copied him. The snowflakes melted on his tongue. So that was what the sky tasted like. Cold. Sweet. Suddenly, something smacked his head, something cold and wet which knocked off his hat. Bending to pick it up made his backside a target. He straightened up, and saw something large and white coming toward him until it struck him in the face. Li Chang laughed. He spread his arms and invited Li Yu to join him. Li Yu scooped up some snow and flung it; it flew barely three feet from his hand.

"You have to pack it first, little brother," Li Chang said. By that time, snowballs were flying every which way. Li Yu was feeling warm again from all the exertion, and it was a pleasant diversion from his dashed Gold Mountain dreams.

Months passed. The Chinese miners, including Li Chang and Li Yu, worked purposefully, but often came up empty-handed. Li Yu threw down his mining tools and flopped on the ground with his face to the ground.

"Hello, down there in China! Is anybody listening? Because I'm crying," Li Yu shouted. "Hello, mother. Hello, my wife. I miss you. What are you doing right now? Happy birthday. I've been working hard for you, and I hate it."

Li Yu whispered to himself with tears rolling down his face, "Sometimes, I forget my family and wish to go to other women. I want to drink all night. Maybe I should start gambling. I don't even look Chinese anymore. I'm coming home. I'm not coming home. I want to be home," Li Yu said.

Li Chang also had days when he doubted why they had come to America. Sure, it was about searching for gold, but also for the adventure and to get away from the violence and poverty of China.

"Li Yu, do not pray for an easy life, pray for a difficult one with the strength to endure it," he said.

Then, finally, gold! Li Yu wrote to his wife Sun Wei:

> I have found a wondrous country, really gold, and I have gotten two bags of it, one of which I have made into a ring. I will send it to you soon.

Eight months later, Li Yu received a reply from Sun Wei.

> I have received the ring and will give it to our son Li Wu. That ring on his finger proves that the Gold Mountain exists and that you, my husband, are there and doing well for us. Your mother says return home soon. We know Li Chang is watching over you.

Still, on other occasions Li Yu yelled out, "I want home!" as he pressed against the soil, and smelled the earth. "I want my home. I want home. Home. Home. Home. Home."

ED SHEW

While Li Yu thought of his wife Sun Wei and his son Li Wu, he still asked, "How do I run from what's inside my head?" And he meant Wang Wei. He wrote to her care of the Clerk of the Chinese Benevolent Association in San Francisco:

> My brother and I have struck gold. I wonder when I will see you again. If you get this letter, write to me care of the Chinese Benevolent Association in San Francisco.

Time passed. Like the vast majority of miners, Li Chang and his brother Li Yu never got rich. However, they kept on working. After twenty months, including that one strike that produced the gold ring, Li Chang calculated that they had averaged only $7.28 a day before expenses. Their golden dreams faded into leaden realities. Li Yu concluded that the chances of making a fortune in the gold mines were about the same as drawing a prize in a lottery. But still, every three months or so, they were able to send money home to their mother and Li Yu's wife and his now toddler son, Li Wu.

This life of severe hardship and exposure affected their health. Sometimes there was Chinese tea, dried meats and vegetables, but mostly they had to eat hard bread and salt pork for two days.

Li Yu felt ill. "I wonder if I have a touch of scurvy by not eating enough fresh fruits and vegetables? It's hard to get healthy food at the diggings. Maybe I need a rest."

By morning, he was feeling worse. "I dream about slurping mom's soup, but mother is so far away," he said.

Wet and cold most all day, the hot sun shone down upon their heads, and the very air parched their skin like hot air in an oven. Their drinking water came from upstream thoroughly impregnated with mineral substances, but at least Li Chang knew to boil it for tea, unlike the white miners who all suffered from diarrhea and dysentery.

Life expectancy was short. Within six months of arriving, one in every five of the miners was dead. Medicine was primitive, but miners also had high rates of suicide and alcoholism (or opium addiction among the Chinese) that testified to the grim side of gold rush life — as did the prostitution and mania for gambling.

The most prevalent and fatal diseases in California at that time were chronic diarrhea and dysentery and lung disease. Men afflicted with these diseases moped about the streets for weeks with looks of death and despair until their strength and money and friends were gone. At the last, they were carried to a hospital to pass a few miserable weeks more in a filthy ward, where they often died in the night without anyone knowing. But no Chinese died in there. Chinese were not allowed by California law to enter hospital facilities.

Li Yu was thankful that his brother Li Chang forced him to drink hot tea even on the hottest of days when he wanted to drink the water from the cold stream. The Chinese maintained strict standards of personal hygiene, too.

After days of labor, exhausted and faint, they stopped and lay down in their clothes, their boots removed and used as their pillows, and wrapped their blankets around them, on a bed of pine boughs or on the ground. Their feet and hands were blistered and lame, and their limbs were stiff. Anxieties and cares wore away the lives of so many men, who had left their families to come to Gold Mountain.

Li Yu, with his temperature rising, said, "I am tired. I am tired of this battle inside of me. I want to be far away from here and everyone! My head is sick, and my heart is faint."

"No matter what, keep moving forward!" Li Chang said to him. "Move forward like your life depends on it...because it does! Brother, sometimes you might have to take a step back to notice the patterns, beliefs and behaviors that are stopping you from moving forward. Find your path! Remember that a goal is not always meant to be reached, it often serves as simply as something to aim at. Now eat."

A notable Cantonese specialty was slow-cooked soup. The soup was usually a clear broth prepared by simmering meat and other ingredients under low heat for several hours.

"I've mixed Chinese herbs and medicines in the soup. It will heal and strengthen your health," Li Chang said.

Li Chang didn't yet trust the Western doctors or Western medicine, not that it mattered, given the ban on Chinese in hospitals. No law regulated medicine, the healing arts, in the land of gold. Anyone and everyone could practice medicine, and sell potions and pills. The only requirement was the purchase of a monthly license like any other tradesman.

In San Francisco, Li Chang had seen a drugstore where the pharmacist's symbols of colored waters outside paralleled the shining wine and liquor bottles on the bar inside. A "doctor" held consultations in the bar and handed out medicines at the same counter where he poured his drinks.

After a few hours, Li Yu started to recover, and he ate a bird that had been shot and cooked by his brother. They trudged along to Weaver's Creek, prospected for an hour, found a spot where they worked with some hope of success. Just below them was a miner from Georgia, who showed them nine pounds of gold he had collected last week with the assistance of two hired men.

Li Chang walled in a spring and made a cradle, too. He removed the stones and top soil, carried the gold-yielding dirt on handbarrows, made of hides, down to the edge of the water, and washed it. From every indication, they had "struck a rich lead." They found gold on the rocks; on one, Li Chang counted 25 scales. Li Chang finished the cradle and washed a little dirt during the afternoon which yielded about $10 worth in all. Alas, their hopes were dashed—again.

Another month passed, Li Chang looked at Li Yu and said, "The gold has become dim!" After all their preparations and hopes, their toil each day, digging down in the channel of the river until the water was up to their knees, giving themselves barely time to eat, they made but $4 each.

They sat down upon the rock and looked at the small ridge of gold in the pan and then at each other. Li Yu started swearing; Li Chang started laughing. Li Chang tried to say something encouraging.

To secure more provisions they headed back to Hangtown (later called Placerville), the seat of law and order where criminals met with swift justice often at the end of a rope, hence the early name of Hangtown. They noticed the body of a nameless young man about Li Chang's age. He was without a companion—alone in his tent. They buried him and left his possessions there. Li Chang thought about his family. Years will pass, and that beloved son, or brother, or husband was expected home. Why didn't he come home?

As they journeyed another mile or so, they came upon an old Chinese man—old for those days of around fifty years old, sitting on the root of a wide-spreading oak tree. He said he had left his wife and seven children at home, whose memory he cherished with great devotion. He said that when he was homesick he did not cry, but it made him sick to his stomach. He was hardworking, but did not have enough money to buy food.

"Are you pretending not to see his needs? He's not looking for praise or pity. He's not searching for a crutch. He just wants someone to talk to—a little of that human touch," Li Chang admonished Li Yu.

Li Chang pulled out two ounces of gold to give to the man, to give him a helping hand. Li Yu objected, but Li Chang over-ruled him. "It's a long, long road. For some there is no return. While we're on our way, why not share?"

And to the old man, he said: "When you are able, remember to help someone else."

Running low of food, Li Chang and Li Yu intrepidly ventured into the diggings of the white miners. Their food now consisted mostly of the flesh of wild animals, of ship biscuit or bread made by the miners, onions, potatoes, dried beans, salt pork, and, from time to time, of salmon. This fish was plentiful in the Sacramento River, and could then be caught with astonishing ease. Fishermen loaded great carts with salmon and transported them still fresh to the mining camps, where they sold them for a high price. The earnings of the fishermen were on a level with those of a gold-striking miner without exposure to the rigors of the miner's life. Li Chang just smiled and thought maybe he should become a fisherman. Or maybe a cook?

When the rainy season drew near, the miners who were fortunate and had struck gold came down from the diggings to spend the winter in Sacramento. Its close proximity to San Francisco offered a thousand comforts which a miner sought in vain in the towns of the interior.

There were undoubtedly many cases of miners, owners of rich claims, who feared to lose them if they abandoned them during the winter, so some miners remained there and some lost their lives, buried under the snow, drowned in the rivers or devoured by wild animals.

In the winter, Sacramento was always crowded, since it was there that the gamblers assembled. Gaming tables were set up everywhere. The amounts wagered on a single card were great, at times reaching five- or six-hundred ounces of gold.

Near the gambling houses, pawnshops appeared, as by magic. Their sole business was to lend money to the victims of the gamblers, who, after losing their gold, pledged their jewelry, arms and clothes in order to seek revenge and of course lose again, eventually finding themselves stripped of their last possession.

While Li Chang wasn't mining he was cooking for some of the white miners. In China, cooking wasn't deemed a woman's job, and Li Chang had the knowledge, skill, patience and experience to cook. He was disheartened when he first came over about the lack of Chinese foodstuffs, and he observed the pork, beans and flapjacks that the white miners preferred. Next came the bread, heavy bread, produced in loaves of every shade of sourness and every tint of orange. Li Chang could see there was a need to bake bread for the miners.

Cooking in the mining areas was of all types, from the extremes of method and neatness to those of neglect and slovenliness. Coffee was too weak or too strong; steaks were of extreme rareness or burned to a crisp. Potatoes were boiled to pieces or were impervious to the fork. Old stews, trembling on the verge of sourness, were thrust upon the meek and suffering stomachs. Li Chang watched all this and decided he wanted to change it.

Li Chang and Li Yu now went looking for another site in which to strike it rich. Their wanderings took them again to the town of Hangtown. The town was one long straggling street of clapboard houses and log cabins, built in a hollow at the side of a creek, and surrounded by high and steep hills.

The diggings there had once been exceedingly rich—men used to pick the chunks of gold out of the crevices of the rocks in the ravines with no other tool than a bowie-knife. But those days were passed, and now the surface of the whole surrounding country showed the scars of the hard work which had been done. The beds of the numerous ravines which wrinkled the faces of the hills, the bed of the creek, and all the little flats alongside of it were a confused mass of heaps of dirt and piles of stones lying around innumerable holes.

The original course of the creek was completely obliterated; its waters were distributed into numberless little ditches. The bare stumps of what once had been gigantic pine trees dotted the naked hillsides. There was a continuous noise and clatter, as mud, dirt, stones and water were thrown about in all directions; and the men, dressed in ragged clothes and big boots, wielded picks and shovels and rolled big rocks about.

The street of Hangtown was in many places knee-deep in mud, and was strewn with old boots, hats, sardine boxes, empty bottles, worn-out pots and kettles, old ham bones, broken picks and shovels, and other rubbish. Wagons, drawn by six or eight mules or oxen, navigated along the street, or discharged their strangely-assorted cargoes at the various stores, manned by men in picturesque rags, with large muddy boots, long beards and brown faces.

By the time of their arrival at Gold Mountain in 1854, the "easy pickings" were mostly gone; the streams were "panned out." But the optimistic Li Chang always encouraged Li Yu.

"We're bound to strike it rich," he said. "And even if we don't, our families are still better off with the money we've been able to send them. Whatever happens, we're richer for finding America, the land of the free."

Trekking onward, down the river about two or three miles from Hangtown, was a camp of some Chinese. There were about 150 of them there, living in a perfect village of small tents, all clustered together on the rocks. They had a claim in the bed of the river which they were working by means of a wing dam. The dam first ran half way across the river, then down the river, and back again to the same side, thus damming off a portion of its bed without the necessity of the more expensive operation of lifting up the whole river bodily in a "flume." The Chinese dam was 200 or 300 yards long and was built of large pine trees laid on top of the other.

There were Chinese of the better class among them, who no doubt directed the work and paid the other Chinese a fair wage, $2 or $3 a day. The Chinese camps were wonderfully clean compared to other camps, and as they walked through, they saw many of the miners at their toilet, getting their heads shaved, or plaiting each other's pigtails.

But most of them were at dinner, squatted on the rocks in groups of eight or ten around little black pots and dishes, from which they helped themselves with their chopsticks. In the center was a large bowl of rice. This was their staple, and they devoured it most voraciously. Throwing back their heads, they held a large cupful to their wide-open mouths, and, with a quick motion of their chopsticks in the other hand, the rice flowed down their throats in a continuous stream. Li Chang decided he wanted to cook the Chinese food he himself so craved.

"Perhaps," Li Chang said to Li Yu, "We should become part of a team mining gold. Maybe work for someone else in our quest for gold."

Many Chinese benefited from the fact that they were willing to work together in groups. When one group discovered a forty-pound nugget, they prudently chiseled it into small pieces to sell along with their gold dust, because so many small nuggets would ensure both that each man received his fair share and that the find would not draw attention to the group.

Other Chinese prospered not just by luck or hard work, both of which were always needed, but by resourceful use of technology. The Chinese introduced the water wheel to American placer mining. This device, modeled after irrigation techniques used by rice paddy farmers back home, allowed the pumping and sluicing of water from the river, which was then used to wash gravel from gold.

The men of China, who were so much further from home than the white miners, were much more capable of enduring and surviving their hardships. And they were more tolerant of their sorrows. It may have been the wisdom learned from older traditions of exile, but it may also have been simple necessity.

Most of the immigrants from Kwangtung province, almost all men, were part of communities from the same villages and clans. They knew one another, and one another's families, were able to work together in ways the more individualistic Americans and other immigrants did not.

At night, a lively bachelor culture sprang up in these scattered mining camps. The miners formed bands and played Chinese music with instruments brought over from their homeland. The Irish miners called the music, the "wailings of a thousand lovelorn cats, the screams, gobblings, braying and barkings of as many peacocks, turkeys, donkeys and dogs."

The Chinese miners also gambled, gambling being possibly the greatest Chinese vice in the American West. "About every third Chinaman runs a lottery," American storyteller Mark Twain remarked. In gambling shacks, loud, excited groups of Chinese bet on dice, lots, and tosses of coins. A white miner complained about the noise, which began soon after dark: "We don't know and don't care how many years they claim to have been infesting the Earth, and only wish they would go to bed like decent people and stop playing their infernal button game of 'Foo-ti-hoo-ti,' so a fellow can get a nap."

Li Chang and Li Yu both vowed to change their appearance and mental outlook. Although very hard, it was a plan and perhaps could change their luck. First, Li Chang and Li Yu decided to replace their Chinese conical hats with cowboy hats. They already wore the sturdy American boots. But they kept their blue cotton shirts and broad trousers. Most importantly, in order to return home to China, they retained that one vestige of Qing tradition: the long, jet-black queue that swayed gleaming down their backs. This pig-tail grew from just two or three inches of surface; the rest of the head, particularly the front, was shaved bald.

China was a land where elders were respected and one's betters were revered. America, by contrast was untamed. Anything went. Li Chang challenged Li Yu: "Cooperate with others to accomplish a common purpose. If people see they have the same goals as you, they will be on your side. And also, if you just learn a single trick, Li Yu, you'll get along a lot better with all kinds of people. You can never really understand a person until you consider things from their point of view, until you climb inside of their skin and walk around in it."

Thus concluded Li Chang's brotherly talk. A smiling Li Yu, the aspiring writer, shook his head at his brother's ramblings. "You're talking about 'reciprocity.' What you don't want done to yourself, do not do to others. That's what Confucius said."

Li Chang was realistic. "Fortune might be right around the corner, but so too is failure, and we learn from failure not success," he reminded Li Yu. "The more we take the less we become."

The Li brothers escaped from the realities of their conditions in correspondence with home, in community with fellow Chinese miners, at a gambling table, a smoke of opium, in a bottle of whiskey or the temptations of the flesh on Saturday night.

"Brother, I have promised and committed to remain faithful in body and spirit to my family left behind, but I'm constantly tested by the struggles and temptations of the moment," Li Yu said. "And foremost, I think I'm going out of my head with guilt. Sun Wei is my wife, but I cannot get Wang Wei out of my mind and about the way life could be. How did I become such a bad person?"

Li Yu was torn. He closed his eyes, now thinking of Sun Wei, and caressed pages from an old letter; he searched his heart for a trace of love still there.

"I understand," Li Chang said. "The greatest conflict you will ever face will be the conflict with yourself. But now let's go into town."

4

The Inhumanity

"We have not much of a chance at all—a Chinaman's chance." This time, even Li Chang did not rebuke the assertion of his younger brother Li Yu.

Li Yu was nursing another dreadful cold at their camp when Li Chang, with his chest pumped out, brought down from the Yuba River a bag of gold weighing 8.5 lbs. It was the most beautiful gold they had ever seen.

Li Chang spoke to the heavens. "No more gnashing of teeth and pulling hair over Fool's Gold. No more muddy waters, sifting through grit and grime. No more sloshing in bitterly cold rivers seeking all that glitters. The elusive metal is found."

A gang of bushwhackers led by a man named Mitch "Wild Thing" Williams accosted Li Chang but neither threats nor persuasion could induce him to reveal the precise place where he had found the gold.

"You're gonna get a hundred lashes, but we'll let you off with thirty if you tell us where your gold strike is," Williams bellowed.

"Never," cried Li Chang.

The slanting rays of the early spring fell upon the scene, and the cool air filled the valley with an almost invigorating atmosphere. Li Chang was stripped naked and tied left-hand and right-foot to a dead tree. Williams, who wielded a stout strip of rawhide, was a large, muscular man, whose sinewy arms yielded enormous strength. He had been a gold miner for three years, but he was a farmer by occupation and had driven an ox team across the plains in search of Gold Mountain, so he was well-schooled in the use of the whip.

Swinging the whip over his head and bending his body to give it full force, Williams started the lashing immediately. One, two, three—in quick succession. Li Chang tried to bore a hole into the slim tree trunk, gritting his teeth and concentrating on not breaking down. Four, five, six, seven—they kept coming thick and fast. At first the pain wasn't too much, but soon Li Chang squirmed in agony as the torturous strokes increasingly lacerated his back, each blow tapping the blood in his veins. The blows rained down on his body, from the shoulder blades to the calves, then back up again. With each blow, the skin, once tough as leather, softened and the pain grew so that his back felt like it was on fire.

Li Chang summoned up all his control not to move. He didn't realize the human body could generate and tolerate such pain. He had never felt anything like this before.

At about twenty, he lost count because of the pain, but someone else was counting each stroke out loud in Chinese. His Chinese tormentor was the never-to-be-trusted Chen Hu from the *Libertad*. Li Chang gritted his teeth even more and closed his eyes.

The last few strokes were agony, bloody agony. The "Wild Thing" seemed to be the only man unmoved by the horrible spectacle.

It was a sickening sight to behold. Then just as quickly as it started, it was over. Fifty to sixty seconds was all it lasted. The thirty lashes were inflicted. Finally, Li Chang revealed the location, and he was left to die, still tied up.

CHINESE BROTHERS, AMERICAN SONS

"Free me," Li Chang cried.

"I'll tell you what I'll do," Williams said. "I'll leave you tied up here naked. First, it'll just be bugs eating at you. One day, maybe two. That sun's gonna be cooking you. And animals... they're gonna pick on your stink. They'll come looking for something to eat."

The mosquitoes with their long bills went at him, and in less than an hour his whole body was covered with blood. Writhing and trembling from head to foot, Li Chang finally fell unconscious. His gold, Li Yu's gold, their gold, was gone.

Li Chang, broken and battered, survived. Li Yu dragged him back to their camp where the persistent itching from the mosquito bites on his wounds drove him crazy.

Now the Li brothers saw first-hand frontier justice. Nothing was done.

In 1854, the California Supreme Court, in the most significant government action against the Chinese, ruled in People v. Hall that Chinese were barred from testifying against whites in court. Chief Justice Hugh Murray noted that the Naturalization Act of 1790 prohibited Chinese and other nonwhites from becoming U.S. citizens; Murray then justified his decision as being necessary for social stability. If the Chinese were admitted as witnesses in court, he said, the state would "soon see them at the polls, in the jury box, upon the bench, and in our legislative halls." Where would it all end?

Once the white miners understood that they could terrorize Chinese camps without fear of legal consequences—that the law in effect immunized them—they posted signs warning the Chinese to leave immediately or be subjected to "39 lashes and moved by force of arms." White miners torched Chinese tents and mining equipment. The ruling opened the way for almost every sort of discrimination against the Chinese— assault, robbery, and murder, to say nothing of lesser crimes, so long as no white person was available to bear witness on the Chinese miners' behalf.

In the absence of any effective rule of law, brute strength prevailed. A Mexican named Joaquin Murieta whose gang descended on one Chinese camp, rounded up the miners, and tied their pigtails together. Slowly, deliberately, he and his men tortured them until one of them disclosed where they had hidden their gold dust. At which point, Murieta slit all their throats with a bowie knife. Ironically, Murieta had only turned to a life of crime after white miners beat him, hanged his half-brother and raped his sister. After these atrocities, he declared that he would henceforth "live for revenge and that his path should be marked with blood."

In addition, two years before the Li brothers arrived, the California legislature in 1852 had enacted two new taxes. The first discouraged other Chinese from coming to the United States. The commutation tax required masters of all vessels arriving in California to post a $500 bond for each foreign passenger aboard. Because the bond was commuted with a payment of a fee from $5 to $50, most ship captains simply added the fee to the price of passage. The resulting revenue, extracted from the sweat of the Chinese laborer, went to California hospitals, but while the Chinese ended up paying over half of all commutations taxes, they were barred from public hospitals.

The second tax was the foreign miner's tax imposed by the state of California that penalized Chinese already working the gold mines. It stipulated that every Chinese miner working a claim must pay a monthly license fee in gold dust, a fee which was arbitrarily increased over the next few years.

Some collectors backdated the effective date of the license; that obligated the miner to pay money he did not even owe.

Others pocketed money from miners and gave them bogus receipts, leaving the miners vulnerable to legitimate collection efforts later on.

Taxes on foreign miners became commonplace, because gold in California was reserved for the American whites. The Chinese, more dissimilar than other immigrant gold rushers, were singled out for particularly harsh treatment. The Committee on Mines and Mining of the California state legislature declared that "their presence here is a great moral and social evil—a disgusting scab upon the fair face of society—a putrefying sore upon the body politic—in short, a nuisance."

The Li brothers, and all Chinese of the Gold Rush in California, suffered from the bigotry of the Anglo majority. But in the case of the Chinese, it was not always easy—and historically it may be beside the point—to distinguish racism from ethnocentrism, xenophobia, and plain incomprehension.

Most Americans in the 1850s had scarcely a clue what to make of the Chinese. Prior to the Gold Rush, few Americans had ever encountered a Chinese outside the pages of Marco Polo. As a people, the Chinese were almost as exotic as aliens from another planet. The majority of Chinese, of course, were non-Christians, which made them immediately suspect in an era in America when even Catholics were eyed with suspicion.

Many of the Chinese spoke little or no English, and although this by itself did not distinguish them from thousands of Chileans and Mexicans and French and Belgians in California, the Chinese language and especially the Chinese script were downright bizarre next to the speech and writing of Mother Europe. Chinese dress and hairstyle—the long pigtails, or queues—evoked endless comment, and made the Chinese easily recognizable at a distance. Their use of opium put additional distance between them and others in California. How ironic that the Chinese were despised for their use of opium when American merchants joined the British in selling this addictive, lethal drug to them in China!

Stranger still, and more suspect, were the odd ways in which the Chinese ate food. They ate dog meat! And it was said that the Celestials devoured mice and rats, too. They refused to eat the normal diet of beans and beef that the white miners consumed. Instead, they imported food from China: dried oysters, dried fish, dried abalone, dried fruits, dried mushrooms, dried seaweed, dried crackers and candies, and an endless variety of roasted, sweet and sour, and dried meats, poultry and pork, rice and teas. These feasts of "Un-Christian foods" prepared by their own cooks and the brewing of barrels of tea to be served all day long in tiny cups such as "ladies see fit to use" had the Yankees imagining dark, mysterious rituals.

In an era when racial thinking was unabashed and nearly universal, most whites had no difficulty classing the Chinese as inherently inferior. White miners generally viewed Chinese miners with disdain and contempt, and some with hatred.

The white 49ers, as the miners were called, saw a lack of "manhood" in the men from Kwangtung province not only in their diminutive size, but in the ways they dressed and bathed. In the rugged frontier camps, after work, the Chinese miners religiously washed in hot bathtubs made from whiskey kegs.

"Look at them midgets, wouldja? Gettin' all soaped up like a buncha women. Yeah, those monkeys sure do smell purty with all that flower water," taunted the white miners.

Trying to combat the racial tensions of the time was the Chinese Benevolent Association, also known as the Chinese Six Companies in San Francisco. It was organized by dialect and region from which the workers had migrated from; it provided mutual protection and assistance, and the particular obligation was the return to China of the bones of any Chinese who died in America, that they might be honored by their descendants. It represented interests to civic authorities and presided over disputes among members.

In the late 1850s, as the Chinese population grew, an anti-Chinese movement mounted. Pun Chi, a young Chinese merchant, wrote an appeal to Congress in Washington, seeking help against growing anti-Chinese sentiments in the West, reminding Congress that Chinese migration had been encouraged and that migrants deserved legal protection once in the United States:

> We are called 'coolies,' contract laborers who work for pittance and thereby undermine the wages of honest Americans. There are among us tradesmen, mechanics, gentry (persons of respectability, and who enjoy a certain rank and privilege) and schoolmasters, who are reckoned with the gentry, and with us considered a respectable class of people. The poor China man does not come here as a slave. He comes because of his desire for independence, adventure, and to help his family back in China. We are not thieves and enemies, but we are treated with unusual contempt and evil. We are murdered, and our businesses are ruined. You load us with increasing mining taxes and devise means to wholly expel us. It is hard for the spirit to sustain such trials. We generally stay to ourselves unless it is to provide services to stage companies and other interests, amounting to several millions of dollars per year, can it be affirmed that we are of no value? Our conduct is very different from the lawlessness and violence of some other foreigners. Were it not that each so little understands the other's tongue, and

mutual kind sentiments are not communicated, would not more cordial intercourse probably exist? The Americans shouldn't pass laws against the Chinese. Let us stay here—the Americans are doing well to us, and we will do well to them.

Pun Chi's plea fell on deaf ears both in Washington and in Sacramento, the capital of California. While the Chinese mining life was very similar to life for all in the American West—rough and lawless—an English and Chinese phrase book published in San Francisco, harshly reflected the Chinese experience through its selection of what a Chinese prospector might need to be able to say in English:

He assaulted me without provocation. He claimed my mine...
He tried to extort money from me.
He falsely accused me of stealing his watch
He was choked to death with a lasso, by a robber.
She is a good-for-nothing hussy.

When the veins of gold gave out, the Yankee miners blamed the Chinese for their loss and encouraged "Uncle Sam to stop the coming of the Chinese." They were angry and confused about how these "little men" could work as hard as and more successfully than Yankee miners almost twice their size. Li Chang was hardly five foot tall and weighed no more than 120 pounds. Li Yu, the youngest, was 5'4" and a "hefty" 140 pounds. The Chinese successfully reworked claims given up as worthless by others, and this lead to jealousy and hatred and numerous acts of violence.

The California Gold Rush was one of the most important events of the 19th century and its influence on migration, transportation, economic development, politics, and culture was deep and lasting. Part of the equation was its legacy of violence, something familiar to all Americans.

There were a reported 219 homicides in California during the first six months of 1855. Dark images of senseless brawling, murder, widespread gambling, drinking and prostitution, and ethnic strife were everywhere in California. Miners brought with them a bachelor culture of violent masculinity and a shared history of private vengeance, defense of personal honor, and rough-and-ready justice. The widely-held belief and recurring theme that violence solved personal and society problems was a legacy of these gold seekers.

The colorful names of the mining camps reflected the rough masculine society of the gold miners: Drunkards Bar, Poker Flat, Hangtown, Whiskey Gulch, Murderers Bar, Dead Shot Flat, Git Up and Git; Hells Delight, Garrote, Robbers Roost, Wild Yankee, Rough and Ready, Dead Man's Bar, Brandy Flat, and inevitably, Whorehouse Gulch. Because of the scarcity of women, prostitution of course flourished during the Gold Rush.

But not everyone had a vicious streak; a large number of miners were former merchants, mechanics, and farmers, so while mob rule was often the norm, every mining camp had its share of peaceable men to balance off the forces of violence.

Li Chang told Li Yu of the Miners' Ten Commandments, rules to live by the camps, regardless of race:

1) Thou shalt not steal his horse, donkey or mule.
2) Thou shalt not take away his pick, shovel, or a pan or other tool without his leave.
3) Thou shalt not borrow those he cannot spare; or return them broken, nor trouble him to fetch them back again.

4) Thou shalt not talk with him while his water rent is running on.
5) Thou shalt not remove his stake to enlarge thy claim.
6) Thou shalt not undermine his bank in following a lead.
7) Thou shalt not pan out gold from his "riffle box."
8) Thou shalt not wash the "tailings" from his sluice's mouth.
9) Thou shalt not pick out specimen from the company's pan to put them in thy mouth, or in thy purse.
10) Thou shalt not cheat thy partner of his share; nor steal from thy cabin mate his gold dust, to add to thine.

There was an unwritten rule that a commandment breaker, when discovered by his fellow miners, would be hanged or given fifty lashes, or his head was shaved and his cheek branded. Nearly every white miner owned a mule or some other animal to pack his tools, blankets and provisions on when moving from one gulch or diggings to another. But the Chinese miners mostly had no such beast of burden.

But a Chinese miner named Chu Wen reported to the American sheriff that a fellow Chinese miner Shen Liang had stolen his mule. Of course, nothing was done by the sheriff. But several white miners, bitter from gold dust failure, found out about the crime of mule stealing and hung until death both Shen for the theft and Chu for being "uppity" for having a mule. The American sheriff was an emotionless observer.

It was not so easy to avoid trouble during the Gold Rush. The mining camps mushroomed so quickly that brothels, gambling tents, fandango halls, and saloons were built on main streets, next door to legitimate businesses. Men of all social classes, from the Texas ruffian to the Boston gentleman, rubbed shoulders in the same gold fields, saloons and gambling halls. Thus, the average gold seeker, even if he did not shoot or stab anyone, was often in places where men were shot or stabbed.

"Two men get killed; nobody bats an eye. A stupid horse gets stolen, the thief must die," Li Yu said.

"Every day we see the violence around us," Li Chang said to his brother. "While there is very little that we can do about it, take care of yourself and make the change you want to see within others. You may not be able to influence the world, but you can be a better person, and a testament of the change."

It was not easy for the Li brothers walking through this land of broken dreams. Every day heartaches grew stronger. Still, for a surprising number of Chinese miners this was a one-way trip. Many remembered their homeland as a treasured past but found their future in America, even after their original dreams upon landing on the shore of California had faded. The life that beckoned them was one of hardships they had not expected, and of insults and horror they did not understand and could not control.

Violence was everywhere in California, and for the Li brothers, a constant reminder of the violence of the China they had fled. Li Chang wisely told Li Yu: "Never become immune to the violence. You have a son that will look up to you. You must show him the way. Be a man of humanity."

5

THE CHINESE FOOD CULTURE

The Chinese eat everything with four legs, except tables, and everything that walks, swims, crawls or flies with its back to heaven is edible.
—*A proverb from Kwangtung province in southern China*

THE SEARCH FOR California's Gold Mountain was made without women. Most miners were single or chose not to bring their wives and children to this raw frontier land. Single men, with a ready supply of cash, were without wives to cook for them and to service their other needs. In those early years of the Gold Rush, women were scarcer than the precious dust.

Li Chang and Li Yu knew they had come to a country with very few Chinese women, but they found it to be a land with few women of any race. In 1850, women numbered only one out of 12 Californians. In the mining region, two out of every hundred were female. Many of the new female immigrants were prostitutes from Latin America and Australia. In 1852, one in ten people in California was female; by 1860 the number had increased, but women were still only one in four.

The mere rumor of a female newcomer was enough to empty campgrounds, saloons and hotels, causing a stampede. In the mining regions, "Every man thought every woman in that day a beauty," wrote one California pioneer woman. "Even I had men come forty miles over the mountains, just to look at me, and I was never called a handsome woman, in my best days, even by my more ardent admirers."

In fact, it was as unusual to see a woman, Li Chang remarked, as it was to see an old man. But because women were so scarce, many 49ers treated them not just with respect but with reverence, for they represented the mothers, sisters, daughters, wives and sweethearts left at home.

There were stories of women making more money selling homemade pies and doughnuts than their husbands made mining.

Dance halls appeared early and spread quickly throughout the Gold Rush land. They usually offered games of chance too, but their chief attraction was dancing. The customer generally paid 75 cents to $1.00 for a ticket to dance, with the proceeds being split between the "dance hall girl" and the saloon owner. After the dance, the woman steered the miner to the bar, where she made an additional commission from the sale of a drink. These women made so much money that it was very rare for them to double as a prostitute. In fact, many a former "soiled dove" found she could make more money as a "dance hall girl." Her job was to brighten the evenings of the many men of the western towns.

With these demographics, brothels inevitably flourished too. Some enterprising women charged more than a $100 a night—the equivalent of the price of a house or about a year's wages in other parts of the country.

"She must be a lot of woman. One hundred dollars a night!" Li Yu said in disbelief.

"Certain women have a way of changing boys into men, and some men back into boys," Li Chang said.

Entrepreneurs in the world's oldest profession rode furiously on horseback from camp to camp, trying to fit as many clients as possible into their schedules.

But more than all of that, the miners had to eat. As he dreamed of one day opening his own restaurant in San Francisco, Li Chang bemoaned the fact that, "I guess I'll have to tailor my menu to please the tastebuds of unadventurous American diners suspicious of foreign and unusual foods."

"Big Brother," Li Yu said, "You'll have to serve gristly steak and a plate of pork and beans." Their staples from home such as dried fish and preserved ducks' eggs were far from appetizing to the miner's palate.

"I'm willing and able to cook American food," Li Chang said, "but I refuse to accept the concept that the art of cooking lies only in taste. For us Chinese, the most important elements in food appreciating are color, appearance, aroma, flavor and texture. All of these elements must be combined to make a harmonious whole: it is the ability to create this harmony that I believe to be the art of cooking."

Li Yu rolled his eyes and laughed.

But Lie Chang's voice showed commitment. He was describing the influence of Confucius a philosopher and teacher from 2,500 years ago, on the art of cooking. Confucius attached great importance to food and described it as one of the three basic conditions, along with an army and trust, for founding a state.

Li Chang, savoring the aroma in his mind, explained further to Li Yu the exotic dishes he learned to prepare as an apprentice chef for a noble in Beijing and as a chef for wealthy merchants in Canton. Could he one day have people in America enjoy some of the dishes that made up a typical Confucian banquet?

On the topic of food culture, Confucius laid down some pretty simple and logical principles, aimed at ensuring each dining experience depended on the proper mixing of all ingredients and condiments in order to have the right balance of colors, textures and aromas.

Confucius placed a lot of importance on the art of cooking and enjoyment of food in life. Blending of food also resulted in harmony and that was an important part because without harmony, foods could not taste good. Ginger gained a favorite place, as it helped to reduce internal heat and fever in the body and assisted in digestion. He developed dining standards; food should be served in small pieces. Knives were never kept on the table, a rule still obeyed, as it showed disrespect towards their guests. Confucius also gave more priority to vegetables than to meats. To avoid overeating, he said it was important to eat only at mealtimes. On the American frontier, this was hard to do.

Li Chang explained to Li Yu that China had three vital qualities that gave rise to a great cuisine. First, the fertile land, the mountains, deserts, plains, lakes and mighty rivers produced an array of foods. Second, the Chinese people were industrious; they extracted every possible bit of goodness and nutrition from every scrap of land. Third, there was China's elite whose discriminating taste, gave birth to the gourmet. Food became not only a complex tool for ritual and attainment of prestige, but an art form, pursued by men of passion.

Famous Confucian dishes included "Four Edible Birds' Nest Dishes," fried chrysanthemum shrimp dumplings, decorated duck custard, and toffee dates. Yet, "Coarse rice for food, water to drink, and the bended arm for a pillow — happiness may be enjoyed even in these," Confucius said. Because the art of cooking encompassed more than food to the Chinese—food, and its enjoyment, and friends were inseparable; they promoted peace and harmony in society.

"The giving and sharing of foods with friends and family are an important part of the Chinese culinary tradition," Li Chang said. "I hope one day to bring to the American West."

Another food-related principle that the great thinker adhered to was, "never eat alone, which explains why we like to share our food with friends," Li Chang said. "The peak is neither eating nor cooking, but the giving and sharing of food. Great food or simple food should never be taken alone. A good cook can create dishes that will heal the diner. The right foods can ease the mind and heart. I strive to cook like that. But there's one more. The most important one of all is community. Every meal eaten in China, whether the greatest banquet or the poorest lunch eaten by peasants in the field or in a clay hut, is shared by the group. The food is in the middle of the table."

"Now it is time for me to go to sleep, little brother, and for you to go to the post office," said Li Chang. Letters were almost as precious as gold, and sometimes as hard to find.

Li Yu arrived early at 1 a.m. to find about fifty persons were already there. Taking his place in line, Li Yu waited until the post office opened. Now the line had grown to several hundred people. Then according to name, each one was assigned to different queues. Finally, the wait was over; Li Yu was at the "L" window. Now the big line facing the delivery windows extended halfway around the block. At last, the busy clerk looked over a big pile of mail.

"Nothing," the clerk yelled to Li Yu.

Crestfallen, Li Yu then went to the big line again—another four-hour wait, then to the Y delivery line, no wait there. He had forgotten—in America, the surname was after the first name. His mail was with the letters addressed to "Y."

Li Yu hurried back to camp and scanned the familiar writing. With a strange tremor he dutifully read the letter from Sun Wei, the wife he hardly knew.

Your mother Cheung Yee has died—quietly in her sleep without pain. With the money you send us, there is no more hoarding of every grain and every stalk of wilted vegetable for us. Before, an egg was a miracle. No more, thanks to you, my husband, and your brother, Li Chang.

Up to the end, once or twice a week, Ma cooked for us. She made the dishes she loved from her childhood, fried tomatoes and tofu, hot and sour cabbage, soup noodles with pickles. She was so proud of you. Me, too.

Li Wu and I are fine; we miss you.

Li Yu wept. Li Chang pushed Li Yu's head under his chin and stroked his brother's head, still perspiring after the six-mile walk back to camp.

Li Chang now went right to work. He knew that if someone was grieving, cook with green onions, ginger, coriander and rosemary. Theirs was the pungent flavor which drew grief up and out of the body and released it into the air. Chicken in boiling water with some salt, ginger and green onions. Get the wok going with some oil. Add some ginger to hiss and rumble; add some green onions. The fragrance flowers instantly. He shut down the flame and poured the boiling, crackling oil over the chicken. Then he sprinkled cilantro leaves on top.

"Now it's ready, try it," Li Chang said to Li Yu. "It's cut bone-in. Can't get the flavor without the marrow. Just spit the bones out."

Li Yu plucked a morsel from the side of the bird, low on the breast where the moistness of the thigh came in, and tasted it. It was soft as velvet, chicken times three, shot through with ginger and the note of onion. Small sticks of bones, their essence exhausted, crumbled in his mouth.

"These flavors are for you, my brother, to benefit you. Ginger and cilantro and green onions; they're powerful. Very healing. I was trained in China to perceive the diner, and cook accordingly. Feed the body, but that's only the beginning. Also, feed the mind and the soul," Li Chang said.

Li Chang asked several white miners camped not far from their camp to join them. They each wore hats, spoke with a Dutch accent and each was bearded. Li Yu plucked tender pieces from the rich underside of the bird. It tasted so good, so necessary to him, that he quickly ate all the food in his bowl while Li Chang sat across from him, watching him. After this meal shared with fellow miners, Li Chang said to his brother, "Sadness may be forever, but our grieving is gone. Let's go into town."

They made a ten-mile trek into Coloma, during which Li Yu thought of his wife Sun Wei and his son Li Wu. He and Li Chang had been providing for their mother, his wife and son, but now there were only two people to send money to. He reasoned they would be better off now.

"Should I return to China?" he asked himself. "I didn't marry for love but I do miss her. What is my son like? Does he favor me?"

Li Chang, now almost jogging and eager to reach Coloma, asked Li Yu, "Now, what? Are you thinking of going home?"

Li Yu avoided the thought and asked Li Chang to continue telling him about cooking and its importance. "How did you decide to become a cook?" he asked.

Li Chang recalled that when he was fourteen, the family was starving. The decision was made to sell one of the children. Usually a family sold a girl, but there were no girls. Li Yu was just four years old; no one wanted him—too young!

CHINESE BROTHERS, AMERICAN SONS

Li Chang, now sixteen, said he would go. It was time for him to be a man. At least with this move he knew he would eat. There was a reason why families as poor as theirs sold their children into the restaurant trade. It was slavery, but it came with hot meals. And if the young one proved gifted, there was nothing really to stop him from reaching the top. In China, with food, a man could advance on merit alone, without money, lineage, or education.

For Li Chang, being sold was his life's beginning. A broker resold him into the employ of a nobleman's palace in the capital, Beijing. An incredible variety of food was created in or brought to the palace. There were five divisions: meat, vegetarian, cereals—which meant rice, buns and noodles—snacks and pastries. Game, birds and seafood of all description, and also fruits and vegetables specially chosen at dedicated farms, each piece plucked from the bottom of the plant, the place closest to the root and thus to life.

The repertoire of the nobleman's palace kitchen covered 4,000 dishes. The most important creations—those most favored by the imperial family—sometimes became the lifelong concentration of one celebrated cook.

By chance, Li Chang's new life in a palace kitchen in Beijing brought him into contact with Wang Hu, the greatest chef of his generation, who prepared food for the Empress Dowager in the Imperial Palace. The Empress Dowager, for all the many elaborate dishes prepared for her, cared only for little cakes that comforted her and carried her back to other times. After every meal, the delicacies not consumed were packed into lacquer boxes, and carried to the homes of princes and high officials. Li Chang saw them, tasted them and found a way through the chief chef of his kitchen to spend some time working for Wang Hu. Wang Hu saw that Li Chang had talent and Li Chang learned from him.

Sometimes, he saw Wang come up to a pot when he believed no one was looking and add in a secret pinch of something from his pocket.

Lord Wang encouraged Li Chang to educate himself. "You must read the food classics," he said. "No Chinese can call himself a chef without doing so."

Lord Wang gave Li Chang passage to a higher world. Yet what he read was not recipes; they were almost never written down. The way of cooking a dish was always secret, and exclusive, and the only way to learn it was by watching.

Wang was wiser than any alchemist. His dishes brought him all the glory under heaven. And he did it just as easily from coarse simple food as from rare delicacies. Wang often said that the best food was simple and homey. That reminded Li Chang of when he was young back home, and he felt good.

Sometimes, the noble for whom the apprentice chefs cooked or his guests gave tips to the kitchen staff. One day, a beautiful aristocratic girl came over to Li Chang, and with an amused look reached into her purse for coins. When she unfolded her hand, he saw five coins. He saved such gifts for when he saw his family every other year or so.

"Are you still with me?" Li Chang asked.

"I shall never forget this time spent with you," Li Yu said. "Go on. More."

Li Chang recounted one October day when he returned to his family's old farmhouse and turned panting along his own pathway. The first thing he saw was his mother sitting outside the doorway on a stool, scrubbing cabbage.

"My son," she said slowly, half stumbling with surprise and wonder. "Li Chang has returned!" Then she leaped up and threw her arms around him.

"Ma," he said, the single syllable strangling out of his mouth.

She was so small and frail; while about the same height as Li Chang, he had not realized how much stronger he was. His skin was scrubbed, his queue plaited.

"Come," she said, and pulled him quickly in through the low, stooping doorway. As his eyes adjusted to the dimness of the clay-walled room, his brother (now taller than him) appeared from the shadows, eyes large, barely believing. It was as familiar as a dream: the cracked basin, the faded flowers on the bedding, his mother's dented pans. His father had died four years earlier. He had another father now—his benefactor, Chef Wang. His life was Wang's.

"I can't stay," Li Chang said. He gave his mother and Li Yu a squeeze. They were thin, not flush with good food as he was.

Li Chang took her elbow, opened her hand, and dropped in all five of the coins.

She looked at him. "Where did you get it?"

"I earned it." He was as the sky then, a man who ruled the world. He bent over it with her. "Is it enough for the winter?" Li Chang asked.

"Yes, more than enough," his mother said.

Her eyes filled with gratitude as she slipped it into a secret pocket she kept within her clothes. Then she let out a small cry of thankfulness and dropped to grasp him by his knees.

"Ma, stop," he said. He pulled her up, but his heart swelled with happiness.

"I must go," he said. "Take care of Li Yu."

Li Chang ran back through twisted lanes and dusty pathways where as a child he had played. It was the whole world to him then—neither good nor bad, rich nor poor. Old men played mahjong by the trees and lounged on wooden steps as they always had, bulky wadding inside their socks for warmth. Small children wore clothes handed down and mended. Old ladies

ED SHEW

walked in gray cotton with their hands behind their backs. And here he was, passing in bright silks with leather on his feet. How ironic, Li Chang was sold to help his family, and now Li Chang was still helping his family.

After being sold, Li Chang didn't become rich or powerful as Wang Hu did, and the noble in whose kitchen he worked fell on hard times and died. The indentured servants including Li Chang were all discarded. Li Chang returned to Canton and for a time cooked for wealthy merchants there before leaving for America with his brother.

Li Yu reached for Li Chang's hand. He gripped it tightly. They were never closer than at that moment. Whatever happened, they would survive together.

Miners seldom took days off, but when they did, those days offered a break from the drudgery and the competitiveness of mining. Li Chang and Li Yu stayed to themselves, joined other Chinese miners or ventured into the mining towns of the white community. Along with a chance to rest, they read, wrote letters, bathed and washed clothes. All the miners spent some of their hard-earned gold dust. They congregated at gambling houses, and houses of ill-repute, dances and even the occasional circus.

On this day Li Chang and Li Yu went to an exhilarating miner's Sunday in Coloma (Sierra Nevada goldfields). The street was alive with crowds of milling men, passing and re-passing, laughing and talking, all in the best of humor: Negroes who had escaped from the slavery of the southern states swaggered with the expansive feeling of run-away freedom; mulattoes from Jamaica trudged arm-in-arm with Kanakas from Hawaii; Peruvians and Chileans claimed affinity with the swarthier Mexicans; Frenchmen, Germans, and Italians fraternized with one another and with cockneys fresh from the shores of England;

an Irishman traced his past through Australia; Yankees from New England chatted and bargained with genial Oregonians. Here they were, among the few Chinese scattered here and there through the crowds, their pigtails and conical hats now replaced by cowboy hats. Last of all, a few Indians, the only indigenous creatures among all these exotics, lost, swallowed up—out of place, "*rari nantes in gurgite vasto.*"

It was a scene that no other country could replicate. Persons of all colors, races, religions, languages, size, capability, strengths and morals were there, within that one small town in the mountains of California. All there with but one purpose and one desire—to have a grand time.

The street was one continuous din. Thimble-riggers, French monte dealers and string-game tricksters were shouting at every corner: "Six ounces, gentlemen, who can tell where the little joker is?" or "Bet on the jack, the jack's the winning card! Three ounces no man can turn up the jack!"

Above all this clamor was the shrill voice of a down-east auctioneer who, perched on a large box in front of a very small canvas booth, was disposing of the various articles "all at a bargain." Behind a smaller box, to the left of the Yankee, was a German Jew in a red cap and scarlet flannel shirt, busy with his scales and leaden weights, weighing out the "dust" from the various purchasers.

What a ragged, dirty, unshaven, good-natured motley crew!

For Li Chang and Li Yu, it was as if they were back home in Canton visiting the markets. "Here's a splendid pair of brand-new boots! Cowhide, double-soled, triple-pegged, water-proof boots! The very thing for you, sir; going for only four ounces and a half! And gone—for four and a half; walk up there and weigh out your dust," the auctioneer said.

Li Chang, having bought the boots, drew out a long and well-filled buckskin bag and tossed it to the expectant Jew with as much carelessness as if it were ordinary dust.

"Weigh out the boots and eight lickers," Li Chang said in his best cowboy accent. Then he turned to the men watching nearby, "Come, boys, and call for what you like; it's my treat."

"Vat ye takes?" asked the Jew, who also served drinks to his customers.

"Brandy straight," "brandy punch," "brandy sling," "gin cocktail." And thus they went on, each calling for a different drink.

The stalls along the street were selling almost everything imaginable. Butcher-knives for crevicing, tin pans, shovels, picks, clothing of all colors, shapes and sizes; hats and caps of every style; coffee, tea, sugar, bacon, flour, liquors of all grades in stiff-necked bottles— in a word, almost everything that a miner could want, and all moving at a furious rate. But alas, no Chinese imported food. That would have to wait for the bi-monthly shipment Li Yu received or when Li Chang could find a Chinese grocery store in San Francisco or Sacramento in the winter.

Suddenly, there was a great noise of shouting and hurrahing away up the street, and the crowd heaved and separated upon both sides. Li Yu jerked his head around and saw a dozen half-wild, bearded miners, fine, wiry, strapping fellows on foaming horses, lashed to the utmost, and giving the piercing scalp-yells of the Comanches. They suddenly halted in front of Winter's Hotel, and most dismounted and strolled into the barroom for drinks and pleasure, while a few remained outside displaying acts of daring horsemanship.

They picked up knives from the ground while at full gallop, Indian-like whirling on the sides of their steeds, then up and off like the wind and, while apparently dashing into the surrounding crowd, suddenly reined in their horses upon the haunches. They whirled them up upon their hind legs, then with a stop, dashed off as furiously in the opposite direction.

These were Doniphan's wild riders, who could best even the Mexican caballeros in their feats of horsemanship. The scurrying miners cheered them on with great enthusiasm. Li Chang just smiled at Li Yu and said, "That beats the jugglers at our market in Canton."

They heard a ragged and hairy preacher, who spoke well and with conviction. He warmed everyone with his fine and impassioned delivery. He closed with a benediction but prefaced it by saying: "There will be a divine service in this house next Sabbath—if, in the meantime, I hear of no new diggings!" he laughed.

Nearby was the hotel par excellence of the town. Li Yu easily recognized it as such by its long white colonnade in front, and its numerous windows in the upper story. A large saloon occupied the whole front of the building. There was a perfect Babel of noises from inside. English, French, Spaniards, Portuguese, Italians, Kanakas, Chileans, all were talking in their respective languages. Glasses were jingling; money was rattling. Two fiddlers in a distant corner scraped furiously on their instruments.

Li Chang suggested that he and Li Yu split up—to better enjoy the town.

Crowding inch by inch into one of the many groups, Li Chang found himself at last in front of a large table, neatly covered with blue cloth, upon which was a mass of Mexican silver dollars piled up in stacks. Immediately facing him was the banker, a well-dressed, middle-aged, quiet little man with a demure face. Beside was the croupier, just a boy, whose duty was to take in the winnings and pay out the losses, which he did with wonderful dexterity.

Fronting the dealer was a large Chinese box of exquisite

construction. Upon it were several large piles of native gold, and a dozen or more buckskin bags of all sizes and conditions containing gold dust.

Dollars and half-dollars were piled upon the purses. A close observer could read elation or depression in the anxious eyes of the players as the weight in these bags rose and fell. The purses were in pawn; the dollars and half-dollars were the counters wherewith the banker numbered the ounces or half-ounces that were owed to the bank.

As his winnings mounted, Li Chang called out, "Drinks on me!"

"Twenty-two, you're busted," laughed a fat-faced man of Spanish descent in a red shirt and Chinese cap to Li Chang.

"Twenty to your nineteen, you lose again, Chiney man," the dealer screamed. Li Chang cast a furtive glance around to see if Li Yu was in the vicinity.

He shuffled on, from table to table. At another game, he observed a luckless young Negro man, maybe a runaway slave from America's south. The pointy-nosed dealer rang out, "three Jacks to your pair." Then he rejoined Li Yu.

"Bad news, little brother," Li Chang said. "I was attacked by some drunken miners. The $50 we were to send home, and also my new boots are gone."

Now they only had enough money left to buy dinner. Fortunately, they had already bought next month's provisions; Li Chang promised to pick up a few extra dollars by cooking for some white miners.

Li Yu said nothing.

By this time, the gurgling stomachs of Li Chang and Li Yu warned them it was supper time. There were an endless number of eating-houses and booths. Which one to choose? But there was no Chinese food in sight. And now the crowd was streaming to the other side of the river. They soon found themselves in front of "Little's Hotel," the largest frame building on the right bank of the river, serving the triple role of post-office, store and tavern.

Here they found more miners, who, like them, were in search of one good dinner for the week. Around the table was a collection of ten uncouth men. The contrast between the snow-white tablecloth, china dishes, silver forks and spoons and the unwashed, half-famished, sunburnt crowd of hungry and bearded miners was startling. Li Chang smiled and wondered how he and Li Yu, the only clean shaven ones, had come to be amongst them. But they felt comfortable to be there.

All too often the Li brothers ate alone. Very often, no white person would share a table with them. Thus, Li Chang reminded Li Yu, "If you don't have a seat at the table, you're probably on the menu. Be careful."

Although, the meal was not as good as Li Chang could cook, the dinner of two-inch beef steaks, roasted potatoes, corn-on-the-cob, fresh rolls and cherry pie was still delicious, and everyone appeared heartily to enjoy it. But too often, Americans did not understand that a meal was more than just food. People needed venues in which they entertained each other, sit and converse, negotiate, extract information, and offer and ask for help. This was how things got done, Li Chang believed.

It was always this way. A favor was bestowed, in the form of a great meal, and favors were offered and asked in return. Then there was the social side of life: families and groups of friends needing a place to gather, lovers a place to meet. All of them would come back for more.

6

The Renewed Search for Gold Mountain

Li Chang and Li Yu quickly learned that there was no single Gold Mountain. The gold that there was, was scattered around all the mountains. Some of it was in the ground. Some of it was washing down the river. Li Yu felt so stupid. The Gold Mountain was a fancy, poetical name. It was not the literal truth.

At the start of the gold rush, miners found gold by just dipping a pan into the river. For too often, Li Yu dipped his pan into the cold, swift water. swirled the water out, sifted through the mud and pebbles and found only rocks.

He couldn't hold it anymore, "Where are the melon-sized nuggets?" He asked himself, "Why did I listen to these fantasies?"

Li Chang looked dirtier and more tired than he had ever been at home. But Li Yu had to admit that although Li Chang was small, he could work. Like him, Li Chang was used to working long days, whether it was at home during harvest and planting time or in the kitchen of a nobleman. Li Chang saw their reflection in the water when they washed up. "We came here to get away from the dirt of peasants, and now look at us," Li Chang said with a laugh.

Li Yu had never felt more sore or tired. American soil looked like Chinese soil, but this hard land seemed to grow heavier and heavier with every shovelful.

CHINESE BROTHERS, AMERICAN SONS

They found limited success on their own, so they joined a small mining company run by a man known as the Dragon. He was Chinese, about forty years old, bald with sleepy eyes. He provided food for his workers.

Li Yu stuffed himself. All the vegetables and meat were salted or pickled, but there was lots of it. Basically the cook boiled a big wok of rice and then put pickled vegetables and salted fish and sausages on top. The steam from the rice cooked the sausages and fish at the same time. A kettle of tea heated next to the wok.

"This sure beats weed soup," exclaimed Li Yu. It was more food than he'd ever had at home or when they mined alone, and Li Chang said they would have meat every Sunday, usually a chicken but sometimes pork or even beef. For breakfast, they had rice porridge with sausages and crullers. Li Yu had never eaten so well in the morning.

They went over to the river. They heard the roar from the rapids about 500 feet upstream. Here the river had widened and the water slowed. Li Chang said it was a natural spot for the gold to drop out of the water. The Chinese mining company of about twenty men constructed what the Americans called a wing dam. They built a wall from the riverbank out into the river. Then they built another wall at right angles to the first, cutting off an area of the riverbed. From that they would pluck their gold nuggets, Li Yu said. No, Li Chang said. The gold will be dust.

Another miner Tse An asked Li Yu to write a letter to his family; he, too, was from Canton. His face reminded Li Yu of his dead friend from the ship coming to America. He had the look of a hungry man, hungry not for food but for home. Li Yu didn't want any payment, but Tse An insisted he take this American penny.

Li Yu looked so sad. Li Chang asked him what was wrong.

"I have let down my family," Li Yu said. "I am not successful."

Before Li Chang could comfort him, another man came over and also asked Li Yu to write a letter for him. And then there was a third. Word had spread through the camp. Even the cook came to Li Yu to have a letter written.

Li Chang interrupted Li Yu's letter writing.

"You have a gift," he said. "You can turn a phrase into a powerful weapon for good or a remedy that ails the human spirit. Say what you want to say and let the words fall out. But that is not enough. When the times are right, be fearless in action, too."

"I don't know if I can," Li Yu said to Li Chang.

"Your deepest fear is not that you are inadequate. Your deepest fear is that you are powerful beyond measure. Don't give fear the power to silence or stop you. Remember, wise action and not false bravado is the key," Li Chang said.

By the time Li Yu had finished writing all the letters, Li Chang was already asleep, but Li Yu saw a contented smile on his brother's face that was mirrored on his own face as well. It was nice to feel needed, to be helpful and have some purpose. Li Yu's handful of pennies began to grow into a small pile. Li Yu thought he would just mine for gold, but maybe America needed strong minds just as it needed strong backs. Perhaps there was a place for him here after all.

The next time Li Yu went into the Dragon's tent, the Dragon said he had seen Li Yu writing letters and asked if he could use an abacus as well. Li Yu said that he could, a little.

Li Yu learned the Dragon's bookkeeping system, and he found out that while he and Li Chang made $2 a day, $60 a month (plus a bonus if more gold than expected was discovered), Li Chang was only sending home $10 a month. Where was the rest of the money going?

They were not in debt. Li Chang and Li Yu were among the

few who had bought their own tickets to get to America. Many others were still paying theirs off. The Dragon deducted a certain amount each month for them and sent it to San Francisco to be passed on to the various people who owned the notes.

Finally, a letter arrived from Li Yu's wife, Sun Wei:

> How are you? It has been terrible here in China. Floods have ruined the first rice crop. We thank you for the money you send to us. Other villagers are not so lucky. We have survived thanks to you. We are helping our clan members who are not so fortunate. Could you send more money? Everyone blesses your name.

An American tax man appeared demanding payment from all the workers. One of them, their friend Tse An, had no money and begged the tax collector to give him time. The tax man slipped a knife from a sheath and pressed the tip against Tse An's arm. Finally, Li Chang and a couple of other Chinese miners scraped together a few dollars to help him.

The reality was still clear. They were in a strange country where the Americans did anything they wanted to them. Li Yu longed for home. He wished he was safe.

At the mining company, the Dragon let them have every Sunday off, an American tradition. On that day, Li Yu wrote letters for the other men. Li Chang sat with his brother, mending the tears in their clothes. Li Yu wrote everything in the letters as dictated by his customers, from general wishes to stories that made him want to cry. Fathers wondered about their children. Husbands wanted to know why they had not heard from their wives.

For Li Yu, he was grateful to know that his family was doing well in China and that his son Li Wu was now almost five years old and growing and talking even more. He yearned for the day when he could see Sun Wei again and for the first time, Li Wu.

But still Li Yu added, "I still stay up thinking of Wang Wei. All I have are dreams of her. I wake up in the night with a fear so real. I search through every open door. I spend my life waiting for a moment that just won't come."

"Don't waste your time waiting," Li Chang replied. "You're grieving for the loss of someone who never existed. At some point, you have to realize that Wang Wei can be in your heart but not in your life."

Li Chang gently put his hand on Li Yu's shoulder and said they should enjoy the Sunday. He was the opposite of their father, who could not stand to be idle or see his children idle. Li Yu told his brother he had to write letters until mealtime. They were both looking forward to their noonday meal which would include chicken. The cook had been plucking the birds that morning and there were little white feathers all over like flower petals.

After Li Yu's Sunday letter-writing, he found Li Chang waiting outside with a horse. Li Yu wasn't sure if Li Chang was riding the horse or hanging onto it. His hands clung to the mane as well as the reins. But the horse wasn't going fast. In fact, it was plodding slower than a water buffalo on a hot summer's day. He had rented it, and he told Li Yu they were going for a ride.

But first he wanted to change Li Yu's clothes. He gave him some packages that had been tied to the saddle. Li Yu already had an American cowboy felt hat with a soft brim and boots, and now Li Chang gave him a shirt, a warmer coat and woolen pants. They were expensive. The heavy red flannel shirt fitted fine and the pants had already been taken up by Li Chang.

Though they wanted to go to the top of the hill for the view, Li Chang had trouble turning the horse, which clopped along with a mind of its own. To save his brother's pride, Li Yu commented that the scenery where they were was pretty nice already. Li Chang seemed grateful as he let the horse pick its own path. Tall trees grew on either side. Through the branches, they caught glimpses of cascading waterfalls pouring into the aquamarine American River. The sunlight reflected off the surface in hundreds of curving smiles with brightly-colored wildflowers everywhere. Little did they know that they would see that same American River from an even more majestic viewpoint almost a decade later.

The strangest thing they saw that day was a small open field. There were dozens of sticks crossed like the Chinese word for ten. They were at an American cemetery. A service was going on, American miners were in their best clothes and their hair was slicked back.

These were places mostly forgotten in a year or two, left to the aspens, junipers, pines and sagebrush. There was a sense of desolation and removal from the world and its frantic gold-rush pace. Tree roots pushed up the soil. If the dead were fortunate enough to have been buried in a wooden casket, they had sunk by now.

Li Yu thought again of the many Chinese who didn't make it to America, whose bodies had been thrown like so much garbage into the ocean. Li Chang wrapped his arms around Li Yu. "I'm glad you're here with me," he said.

They returned the horse to town. It was a Sunday, and it was filled with miners from all over. There were all sorts of gambling games going on. Cheerful men were selling liquor everywhere. From other tents they smelled meat cooking and men sitting at a crude table shoveling food into their mouths as fast as they could.

Li Chang headed for the drayer's to return the horse. It was a tent with a corral next to it. Annie, the owner, was an American woman, the first woman he had seen in a long time. Li Yu stared a little too hard, and Li Chang scolded him. Li Yu liked her red hair. She had a good laugh and even gave Li Yu some beef jerky.

At the outskirts of town, about a dozen Americans surrounded them. All of them were wearing guns and knives. Li Yu felt so alone; he stood as stiff as wood. Li Chang grabbed his shoulders and turned him around towards the camp. He whistled to Li Yu to walk and to not show that he was frightened. It would only encourage them to do something.

As Li Yu trudged forward, the jeering started. Suddenly, a huge bearded giant blocked their way. He smelled bad, too. They tried to go around him, but he flung out his arms, as thick as a tree trunk. Then he yelled at them. They didn't know what he said. All Li Yu could see were the rotted teeth in his mouth. Li Chang gave his brother a push while he distracted the giant.

Li Chang was surrounded by the bullies. However, all they wanted to do was scold Li Chang. Li Chang saw Li Yu further down the road heading back to the camp and waved his hand frantically for him to keep walking.

Still, Li Yu felt like a coward when he turned his back on his brother. He did not look back to see if they followed him. He forced his legs to move one step at a time. But his ears strained for footsteps following him.

Li Yu didn't stop until he reached the edge of their camp. Thankfully, Li Chang arrived about fifteen minutes later. He had a couple bruises on his face. Li Chang explained that American miners blamed the Chinese for everything that had gone wrong in their lives — from lower wages to rain and even warts.

"Gold is a curse," Li Chang said. "It twists people's minds and makes them act like beasts."

Li Yu began to think his brother was right. Li Yu shivered, but not from the cold. America was so lovely, and yet so frightening.

CHINESE BROTHERS, AMERICAN SONS

Despite the growing dangers they faced searching for gold (even working for a company), Li Chang seemed content, Li Yu observed. With all its risks, America suited an inventive person like Li Chang. Tired of the salted fish they got in camp; it was his idea to take Li Yu fishing. He fashioned some straight branches by stripping them like they were poles. He took a ball of string from his pocket, got some nails and used a rock to bend them into hooks. When the two poles were ready, he handed one to Li Yu, and they dug worms out of the soil, walked to the stream and cast their lines into the water.

As they sat in the sun by the sparkling water, they forgot for a while about the American tax men and the bullies.

After fishing, they stopped by their camp. Li Chang gave six fish to the cook and playfully said, "Steam them with lots of ginger and green onions."

They then rode back into town. The casual crowd was gone, and the bullies were out. When they returned the horse, Li Chang told Li Yu to stick close to him. Li Yu kept telling himself not to be afraid. Li Chang acted like they were out for a stroll. He was like a whole different man here. Li Yu wished the clan back in China could see how much courage he had. Li Yu hoped he could be brave like his brother.

In China, water chains with troughs and paddles carried water from streams to nearby fields and irrigation ditches, and Li Chang knew how to build them. One day the Dragon had a letter to mail and someone had to take it into town. Afraid of the Westerners, no one wanted a break from work. The Dragon knew this, so he had already prepared some straws in his back pocket. He told them that the one who drew the shortest would go. The Dragon didn't want Li Chang and Li Yu to go because he wanted them to continue working on the water chains. The faster they got the gold, the faster they could go home. But Li Chang insisted on trying. He wanted to be fair to the others. And since he did it, so did his brother.

Naturally, Li Chang's luck held true and he drew the shortest. He returned from town with his shirt torn and cuts and bruises on his face. But at least he was alive, Li Yu said. The Dragon tended to his wounds. When Li Chang took off his shirt, Li Yu saw that his body had even more cuts and bruises. The bullies had jumped him without warning after he mailed the letter.

Li Yu suggested reporting them to the local magistrate and the Dragon looked at him like he had said the most stupid thing. It was no use going to a law enforcement officer, he said, because Chinese were not allowed to testify in court. Chinese were not people to the Americans. If an American jumped one of their claims or robbed a Chinese, it was not a crime — not unless another American saw it and testified. No more going into town. Suddenly, Li Yu felt the Gold Mountain was even more out of reach.

A wooden crate arrived in the camp. The Dragon pried off the board and lifted out a huge chamber pot. He turned it around in his hand. There wasn't a chip on it. The Chinese miners guessed that the Dragon didn't want to use the latrines anymore at night and Li Yu figured that the Dragon must be too scared to go out in the dark. How could they work for a man who was too scared to leave his tent?

Li Yu was in the tent with the Dragon when they heard shouts of "robbers." He began to snatch up sacks of coins for the payroll and made to run away but the Dragon calmly told him to put the money back down and step to the back of the tent. Li Yu hated the thought of losing all their hard-earned money. He told the Dragon he could get under the tent and escape with the money. The Dragon snapped at him to do what he said. Hastily he dropped the sacks back onto the table.

Suddenly, the flap was thrown back and three robbers, all masked, stood there. Their eyes and hair color said they were Americans. Beyond them, Li Yu saw the angry miners and his worried brother. Two of the robbers stayed outside with drawn guns while the third strolled into the tent in broad daylight as if he didn't have a care in the world. He spoke American and demanded the money.

Angrily, the Dragon ordered the robbers to get out. The robber hit the Dragon so hard with his pistol that he fell down. Li Yu shouted in English for the robbers to stop and go away. The Dragon yelled back in Chinese for him to be quiet. Then he pointed to the table and told the robber to take the money and not hurt him anymore. The robber picked up the sacks of coins and stuffed them into his pockets, then walked back out of the tent. His laugh grated on Li Yu's ears like a plane on wood.

For someone who had just been beaten and robbed, the Dragon seemed very calm. Li Yu brought a jar of salve from near his sleeping mat, and he told Li Yu to listen to him next time.

"The robbers are like landlords coming for the rent," the Dragon said.

"It's not fair," Li Yu said, but to his surprise, the Dragon just chuckled.

"The thieves got dimes and pennies. Why did you think I had stunk up my tent with the chamber pot? When trouble started in town, I knew it was time to get ready."

He made Li Yu promise not to tell anyone—not even Li Chang—what he next showed him. Then he reached into the chamber pot and pulled up a packet wrapped in oil cloth. This was his strongbox. That was why he had such a big chamber pot. Robbers would never look in there.

His workers had been wrong about the Dragon. "Where there's no law, you have to use your wits," the Dragon said. He explained that he couldn't make the theft look too easy, or they would become suspicious.

The Dragon was a fitting name for his boss, thought Li Yu. In the Chinese Zodiac, the Dragon is the mightiest of the signs. Dragons symbolize character traits such as dominance and ambition. Dragons prefer to live by their own rules and if left on their own, are usually successful. They're driven, unafraid of challenges, and willing to take risks.

Giving Li Yu a stern look, the Dragon cleaned his hands. If the Chinese killed any white man—even if he was a robber—they would be lynched. All the mob cared about was the color of the victim's skin. And then the Dragon said something that Li Yu wanted always to remember: "You don't have to fight back; the real strong man has the guts not to fight back, takes it and lives on. The family always comes first. Your ghost can't send them money."

Li Yu hated that there was nothing to be done. But it was true that family came first. It wouldn't do them any good if he got himself killed. The sooner he got back to China, the better.

The crews built what they called the Great Wall out of logs and planks. But the river hated being obstructed. It bashed against the dam. The workers shouted and shivered as they hammered boards against the logs. They had to constantly submerge their heads since most of the logs were underwater. Then the first part of the wing dam was done. The last log was set, but there was still quite a bit of water flowing through.

Later they hauled baskets of soil to the river. The dirt was almost like clay, so it was heavy. They dumped it over the face of the Great Wall faster than the river washed it away. Then they added boughs that were saved from the trimmed trees. Even so, the river was determined to keep to its old bed. It found cracks in the structure and sloshed around inside it.

CHINESE BROTHERS, AMERICAN SONS

They brought in Li Chang's water chains and set them up. The chain was turned by pedals and everyone took a turn to work it, ladling the water out. The water level slowly dropped behind the Great Wall and now they could see the bottom of the stream. Li Yu looked for gold, but all the specks he saw were fish.

The water level dropped further over the next three days and Li Chang and Li Yu began to build rockers, rectangle boxes with a slight slope to the bottom across which cleats were nailed. One end of the box had a screen cover into which the water and mud was poured. It went through the box, over the cleats and exited from the open end. The whole thing rested on curved boards so it rocked back and forth, which is how the machine got its name. If you were lucky, there were specks of gold lying in the opening at the end of the rocker.

Li Chang high-stepped through the mud and wet gravel until he was in the middle of the area behind the Great Wall. It was there that his nose told him to dig. He then high-stepped back to the bank where a rocker stood. He dumped the test shovelful onto the screen cover, then he dumped a bucket of water over it. The dirty water traveled down the angled bottom and gushed out the open end. Li Yu didn't see any melon-sized nuggets lying in the screen box. All he saw were small rocks and bits of gravel and he was disappointed. But Li Chang ran a finger along one of the wooden cleats, and then held up a gleaming fingertip. The little flecks on it gleamed like stars. Li Yu didn't think he had ever seen anything as pretty. He was reminded again and understood how gold could sink its claws into someone. Everyone let out a whoop and a roar. The sun reflected off the wet riverbed, so it shone as if it were all gold. All their worries evaporated like the mist rising from the mud.

They went on digging, down another three feet. Still more gold. They began to eat better. A wagon came to them with using sophisticated methods to extract the gold. Hydraulic miners used giant water nozzles to wash away entire hillsides.

They should have stayed in China, Li Chang said, rather than work for such an operation that destroyed the Earth.

Then, surprise! Li Yu saw Jimmy Smits and his friend Brian Sullivan toiling up-river from the company's camp. Smits handed him a bunch of fresh new pencils. All Li Yu had from his last shipment were stubs. He felt a little guilty that he didn't have anything to give them in return, so he told them to wait a moment while he got some tea for everyone. He was going to trade some Chinese beef jerky for the letter writing pieces. It was sweet as well as salty, different from American jerky.

He and Li Chang talked with Li Yu's American friends. The Americans were having trouble finding gold and were thinking about trying their luck back in San Francisco. The merchants were the ones getting rich, they said. They could charge a fortune just for one egg.

"The miners dig up the gold, but we don't get to keep it. Most of it goes to storekeepers for food and other things," Sullivan said.

"But when the gold plays out, prices will fall back to normal," Li Chang countered.

"The real money is in the land," Smits said.

Li Yu thought of the rich lands they saw as being "perfect for rice."

Smits said he was going to start a farm here to grow fresh vegetables. "Too many Americans get sick from scurvy without them."

Smits asked about Li Yu's wife and son. Li Yu didn't think he would ask her to risk such a dangerous trip to America. Besides, he and Li Chang were sending money to them and he still expected to return home. He was not going to turn his back on China. His clan had been there in Kwangtung province for hundreds of years. Many generations were buried in its soil.

But Li Yu did not have a strong yearning to see Sun Wei. "I guess I always knew inside," he said.

Li Yu heard a commotion in the camp. It was an American. He didn't recognize him at first. But when he saw the slips of paper in his hand, he figured it was the tax collector.

The Dragon tried to protest, and the American unhooked a whip from his belt. When he shook it out, it was as long as a man is tall and as lethal as a cobra. And when he cracked it on the ground, bits of dirt flew everywhere. He demanded to be paid the taxes.

Sullivan stared at him hard. He whispered to Li Yu and Smits that the man was no tax collector. He was another miner who had just lost his money in a poker game with his cousin the night before. Smits wouldn't back down. He would tell the magistrate. Sullivan was an American too. He could testify in court. The bogus tax collector gave up.

Though an icy breeze was blowing from the water and the tea had almost frozen, Li Yu didn't feel cold anymore.

Li Yu could not stand it any longer. He asked the Dragon where all the gold went that was stored in the chamber pot. The strongbox and chamber pot were only big enough to hold a day's worth of gold. So the Dragon must be storing the hoard elsewhere. Underneath his straw, sleeping mat, the Dragon and Li Yu dug. A jar was exposed and Li Yu opened the lid to see it was filled with little sacks of gold dust and nuggets. There were also molds for something long and thin. It took Li Yu a moment to realize they were for chopsticks. The Dragon wasn't cold at all when he was burning all that firewood. He was melting the gold into the shape of ordinary-looking chopsticks. Then he blackened them so they looked just like the real thing.

The Dragon shipped them out on the same wagon that brought their supplies. He said that a couple times, Americans had searched the wagons, but he always put real chopsticks on top. So far, all the boxes had made it to San Francisco.

Li Yu came down with a severe cold and drank tea Li Chang brought him. The heavy snow prevented them from doing any work that day. As he rested, he thought about Li Chang and decided he would make someone a good father. Li Yu wondered about his own son and wife in China. Li Yu asked his brother why he had never married.

"Why should I marry? One marries to have children, but I already have two children, you and my cooking," Li Chang said.

An American doctor came to see Li Yu. Now he seemed to be on the mend, and he survived another winter in America. Even Li Yu loved this land in the spring. The fields were green after the winter rains, flowers sprouted everywhere. He just stood outside the tent and smelled all the young, growing things.

He remembered that smell. It was the planting smell. It was the time when the fields were flooded again and the young Li Chang and Li Yu took rice seedlings from the sprouting tubs and planted them in the muddy water. They hoped that everything would grow and their bellies would be full in the coming year, for a change. For this coming year at least, his family far away didn't have to worry. There was the gold and their earnings, now safely in San Francisco.

But Li Chang said it was even more dangerous now that the Americans' claims were playing out. American miners resented the fact that the Dragon's company was still getting a bit of gold from its wing dam.

"It's not our fault that the white miners picked wrong," Li Yu said. "And anyway, it hasn't been their country for long. They took it from the Mexicans, and the Mexicans took it from the

Indians."

"I hope the rest of America doesn't see it that way," Li Chang said.

"The rest of America doesn't mean crap," Li Yu said. "We're in California."

Now Li Yu looked to the sky and saw the swans flying away. He wished he could go with them. He shouted at the swans, "I want to leave all these crazy people behind!"

For the last three nights, the Americans had held rallies just outside their camp, chanting, "The Chinese must go."

No time to brood. Everyone wanted to send letters back home to China. They were scared, which meant they naturally thought of home. Sometimes it was just a few lines that told their families how much they missed them. Most, however, poured out all their worries and fears. Li Yu heard them over and over. He tried to be a machine that just took down their dictation, but he got tired and very scared. The pennies kept on mounting.

Li Yu couldn't sleep. The Americans had another meeting. Their shouts carried through the tent walls. He heard the word "kill" a lot. Sometimes he wished he didn't know some American words.

Li Chang gathered the other Chinese miners together. He told them that last May, mining districts all over the state had driven Chinese out. In some places, the Chinese were allowed to leave with their belongings. In others, they were robbed and beaten but still allowed to go. In a few places, the Chinese never left at all except as bones back to China.

If the American mobs came to the camp to drive them out, Li Chang said they should not resist. Other miners asked why they should not fight back, and Li Chang replied that it would be even more dangerous; they would make the Americans even angrier and then someone would get hurt for sure. They could not win against so many. Especially, when there was no law to protect them.

Li Yu also remembered what the Dragon had said about true courage, about how really brave people put their families before their pride. But it stuck in his throat. He wanted to fight. However, he decided to obey his brother.

"Sometimes it is nothing more than gritting your teeth against the pain, and working every day, the slow walk toward a better life," Li Chang said. "That is the sort of bravery we must have now."

Li Yu prayed that somehow Li Chang would pull off a miracle and they would be safe.

Li Chang said that most Americans hated the Chinese, but he added, "They hate Chinese because they are scared of us, and they are scared for their families just like we would be."

"I still don't forgive them," said Li Yu.

"You don't have to," Li Chang said. "You just have to go on with your life. There is a difference between giving up and knowing when you have had enough."

What we can take ownership of, he said, is "ourselves and our choices. For example, if you are eating with white miners at an American restaurant, be polite and try some of the dishes, but don't polish off that whole plate of beans and salt pork in a futile attempt to assimilate. Unless you want to. Being yourself in a world that is constantly trying to make you something else is a great accomplishment."

Li Yu's American friend Jimmy Smits stumbled into camp. Sweating and panting, he had been running all the way. He told them to get out. A mob was coming to drive them from the almost-used-up claim. The Chinese miners who understood English told the others the news in hushed, frightened voices. Li Yu told Smits to leave. He knew Smits had taken a considerable risk in coming and he didn't want the mob to catch Smits here. Smits said he was going to stay; he had lost his taste for mining. He'd try his hand at farming.

The Americans were coming. Li Yu hid his diary in his pants. It was the one thing he didn't want to lose.

When the mob came, they had torches, in the light of which Li Chang and Li Yu saw the bully faces in front. Behind the front rows, the faces looked different. Many looked embarrassed. They didn't seem to want to be part of the mob. Li Chang reminded the Chinese miners to stay calm and not fight back. Then he announced to the mob in broken English that they were leaving.

A dozen Americans started grabbing things. Some of them, though, were ashamed and pulled the looters back. The mob found and kept the strongbox, but there was only a small amount of gold in it. The Chinese miners stumbled away into the darkness amidst gunfire and chants of "Kill the Chinks."

Li Chang yelled to Li Yu, "Stay close!"

7

THE FINAL OPPORTUNITY

LI YU INSISTED they give the gold one more chance, so he and Li Chang set out into the western Sierras, accompanied only by Li Yu's little dog, Rosco.

They were attacked by gold-mining bandits and all their provisions were stolen, except for one rifle and a butcher knife which were overlooked, and a couple of candles, flint and steel, cookware and cups and some spices, tea, coffee and ointment in Li Chang's large coat pockets. They were knocked unconscious and left to die as winter set in, but not before the outlaws severed Li Chang's queue.

Notwithstanding the demeaning origins of the custom of wearing the queue, a Chinese man experienced deep humiliation on having his queue cut off against his will by a white person. With his queue gone, Li Chang knew he could not return to China.

"Can you ever forgive my greed?" Li Yu cried out "What have I done to you? What will you do?"

"I think I'll grow a moustache," whispered Li Chang.

Li Chang now wore a look of serene contentment. "Don't worry little brother. I am at peace. My decision to stay has been made. I'm alive, and you are, too. I'm hungry."

Fortunately, they found an abandoned cabin, a long-ago

encampment for someone who had struck it rich, thought Li Yu. They were close to starving, but Li Chang could make something out of nothing. He hunted around inside the cabin, and found several naked leg-bones of deer, long since stripped by dogs and wolves. These he gladly gathered, cracked open a couple and found in each a yellow shriveled string of marrow. He warmed some water found in a discarded jug in the cabin, washed the bones and boiled them, producing a very cheesy-tasting broth which he seasoned with salt and pepper. Li Yu greedily swallowed it down.

A large mixed flock of geese and swan flew over to the northwest, too far away to shoot. Geese always set Li Yu's pup Rosco barking. They must eat. What about Li Yu's faithful dog, his poor little Rosco, who had shared his sufferings? Could they make of him one meal and then die regretting it? Li Yu would not, and neither would his brother.

Outside, they found the carcass of a long-ago killed deer. Li Chang examined the deer-skin and found on the flesh side some very small strips of dry meat but the strips were full of worms. He carefully opened them, and with his butcher knife, scraped out the insects and tore off the bits of meat. He boiled them with two old cracked leg bones with another inch of tallow from a candle. He made Li Yu a broth and served it with coffee. Then they ate the coffee grounds with salt.

They were so tired they couldn't move and soon dozed off. They heard a wolf bark. Li Yu took his gun and set out to look for some game. He saw the tracks of a grizzly bear, perfectly fresh in the mud and snow. Deer tracks went in all directions. But no luck. The next day, Li Yu again took his gun and went to try for game of any kind. It started to rain; he got three hundred yards and he found himself too feeble to proceed. So he returned to the cabin and discovered a deer's head under the eaves of the cabin;

a long time ago it must have become wedged in the logs and had died there.

"Ha! We have food!" Li Yu screamed.

It was half-decayed and consumed by worms and insects, but Li Chang took it to a stump near the cabin, chopped it with his butcher's knife and cut out the shriveled tongue. He gave the head and root of the tongue to the tail-wagging Rosco and put the other half of the tongue in a kettle to cook. While this was boiling, Li Yu reinspected the skins and found one of a fawn with the hoofs and fetlock-joints attached. These he cut off, and Li Chang threw them also in the kettle. Li Chang made tea and thanked Confucius that they had another meal, with some solid food.

Li Yu wrinkled his face while slowly digesting the food, which possessed a queer taste, and was probably, in different circumstances, quite disgusting. But Li Chang and Li Yu also recalled the days of famine in China and their mother's weed soup.

Now all that Li Yu and Li Chang had were two tallow candles and a dozen acorns, just found, that the wild animals overlooked. Li Yu hoped to be able to walk better soon. Li Chang rubbed his brother's legs several times a day with camphor and cayenne, both of which they were lucky enough to possess. If they decided to leave the cabin, they would be facing at least three nights' exposure to cold, wild animals and maybe Indians. In Li Yu's feeble condition, Li Chang did not know if they would make it. Li Yu told Li Chang to go on without him, but Li Chang refused.

"I'm strong enough to carry you," Li Chang said.

They decided to leave and prepared to do so. They had to reach water. They packed the two tallow candles, now just one-inch nubs, cookware and cups, flint and steel, spices, tea, butcher's knife and rifle and set off, and within about 800 yards they found a small stream. They unloaded their gear, started a fire and made tea. They drank a cupful each.

Li Yu, while he was sitting down and leaning against a tree, proudly shot a small bluebird. He gave the feet and entrails to the begging Rosco. Li Chang slightly grilled the bird and gave most of it to Li Yu to eat. They proceeded—exceedingly stiff and weak—and resting on rocks, it seemed, every fifty paces. They descended a very rugged and crooked path to a stream which they barely managed to cross without falling in, jumping from rock to rock, with the aid of a pole. Then they ascended a hill, on the western side, climbing about 300 yards and then another 100 yards more before they gave up.

When they had recovered, Li Chang took out one of the candles, salted and peppered it and gave it to Li Yu to eat. Li Chang cut up a piece of rawhide and gave it to poor Rosco to gnaw on. He also gave Rosco the candlewick.

They next came upon an abandoned camp and found some seeds that had been spilled on the ground. Li Chang noticed nearby a few very small sprouts of cabbage, lettuce and radishes—none over two inches long. They got down on their hands and knees and carefully gathered them and ate them, roots and all—and some grains of sand, too. It was the sweetest cold salad they had ever had.

"Better than mom's weed soup," smiled Li Chang to Li Yu.

Another sleepless and cold night, with the wolves howling ever so close. They proceeded the next morning and saw a group of men they first thought were Indians. Li Chang cocked his brother's gun and quickly walked towards them. They were Chinese. He saluted them, staggered, fell and pleaded for something to eat for himself and Li Yu. One of the men gave the brothers some tea and some dried pork with stale bread. The food was soon devoured. They traveled on with these men for fourteen miles—seven to Steep Hollow—and seven the other side of it. Li Chang had to drag Li Yu's feeble body—at least mentally. Alone, Li Yu would not have made it.

It started to rain, which prevented the Chinese men from continuing their journey, and they fastened blankets up to create a sort of tent to sleep under. They huddled together under the shelter from the rain, and invited the Li brothers to join them, but there was no room. Li Chang and Li Yu were satisfied to rest their weary heads and shelter their shoulders only between their saviors' legs. Their bodies from their waist to their feet were just fine outside the tent.

Li Yu gave Rosco a pork bone.

They talked with the men about their experiences since leaving China, and one by one, it became clear that most of these men from China had made the decision to forgo their mining stakes and instead look for a place in a city or some other enterprising venture to call their own.

Li Chang told the Chinese huddled under the tent, "I've come to think of California as home. And all the animals are my kin. Sometimes the land is so beautiful it takes my breath away. And the thought of leaving it makes me ache inside. If only we could get along with our neighbors."

"What are we to do now?" the Chinese men asked Li Chang.

Li Chang said Americans wanted to build levees to reclaim some of the Sacramento delta and turn it into farmland. The mountains had been pouring rich soil down the river for millennia, but that kind of work was too hard for Americans. It might not pay as well as mining, but there would be a lot of jobs for the Chinese. That cheered everyone up. They could still send money home. It was not going to make them rich, but it was still something. American money was still worth much more in China. The important thing was that with that kind of labor, the

CHINESE BROTHERS, AMERICAN SONS

American bullies would not be jealous, Li Chang said.

Though not afraid of hard work, Li Chang and Li Yu just didn't see themselves piling up dirt to make levees. It would be like they were in prison. Li Chang wanted freedom and to better himself. He wanted a new adventure. Li Chang and Li Yu had tried gold mining alone and with a group. It was time to do something else, Li Chang said to Li Yu. He wanted to go to the city and use the culinary skills he had learned in China.

"I believe in the power of food to bring people together," he said.

They said goodbye to the Chinese men and trekked off towards San Francisco. They found an abandoned shack with no roof but a fireplace, and Li Yu got a good fire started. They lay down in the blankets that the Chinese men insisted the Li brothers take with them. As Li Yu stared at the flickering flames, he thought of his mother and his wife. He used to squat by the front of the stove feeding the fire while they cooked. They used to hum a tune, and the flames before him seemed to dance to the same melody. Their mother was now gone. When would he see Sun Wei again? And where was Wang Wei?

Li Yu must have slept for quite a while, because the fire was now dying. There were little dots of light all over the dirt floor of the cabin. They looked like the torches the mob had carried. What was reflecting the light? He crawled out of his blanket and crept across the floor with his nose almost touching the dirt. He smelled gold. There was gold dust scattered all around them.

Why didn't the owner pick up the gold? Li Chang suspected this area had been worked in the early months of the gold rush. There had been plenty of easy gold back then, and probably the owner thought the floor wasn't worth the time and that there would be whole nuggets just waiting to be picked up down in the river.

"Maybe even as big as melons," Li Yu laughed.

They built a rocker from one of the walls of the shack. It took a half day to build it. Carefully, Li Yu carried a shovelful of soil by the fireplace. He used his hat to pour water in. He didn't see anything. He leaned his head this way and that, studying the wooden cleats from all angles.

"Wait," Li Yu said. "There's a faint gleam of light." He ran his fingertips along the edge and held it up. Bits of gold clung to it. It took only a day and half to get a small pouch of gold.

"We'll make our melon-sized nuggets the hard way, one flake at a time," Li Chang said.

Now, it was on to the next abandoned claim as they headed towards San Francisco. While they worked, gathering the leftover gold flakes, Li Yu told his brother about some investment schemes he had heard about from his friends and mentioned in some of the miners' letters, including running a restaurant. Li Chang agreed that a restaurant might be a good idea for him in the future, financed by their new-found gold holdings.

Li Chang and Li Yu continued their trek through the western Sierras towards San Francisco. The gold industry was declining and the gradual abandonment of placer mining even by the Chinese provided abundant pathos. They saw it in the many towns and camps where empty buildings in disrepair stood in rows, and no nailing-up of blinds or closing of doors could hide the emptiness. The cheap squalor of the Chinese streets added misery to the scene—even the scent of pure mountain air was overcome by the odors of complete wretchedness. Pigs prowled the streets. Every deserted cabin told a story of an effort that had ended in bitter failure. The stranded men who lingered had a melancholy look as of fish washed ashore and left to die.

Li Chang felt even more that it was time to move on. He and Li Yu walked into Hangtown. They found only one family remaining, too desperately poor to leave their home. All the other buildings—general store, church, post office, the half-dozen saloons, and many dwellings—stood with wide-open doors, their cloth walls and ceilings torn down to make squaw petticoats. With this slow decay, the venturous, both good and bad, had drifted off to other gold mining territories. Or they returned home and took other jobs. Or they perished, leaving no one to regret the passing of their lives.

Li Yu saw an old gray, bearded man sitting on a bench outside a general store. He described Wang Wei to her. The old man said, "Yes, she's been here." But his memory wasn't clear. "Was it yesterday? No, wait the day before."

Still traveling the Sierra foothills, getting closer to San Francisco, Li Chang saw the old, rude scars of mining; deep trenches yawned, disordered heaps charged the ground, yet they were no longer bare. Time, with friendly rain, and wind and flood, slowly, surely, leveled all, and a compassionate cover of greenery weaved a carpet fresh and cool from mile to mile. Nature thus gently healed the humble Earth. There was hope that man could be molded and changed, too, Li Chang told Li Yu.

Li Chang now knew, again, more than ever, that it was time to move on. How could he have known that he would be back in the Sierras a decade later changing the course of his new nation?

As they fought on through the rain, it was clear to Li Chang that Li Yu was thinking of Wang Wei, a woman he knew not at all, and his son, a boy he had never seen.

"A fool will lose tomorrow by reaching back for yesterday, but I will find Wang Wei for you and then you can choose for yourself," Li Chang promised.

Li Chang and Li Yu finally arrived in San Francisco. They made their way along the now well-built and well-lighted streets, as alive by night as by day, where boys in high-pitched voices were already crying out the headlines of the latest San Francisco papers. Between 1 a.m. and 2 a.m. in the morning they found themselves comfortably in bed in a luxurious room in the Oriental Hotel, which stood, as well as they could learn, on a filled-up cove not far from the spot where they had arrived on the *Libertad* five years before.

When they awoke in the morning, they looked out from their windows over the city of San Francisco, with its storehouses, towers and steeples, its courthouses and theaters and hospitals. They saw its wharves and harbor, with its 1,000-ton clipper ships, more in number than were sheltering in Canton or Boston on that day. San Francisco was now one of the capitals of the American Republic, and the sole trader with a new world, the awakened Pacific.

When they looked eastward across the bay, the Li brothers saw a beautiful town on the fertile, wooded shores of the Contra Costa with steamers and ferryboats, large and small, plying back and forth. They saw capacious freighters and passenger carriers serving all parts of the great bay and its tributaries, the lines of their smoke marking the horizon.

When they saw all these things, and reflected on what they had once seen here and what now surrounded them, they could scarcely keep their hold on reality. But this was real.

"We are fulfilled," Li Chang said to Li Yu. "The possibilities in America are endless."

They now walked with a proud stride, an uplifted open countenance.

They awoke early in the morning to meet the clerk in the American bank who weighed and recorded their deposits. The clerk was very curious. He wanted to know if they had made a big strike. They decided to just smile and say as little as possible.

Once they got their bank draft, they went over to Chinatown

to the benevolent association headquarters for their district back in China and remitted some of the money back to China. Li Yu hoped they would hear quickly from the family that their money was received.

Li Chang handed the clerk the draft from the American bank; the clerk's eyebrows shot up. It was not a small sum. He held the paper up to the window and studied the signature every which way to see if it was a forgery. Li Chang told him to check with the bank. The clerk sent an assistant scooting over there. The draft was good, the assistant told the clerk.

The clerk remembered the Li brothers and told Li Yu the job offer was still open.

"Not now," Li Yu replied. "Maybe later."

They were staying in Chinatown's finest boardinghouse. It had real American beds, no straw mats on the floor. Li Yu felt rich. The room was above a restaurant. Such wonderful smells came from the kitchen. His mouth watered.

They bathed and then they went to a street-side barber. The barber carried a bamboo pole over his shoulders from which he balanced a stool, furnace, water, razors and assorted brushes. Li Chang was impressed that the itinerant barber always managed to keep the water boiling.

"This is a real barber," said Li Yu. "How we stood the torture of a scrape without the soothing influence of soap is a mystery to me."

Li Yu had the crown of his head shaved and sides trimmed; his pigtail glistened. For Li Chang, since his pig tail had been chopped off by the gold-mining thugs, he had his head shorn bald. They then had the wax scooped out of their ears. A real deluxe job, just like for rich gentlemen!

They wanted to celebrate the fifth anniversary of their arrival on Gold Mountain.

Li Chang said, "We eat."

Before starting their meal, Li Chang went outside and invited others to share the banquet with them. Li Chang reminded his brother that the high point of every meal was never the food itself, but always the act of sharing it, with friends and family, or with strangers.

To their new Chinese and American acquaintances, Li Chang made a toast: "Food and friends are inseparable. To Confucius and to our community!" The tea cups clanged together.

Enough of that, thought Li Yu as he held his bowl to his mouth and shoveled as fast as he could, chewing crackly pork and pressed duck in one bite, gulping it all down while indiscriminately jabbing for more from the center dishes of pea pod greens, bitter melon, stuffed black mushrooms and celery cabbage. He ate as if food was scarce and he would be left behind as the runt pig. Li Yu picked up the almost-empty soup tureen and drank directly from it. Then he threw down his bowl and chopsticks, and spit the bones "*p-foo*" out on the table.

Li Chang laughed. "At my restaurant you will show some manners or I will feed you nothing but beans and salt pork," he said.

After this refreshing interlude, Li Chang disappeared on what he said was an errand.

Later, there was a letter from home, too. Finally. Li Chang opened the envelope. Inside was a letter wrapped around another envelope. He gave Li Yu that page because it had his name on it. As Li Chang read the gossip in his letter, he chuckled occasionally or muttered a few words.

Li Yu opened his envelope and unfolded the letter from his wife, Sun Wei:

Whatever you do, do not let your brother read this

letter. I knew if anyone could keep you alive, it would be your brother. He volunteered to leave the family because they were poor. And he gave them money while he was learning how to cook up north. Not only are both of you safe, but you have also helped us so much. We are not hungry now, even though we have not been able to buy a small plot of land of our own as you thought we would.

We have not been receiving all the money you said you have sent.

We love you. We want you to come home. Of course, it has to be all right with your brother.

Li Chang said his brother should go home, since his wife wanted it. But Li Yu said he wanted to stay.

"All I know is the way I feel. I've made my mind up," Li Yu said. "I'll live my life alone. I guess I've always known I would say goodbye to Sun Wei. What's wrong with me?"

He agonized over his feelings. And what was happening to the money they had sent to their family, he wondered?

Li Chang didn't mention himself going back. He knew that going back to China was no longer an option for him. He said he might try and open a restaurant, but he was affected by the ambivalence about becoming American that many Chinese immigrants carried with them.

"So much American ethnic history is either told as a sentimental romance like Gold Mountain, or as a litany of the wrongs done to the newcomers," he said to Li Yu. "We know the true story is somewhere in between. It's about excruciating dilemmas and a tug-of-war between the old world and the new."

Li Yu couldn't sleep. He, like his brother, remembered the good people he had met here on Gold Mountain. He thought of the beautiful waterfalls and meadows and other wonders he had seen. Those were the real treasures, not the gold.

And there were his friends, Jimmy and Brian, who like him had become men. He'd miss them as much as he missed his clan in Kwangtung province. Maybe more. They were all dreamers, and they were all risk-takers. They were his clan in spirit if not in blood.

"But I've got a wife and child," Li Yu said with some tinge of regret, "Who I have faithfully supported these last five years."

They had come for both adventure and riches, but they had stayed and sunk their roots, tenuous as they were. "I'd feel like a coward if I went back to China now," Li Yu said.

He was too excited to sleep now. He thought about life in Kwangtung—the endless days of drudgery and backbreaking work in the rice paddies. There, even a rich person couldn't ride on a horse to waterfalls and meadows of flowers. It was not dignified. And there were so many things people were not supposed to do in China. He could not even scratch when he itched. That kind of life now seemed to him tighter than a too-small jacket.

"Here on the Gold Mountain, I'm free. I can scratch all I want. And I can get all the books I want in San Francisco," Li Yu said.

And then it hit him. "The swans have two homes, why can't I? I'll go home for a short visit. Then I'll come right back to the Gold Mountain."

8

THE STREETS OF SAN FRANCISCO

LI YU NEVER asked, but he knew. His brother Li Chang had squandered all of the money. There would be no fancy San Francisco Chinese restaurant with tables and chairs of mahogany and china of porcelain for Li Chang to own and to cook in.

Still, work was plentiful for young men who did not choose to try their luck in the gold fields or who, like the Li brothers, had done so.

They could hire out as day laborers or household servants, take construction jobs or peddle food and other items in the street. Even though the income from such work was low, it was more than the starvation pittances on which most Chinese tried to survive in China.

In California, the Chinese could also find other work as gardeners, errand boys, factory workers, fishermen and tenant farmers. Like most immigrants in the past, some started sending back letters to their families in China, urging their wives, children, parents, brothers and sisters to join them.

There was a need for Chinese barbershops. Shaving the frontal area of the head and braiding the rest of their hair into a single long plait or queue was a complicated process. Under Chinese law an immigrant who cut off his queue or had it chopped off, as Li Chang had, could not return to China. This law remained in effect in China until 1911 when the Manchu dynasty fell.

The Chinese not in mining lived in San Francisco clustered in a ten-block area known as "little China," "little Canton," or the "Chinese quarter." Later it was known as Chinatown.

Some Chinese, like Li Chang and Li Yu, hammered a shanty together using local materials, while others used prefabricated wooden structures brought over from Hong Kong. Inside these shacks, the Chinese created a rough semblance of home.

Because tradition generally kept married women at home in China, caring for their children and their in-laws, and because single women did not travel alone, Chinatowns were largely bachelor societies.

By early 1852, over 20,000 Chinese had arrived in San Francisco; in 1865 the number had swelled to 50,000 in the whole state. For most, San Francisco was the port of entry before they wandered out into the gold fields, and in the late 1850s, an increasing number were returning to San Francisco. Plenty of money could be made from meeting their dietary preferences, and not surprisingly, thriving businesses catering to Chinese needs soon developed.

Most importantly, Li Chang had a place to cook and customers to cook for. He built a brick stove and chimney like those in his homeland — a brick bench packed with earth, constructed near an inside window of their one-room shanty to permit smoke to escape. By day the room was a kitchen; at night it was where they slept. Diners ate under a tent in the alley. Li Chang's Miners' Restaurant was born on Chinatown's edge.

Li Chang called his "restaurant" his "Big Opportunity." It helped that Li Yu prepared a sign on a long piece of cloth, and with ink and brush wrote "RESTAURANT — WE SPEAK ENGLISH." Then Li Yu helped Li Chang up the ladder. Thump, thump, thump, thump. He nailed the sign to the restaurant.

CHINESE BROTHERS, AMERICAN SONS

Li Yu said, "The sign is beautiful."

Chinese grocery stores, providing the locals with foods imported from China, quickly followed. The stores were filled with dried mushrooms, seaweed, tea, ham, dried fish, and duck, and vendors hawked fruits and vegetables in reed baskets suspended from bamboo poles. Small shopkeepers spread game meat on sidewalk mats. The area reeked of fish as Chinese fishermen who worked along the bay sold their catches to miners and the burgeoning food industry.

Li Chang, reminded of the markets back home, visited the neighborhood markets once or twice daily to ensure that he served the freshest meats, fruits and vegetables to his customers. Homemade tofu, eggs, live poultry and dogs ready for slaughter might also be available along with lots of dried medicinal foods. He might buy a whole chicken, and the market owner would take his cleaver and chop it into a hundred pieces so it was ready for Li Chang to cook in his wok—with the head and feet in a bag on the side. Clutching his American dollars and coins, he bartered and laughed endlessly with his fellow Chinese entrepreneurs. Generally, Li Chang could barter down about 30 percent off the original price.

"Five cents for three apples, too much, I'll take six apples for that price. And then you can come by for some American apple pie," Li Chang chortled.

Chinese restaurants soon became beloved by San Franciscans of all races and in short order became a selling point that encouraged Americans to visit the city. They ranged from the restaurants which were little more than cheap shacks, such as Li Chang's Miners' Restaurant, to upscale establishments fitted out with regal décor—wood screens imported from China, gas lamp chandeliers, marble and carved furniture where customers enjoyed rare delicacies such as bird's nest soup and shark's fin.

For the most part, Li Chang wanted to keep his cuisine Cantonese, the culinary style of Kwangtung province, with dishes characterized by a tender and slightly sweet taste with sauces light and mellow. Cantonese cuisine included almost all edible foods in addition to the staples of pork, beef and chicken, snakes, snails, chicken feet and duck tongues.

"Chinese food is defined by the flavor principle of soy sauce, ginger, garlic and green onions," Li Chang explained to anyone who would listen. Cooking methods included stir-frying and steaming. "And the most important thing is rice. For true Cantonese food, everything else is a side dish," he said.

Not all the dishes Li Chang served, however, were traditional Chinese fare. Late one evening, a group of drunken white miners entered Li Chang's Miners' Restaurant demanding service. On the verge of closing for the night, Li Yu prudently told Li Chang to feed them and avoid trouble. Li Chang, who had shown he could make something out of nothing, stir-fried the remaining table scraps in his wok—a mélange of fried vegetables, meat, and gravy—and called it chop suey.

The miners raved about this new Chinese delicacy, and soon people all over San Francisco were clamoring for it.

Most of the Chinese immigrants were semi-literate or illiterate, so letter writers such as Li Yu were vital in Chinatown society. Building upon his writing to his wife and their mother, letter-writing for the miners and for the Chinese Six Companies, Li Yu became a quick study in the English language and found his talents much in demand. Li Yu had only a basic education in Chinese, but he had been voraciously reading the books Li Chang gave him since he was young. Li Yu also picked up languages quickly, and became fluent not only in English but also in Spanish.

For a small fee, now three cents a letter, Li Yu wrote letters in calligraphic Chinese script by brush and ink or by pencil — the customer's choice. Letter-writing proved to be a reasonable source of income for Li Yu as there were so many illiterate immigrants waiting to write to their families at least once a month. He helped pen the thoughts and feelings of the coolies and peasants on a strange shore. He also read out return letters for the illiterate. When restaurant business was slow, Li Yu set up on a table at his brother's restaurant.

It was very important for Li Yu to be accurate while reading or writing letters. Apart from writing letters, people approached Li Yu to compose spring couplets, invitation cards, leases and marriage certificates.

Organizations like the Chinese Six Companies took care of the banking needs and handled remittances home. The companies also dutifully sent the bones of the deceased back to their families in China for burial in the soil of their native villages.

In order to expand his non-Chinese clientele, Li Chang worked at learning how to cater to American tastes. The location of his humble restaurant in an often muddy alley on Chinatown's fringe, as well as the restaurant's name, encouraged non-Chinese customers to sample the food. To save space, Li Chang moved the kitchen outside — four posts stuck down into the ground and covered over the top with factory cloth — no floor but the ground. At least now the diners had a roof over their heads and a floor under their feet. Sometimes he made mince pies and apple pies and squash pies. He tried his hand at mince turnovers and donuts. He made biscuits and, now and then, Indian Johnny cake (corn meal flat bread).

During the busy times each day, Li Chang set two tables which were about ten feet in length parallel to each other with four benches surrounding each, and Li Yu did all the little fixings such as filling pepper boxes and vinegar cruets and mustard pots and butter cups. Li Chang still longed for the day when he could cook for more Chinese people, or at least make more Chinese food, but as the weeks turned to months and then into years, Li Chang realized he had found his niche with his little restaurant serving a curious mix of American and Chinese dishes.

Li Yu was often still homesick. Or maybe it was guilt. He continued to send money to Sun Wei, and his son Li Wu, but he seldom wrote his wife. It had been years since he had waved good-bye to his wife. He still thought of Wang Wei, of holding her. "When will this strong yearning end?" he thought.

Li Chang, when not cooking, found time to mingle with his patrons and shared his Confucian wisdom of cooperation and working well with others to accomplish a common purpose. When lonely young and old men arrived at his restaurant, he would often counsel them: "We're all interconnected. If you help others, they will help you. And you don't have to say 'yes' to every request. It usually only takes a few minutes to give what is needed. You want the affection, gratitude and loyalty from others, not indifference. All that is required is a generous heart and a caring frame of mind."

The air around Li Chang and Li Yu each day was undeniably alive with good smells and the sounds of the patrons chattering happily. Each table was filled at all meals. Li Yu strode back and forth, steamer baskets filled with dumplings and trays held high. Bubbles of laughter floated around them. Slowly, Li Chang took great pleasure in the simple sight of his simple restaurant filled with loud, happy, and contented Chinese and Americans, too.

The girl looked up, as if she knew Li Yu. When he saw her face, not to his surprise, he felt a tear fall from his eyes. He moved towards her, legs trembling, through the pools of kerosene light and the clanging dishes and strident voices. Yes, his heart skipped

CHINESE BROTHERS, AMERICAN SONS

a beat. She leaned toward the steam basket he was carrying and the delicate, translucent wrappers filled with a savory mince of vegetables. The aroma encircled her, and she averted her eyes.

"Thank you," she said. But, alas, it was not Wang Wei.

Li Yu smiled, but the tears inside him were burning.

"The years roll by, all things change, but there's always the one," he thought. He felt all alone.

Li Chang's cooking experience for white miners was the cause of him venturing into American food while still cooking the exquisite cuisine he had learned in northern China and practiced in the homes of wealthy merchants in southern China. And he believed that Americans enjoying the food he prepared was a way to connect to the people in California.

Li Yu was continually amazed. Li Chang's hands were as precise as any seamstress. He wielded a sharp knife, cutting through vegetables, sliced thin enough to float up and away like feathers in a breeze. Li Chang rolled up his sleeves and proudly showed off his scars. Serious Chinese cooks always had a signature pattern of different shades of burn marks extending past the wrists all the way up the forearms. Just reaching across the flames, cooks like Li Chang were burned by spattering oil and wayward pots, each leaving their own special mark.

There were few foods more proletarian than the simple dumpling, and Li Chang made all kinds, buns filled with either meat or cabbage. That was alright. A great dish could be made with a cabbage, one of the simplest ingredients. Li Yu also knew there was nothing tastier, in its own way, than a fragrant, light-as-a-cloud meat bun. He helped make them day after day, week after week, for years.

As Chinatown grew, it began to be hemmed in by other neighborhoods. The streets and lanes became increasingly dark and twisted. Whites were both fascinated and repelled by the dim alleys. The alleys were home to tearooms, as well as gambling houses, where the Chinese residents spent their limited work-free hours playing Chinese games such as mahjong and fan-tan, along with dominoes, dice and poker, which they had learned from Americans.

Opium was used among the Chinese, but because of the urgent need to save money to send home, most of the newcomers took narcotics only on Sundays and other nonworking times. Supplying the lonely bachelor society with drugs and prostitutes was the province of the secret societies known as tongs. The word originally means "hall," or organization and tongs were known to exist in San Francisco as early as 1852. They also served as illicit versions of the Chinese Six Companies, offering members financial aid and protection not available elsewhere for housing and business problems.

Through it all, Li Yu's thoughts turned constantly to Wang Wei, the girl he had been so mesmerized by and enamored with in that Chinatown basement years ago. She had changed his life in a moment. He would never be the same again.

"I still remember her. Does she still remember me? I know you're out there somewhere," Li Yu said.

He gazed at people, some hand in hand. He looked left and right for her in the crowded San Francisco Chinatown streets. He hunted for her face and always came up empty. Where was she? He still wanted to help her, he needed to help her. Li Yu reminded Li Chang of the promise he had made. "Not now, but later."

Li Chang, for a $100 fee, amounting to over two month's profits from his restaurant, enlisted the help of the Chinese Six Companies that he knew to be involved in procuring Chinese girls in the sex trade. He also asked Jimmy Lin, the Chinese clerk who worked for one of the benevolent associations of the Six

CHINESE BROTHERS, AMERICAN SONS

Companies, to aid in the search. In exchange for Lin's help, Li Yu agreed to write two love letters a year for Lin to send to his wife back in China. Such letters were best in calligraphic Chinese script and Lin wanted to include poems urging his wife to join him in America.

The only information Li Yu had to help in the search was that the girl of his dreams was named Wang Wei and that she would be about the same age as him, early twenties or maybe a bit younger. But she could be anywhere, and maybe was even dead by now. Li Yu felt alone and he kept up the fool's game of looking for her. In his spare time, he sometimes visited Chinatown's brothels searching for her comfort, but instead partaking of the other pleasures on offer.

As the Chinese population grew, so did consternation among certain whites. Fearing assimilation, an exclusionary law to bar future Chinese immigrants was discussed in the press, but not enacted until much later. One newspaper, the *San Francisco Daily Alta California* was virulently racist. The Chinese or "Celestials," it asserted in a series of editorials, were "morally a far worse class than the negro. They are idolatrous in their religion—in their disposition cunning and deceitful, and in their habits libidinous and offensive."

White men constantly compared the Chinese to another subordinate group, white women, and despised the Chinese even as they used them. The Chinese were small, with delicate hands and hairless faces and long, braided hair. One writer called them "half-made men."

An English phrase book published in San Francisco taught English speakers how to say phrases in Chinese such as: "Can you get me a good boy? He wants $8.00 per month! He ought to be happy with $6.00. I think he is very stupid. Come at seven every morning. Go home at eight every night. Light the fire.

Sweep the rooms. Wash the clothes. Wash the windows. Wash the floor. Sweep the stairs. Trim the lamps. I want to cut his wages."

Two phrases that never appeared in these English-Chinese phrase books were, "How are you?" and "Thank you."

Chinese booklets for learning English phrases included, "He does not intend to pay me my wages," "He tries to extort money from me," "He assaulted me."

It was a brisk, sunny spring day in 1862, Li Yu ventured out of Chinatown. He wished to see the newly-elected governor of California give a speech. He listened intently and with fear as Leland Stanford called the Chinese the "dregs" of Asia, and a "degraded" people.

Stanford begrudgingly conceded that the Chinese had the redeeming features of a strong work ethic and inventiveness. "But they are not of that kind that Americans can ever associate or sympathize with. They do not mix with our people, and it is undesirable that they should, for nothing but degradation can result to us from the contact. It is of no advantage to us to have them here. Those slanty-eyed heathen can never become like us."

The crowd was worked into a fist-pumping, venom-yelling mob chanting, "Chinks go home! Chinks go home! Go back to China!"

Now holding back his anger, Li Yu attempted to leave quietly but he was subjected to a racist and brutal attack. Initially, he was just jostled and pushed and spat upon by the mob. But now his shirt was torn off. Four thugs punched him to the ground. They kicked him repeatedly in the head, face and body, even his groin, while laughing and taunting him with demeaning words: "chink," "chopstick," "ching chang chong," "coolie," "slanty-eyes."

One of Li Yu's attackers stomped on his chest. He writhed,

screaming in agony on the street. No one intervened. The police never came. Then the beating came to a merciful end. One man in the group shouted for them to leave and they all ran off in different directions. Li Yu crawled into a darkened alley between two buildings.

"Coward! Coward! Coward!" Li Yu screamed at the top of his lungs. He took a bag of fruit he was carrying and slammed it hard and harder against the urine-stained walls, covered in racist graffiti — "Go Home Chinamen." Eventually, he said, "I am such a coward, I am such a coward." But he knew he couldn't have fought back. He would have been killed. He sobbed uncontrollably as he lay in a pool of his own blood on the muddy, stinking earth.

Race did matter. The slights, the snickers, the silent and not so silent judgments and, yes, the verbal and physical abuse, reinforced that most crippling of thoughts: "I do not belong here."

It was proof, Li Yu believed, that contrary to what his brother Li Chang envisioned, the Chinese were never going to be accepted. He now wished he had heeded Li Chang's warning that "Chinese should not go outside of Chinatown."

Li Yu now sat up, and then stood up. Limping with tattered bloody clothes, he headed back to Chinatown. He walked through dark alleys smelling of opium and burning coal, because he didn't want anyone to recognize his shame.

He peered through a dusty window. It was not broken like the last time. But he could see and hear young women, yes, girls, being stripped of their clothes and dignity — of their very life, in that basement on that platform of surrender. Some were screaming; others were crying, still more had their heads lowered. Their faces were lifeless and expressionless, an empty stare indicating their hopelessness.

Everything just took him back to when Wang Wei was here. And with tears rolling down his cheeks, he didn't flee, he didn't hesitate. And Li Chang was not around to discourage him. He burst into the room, hog-tied the lady procurer and ordered the women to leave.

"Go!" he shouted. "Find a job in the cannery, a laundry. Hire yourself out as a servant. Find a good man who will take care of you. Don't let these wicked people win, don't let them destroy you."

Most understood and fled like little mice. Others with nowhere to go, nowhere to run, stayed; they were emotionally numb.

The next day, he got the news. Jimmy Lin had found records of Wang Wei's sale. On November 10, 1854 she was sold to a wholesale grocer with the initials "M.H." who gave his residence as Placerville, according to the ink-stained ledger. With his head still spinning and his ears still ringing, Li Yu was both heartened and disheartened by the news. "Hangtown!" Li Yu cried out in agony.

But the most wondrous thing then took place.

"You remember that letter you sent, I think, about eight years ago?" Jimmy Lin added. "Well, you might have gotten a response. I thought I had lost the letter. I didn't know where you were on Gold Mountain," The envelope was postmarked "Placerville, CA." The date was indecipherable; the contents weren't much better:

> Li Yu,
> It's a miracle, but I'm still alive and your letter has reached me. I live in Placerville. Have you found much gold? I doubt you will ever receive this letter. I am moving with (indecipherable) who brought me to

CHINESE BROTHERS, AMERICAN SONS

Sacramento.
(indecipherable)

Wang Wei must have been sold to be someone's wife or servant. At any rate, not a prostitute; thus, she may be alive, Li Yu reckoned. "Hangtown is a ghost town now. Where is my Wang Wei? We are not human to Americans."

But with hope still flickering, Li Yu wrote:

April 12, 1862, Wang Wei
c/o M.H., grocer, Sacramento, CA.
Yes, it is a miracle. I'm still in California, too. I help my brother who has opened a restaurant in San Francisco Chinatown. I write letters for homesick Chinese men to send to their wives or mothers in China. I have never forgotten you. You are safe in my heart. Look above; the moon represents my heart. If you get this, write to me c/o Jimmy Lin, San Francisco, Chinese Six Companies, Li Yu.

9

The Transcontinental Railroad, "From Sea to Shining Sea"

In the early 1860s with the country in civil war, the discussions in California and in the halls of Congress about what to do with the Chinese had little immediate impact on the daily life of Chinese Americans. For most of them, the right to suffrage or election to public office was the last things on their minds; their ambition was not to be part of the governing class, but to just earn a living. But this was the beginning of bad times for the Chinese in California. Mobs ran wild through the streets, pelting Chinese with rocks and filth. Drunks and hoodlums set fire to Chinese-owned laundries and cigar factories, emptied chamber pots on their doorsteps and howled indecencies at Chinese funeral processions.

The antagonism toward the Chinese on the West Coast, however, was not broadly reflected in the corridors of federal power. Many in Washington saw the Chinese as a valuable source of manpower. The war coincided with a grand plan to construct a Transcontinental Railroad, and American capitalists, while initially skeptical, eventually eyed the industrious Chinese as labor for one of the most ambitious engineering feats in history.

Li Chang had found his niche in life; his restaurant was

prospering. He had his customers to whom he imparted his Confucian wisdom. He even saved a little money. He was happy. Li Yu was also happy, to a degree. But he knew he had to find some kind of peace of mind to ease his loneliness.

At the peak of the Civil War, with unity on President Abraham Lincoln's mind, he sought a way to connect and secure the great expanse of the nation, to make it one, from sea to shining sea. The answer was the Transcontinental Railroad, and Congress, now without southern opposition due to its secession, passed legislation in July 1862 to finance the venture.

Dreamers had first began talking about a route to the Pacific in the 1830s. Lincoln was adamant when he took office in 1861 in his belief that the railroad was absolutely necessary, despite the naysayers arguing about who would pay for it and who would build it. The new line would encourage communities and outposts on the frontier, provide settlers with safe, dependable and affordable passage westwards. Most importantly, it would tie the new states of California and Oregon, rich with natural resources and trade potential, to the rest of the country. A Transcontinental Railroad would bring the entire nation closer together, would make Americans across the continent feel like one people. That was what Lincoln hoped. And indeed, "Abraham's faith moved mountains," as one political pundit said.

There were only two potential routes — one over the Rockies and another more southern route through Apache and Comanche territory. Both were death traps. From anywhere east of Missouri, it was almost always better to travel to California by sea. The route involved boarding a vessel and traveling around South America's tip or taking a ship to Panama in Central America, traveling by wagon across the isthmus, and then riding a steamboat headed north.

Before the Transcontinental Railroad, to get from the east

to the west coast of America was five or six months of misery in a horse and wagon. That is, if the travelers made it. The trip was dangerous and crossing the continent meant braving death by disease, Native Americans, cut-throat mountaineers, wild animals, starvation, thirst, unbelievable heat or freezing cold. Rich farmland, gold and silver were waiting to be mined and taxed, but what was needed was a railroad to move more people west and natural resources safely and profitably to the major markets back east.

Two companies divided the task of actual construction of the railroad. In 1862, the Central Pacific Railroad headed by the "Big Four"— Leland Stanford, Collis P. Huntington, Charles Crocker and Mark Hopkins—was awarded the contract to build tracks eastward from Sacramento, California while its rival, the Union Pacific, was awarded the path westward from Omaha, Nebraska, which was already connected to the East through existing rail lines. After an expected bitter contest, the goal was to meet somewhere in the middle, connecting the nation with a continuous stretch of railroad tracks from the Atlantic to the Pacific.

The Pacific Railroad acts of 1862 and 1864 granted land and government bonds to these two companies on the basis of how many miles of track they laid, setting the stage for a wild seven-year race. Besides land grants along the right-of-way, each railroad was paid $16,000 per mile built over an easy grade, $32,000 per mile in the high plains, and $48,000 per mile in the mountains. These terms encouraged the companies to construct many extra miles of track, direct the line toward property they owned, and in many other ways exploit the poorly-written law to their own benefit.

The Union Pacific's job—laying track over the plains—was much easier, while the Central Pacific had to go over and through

CHINESE BROTHERS, AMERICAN SONS

and around steep mountains and across a parched desert. The line had nearly 2,000 miles to cross with great stretches of desert where there was no water, plus vast areas without trees for ties or bridges, stones for footings, or game for food.

There were three mountain ranges, the Rockies, the Wasatch, and the Sierra Nevada. The wind howled and the snow came down in great quantities, the creeks and rivers ran through 1,000-foot and deeper gorges, the summits were granite. Neither man nor animal lived there. Over most of the route, there were no cities except Salt Lake City, no settlements, no farms and no water pumps.

It took the backing of the government to make it happen, because only the government had the resources—money and land—to finance the project. "A work of giants. And Uncle Sam is the only giant I know who can grapple the subject," said William T. Sherman, a Union general.

The Central Pacific was required to complete fifty miles within two years and fifty miles each year thereafter, and the entire road was to be completed by July 1, 1876, under pain of forfeiture. That was by no means all of it, but it was enough for Theodore Judah (the railroad's originator) to flash the first words to his Sacramento colleagues by the newly-established telegraph: "We have drawn the elephant. Now let us see if we can harness him."

On January 8, 1863 with much fanfare the Central Pacific had its ground breaking in downtown Sacramento. Charles Crocker introduced Governor Leland Stanford. With thousands watching, Stanford took a shovel and turned the first earth for the railroad. Then Crocker turned a spadeful and made a short speech. "All that I have, all of my own strength, intellect and energy," he promised, "are devoted to the building [of this road]."

On October 26, 1863, Crocker's men spiked the first rails to their ties.

ED SHEW

"If you want to jubilate over driving the first spike," Huntington prophetically said, "go ahead and do it. I don't. Those mountains over there look too ugly. We may fail, and if we do, I want to have as few people know it as we can...Anybody can drive the first spike, but there are many months of labor and unrest between the first and last spike."

By November 10, the first Central Pacific locomotive to arrive in California, named the Governor Stanford, made the first run ever for the Central Pacific. The engine cost $13,688. It was more than ten feet tall and fifty feet long, with four driving wheels of four and a half feet in diameter. The driving rods and pistons were of wrought iron. The bell, made of brass, was painted maroon, green, red, orange and yellow. Gold initials, "C.P.R.R.," were on the red tender. Locomotive and tender, with a full load of wood and water, weighed 46 tons, making the Governor Stanford the biggest man-made thing in California.

Until 1865, the Central Pacific operated mainly on the Big Four's money or on loans. In 1863 and 1864, not a penny in aid reached the railroad. The only other work actually under way was the construction of the bridge over the American River at Sacramento. Getting laborers was devilishly difficult. Mining was more to the laborers liking than the discipline of railroad work. They were indifferent and independent and their labor was priced high. It was believed that there were not enough workers in California for the rapid construction of the railroad, and the labor as it existed could not be depended upon.

With the rail head now sixteen miles out from Sacramento, Li Chang and Li Yu paid a visit from San Francisco, restless and seeking adventure. They saw the graders at work and were filled with admiration for these men, but also satisfied to know that they were capable of performing such demanding tasks too. Engineers might do the surveying while Crocker oversaw the whole and bossed it, but it was the men who did the work—bending, digging, shoveling, throwing the dirt up on the embankment, bringing in the ballast by the cartload, and dumping it. It was those workers who impressed Li Yu and Li Chang.

Experience working on the rails, they had none, but experience in backbreaking manual labor, they had plenty, from rural farming in China to mining in the goldfields. Li Yu haltingly said to his brother Li Chang, "Let's join the railroad. I think you could cook for Chinese there; you're getting tired of cooking chop suey for whites. Besides, I'm getting tired of writing those damn letters."

"Little Brother, you followed me to Gold Mountain; I'll be by your side as we help build the path for the Firewagon," Li Chang replied.

First, they took a detour to Sacramento, now a city of 15,000 people, and Li Yu persuaded Li Chang to look for Wang Wei. The brothers searched all the grocery stores, but no grocers with the initials MH were found. They asked passers-by if there were any white men with Chinese wives or Chinese servants. They came up empty-handed.

Li Chang talked to Jimmy Lin's counterpart, Young Kwong Hoy, at Sacramento's China Six Companies and asked about young women sold into the slave trade. Often, young Chinese girls started as house servants. Their lives controlled by their masters; they were often sold from family to family.

"Even if I knew of her, you couldn't afford to buy her back," Young scoffed at Li Chang's inquiry. "I can tell you're just another Gold Mountain has-been."

"I know you say 'you'll get over it,'" Li Yu said wearily. "But I know it's not true. I cannot forget her; I won't forget her. It doesn't matter how hard I try. I can't let go. Wang Wei's a part of me. Do you understand?"

"What would you do if you found Wang Wei?" Li Chang asked. "You're still married to Sun Wei. You may be looking desperately for something that's not actually there, and if you do find her, she may not want you. But I will still help you. Don't stop believing. Your tears of love will not be wasted. Trust me."

Li Yu penned, in his mind, this final letter to Wang Wei c/o M.H., grocer, Sacramento, CA, on March 8, 1864.

> We searched for you in Sacramento, but no luck. Now my brother and I are joining the effort to build a railroad across America. If you get this write to me, please write c/o Central Pacific Railroad,
> Li Yu

Li Chang and Li Yu were hired on sight and were among the earliest hires, and the first Chinese hires. They arrived in the spring 1864. The prevalent view was that there were not enough workingmen to do all the labor of building a new country. Some of the consternation came from the civil war which would decide whether or not black people would continue to work for nothing.

"This is the first time we have worked for and with westerners," Li Chang reminded Li Yu.

"I know there are a lot of racists ready to find fault with us, and put us down because we look different, but we hold our heads high and ignore them," Li Yu said. "We've got to be proud to be different or else it won't work."

Li Chang nodded, but added, "Remember that not every unfavorable interaction you may have with a white person is a result of racism or bigotry. Sometimes, when we are expecting something, we often find it where it isn't. Consider: if this person were the same race as me, would we have reached the same outcome? If the answer is yes, you can be pretty sure there is no racism at work. But even if the answer is no, also remember that having different cultural backgrounds can lead people to different expectations of behavior."

"You are wise, my brother," Li Yu said. "But I sometimes wish I was white. I thought I had self-esteem and a strong Chinese identity, but I feel like a failure."

"No, brother, you haven't failed. I know you have pride in yourself and your heritage. But when being Chinese is devalued by society, the task is indeed harder," Li Chang said.

"If someone is mean to me or makes me feel bad, I'll prove them wrong," Li Yu said. "If someone insults me, I'll hold my head high, and walk past them and smile. I'll say 'I'm happy that I'm Chinese and I think you should be proud of your race to.'"

"If someone speaks to you in broken Chinese, say, 'Why thank you, I'm proud to be Chinese.' Keep your integrity by continually showing that you are proud of who you are, how you look and where you came from," Li Chang told him. "Our race is just one aspect of who we are and we must still work to be accepted. We need to interact with our white co-workers and make more friends with people who aren't like us."

"I guess we can talk about our families and the farms we left behind," Li Yu said. "I hear the Irish workers came to America because of a great famine. Maybe I can a find another friend like Jimmy Smits?"

Li Chang and Li Yu were given daily instructions by a white foreman, but he and the rest of the Irish crew basically ignored them. Often times, they worked alone. They were invisible. They were spoken to only as needed.

Li Chang and Li Yu's first job was to fell a redwood tree which was thick enough to divide into three or four beams. The tree finally swayed and slowly dived to Earth, creaking and screeching like an animal. They were so awed, they forgot what they were supposed to yell.

They blew up the tree stumps with gunpowder. "It is like uprooting a tooth," Li Yu said. Li Yu still believed there might be gold in these mountains, and he rushed over to the root hole to look for gold veins and ore.

They began each day at dawn and continued until dusk. When they weren't felling trees, side by side, Li Chang and Li Yu worked with heavy sledge-hammers that they slammed into the rail spikes till their blistered hands bled. A cart full of tools and supplies trailed up and down the rail line as the workers hammered away under the beaming hot sun and chilling winds.

"We must do our job well to quench any doubts about our ability," Li Yu said. "We will show the Americans that Chinese can help them build this railroad."

Li Chang patted his brother on his back. "We can do more than that, when the time is right. Our Chinese culture tells us that speaking out is rude and not knowing one's place, especially to someone in authority."

"But individualism is a part of American culture, and assertiveness is necessary for communicating and getting what we want," Li Yu said. "You want a brother who has the guts to fight back."

"No, I want a brother who has the guts 'not' to fight back," Li Chang answered.

As the gradings up the river got closer to the gold and silver deposits, more men stampeded off the job. So Crocker decided to get involved himself. He pulled off his coat and shouted, "Come on boys, follow me!" He put all of his 250 pounds into it, bringing energy and dynamism to the job. But workers and funding were still lagging.

CHINESE BROTHERS, AMERICAN SONS

Later that year, Crocker found a new construction boss, the profane, hard-driving James Harvey Strobridge, to run the crews, most of them Irish. Strobridge was 37-years old, out of Ireland, over six feet tall, made of solid iron but agile and energetic. He cursed the men and lost his temper at any moment. He had worked on railroads in the East, and his style was to intimidate workers. If intimidation failed, he regularly fell back on physical violence.

"These Irish workers are not so much human beings as creatures," Crocker said.

"Yes, you cannot talk to them like gentlemen," Strobridge replied. "They are about as near brutes as they can get."

Crocker quickly placed Strobridge in charge of the entire construction program. He was a man of ability and command, with a willingness to take responsibility and initiative under adverse circumstances.

The Central Pacific started with Irish laborers. This particularly suited Strobridge who had worked with the Irish before. But there weren't enough Irish in the West, and they developed what Stanford and his partners saw as an inflated sense of their own worth.

"Some of the Irishmen are talking together," Crocker said. "There is some trouble ahead."

The "trouble" materialized in the form of a committee of workmen who requested an increase in wages.

"We'll go over to Auburn and get some Chinamen and put them to work," Crocker said to them. That quieted the demands for higher pay.

Railroad work was hard, and the management was chaotic, leading to a high attrition rate. The Central Pacific managers puzzled over how to attract and retain a work force that was up to the enormous task. In keeping with the prejudices of the day, some Central Pacific bosses believed that all Irishmen would spend their wages on liquor and that all Chinese were unreliable. Yet given the critical shortage, Crocker suggested that reconsideration be given to hiring Chinese. He encountered strong opposition from Strobridge.

But Strobridge had never-ending problems finding dependable men to man the grading and track-laying crews. California still had a small population, and most laborers preferred to work near the comforts of a town or out in the goldfields. There was more bad news. Strobridge lost the use of his right eye at Bloomer Cut, when there was a delay in the detonation of some black powder and it ended up exploding in his face. Still, construction continued, even though in the winter of 1864-65 the Central Pacific was down to about five hundred workmen.

The surrender at Appomattox in April 1865 ended the civil war and nixed the idea of using Confederate prisoners, so the Central Pacific distributed handbills all over northern California advertising for 5,000 workers immediately with good pay on offer.

> Wanted, 5,000 laborers for constant and permanent work, also experienced foremen. Apply to J.H. Strobridge, Superintendent. On the work, near Auburn.

Many applied, few stayed. What the white men wanted was what they had come to California to get—easy money. Why toil for wages when an instant fortune was still a possibility in the mines? Many of the men who did sign on were, in the words of Strobridge, "Unsteady men, unreliable men; they stay a few days. They stay until pay day. Get drunk, and clear out."

CHINESE BROTHERS, AMERICAN SONS

The Central Pacific was not offering them easy money, and new silver strikes in Nevada promised riches. The prospective rich men needed some cash to get there and a week's work on the Central Pacific would suffice. So, of the almost 2,000 laborers who signed up to work for Strobridge, only 200 were still there a week later.

Strobridge still had misgivings about Chinese workers. But Crocker and he were getting desperate; they had money burning in their pockets but no workers.

10

The Recruitment of the Chinese

In February 1865, a month after the Central Pacific's all-but-useless call for labor, Charles Crocker met with James Strobridge and again raised the question of hiring Chinese. He said some twenty of them had been working, and well, on the Dutch Flat and Donner Lake Wagon Road. "Stro," as he was known to his friends, was opposed.

"What do Chinese know about railroad construction? They cannot do the work," Strobridge declared. "They average 120 pounds in weight and only a few are taller than 4 foot 10."

The foremen hired by the Central Pacific did not believe the Chinese could endure the building of the railroad. And it was true—on average they were skinny and looked like weaklings. The foremen made fun of their straw hats, pajama-like clothes and the long queues down the center of their backs. "Coolies" and "Chinks," the foremen called the lowly Chinese workers. One of the foremen was called Kirby, once known as Mitch "Wild Thing" Williams. He frequently used his whip on the Chinese railroad workers.

From the beginning, the white railroad men ridiculed the Chinese as too "effeminate" to do a "real man's work," such as laying iron rails. They were too "delicate." They had "too small hands." "The Chinese marched through the white camps like a

CHINESE BROTHERS, AMERICAN SONS

weird procession of midgets," said one historian.

Strobridge, a stubborn Irishman from Vermont, insisted the Chinese were too "frail" to swing a jack hammer, but begrudgingly, in the end, he had to put the Chinese to work. He first gave them light and unskilled jobs, like filling dump carts. Yet when Irish stonemasons went out on strike, Crocker ordered Chinese replacements. Strobridge objected that he couldn't make masons out of Chinese.

"Did they not build the Great Wall of China, the biggest piece of masonry in the world?" Crocker replied.

Strobridge acquiesced, and Chinese crews were soon laying stone.

Crocker was not without his prejudices. He claimed it was impossible to tell Chinese people apart. "They are just like Indians," he said. "Did you hear about the look-a-like competition in China?" he asked Strobridge with a laugh. "Everybody won."

"How do Chinese parents name their children?" Crocker added. Before Strobridge could answer, he said, "Throw a pan down the stairs, ching, chong, wong."

Concerned about paying double wages because of the difficulty he had distinguishing between the Chinese workers, Crocker devised a scheme to employ and pay them in teams. The Chinese were organized by the Central Pacific into gangs of twelve to twenty men, one of whom was selected as headman and another as cook. The headman collected all the wages and gave some to the cook to purchase provisions from the Chinese merchants. Other amounts went for clothing and opium. The Chinese laborers used the drug to relax on Sunday, their only day off. At the end of the month, each worker got his share of the remaining cash, $20 or more. Each gang had a white, usually Irish, foreman, and the whites initially monopolized the skilled work, such as trestling, masonry, and the actual lay-railing.

ED SHEW

Crocker's assistant chief engineer, Lewis Clement, described him as follows: "He is a business man in the full sense of the word—prompt, methodical, fearless and confident. He kept his word, but he is very quick to act, and sometimes acts too quickly—he acts and then considers it afterwards. He has a job no ordinary man can do."

Crocker was a big man, but not an imposing one, despite his bulk. He was less than six feet tall, with a fair complexion, and at times beardless.

"I suppose," Clement said, "that there is not a mile of road construction that he has not gone over the ground, either on horseback or with a wagon; he always wants to see what has to be done and what is being done." He was out in every kind of weather, "and it makes no difference whether it is an American horse or a bucking Spanish pony." Clement admitted that Crocker "is a large eater and a man of very strong prejudices."

Crocker's next move was his canniest. With no other way of meeting the requirement for 4,000 laborers, in 1865 he began hiring Chinese workers. Fortunately for the Central Pacific, Chinese immigrants provided a vast pool of cheap, plentiful and easily exploitable labor. By 1865, the number of Chinese in California had reached close to 60,000—at least ninety percent of them young men.

The first fifty Chinese workers taken on excelled at their work, to the surprise of many, but not to the Chinese. They were fast learners so the railroad quickly gave them more responsibilities like doing rock cuts. In time, the company hired another fifty Chinese, and then another fifty, until eventually the company was employing thousands of Chinese laborers.

Needless to say, this reminder that the white workers were easily replaced did not contribute to harmony between the whites and Chinese.

CHINESE BROTHERS, AMERICAN SONS

Strobridge appreciated what the Chinese did, and after a month's work, he conceded that the Chinese had performed superbly. They operated as teams, took almost no breaks, and stayed healthy and on the job.

After a few more months with them, Strobridge said, "They learn quickly, do not fight, have no strikes that amount to anything, and are very cleanly in their habits. They will gamble and quarrel among themselves most noisily—but harmlessly." The Chinese grew to respect him. Those who had learned English called him "Stro" the "One-Eyed Bossy Man."

He could see as well with one eye as most men could with two, and when, as happened occasionally, there was trouble among the Chinese workers, Strobridge could pick out the ringleaders with a glance. He confronted them, usually with an ax handle, and they gave way and he prevailed. Li Yu sometimes spurred on his Chinese work gang by clapping a hand over his right eye and striding about as Strobridge did, implying that "Stro" was about to appear.

"Men generally earn their money when they work for me," Strobridge said.

Finally, on the day the Chinese were at last permitted to work at grading the roadbed for the tracks, the Chinese workers' right of way was longer and smoother than any the white crews had ever created. The Irish workers were embarrassed; the Chinese men were so inexperienced that many of them had never been on a railroad or even seen one.

Enraged, the white crews vowed to avenge their shame. In the days that followed, they not only worked at top speed, but voluntarily halved their lunch break. Still, at the end of a week, the roadbeds of the Chinese were still the longest of any gang on the line. They moved the earth and rock rapidly. The praise they received only increased as time passed.

ED SHEW

Crocker was frustrated in his strenuous efforts to put more Chinese on the Central Pacific's payroll. "We are scouring the state for men to put on the Truckee, but they come in very slow."

On May 13, 1865, the same day the train carried passengers and freight to Auburn, Huntington sent a telegram to Stanford: "I received yesterday $1,258,000 United States bonds for account of CPR of California." That represented the government's loan to the Central Pacific for work completed in 1864, for the thirty-one miles from Sacramento to Newcastle.

With the money received and progress being made, everything was looking up. Business was constantly growing; in the first ten months of 1865, the company earned $313,404 from mails, passengers and freight on the line section so far completed. The total workforce was up to 2,500 (mainly Chinese) and on the rise despite continued desertions to the mines. The Central Pacific charged ahead. What it needed to keep up the momentum was more workers. The muscular young men from China were given the jobs that the whites abandoned. The Chinese now did grading, made cuts and fills, blasted, felled trees, and eventually the most arduous tasks such as drilling the holes and putting in and lighting the black powder and driving tunnels.

"Wherever we place them, we find them good," said the delighted Crocker. "And they work themselves into our favor to such an extent, we find if we are in a hurry for a job of work, it is better to put Chinese on it at once."

Even the stubborn Strobridge barked, "Send up more coolies."

White laborers, however, believed that Chinese diligence forced everyone to work harder for less reward. For $30 a month—less board—the Chinese railroad laborers worked six days a week, ten to 12 hours a day.

"We pay you $35 a month and board and $30 a month to Chinamen and they board themselves," Crocker told a white laborer.

"That is pretty good wages," the white laborer responded. "But if it wasn't for those damned Chinamen we would get $50 a month and not do half the work."

White workers were resentful of the skill and strength of the "little yellow men" whom they contemptuously compared to midgets and monkeys.

By the turn of 1866, the Central Pacific had 7,000 Chinese on the payroll, men aged from thirteen to sixty, working alongside just under 2,000 whites. Thus, nearly 80 percent of the Central Pacific's workforce was Chinese. But contrary to myth, they were not brought over by the boatload to work for the railroad – they were already in California.

There was whispering among the Irish laborers about driving the Chinese off the job, but when Crocker got wind of this, he threatened to replace all the remaining whites with Chinese if they didn't accept working alongside the Chinese crews. The ultimatum may not have cured the anger of the white crews, but it sufficed to quell rebellion.

Eventually the white workers were placated with the knowledge that they alone could be promoted to the position of foreman. More Chinese workers and fewer whites made for less competition for foreman positions among the whites, and foremen were paid several times the wages of a laborer.

Delighted by the productivity of the Chinese, railroad executives became fervent advocates of Chinese immigration to California. "I like the idea of getting over more Chinamen," Collis Huntington, one of the "Big Four" at the Central Pacific, wrote to Crocker in 1867. "It would be better for us and California if there should a half million come over in 1868."

In awe of the strength and skill of the men from China who did this work, Albert Richardson of the *New York Tribune*, described the scene: "They (the Chinese) were a great army laying siege to Nature in her strongest citadel. The rugged mountains looked like stupendous anthills. They swarmed with Celestials, shoveling, wheeling, carting, drilling and blasting rocks from earth…"

The large number of Chinese made white workers uncomfortable. Li Yu offered this observation: "We're persecuted not for our vices but for our virtues."

"Many whites and Chinese hate each other, because we misunderstand and fear each other," Li Yu observed. "And we fear each other because we do not know each other. And we do not know each other because we are separated from each other. We Chinese are also to blame; we want to stay to ourselves."

"Yes," Li Chang said. "We need the ability to put ourselves in others' shoes, and the will to enter their world through the power of imagination. Without this empathy there can be no genuine dialogue, and we will remain isolated and alien and segregated."

"But we, the Chinese, are looking for more than that," Li Yu said. "We want peace, and real peace is not the absence of conflict and aggression. It has always been the presence of justice."

"Not everything that is faced can be changed, but nothing can be changed until it is faced," Li Yu said, looking over towards Crocker and Strobridge.

11

ATTACKING THE SIERRA NEVADA MOUNTAINS

CALIFORNIA WAS THE land that Americans could scarcely get to or out of because of the granite wall between it and the eastern United States. It was as if the mountains were designed to divide California permanently from the remainder of the country. They were too big, too snowy, too steep, too rugged, too extensive, and too formidable ever to be crossed. The Central Pacific's workers had the dangerous task of ramming tunnels through these mountains to allow a train to get through the Sierra Nevada Mountains. Some engineers, watching from afar, said it was impossible.

As the principal topographical feature of the American Far West, the Sierras rose from 1,000 feet on its western slopes to over 10,000 feet with many peaks exceeding 14,000 feet. Many of the summits were enveloped in glaciers. And if and when the Sierras could somehow be tamed, tracks still had to be laid across the parched Nevada and Utah deserts.

The railroad workers had to face the high Sierras with their terrible weather, thirty-foot snow drifts, mud slides, and find a way to dig deep rock cuts and tunnels through it all. It was going to be a tremendous amount of work to get this dream built across the mountains.

The plan was to bridge rivers and ravines, carve twenty-foot wide shelves out of sheer mountain faces and cut eighteen tunnels—one of them more than 1,600 feet long—through solid granite. And there was not a manufacturer on the Pacific coast who could provide the Central Pacific with drills, spikes and rails, let alone locomotives or railroad cars.

Charles Crocker looked at the seven miles of track beyond Newcastle. He knew the cuts and fills were as great as any found in the nation. In the thirty-one miles from Sacramento to Newcastle, the grade of the roadbed rose steadily until, after Rocklin, it reached 105 feet to the mile and then 116 feet per mile, the steepest allowed by Congress, and steeper than any other gradient in the Sierra Nevada.

Bloomer Cut, just beyond Newcastle, took months to complete. It was a 63-foot deep cut that ran 800 feet long, composed of naturally-cemented gravel that was moved out one wheelbarrow at a time. As much as 500 kegs of blasting powder were used each day in early 1864—more than was used in most major battles in the ongoing Civil War. The rock was so hard that it was sometimes impossible to drill into it for a sufficient depth for blasting purposes.

After each blast, the men used picks and shovels to fill their wheelbarrows or one-horse carts and move the gravel out. The wedge they cut had almost vertical walls. This was the first of the obstacles for the Central Pacific's workforce to overcome. How many sore, blistered, bleeding hands the Bloomer Cut required was not recorded, or how many damaged backs or crushed knees. But the rigors and dangers only got worse afterwards.

The original plan was to bridge the deeper ravines and gaps between Newcastle (below Auburn) and Illinoistown with timber structures, but now with the Chinese to fill and push the carts, wherever possible earthen embankments ("fills") were used. In a five-mile stretch from Auburn to Newcastle, the only significant wooden structures were the Newcastle trestle (86 feet high and 528 feet long) and a trestle near Auburn at 30 feet high and 416 feet long.

The trestles straddled the gorges along the way with their massive legs, each pair 16-feet apart and made from huge pine trees with their feet sunk into concrete. Central Pacific lumbermen used the huge trees close at hand, giant red firs and others to make the legs. The legs and struts were all lashed together by hand, for there were no steam or power tools. The tons of dirt was all moved entirely by hand.

Over the serrated ridges that make up the Sierra Nevada foothills, the iron rails curved and climbed. The ravines between were filled in with massive quantities of earth or else were bridged with the giant trestles, some of them 100 feet high and 500 feet long. The rickety appearance scared many passengers as they peered down into the depths below the track. But the trestles all managed to withstand the weight of all the locomotives and cars that passed over them.

On June 10, 1865 the rails reached Clipper Gap, about halfway between Auburn and Illinoistown. Toward the end of that summer, the railhead became Illinoistown, fifty-four miles from Sacramento. The elevation was 2,242 feet. From there to the summit was about fifty miles. The grade climbed almost 4,800 feet to 7,042 feet, along the dividing ridge between the North Fork of the American River, which lay to the south, and Bear River, which was to the north.

This was the toughest and the most expensive section, the fifty miles that would be the most time-consuming. It took a full year to reach Dutch Flat from Illinoistown, sixty-seven miles from Sacramento. After that the degree of difficulty increased even further, requiring more blasting, cutting and filling, precipitous gorges to be bridged, massive pinewood stands to be cleared, numerous tight curves to be plotted.

As the grading and then the tracks made their way up the Sierra Nevada, the costs increased and the weather worsened. The ground was kept bare for the graders by having half the men shoveling snow. After storms, the entire grading force was put to work removing snow.

Supervisor James Strobridge divided his work crews into five parts. The largest, some 5,000 men and 600 teams of horses, were sent ahead of Illinoistown to work on Cape Horn. Another 1,000 men were detailed to clear the right-of-way. Smaller teams of 300 to 400 men each were put to work boring the entrances for the first three tunnels.

It was all dangerous work with the air full of flying debris, and the ever-present danger of loosened boulders and landslides. But even more than the European gold miners, the Chinese railroad men enjoyed, relished, even sought out the challenge of the unknown and the adventures offered. Working on the railroad allowed them to find them plenty. But the next adventure was not something anyone foresaw or was prepared for.

Cape Horn was a sheer mountainside towering over the American River 2,000 feet below, rising out of the blue mist. It was named by Californians who well remembered the seagoing difficulties of rounding the geological protrusion at the foot of South America. With an incline of 75 degrees, not even the most sure-footed surveyors would broach it; they merely sighted it on the far end and drew a steadily climbing, wholly theoretical line across the cliff. The plan was to make a ledge where a track could run 1,300 feet above the valley floor. The only way to get the railroad across was to start slow, to carve out a narrow shelf just wide enough for a man to walk. There were no trails or ledges, not even a goat path. The grade could not be bored through a tunnel, but had to be built on the side of the mountain, which required blasting and rock cuts on the sheer cliffs. The mountain had to be sculpted.

The blasting crews chipped away at the 75-degree incline for days, inch by inch. On some days, they advanced less than a foot. Then, over time, it was enlarged until the Central Pacific could send crews out to chisel away the cliff face. They cut the very hard rock by hand, tediously. It was hard, back-breaking and dangerous work performed by, who else, the Chinese. They produced a seven-foot-wide shelf from which a wider platform could be scraped and blasted — and they did it using only picks, shovels, hand drills, wheelbarrows and one-horse dump carts, along with the most unlikely of materials, the humble bendable reed.

One day Li Yu, the headman for his Chinese work group, asked his foreman if he could speak to Strobridge. Li Yu politely waited to speak, still with his western hat in hand unlike most of the other Chinese laborers who still wore the conical straw hat.

"Maybe we can be of some help," he said. "My people, you know, built the Great Wall of China!"

The carving out of paths that clung to cliff sides, like bird nests on inaccessible ledges, was an ancient art well-known to Chinese engineers. In some places, the Chinese dangled supplies down to work sites on cliff faces in reed baskets, attached to ropes secured from the tops of the mountains. Feats of construction such as these had been commonplace in China for thousands of years.

The idea of the men from Kwangtung province hanging from cliffs at dizzying heights and blasting caused Strobridge to sneer in disbelief. But he gave his begrudging approval. He had nothing to lose. It was a safe bet for Strobridge — what could he lose but a few Celestials? So he agreed.

Reeds were shipped out immediately from San Francisco to Cape Horn. The men wove great baskets, large enough to hold one or two workmen, of tall reeds and vines. On the waist-high baskets they knotted four eyelets, in the directions of the Four Winds, and inscribed them with the proper prayers. Ropes were tied through the eyelets and the baskets were slowly lowered from the edge of the cliff down to the elevation of the future roadbed hundreds of feet below.

Strobridge pulled Li Yu aside. "Since this hair-brained idea is yours, you can be lowered in the basket first to set the explosive," he said.

Li Chang insisted on taking his brother's place, shouting, "I am smaller than you. I will set the powder charges." Then he whispered to Li Yu, "You have a wife and child; I have no one."

Strobridge nodded. Lowered in the handmade basket, Li Chang balanced himself against the harsh wind. He made sure the wick on the powder charge was long enough so the workers had plenty of time to pull him up away from the blast. Using a handpick, he dug a small opening and placed the charge carefully into the hole.

After Li Chang lit the wick, he shouted, "Go! Hurry up!"

Li Yu and the workers quickly pulled Li Chang away from the blast. Up above, Li Yu sighed in relief.

Li Chang got to be a basketman because he was thin and light, but most of the basketmen were boys of less that twenty years old. He rode the basket barefoot so that the heels of his boots did not break through the bottom. The basket danced and whirled, and he saw the world turning underneath him. It was a fun feeling, a new experience.

Suspended in the quiet sky, he thought all kinds of crazy thoughts, that if a man didn't want to live any more, he could just cut the ropes or, even easier, tilt the basket and never worry about anything ever again. He would spread his arms, and the air momentarily would hold him as he fell past the buzzards, hawks, and eagles, and landed impaled on the tip of a sequoia.

Gusts of wind spun the light basket. Neighboring baskets swung together and parted. He and the man next to him looked at each other and laughed.

Swinging beside the cliff, Li Chang stood up and grabbed a twig. He dug holes and inserted gunpowder and fuses. He worked neither fast nor slow, keeping pace with the others. The basketmen signaled to one another to light the fuses in unison. He struck match after match and dropped the burnt matches over the side. At last his fuse caught; he waved, and the men above pulled hand over hand hauling him up, pulleys creaking.

"Hurry, hurry!" Li Chang shouted.

Some impatient men clambered up the ropes holding the baskets. Li Chang watched the explosions, which came almost synchronously, echoes booming as in a war. He moved the scaffold to the next section of cliff and went down in the basket again and set the next charges.

This time, two men were blown up. One was knocked out or killed by the explosion and plummeted silently. The other screamed, his arms and legs struggling as he fell. Oh, how Li Chang wished for an arm long enough to reach down and catch them. Much time passed as they fell like lead weights. Shreds of basket and a conical straw hat skimmed down. The winds that pushed birds off course and up over the mountains did not carry men. Li Chang gripped the ropes tightly, and found it difficult to let go and get on with the work.

"It can't happen twice in a row," Li Yu said to Li Chang.

"Yes, the chances are very good that the trip after an accident is probably the safest one," Li Chang replied. They raced to Li Chang's favorite basket, checked and double-checked the four ropes, yanked the strands, tested the pulleys, oiled them, reminded the pulley men about the signals, and Li Chang went off into the sky again.

That night, Li Chang found himself falling through a dream and woke up suddenly. He heard other men call out in their sleep. There was no warm woman beside him to tweak his ears and hug him. But it was only a dream, he told himself. Li Yu heard his occasional screams.

The next night there was a warm wind blowing the stars around. Li Yu sat next to his brother and talked to the moon and to Wang Wei.

"I hope you're on the other side talking to me, too," he thought. "Or am I a fool who sits alone talking to the moon?"

The next day across a valley, a chain of men working on the next mountain, men like ants working to change the face of the world, fell together. But they were very far away. Godlike, Li Chang watched men whose faces he could not see and whose screams he did not hear, roll and bounce and slide down like a handful of gravel. After a fall, the buzzards circled the spot and reminded the workers for days that a dead man was down there. The men threw piles of rocks and branches to cover bodies from sight. The bones of these Chinese men would never return to China.

The mountain face was reshaped; they drove in supports for a bridge. Since hammering was less dangerous than detonations, the men played a little; they rode the baskets swooping in wide arcs; they twisted the ropes and let them unwind like tops.

"Look at me!" shouted Li Chang, as he pulled open his pants, and pissed overboard, the wind scattering the drops. "I'm a waterfall!" On rare windless days, he watched his piss fall in a continuous stream from himself almost to the bottom of the valley.

When the wind blew fiercely, the men suspended the basketwork. Clouds moved in several directions at once. Men pointed at dust devils, which turned their mouths crooked. There was ceaseless motion; clothes kept moving; hair ruffled, sleeves puffed out. Nothing stayed still long enough for Li Chang to figure it all out. The wind sucked the breath out of his mouth and blew thoughts from his brain.

When all was said and done, the rail bed was sculpted out of the face of sheer rock that was Cape Horn. The work took a year and more than three hundred Chinese workers fell to their deaths in the process.

No longer governor of California, Leland Stanford now changed his tune. "We swarmed the mountains with Chinamen," he declared. And it remained one of the best known of all the Chinese labors on the Central Pacific mainly because, unlike the work in the tunnels, it made for one of the grandest sights to be seen along the entire Central Pacific line.

Drilling holes in the cliff, placing the fuses, and getting away in time. The white laborers couldn't do it. The Chinese could, if not as a matter of course, then quickly and easily. At least they made it look easy.

Dangerous as the Cape Horn work was, clearing the roadbed was even worse. One 300-man gang spent a full ten days clearing a single mile of right-of-way. The trees were shipped to sawmills and fashioned into ties and trestling. Then the stumps were blasted from the soil. Ten barrels of gunpowder were needed to free each one. In any one week, the crews used as much explosives as fired at the Civil War's Battle of Antietam.

In a few weeks, the roadbed had been blasted from the rock. The summit, however, still lay ahead. To get a locomotive through that granite would require tunnels. Without them, no locomotive could get over the peaks, even using passes and switchbacks. Tunnels through granite were without precedence. To make it happen, a way had to be found. In late summer of 1865, the Central Pacific went to work on the apparently unsolvable problem.

12

THE SUMMIT TUNNEL

"Hello darkness, say good-bye to Mr. Sun," said Li Yu, now a headman, a leader of a twelve-man Chinese tunnel work crew and his skin as dark as leather. "I feel almost as if the very darkness will swallow me up forever."

The tunnel whispered, but it was just the sound of their feet avoiding scummy patches of ice. The tunnel was like a giant flute, and snow tunnels 50 to 500 feet in length were constructed to connect the outside world to the granite tunnel. The further they went into the snow maze, the more Li Yu felt that the wind's tune was a funeral dirge. Candlewicks seemed to dance like yellow ghosts.

"We shouldn't be here at all," he said. Day or night, Li Yu didn't know which it was. When he slept, he dreamed, often of a temple he had visited as a boy, which had nine rooms filled with representations of the nine hells. There were life-size images of people being roasted over fires, faces with eyes poked out and tongues removed, women ripped apart and men dismembered. He had dug and exploded his way into one of these hells. "Only here there are 16 tunnels, not nine, plus all the tracks between them," he lamented to Li Chang.

"But you can't give in, it's war," Li Chang responded, forcefully but with his usual easy-going smile. "The mountain can kill you in a dozen different ways before you blink an eye and victory is eight inches a shift."

Indeed, this was cruel work, dangerous and claustrophobic. The tunnels smelled of sweat, salt and blood. The Chinese tunnel crews seldom saw the light of day or a blue sky. They walked to and from work inside the snow tunnels, and there they endured their long, grueling shifts in a dim, dank world of smoky lights, ear-ringing explosions, and choking dust.

Seven separate tunnels had to be dug first. The most difficult was the Summit Tunnel. And by the winter of 1866 the tracks still had not reached its mouth.

Before joining this massive and dangerous undertaking, Li Yu had written to his wife Sun Wei and his son, Li Wu. "In America, they have a firewagon that has the strength of 1,000 water buffalo. We are helping the Americans build paths for the firewagon."

His wife wrote back, "You can help me by preserving what we have. Stay and be safe in San Francisco." Li Wu was now twelve years old.

Ideally, the roadbed tunnel through the mountains would have been dug by heavy machinery, but such machinery was unavailable, either because it was too expensive or too difficult to transport to the site. Entire bridges would have had to be rebuilt for such machinery to reach the tunnel locations. Thus, the Chinese were forced to chisel tunnels through the granite using only handheld rock drills, pick axes, sledge hammers, explosives and shovels.

On November 24, 1866, the first train arrived at Cisco Station (thirteen miles from the mouth of the Summit Tunnel). It was loaded with ties, rails, chairs, fishplates, and measuring rods. It took three engines to pull the freight up the mountain. Supervisor James Strobridge had wagons and carts to meet the train, with hundreds of Chinese aboard. All night they loaded the rails and the rest onto the wagons and carts. They also pulled two locomotives off the tracks and put them atop skid sleds made of logs split down the middle and rounded at the ends. They were greased with fat on the bottom to help them slide.

At dawn, the procession toward the summit began. Carts went first, followed by the wagon train. At the rear, hundreds of Chinese tugged at ropes alongside mule teams and horse teams to skid the locomotives over the summit and down the eastern slopes of the mountain. The sight was much more daunting than inspirational. And then the snow came again.

The teamsters and their oxen made their way through new snow that was soft and powdery, and up to their waists or higher, even to their shoulders. Into this, the oxen floundered. Often they simply lay down, worn out, to be roused by teamsters twisting their tails. Bellowing with pain, they scrambled to their feet and went on. One ox had its tail twisted clear off and was thus spared further agony.

Construction chief Charles Crocker established work camps on each side of the summit, to facilitate the round-the-clock drilling, blasting, scraping, shoveling and hauling by the Chinese. He correctly figured there was no night or day within a tunnel.

Inside the man-made caves, shadowy men in the dim light worked around the clock, in three eight-hour shifts, at four separate headings: the first team on the east side, the second team on the west. To speed progress, engineers drilled a vertical shaft down from the top, midway along the projected tunnel line, blasting from the inside out. So a third team worked westward back from the middle and a fourth team worked eastward back from the same spot—both moving outward. For teams three and four, the men were lowered by ropes 100 feet down the 8-by-12-foot man-made shaft.

CHINESE BROTHERS, AMERICAN SONS

The Chinese cut it through by hand and hauled the debris (mainly granite chunks) up the shaft, and lowered timbers down to shore up the lengthening tunnel. Good progress was made for the first thirty days, at which point the job of hoisting rubble from the shaft using a hand derrick became impossible. The problem was solved with a locomotive stripped of all non-essential parts, with wheels removed, and its body taken up on a logging cart driven by ten oxen. It was let down carefully into the sunken shaft and used as a hoisting engine.

That winter, the men in the Summit Tunnel were almost all Chinese, with a few Irish on the west end. Gangs consisted of one white foreman per thirty or forty workers. The winter of 1865-66 was the worst anyone had ever seen in California, and the winter of 1866-67 was even worse. But right through, an average of 6,000 to 10,000 men were working on the Central Pacific railroad. Even with twelve to fifteen men drilling at each face and more than 500 barrels of black powder expended daily, the Central Pacific partners figured it would take fifteen months to break through the Summit Tunnel of just 1,659 feet in length, which was just 113 yards longer than a quarter mile. Progress through the hard rock was excruciatingly slow at one foot a day with hand drills and black blasting powder. The Central Pacific could not afford fifteen months. On New Year's Day 1867, there was still 1,367 feet to go to complete the Summit Tunnel, 26 feet wide and 20 feet high and as much as 124 feet below the surface.

The Chinese usually operated in teams of three at the tunnel facing—one holding the drill, the other two alternating the pounding of the drill—with four teams (a dozen men) working side by side. One man held his rock drill as high as he could, another held it at waist level, another down at his toes. The man with the drill (such as Li Chang) turned it constantly while holding it firm and in place. The men (like Li Yu) who did the pounding did so with sledgehammers weighing from 14 to 18 pounds each. They swung, hit the drill at its far end, dropped the hammer, brought it up again behind them, and swung once more, alternately, many times a minute. They could each drill four holes, one and three-quarters inches in diameter, in eight hours.

Of all the backbreaking labor that went into the building of the Transcontinental Railroad, of all the dangers inherent in the work, this was the worst. The drills lost their edge to the granite and had to be replaced frequently. The Central Pacific soon learned to order its drills in 100-ton lots.

Li Chang held the drill steady or he would get hit by the sledgehammer. Li Yu, swinging the hammer, had muscles like steel. When a 15 to 18-inch deep hole was at last big enough for the black powder, the crew filled it with hay and powder, set a fuse imbedded in sand, and yelled as loud as they could while running out of the range of the blast. Sometimes, the fuse worked, sometimes it didn't. Often the workers had put in too much powder and most of it blew toward them—harmlessly as far as the granite was concerned, but at great danger to the Chinese.

The granite was merciless. Li Yu struck it with his pickax, and it jarred his bones, chattered his teeth. He swung the sledgehammer against it, and the impact rang in the dome of his skull. The mountain that was millions of years old was locked against them and was not to be broken into.

"The Summit Tunnel is the key," Li Yu told his men while even the muscles of their throats strained as they tried to crack the granite wall. "It's the longest, the toughest and the meanest. Either we beat it or the railroad never gets finished,"

Juk Bok, at fourteen, only two years older than Li Yu's son, was one of the best workers. "I want to help build this railroad, show Americans we belong," he said. "I refuse to be a farmer like my father in China. He's such a coward. Unlike you, he didn't want to come to America."

"Don't you ever say that again about your father, because he is not a coward," Li Yu said. "You think I am brave; well, your father is much braver because he carries responsibility, for you, your brother, your sister, and your mother. And this responsibility is like a big rock that weighs a ton. It bends and it twists him until finally it buries him under the ground. Nobody says he has to do this. He does it because he loves you, and because he wants to. I have never had this kind of courage. Farming, working like a water buffalo every day with no guarantee anything will ever come of it. That is bravery."

He put his hands on Juk Bok's shoulders. "Juk Bok, you know I'd cut off my leg before I would let anything happen to you," Li Yu said.

Li Chang smiled approvingly of Li Yu's fatherly gesture.

The Chinese tunnelers, who were accustomed to spending their days outdoors and sharing crowded quarters at night, camped in thin canvas tents, under 10- to 20-foot snow drifts. For month after month, they lived like seals, huddled together wearing padded cotton clothes. Several of the camps were swept away by avalanches in the arctic oblivion of those mountains, and the dead were not recovered until the snow thawed.

In a little tent, ten by twelve feet, a half dozen or more Chinese ate and slept together. Tents went up at the facings of each tunnel or near the site of grading or near other work places. But each gang had a cook, and they ate a healthy diet of well-cooked and tasty food before and after each shift, unlike the white workers.

The Central Pacific provided the Americans with boiled beef and potatoes, beans, bread and butter, and coffee. If they wanted to spend their own money, the company kept stores that offered dried fish, fruit, tomatoes, eggs, beets, turnips, pickles and more.

The Chinese paid for all their food. They got an astonishing variety — oysters, cuttlefish, finned fish, abalone, Oriental fruits, and scores of vegetables, including bamboo shoots, seaweed, and mushrooms. Each of these foods came dried, purchased from the Chinese merchants in San Francisco. Further, the Chinese ate rice, salted cabbage, vermicelli, bacon, and sweet crackers. Very occasionally they had fresh meat, pork being a prime favorite, along with chicken.

The food helped keep the Chinese healthy. And Li Chang now had Chinese people to cook for when he occasionally assumed those chores. The water they drank was even more important. Like the miners before, the American railroad workers drank from the streams and lakes, and many of them got diarrhea, dysentery, and other illnesses. The Chinese drank nothing but tepid tea. The water was boiled first and was brought to them by youngsters who carried two pails on a sturdy pole across their shoulders. They used pails or kegs that had originally been filled with gunpowder and were washed clean before the tea went in. In California it was known as "powder tea."

The remainder of the time off was spent, besides sleeping on mats in the snow tunnel quarters, in washing themselves and their clothes, gambling, talking and reading. Not having acquired a taste for whiskey, they had few fights and were not often drunk. They did smoke opium on Sundays, their day off, but they did not stupefy themselves with it.

Leland Stanford, one of the Central Pacific owners, wrote to President Andrew Johnson, "The grading between Newcastle and Colfax was very difficult and expensive, increasing as the line was pushed up the mountain slope. The cuttings have been deeper, the embankments higher, and more rock work encountered, as the line has progressed eastward.... We have encountered and are now laboring upon the most difficult and expensive portion of the line entrusted to us. This, too, at the very commencement of our efforts."

Shoulder to shoulder, hour after hour, the Chinese railroad workers chipped away at the rock, breathing granite dust, sweating and panting by the dim flickering glow of candlelight, until even the strongest of them fainted from exhaustion.

One day, Li Yu came out of the tunnel to find the mountains white with flowers. His outlook brightened. Was it a sign? It was the April rose that only grows in the early spring. Icicles, which Li Chang called "ice chopsticks," dripped from the trees. Li Yu sat in his basket and slid down the slopes.

The days became nights when the crews tunneled inside the mountain, which sheltered them from the wind, but also hid the light and the sky. Li Yu and his crew pick-axed the mountain, the dirt filling their nostrils even through their cowboy bandanas. They shoveled the dirt into a cart and pushed it to a place that had enough ceiling for the mules, which hauled it the rest of the way out. His crew looked forward to cart duty to edge closer to the entrance. Eyes dark, nose plugged, his cough hacking, his job was to mole his way another 1,000 feet and meet others digging from the other side.

Li Yu lifted the hammer high, careful that it did not pull him backward. He let it fall forward of its own weight against the rock. Nothing happened to that gray wall; he slammed with strength and will. He hit the same spot over and over again, the same rock. Some chips and flakes broke off. The granite looked the same everywhere. It had no softer or weaker spots anywhere, it was the same hard gray. He learned to slide his hand up the handle, lift, slide and swing, a circular motion, hammering, hammering, and hammering. He would bite like a rat through that mountain. His eyes couldn't see; his nose couldn't smell; and now his ears were deafened with the noise of hammering.

"When will I breathe properly again?" Li Yu asked, and his thoughts drifted to Wang Wei. He would have liked to have loved Sun Wei, and he continued to send money to her and his son back in China. But his heart was elsewhere. "My burden is to bear a love I shouldn't carry," he thought. Coming out of the tunnel at the end of a shift, he had no idea whether it was supposed to be day or night. He blew his nose fifteen times before the mucus cleared again.

When the foreman measured progress at the end of 24 hours of pounding, the rock had given a foot. The hammering went on day and night. While Li Chang and Li Yu slept, they could hear the sledgehammers of other men working in the earth. The steady banging reminded him of holidays and harvest days; falling asleep, he heard the women chopping mincemeat and the millstones striking. Then next day, everyone worked again to tunnel through the mountain, even the cook Li Chang.

"How much?" Kirby, the white foreman, asked.

"Almost nine inches," replied headman Li Yu.

"Not so good, Chinaman," Kirby barked. "You got to get better if we're going to catch up with the schedule. Tomorrow drill the same number of holes but double-charge them."

Li Yu protested. "No, if we pack too tight, the powder won't burn."

Kirby, however, was unrepentant. "Chink, God's country sits west of the mountains and a whole continent is wanting to get to it; but it can't because of these mountains and your insubordination."

The very next day, a member of another gang under Kirby was blinded.

"What happened?" asked Li Yu of a nearby headman Lin Bo.

CHINESE BROTHERS, AMERICAN SONS

"Li Kang was holding the drill, and I had the hammer," Lin said. "All I know is I hit it good and the next thing the whole world went off. Rocks flew everywhere, bouncing off the walls. Kirby made us double-charge the powder. All the powder didn't burn at the same time. Some went off later."

Other men in "boss suits" occasionally came into the tunnel, measured with a yardstick, and shook their heads. "Faster," they said, "Faster, Chinamen, too slow. Too slow."

The Chinese laborers in the top tiers of scaffolding let rocks drop, or a hammer fall. Ropes tangled around the demons' heads and feet. The Chinese muttered and flexed, glaring out of the corners of their eyes. But usually there were no such diversions. One day was the same as the next, one hour no different from one another—the endless beating against the granite.

Li Yu opened the door of a shack, a 12-by-12 feet log cabin inside the tunnel. There was barely enough room for the three tiers of bunks on three of the walls. Each tier had four beds and each bed was little more than a wooden shelf, with only two feet separating each shelf. It reminded Li Yu of the bunks on the ship coming over. For Li Yu, the headman, and his twelve-man work crew, that meant one man had to sleep on the floor. Li Yu and Li Chang decided to alternate sleeping on the floor and bunk.

In the center of the cabin was a Western-style stove, made of iron and shaped like a barrel. As they entered, its warmth enveloped them like a grandmother's quilt. On the top of the stove was a big pot of hot water while another pot sat on the floor keeping warm near the stove.

Despite the stove's roaring fire, Li Yu could feel all the little drafts in the shack as heat leaked out between the logs. Sheets of English language newspapers, pieces of scrap lumber and even tin were put up in a vain attempt to add another layer. Mud was packed into the gaps, too. Tending the stove was Li Chang, now a wispy little man. Railroad building had stooped his shoulders.

"Your hair was once darker," Li Yu said to his brother.

"My heart was lighter too," Li Chang said.

Li Chang was now in his late thirties—old by those times—but he was as animated as ever as he moved from the chopping block to his pot to the woodpile, while still conversing with the work crew. "Your dinner's turned to charcoal," he said to the workers in a scolding tone while stifling a smile.

Li Chang singled out Juk Bok. "I pity you, boy, having to put up with these tardy ingrates. They'll be late to their own funeral."

After the crew washed one by one, Juk Bok asked Li Chang, "What's there to eat?"

"Rice soup," the crew derisively shouted in unison.

Li Yu rolled his eyes.

"Congee," said Li Chang, his head shaking. "Rice porridge. It's the simplest food, the most basic. But it takes care to make. First it must have that fragrance of fresh-steamed rice. Then the ingredients, maybe some red beans, bean curd, dried oysters and oh, so good, the toppings."

He pointed to the small table next to the stove which was crowded with little bowls he had prepared while the aromatic rice cooked. There were tiny squares of crunchy pickle, slivers of greens, cubes of tofu, tiny smoke-dried fish and peanuts. Now Li Chang added ginger and green onions to the simmering congee. Then he put the pot in the middle of the floor of the shack, surrounded by the little bowls of condiments in a pleasing circle.

They all sat down together; the crew passed their clean bowls to Li Chang. The first one he filled, he handed to Li Yu. Then he served the eldest on down until he served Juk Bok last. Li Chang looked satisfied. The crew knew that Li Chang cared about what they were eating.

Chopsticks flew as they piled ingredients on top of their bowls of congee, and the conversation burst forth like steam from a kettle. Li Chang loved the sound of it. Li Yu mixed his congee with his spoon and tasted it. Oh, so good. The salty and piquant flavors against the delicate fragrance of the rice, the crispy fish against the tofu and the soft gruel.

"Wonderful," he said as he caught Li Chang's eye.

"Anybody can make you enjoy the first bite of a dish, but only a great chef can make you enjoy the last," Li Yu whispered in Li Chang's ear. "Now eat," he said to the crew. "In eight hours, the mountain will be waiting for us." The work crew raised their tea cups towards him.

Li Chang knew that eating was only the beginning of cuisine. Just the start. Flavor and texture and aroma and all the pleasure of taste were no more than the entry way. Really great cooking went beyond this to engage the mind and the spirit. Never cook food just to be eaten, Li Chang had been taught.

They awoke to the breakfast music of coughing—from small, throat-clearing ones to chest-wracking growls. But Juk Bok had already gone.

"I hope he didn't do something stupid; we need to go look for him," Li Yu said. Li Chang noticed that there was a rope tied to the wheel of an overturned cart while the other end disappeared somewhere outside in the snowy, bitter cold landscape. Suddenly the rope went slack and a shadowy figure appeared in the curtain of snow with a lantern in one hand and snow all over his clothes. It was an American, the rope was tied to his waist. Startled, he said to Li Chang and Li Yu, "Are you a relative?"

"Of whom?" Li Yu asked.

"The boy who got lost." The man untied the rope from the wheel. A moment later another man entered, carrying the legs of a frozen corpse. A third man followed carrying the shoulders. Li Yu stared in horror; it was the body of Juk Bok.

"It's some boy," the first rescuer said. "He went out with a handcart to dump some trash and got lost."

Li Yu wept. He had failed Juk Bok; he didn't look out for him as he had promised.

"Thank you," Li Yu said to the Americans.

"I've got a son back in Ohio," the first rescuer said.

For the first time in a long time, Li Yu saw a glimmer of what Li Chang had tried to tell him. "All Westerners are not demons."

Li Yu now more than ever yearned to see his son, Li Wu. But his tears of sorrow were interrupted.

"Chinamen, get back to work!" Kirby bellowed.

Li Chang was startled; adrenaline pumped into his muscles. His heart raced and his breathing was heavy. He studied Kirby's face and a flash of recognition overwhelmed him. He recognized him as the man who had stolen their mining claim, Mitch "Wild Thing" Williams.

But Li Chang became calm. "Should I fight him or run?" he thought.

Before he could answer, Strobridge came upon the scene. "I'll bury the boy at mile marker 100 so you can send his bones home later. Now move on before I dock your pay."

Strobridge spent most of his time that fall and winter near or at the Summit Tunnel—No. 6, as it was called. Strobridge invented games for working faster, gold coins for miles of track laid, for the heaviest rock, a grand prize for the first team to break through a tunnel. Day shifts raced against night shifts, Chinese against Welshmen, Chinese against Irishmen, Chinese against Injuns and black demons. The fastest races were Chinese against Chinese, who bet on their own teams. Chinese always won because of good teamwork, smart thinking, and their need for the money. Also, they had the most workers to choose teams from. Whenever his team won anything, Li Chang added the winnings to his gold stash.

After tunneling into granite for over a year, Li Yu understood the immovability of the Earth. Men changed, men died, and weather changed, but a mountain was the same as permanence and time. This mountain had taken no new shape for centuries, ten thousand centuries. The world was a still, still place, time unmoving. But he also learned that his crew's spirit, while it might bend, was also unbreakable.

Li Chang found the scene from the Dutch Flat Road strangely beautiful at night. He was drawn by the sight of the tall firs drooping under their heavy white burdens but still pointing to the mountains that overhung them.

The fires that lit seven tunnels shone like stars on the snowy mountainsides. The only sounds that came down to break the stillness of the winter night were broken by the sharp ring of hammer on steel, or the heavy reports of the blasts.

In the midst of the seldom-quiet night - or was it day - Li Yu closed his eyes, and Wang Wei was here in his arms.

"Bring me the night, because when I'm dreaming, we don't seem so far from each other," Li Yu said to himself and looked up at the moon.

Strobridge put hundreds of the Chinese to work shoveling the snow away to keep open a cart trail to the tunnel opening. If it had not been for the race with the Union Pacific, the Central Pacific would have closed down that winter, but the fear of losing all Utah and Nevada to their rival drove them on.

Li Chang remained optimistic. He awaited the joyful day when the shrill whistle of the locomotive was heard as the train of cars rattled across the mountain and down the Truckee. And that day was not too far distant.

The tunneling went on, up and down the line. No matter what the cost, the remaining tunnels would be bored that winter.

ED SHEW

On December 31, 1866, the last day of the year, the Central Pacific was able to announce that it was "in daily operation from Sacramento to Cisco." That was 92 miles, within 12 miles of the summit and 5,911 feet above sea level—the highest altitude yet reached by a railroad in the United States, or anywhere else.

The snow tunnels were large enough for a team of horses to walk through. Windows were dug out of the snow walls, to dump refuse and let in a bit of light, also chimney and air shafts. But for the most part the Chinese worked, ate, drank their tea, gambled, smoked opium, and slept in the remarkable labyrinth they were constantly building under the snow.

Falling ice scrabbled on the roofs. The men stayed under the snow for weeks at a time. Snow slides covered the entrances to the tunnels, which they had to dig out to enter and exit. Their world was white tunnels and black tunnels.

There were accidents of all kinds, mainly from the blasting powder. Sometimes the heavy explosions started avalanches, and entire camps of workmen were buried alive. Near the Summit Tunnel, an avalanche carried away some twenty Chinese, whose bodies were found after the spring thaw, still standing erect, their frozen hands gripping picks and shovels. Ears and noses fell off those still alive. Fingers stuck to the cold silver rails. Snow-blind men stumbled about with bandannas over their eyes. How many fingers or hands were lost to the hammers? The cost in human life was enormous.

Outside Tunnel 10, which was drilled through the aptly named Cement Ridge two miles east of the summit, one slide killed "another fifteen or twenty Chinamen." They did not bother to get the body count right.

At another camp with 200 workers, the snow was so deep the Chinese had to shovel it from the roof and make steps to get to the top. They were snowed in, and their provisions got down to corn meal and tea. Had it lasted one week longer they would have been compelled to eat horse meat.

The men who died slowly enough to say last words, said, "Don't leave me frozen under the snow. Send my body home. Burn it and put the ashes in a tin can. Take the bone jar when you come down the mountain. Then tell my descendants to come for me."

"Shut up," scolded the fearless men. "We don't want to hear about bone jars and dying."

"You're lucky to have a body not blown to smithereens," they shouted to the sick and wounded. "How your wives would scold us if we brought back deadman's bones."

Likewise, Li Yu wrote in a letter to a dead friend's wife. "This is the Gold Mountain. We're marking the land now. The track sections are numbered, and your family will know where we leave you."

After one especially harrowing day, Li Yu gazed around the cabin. The crew looked just like corpses in narrow coffins. And overhead the storm winds howled triumphantly; and the snow, the white, white snow piled even higher above them. Li Yu straightened and looked at Li Chang.

"This mountain kills everything," he said. "It kills singing; it kills laughter. Every day we're here, I think we die a little."

But Li Chang shook his head. "Perhaps the mountain can show us if we care about each other, we can get through anything."

Li Chang proudly said he had killed a wild pig. He kept it frozen, buried on the roof of the cabin. "So we eat pork ribs marinated in hoisin sauce, rolled in five-spice crumbles—then they are wrapped in lotus leaves and steamed for hours."

"So soft that the meat falls away in your mouth," Li Yu cooed.

The work crew, now aroused from their bone-tired, melancholy state, conversed with each other as if they were freshly born.

"To Juk Bok!" the crew said in unison while raising their teacups.

"Now eat, men!" Li Yu proclaimed. "Another day lies ahead."

The next day, Li Chang told Li Yu he would work in the tunnel, foregoing his cooking chores. Someone had to replace Juk Bok. Once Li Yu's gang reached the tunnel, everyone sprang willingly into action. No one hesitated. No one held back or complained that someone else was doing more work. A few quick orders sent drill teams to work.

Li Chang held the rock drill firmly. Li Yu swung the 16-pound sledgehammer, twisting from the waist with his whole torso and shoulders, aiming a blow that would have crushed a water buffalo's skull. He did it without effort, delivering one crushing blow after another for twelve hours if he had to. He did it with rhythm.

"Hit it! Attack it!" Li Yu said to his crew.

The sledgehammers began to pound the rock drills in rhythm to his chant. Li Yu looked to the side, looked above him, and looked below. He smiled.

Suddenly, the men began chanting over and over, "We are Chinese. Hit, hit.

Work, work. Get rich. Go home."

The sledge hammers began moving in the same rhythm. The noise all around Li Chang and Li Yu had synchronized to the chant. They were even more working as a team.

Li Chang hollered amidst the chanting, "How are you holding up, men of Kwangtung?"

"They'll hold up longer than this mountain," Li Yu said as he swung again. Li Yu's gang roared their approval.

In the dim lantern light, Juk Bok's tragedy drew them together and perhaps the words of Li Chang and Li Yu, too.

More than a dozen tunnels were cut this way through the

CHINESE BROTHERS, AMERICAN SONS

granite mountains.

At the eastern approach to the Summit Tunnel, the Chinese lengthened their snow tunnel fifty feet in order to get to their quarters and on to work. One of the engineers said that whenever he returned to his shack he had to shovel it out before he could enter. Another twenty Chinese were killed in one snow slide. Individual workers simply disappeared.

In the winter of 1866-1867 to speed up progress, Crocker and Strobridge decided to experiment with nitroglycerin, which was brand-new. Said to be an extraordinary explosive, it was invented in Italy in 1847, and then refined in the 1860s by demolition engineer Alfred Nobel in Sweden. It was five times more powerful by bulk than black powder and thirteen times more destructive. The Railroad Record in August 1866 said that "its storing and transport involve no danger."

Not so, as there were terrible accidents, ignored for the most part by the Central Pacific but nevertheless more than enough to force most companies to swear off it.

On April 16, 1867 Crocker and Strobridge conducted their first tests of nitroglycerin on the hard rock of the Sierra Nevada. One nitroglycerin sample detonated prematurely, ripping apart six workers. It did not take long for press and public to put two and two together. The railroad came under heavy criticism.

During the tests, Li Yu saw a ten-foot boulder in diameter dissolve into powder, a steep bluff disintegrate into gravel, a cliff face slide away like cornmeal. Another time, standing in a clearing, Li Chang and Li Yu watched as the dynamite detonated in the open and they saw the Chinese men in front of them thrown into the air as if shot from a cannon, their conical hats floating skyward. Li Chang shoved Li Yu down, out of harm's way. One of them was killed, many had broken bones, and all were bruised.

"If I had been nearer, it would have killed me," Li Yu wrote his wife. "If I was stiff, it would have cut me in half. Li Chang saved me — again."

But it mattered not to Crocker. His problem was getting his hands on more of the stuff. The state had confiscated all private holdings of nitroglycerin and banned its transportation within California. While Central Pacific workers seemed hopelessly mired in the Summit Tunnel, a British chemist named James Howden walked unannounced into Central Pacific's Sacramento office and declared that he could manufacture nitroglycerin on-site in the mountains, thus allowing the railroad to circumvent the transportation ban. All he needed was the lordly amount of $300 per month and a steady supply of ingredients. Tracking down pure glycerol was tricky, but Crocker agreed to give it a try.

Howden's recipe practically burned through rock. Nitroglycerin required smaller and shallower holes, and fewer of them. Its smoke cleared faster than that of black powder, its debris cleaned up more easily, saving a lot of cumulative time and sweat, and it also worked in wet rock, where black powder did not.

The work now progressed fifty to seventy-five percent faster and the granite was broken into far smaller pieces. At the facings, inward progress increased from 1.18 feet per day with powder to 1.82 feet per day with nitroglycerine. At the bottom of the tunnel shaft, where the workers had their backs to each other as they moved outward, the average daily progress jumped from 2.51 feet with powder to 4.38 feet with nitroglycerine.

"Some are three feet per day. Hurrah for nitroglycerine!" Crocker said.

In early May, there was only 682 feet left between the two headings, east and west. Progress was now 60 feet per week. The dynamite created more accidents and new ways of dying, but if it were not used, the railroad would take fifty more years to finish. Nitroglycerine could explode when it was shaken on a horse or dropped. A man who fell with it in his pocket would blow himself up into bloody red pieces. Sometimes, it combusted even while static. Human bodies skipped through the air like puppets. The smell of burned flesh stuck to the rocks.

Strobridge wanted it banned. Crocker ignored the dangers and continued to make and use nitroglycerine, but only for Summit Tunnel. Only the Chinese — a people experienced with fireworks — were willing to handle this unpredictable explosive.

"Remember Uncle Long-Winded Leung. Remember Strong-Back Wong. Remember Brother Lam and Uncle Fong." Li Chang and Li Yu lost count of the number of dead. The Chinese used Sundays to look for the bodies. Kirby and the other foremen, at Crocker's direction, gave them no work time to search, because they were so far behind schedule.

The unlucky dead were stuffed into rock crevices or beneath trees. The lucky ones were buried in boxes made of crude thin planks hastily nailed together. There were a lot of victims from that winter who were never found. Whether it was good luck or bad luck, the corpses recovered were buried next to the last section of track they had worked on. So it was with Juk Bok. "May his ghost not toil," Li Chang said over his grave.

Generally, the funerals were short. "No time. No time," said both Chinese headmen and white foremen.

Chinese ghosts like straight lines of access, and the railroad was as made straight as they could build it, but no ghosts sat on the tracks; no strange presences haunted the tunnels. The blasts scared even the ghosts away.

The Central Pacific's Chinese workers moved ahead under the direction of build-at-all-cost Charles Crocker and the brutish James Strobridge. Both of them felt the Summit Tunnel would be ready for track by October 1, 1867.

The Chinese pecked, drilled, and hacked through the tunnel, but conditions grew dangerously worse. Now most Chinese labored from sunrise to sunset, or sunset to sunrise, six days a week, in twelve-hour shifts. Only on Sundays did they have time to rest, mend their clothes, talk, smoke, and of course, gamble. Gambling was as addictive for Chinese railroad workers as whiskey among their white counterparts. The tedium of their lives was aggravated by systemized abuse and contempt heaped upon them by the railroad managers and foremen. Many Chinese endured whippings from some of the foremen, who treated them like slaves. Naturally, resentment gradually built up in the camps.

One day, Li Chang lost two right toes when his pickax struck a rock that still had some residual blasting oil or nitro on it. Li Yu was cut by flying chips and his right cheek, already scarred, bore an even larger mark for the rest of his life. In that, they were the lucky ones.

"Sacrifice is a part of life," Li Chang said to Li Yu. "It is supposed to be. It is not something to regret but something to aspire to."

But the Chinese had just about had enough.

13

The Strike

Twenty charges were placed and ignited. "But only eighteen blasts went off," Li Yu yelled.

Foreman Kirby still ordered the Chinese to enter the cave of the Summit Tunnel to resume work. They obeyed and seconds later, the two other charges suddenly exploded. Chinese bodies flew from within the cave as if shot from a cannon.

Four Chinese were found dead, but Li Chang was nowhere to be found. Still searching hours later, at the end of the Summit Tunnel, Li Yu spotted a figure lying among the rocks. He leaped over the rubble, nearly falling on the icy floor, and shone the lantern on the body's face; it was bloody. Around the head there was a dark-red pool that was frozen. It was Li Chang.

On his knees, Li Yu took his brother's wrist in his cold hands. The skin was still warm; a pulse could be felt. Li Yu rubbed it and felt Li Chang's pulse grow stronger — as if he were taking energy from the touch of Li Yu's hand. "My brother, you are alive!"

Li Chang felt blissful sensations. He had been near death. He was moving very rapidly down a long, dark tunnel. He seemed to be floating. He saw faces which came and went and who looked at him kindly, but did not communicate. He did not recognize them. As he got nearer to the end of the tunnel, he seemed to be surrounded by a wonderful warm glowing light.

Li Yu finished bandaging Li Chang's wounds and felt his wrist again— his pulse was stronger than before. Breathing a sigh of relief, Li Yu said to his dazed brother, "There was an accident. Fortunately, most of the rocks hit your hard head, not your body."

"Yeah, lucky," Li Chang said smilingly to his brother in between the grimaces.

Li Yu's crew had now gathered around the two of them. They were all scared.

"We need to keep working to reach that other side," Li Chang said to Li Yu. "We feel trapped and the darkness can choke us. We're far from our homes. But all that matters is getting through the tunnel."

"This journey through the darkness seems like it will never end, it requires a lot of self-control," Li Yu replied. "Our journey is turning into a nightmare."

The men shouted, one after the other: "I don't like this. This stinks. This is so unfair! This is horrible. I can't believe that I'm still stuck in this fucking, god-forsaken place!"

"Yes, we may be sorely tempted to give in to despair, to throw up our hands and say, 'That's it, I quit!'" Li Yu said.

But what could they do? The Central Pacific would not let the Chinese leave.

"We are just in a tunnel, not a bottomless pit," Li Yu told his men. "This tunnel has a beginning, and we know that it has an end. If we keep moving forward, doing our part, helping each other, we will eventually make it through."

"So maybe we'll take a break to catch our breath," Li Chang added. "We can grumble, and maybe even engage in some good old-fashioned anger. But eventually we'll make the choice to start moving again."

"We will find a way, or we'll make one. And on we go," Li Yu said.

"Yes!" hollered Li Yu's crew. Other Chinese workers were a bit more restrained, but most nodded with approval.

"Can you walk?" asked Li Yu. Li Chang shook one leg and then the other. Dazed, he trudged through the treacherous tunnel with every muscle in his body stiff as he stepped around the rocks. The light from the swinging lantern seemed to ripple along the rough-hewn floor as if in a tomb, pulsing like living tissue.

"Get back to work," Kirby said as if speaking to a dog.

Li Yu stared back in disbelief. "You're not ordering us back into that deadly tunnel straight after just what happened," said Li Yu. "No."

"I said get back to work," as Kirby aimed a kick towards Li Yu. He jumped to avoid Kirby's black steel-toed boot.

"No," Li Yu said matter of factly, carefully and slowly. "We need a short break. Otherwise, my brother and I quit. We quit."

Kirby's face went blank, as Li Yu said it again, "We quit."

Li Chang, barely able to stand, said to his brother, "They won't let us leave."

By now, other workers, engineers, bosses and some Irish workers, shoved their way to the front and formed a line between them and the rest of the Chinese railroad workers, including Li Yu's crew.

Kirby unbuttoned his coat exposing a whip coiled in his belt. "Go back to work," he said.

Li Chang staggered in the direction of Kirby. "I'll talk to him," Li Chang tried to reassure Kirby. He tripped and fell to his knees, too weak to get up.

Kirby lifted the coiled whip from his belt. "Chink, you're scared of the mountain when you really ought to be scared of me." He shook out the whip so that it looked like a long, black snake. "I'm telling you one last time. Get back into that tunnel."

Li Yu proudly said, "I am a free man. Isn't this a country where you fight wars to be free?"

Kirby raised and lowered the whip. "Not on my mountain," he said.

As Li Yu turned his back on Kirby, he heard the crack and instantly felt a fiery pain across his back. The whip ripped through the thick padding of his coat and his shirt as if they were paper. Another lash and Li Yu was sent sprawling face-first. He saw his own blood. He felt another lash.

Behind the line of white men, there were now maybe a hundred or more Chinese workers with pickaxes, shovels, rock drills and sledge hammers. "Stop working, we outnumber them," Li Yu implored.

Kirby gave Li Yu eight more bone-rattling, skin-tearing strokes. He whipped to make him scream, to make him shut up. When he cracked his whip for the eleventh time, Li Yu's screams of agony were reduced to a whimper. The writhing of his body was no more.

The rest of Li Yu's crew was let through to pick up the crumpled bodies of both Li Yu and Li Chang and they took them back to their log shack.

The next day, when they returned to work, Li Yu understood more than ever the importance of the thoughts that Li Chang shared with him while mining, while cooking at his restaurant, and now while building this railroad.

"Alone we can do so little, together we can do so much," Li Yu said to his crew. "All we have is one another. We have to cooperate if we're going to build this railroad and get off this mountain alive."

Li Yu's crew worked even more smoothly and efficiently than before. The way Li Yu had been whipped and Li Chang's injuries showed them how they had to depend on one another.

CHINESE BROTHERS, AMERICAN SONS

Sometimes it was a real pleasure to take a sledgehammer to the mountain. Li Yu's crew pretended the rock was Kirby. Outside, the sky was just as angry as the Chinese workers. The storms just kept piling on. Sometimes, fuel and food supplies ran low. A bowl of Li Chang's congee became a luxury, even without the condiments. In the end, Li Yu's crew was down to eating what the white men ate—watery cornmeal.

One morning, they got up amidst much coughing. Breakfast was weak tea and, yes, cornmeal. But Li Chang had bartered with an Irish worker for some honey to make the corn meal porridge taste better. He even made mush of some of the cornmeal, making patties which he fried and topped with honey.

All around them, Li Yu heard the usual breakfast music of coughs—from the dry, the moist, the brassy, the hoarse, the wheezy, the barking and the ones who coughed as if someone was choking them to death. But they all persevered. They ate. They laughed. They sang. They thought about their families. For them, "failing the family was far worse than any personal pain." But Li Yu felt he had planted the seed for what was about to come.

With the introduction of nitroglycerine, progress at the Summit Tunnel was much faster. Nevertheless, Crocker, Strobridge and the foremen, especially Kirby, drove the Chinese workers even harder, forcing them to work longer and longer hours as the days, too, grew longer. Of course, daylight meant little inside the tunnel.

Li Yu's tunnel crew and the other Chinese crews were now working seven days a week with twelve-hour shifts each day. One early summer day when Li Yu arrived at their tent after his shift, Li Chang, who had earlier returned to begin supper, said he had found an envelope with Lu Yu's name written in English slipped under the flap of the tent.

ED SHEW

"Who's it from?" Li Chang asked. Li Yu looked and found it was from Jimmy Smits, who wrote:

It's been years since I saw you last. Just joined the railroad a couple weeks ago. You're a legend for standing up to Kirby. Even we white guys heard about it.

I thought you should know, if you don't already. I earn $35/month while I hear you earn $30/month. I get my meals free; you pay for your food and tools, I heard.

Well, I guess you're a man now. Also, work's not too bad, I don't work in the tunnels like you and I work only eight hours/day. Did you know that Central Pacific policy is no one should work more than 8 hours straight in the tunnels? I guess that doesn't apply to the Chinese.

Farming was not for me. Maybe I can catch up with you on the desert work. Hope you're still writing.
YOUR FRIEND, Jimmy

Li Yu read this letter to his crew. Li Chang, as the cook, knew how much was spent on their food. "When you deduct the charges for food, we only make a third as much as they do," Li Yu told his crew.

One of them, Yao Ming, was particularly incensed. "It kind of sticks up your ass doesn't it?" he said. "We do all the dirty work. And the dangerous work, too. At Cape Horn, only the Chinese hung from those baskets, and I was one of them. I was young, fresh off the boat. What did I know? I wound up dangling over a cliff in a basket, swaying on a rope while I hammered away with a chisel, with only a basket bottom between me and a fall into forever. I prayed the crew would haul me up fast enough after I packed the hole and lit the fuse. Do you remember, Li Chang?"

Li Chang nodded. Li Yu knew what he had to do with this information. He could not be silent. He got out his writing pencils and found his notepad. He told the other Chinese railroad crews how underpaid they were compared to their white counterparts, and that the railroad was requiring them to work longer hours than non-Chinese workers. He decided to post the flyers in a prominent place, maybe near the tea barrels.

Getting into the spirit, Li Yu's crew offered him more sheets of paper. "I will get writer's cramp after the first ten," Li Yu laughed.

Yao Ming said, "I can write too, tell me what to say." Li Chang noted that the selfless spirit was spreading.

"And those who can't write will post the flyers," another crew member shouted.

Li Yu said to Li Chang, "It isn't just work that binds the crew together now, it's an idea."

The next morning the crew talked about the flyers. It was all they thought about. It was still on their lips as they returned to their tent after another twelve-hour day.

Charles Crocker, James Strobridge, Kirby and other foremen were huddled together. Crocker was constantly in the railroad car at track's end burning up the telegraph to Collis Huntington, Leland Stanford and Mark Hopkins, the other three of the Big Four directors.

Li Yu heard that Kirby was suggesting the Central Pacific offer the Chinese five dollars more each month. But as Yao Ming said, "That still doesn't equal the Westerners. We pay for our own food. I'd settle for just working eight-hour shifts in the tunnel."

Talk of a small pay raise only increased the anger of the Chinese. Working in the tunnel, the Chinese wore their anger like a ball and chain. Taking a break from the tunnel due to a cave-in, Li Yu's crew was outside grading the slope on one of those days when the heat just bounced off the rocks and tea never quenched their thirst. The dust coated their throats.

Yao Ming was singing a song, despite all the dust. He sang about a woman at home wondering about her husband overseas.

"Quit making that noise," Kirby shouted. "Try digging faster."

Kirby's words stung no worse than a hundred things he had said before, but tempers were running higher than the heat. They now knew how underpaid they were.

Yao Ming ignored Kirby. His voice grew clearer and sharper.

Kirby said, "I told you to shut up." He pulled back his knee-length coat that he wore even in the heat, displaying the coiled whip hanging from his belt.

"Singing makes the time go by faster," replied Li Yu defiantly.

"If you worked, time would go by even faster," Kirby said.

Li Yu put his hands on the shovel handle. "Our shift was over three hours ago."

Li Yu's crew understood enough English to know what was happening. They followed Li Yu's example. Shovels and pickaxes clanged to the ground.

"I can find another headman," Kirby declared.

In unison Li Yu's crew cried, "Never!"

Squinting, Kirby stepped backward as he kept all of the gang in front of him.

Li Yu lifted his shovel. At first, Kirby smiled smugly, thinking that Li Yu was going back to work. However, Li Yu set the shovel on his shoulder and started toward the path leading to their tent.

Kirby's astonishment turned to anger. "Where are you going?" he demanded.

"The shift's over," Li Yu said.

CHINESE BROTHERS, AMERICAN SONS

Hand on whip, Kirby stopped directly in front of Li Yu. As if talking to an animal, he shouted at Li Yu: "Stop!"

Li Yu, still pained by the unhealed scars on his back, stared back at Kirby. "Try whipping every one of us. Then try to build your stinkin' railroad yourself."

The muscle on Kirby's cheek twitched. Li Yu expected the whip. Then Li Yu heard footsteps. One by one the rest of the crew joined Li Yu, some ambling forward — others trudging forward — but all united.

"This is for you, brother," Li Yu whispered as he stepped away from Kirby's glare. Li Yu heard his crew following him.

"Come on." Li Yu beckoned to headman Li Hong's crew who were next to them. "The shift's over. We eat."

Laughing like schoolboys on a holiday, the men of that crew shouldered their tools as well. As they fell in line with Li Yu's crew, they called to the others. Kirby's helpless shouts were ignored as small streams of men trickled down the mountainside to merge into a strong river that poured right into camp.

The Chinese railroad workers didn't go to sleep after they had bathed and eaten. A festive atmosphere reigned. They had time to rest their backs, visit one another, and play mahjong. Li Yu wrote some letters for other workers that he had delayed.

Surprise! At Strobridge's urging, Crocker let the 12,000 man labor force, of whom almost 10,000 were Chinese, off on Sunday. White employees always took Sundays off anyway, but the Chinese laborers, working twelve-hour days, hadn't been off in months. Headmen were nervously talking about a possible strike.

The American foremen couldn't sway the Chinese with the whip so they tried to do it with food. The Western cooks killed fresh chickens and pigs. Instead of salted and pickled foods, Li Chang had meat to roast.

The mountain air was filled with the smells of feasting; the talk turned to their unanimous determination to return to China after working on the railroad. "I'm going to build a three-story house—just like the ones in San Francisco," said one of the crew.

Another man in the crew, a singer, said, "I'm going to build a theater and put on plays."

Li Chang said, "I'm going to open another restaurant in San Francisco, and this time serve only Chinese food."

"Let's hold our reunions at Li Chang's restaurant," Li Yu said. "It will be 'all you can eat.' How about that for a new concept in dining?" Li Chang shook his head.

"I'm going back to China and pass the government exams so I can rule over the likes of all of you," Yao Ming bravely said as chicken bones bounced off his head.

Turning serious, Li Yu told his crew about a meeting he had Sunday morning with other Chinese headmen to discuss a strike. Li Yu said, "Today, we got away with walking off the job because Strobridge and Crocker weren't around."

"But they'd be up here if we went on strike," Yao Ming said. Members of the crew nodded. They were all afraid of the potential consequences.

"Silence never won rights," Li Yu said. "They are not handed down from above but are forced out by pressure from below. If we stay united, the Central Pacific will be helpless. They can't whip us all; that would put them behind schedule as much as a strike."

The crew members nodded and said, "That's right."

Encouraged, Li Yu went on. "How many of them are here? We have them outnumbered. Their arms would wear out before they could finish whipping us."

Li Hong's crew had joined them for Li Chang's roast chicken and roast pork, but the more they all talked, the more interested they were in taking the pickaxes and showing the Westerners. Li Yu wouldn't have it.

"Violence will get us nowhere," he said. "Only the gallows or if we're lucky, jail. We need to spread the word more first. Then, at the last resort, we strike."

In mid-June, the Chinese workers celebrated the summer solstice by wrapping barley and beans in tea leaves. The way that the red string was wound and knotted revealed what flavors were inside — salty barley with pickled egg, beans and pork, or gelatin pudding. This time, one of the literate men slipped a piece of paper about the strike plan into each one, and Li Chang tied the bundle with a special pattern of red string. In the fourteenth century, information on the time and place of the revolution against the Mongols had been hidden inside autumn moon cakes.

Li Chang looked from one face to another in admiration. Of course, if there were no Chinese, there was no railroad. They were indispensable. And they were free men, not coolies, calling for nothing more than fair working conditions.

The white railroad officials and foremen were not suspicious as Chinese railroad maintenance workers moved up and down the tracks delivering the bundles tied together like lines of fish. They had exchanged gifts every year. When the summer solstice cakes came from other camps, the recipients cut them into neat slices by drawing the string through them. The orange jellies, which had red dye stick inside soaked in lye, fell into a series of sunrises and sunsets. The aged yolks and barley also looked like suns. The notes revealed urged the other Chinese railroad laborers to join in a strike. Also provided were yellow flags to ward off the five evils — centipedes, scorpions, snakes, poisonous lizards, and toads — and these were now flown as banners.

Laborers removing rock on the western heights between

the Cisco and Strong's Canyon, two of the hardest miles of their route, all threw their picks and shovels on the ground and dissolved into a sullen mob, shuffling back to their encampments. Strobridge's attempts to bully them back to work went nowhere.

Some 3,000 of the graders, road pavers and the indispensable tunnel men joined forces and stopped working. They chanted over and over in English, "Equal pay! Equal hours!"

The foremen were furious. "We're not going to tolerate this. No water and no food until you return to work. If you don't cooperate, we'll send you back to China!" they threatened.

The strike began on Tuesday morning, June 25, 1867 somewhere between mile 92 and 119. The men who were working at that hour walked out of the tunnels and away from the tracks. The ones who were sleeping slept on and rose as late as they pleased. They bathed in the streams and shaved their heads. Some went hunting and fishing. Violinists tuned and played their instruments and drummers beat their drums at the punchline of jokes. Gamblers played their cards and tiles, smokers passed their pipes, and drinkers bet for drinks by playing number games with their fingers.

The cooks made party food. The opera singers' falsettos almost perforated the mountains. The men sang new songs about the railroad. They made up verses and shouted at the good ones, and laughed at the rhymes. Oh, they were singing madly at the mountains.

Strobridge's foremen swaggered into the camp, raking their pickax handles over log walls or poking at canvas tent sides as they ordered the Chinese to come out. And out they came, from the cabins and tents, surging to form an army, 3,000 strong.

Kirby blustered and threatened; but no Chinese returned to work. Li Yu wondered if Kirby and the other foremen might try to take a couple of Chinese and make examples of them, as Kirby had once done with him. For this time, the foremen realized it would not be. There were 3,000 of the workers and only five dozen or so of them. Cursing and swearing, they skulked away.

In the meantime, Li Yu had dispatched men to carry word to all the far-flung camps which might have missed the earlier notification, the now nearly 12,000 Kwangtung men along the line and even across the mountains and down into the desert. To Li Chang's disappointment, though, many of the other camps lacked the spark or the nerve that drove their own camp. The difference, Li Chang thought, was that they didn't have Li Yu to inspire them.

All the while, the Chinese headmen led by Li Yu were at the railroad car meeting with Crocker and Strobridge. The demands were: 1) a raise to $40 a month; 2) no more than eight consecutive hours in the tunnel; 3) no more than ten consecutive hours working outside of the tunnel; 4) not to be whipped; 5) the right to leave the job; and 6) the hiring of a hundred Chinese foremen.

It was surprising that Li Yu managed to organize a strike at all, for there were also reports of frequent feuds erupting between groups of Chinese workers, who fought with spades, crowbars and spikes. But organize a significant number they did.

The scabby white workers refused to join the strike even though the demand for $40/month was more than they were making.

Crocker told Li Yu and the other headmen, "We're raising the pay to $35 a month. Because of your excellent work, the Central Pacific Railroad is giving you a $5 raise per month."

The headmen who didn't know better cheered.

"What's the catch?" said Li Yu.

"You'll still have the opportunity to put in more time," said Strobridge. "Two more hours per shift. Ten hour shifts inside the tunnels and 12 hour shifts outside the tunnels. It's not ten and 12 hours straight," said Strobridge with a straight face. "You have time off for tea and meals. Now that you have nitroglycerine, the work isn't so hard."

Li Yu repeated to them what he had said to his crew. "You aren't thinking of us as humans. We Chinese have families and wives, too. You don't think of the Chinese as supporting people across the ocean, as we are. You think it is just the white man that really needs the money."

The headmen discussed the offer of a ten-hour shift, swearing obscenities in Chinese. "Two extra hours a day—sixty hours a month for five more dollars. Pig-catcher demons. Snakes. Turtles!"

"A human body can't handle it," another headman cried out. "These demons don't believe we have a human body. This is a Chink's body."

Crocker said he would dock the entire Chinese workforce if they did not return to work. "You got an extra $5; I won't give you a cent more. I've reduced tunnel work from twelve to ten hours. Outside the tunnel, it's twelve-hour shifts. The Union Pacific is too damn far ahead of us."

The great majority wanted to give in right then and there.

Li Yu remained steadfast in reducing the hours to eight hours in the tunnel and no more than ten-hour days outside the tunnel. Li Yu rallied the other headmen to ensure they did not give in on the work hours.

The Central Pacific, tottering on the brink of bankruptcy, reacted swiftly and ruthlessly. An enraged Charles Crocker contacted employment agencies in an attempt to recruit 10,000 recently-freed American blacks to replace the Chinese. On the fourth day, the strikers heard that the U.S. Cavalry was riding single file up the tracks to shoot them. They argued whether to engage the army with dynamite. But the troops did not come.

CHINESE BROTHERS, AMERICAN SONS

Finally, for Crocker, the stalemate's ultimate solution was cruel but effective. Food and provisions to the Chinese were halted. Now playing mind games, Crocker did not go near the Chinese for a week. With no food, Li Chang heard optimistic Chinese workers saying, "Don't panic. We'll hold out forever. We can hunt. We can last fifty days on water."

Others objected, "Only magic men and monks can do that."

Ever since the corn meal days, Li Chang had been hoarding cured jerky, fermented wine, dried and strung orange and grapefruit peels, pickled and preserved leftovers. A little bit from each meal. He only had enough extra food to feed Li Yu's crew, but he shared it with Li Hong's crew also. He was not selfish, but he repeated a saying that had guided him in China: "The superior man does not push humaneness to the point of stupidity." His mother had scolded him for feeding strangers.

On the fifth and sixth days, Li Chang organized his possessions and patched his clothes and tent. Li Yu read again the letters from his wife Sun Wei. Her tone had changed in the last couple years. His wife now sounded like his deceased mother except for the polite phrases added (by someone else in different penmanship) at the beginnings and the ends.

"Idiot," Sun Wei said, "why are you taking so long? Are you wasting the money? Are you spending it on girls and gambling and whiskey?"

Li Yu and his crew had now been idle for almost a week.

"I need a new dress to wear to weddings. I refuse to go to another banquet in the same old dress. If you weren't such a spendthrift, we could be building the new courtyard where we can drink wine among the flowers and sit about in silk gowns all day. We'll hire peasants to till the fields. Or lease them to tenants, and buy all our food at the market. We'll have clean fingernails and toenails," Sun Wei admonished Li Yu.

Other relatives wrote to him to say, "Send the money to me. Your wife gambles it away and throws parties and doesn't disburse it fairly among us. You might as well come home."

After a week's worth of skimpy rations settled upon the men, Crocker returned to the work camps. The options as he lay them out: wages $35 per month no more, and hours not negotiable.

Strobridge and Crocker again met with Li Yu and the other headmen. "I will not be dictated to," Crocker said. "I make the rules and not you." If the hungry Chinese workers returned to work immediately they would only be fined, but if they continued to strike they would not get paid for the whole month of June, he threatened.

Crocker effectively starved them back to work. They really began to suffer. The cooks sneaked barrels of hot tea for the protesters to survive during the cold nights.

"We paid for the food, but Crocker's cut it off since it has to come on his railroad," Li Chang said. The Chinese were far from San Francisco, and home was even further away beyond that. With the lack of food and water, they grew weaker. Many of them wondered if the protest should continue.

Finally, one night, the workers gathered. Li Yu said, "The railroad needs us more than we need it, and Crocker needs us alive so they can't afford to let us starve."

His crew encouraged other crews. Li Yu discussed the latest developments with other nearby headmen. Still, Li Yu found that every headman except for Li Hong was afraid. Li Yu didn't blame them. The Chinese were a long way from their own kind and safety. Then Li Chang, not looking at Li Yu, reluctantly stood up. "You will all starve if you continue to strike," he said. "You must not forget why you came here."

Nobody said anything. Then, one by one, the workers nodded. They thought of their suffering families back home and agreed to return to work the next day.

The Central Pacific managers brought in a posse of whites to prevent riots which the Chinese had no intention of instigating. And when the hungry Chinese looked out and they saw this mob of deputized whites and the huge, clench-fisted Crocker, and the evil-looking, eye-patched Strobridge, they realized there was really nowhere to go.

The strike ended on the ninth day. The Central Pacific announced that in its benevolence it was giving the workers a $5 raise, not the $10 they had asked for. And that the shifts would be reduced to ten hours in the tunnel but remain at twelve hours outside the tunnel — and no Chinese foremen.

"We were going to give you the $5 raise all along," Crocker said to diminish the victory.

"No use singing and shouting over a compromise and losing nine days' work," Li Chang whispered to Li Yu.

The strike lasted only nine days. It achieved a small victory, securing the Chinese a raise of $5 a month to $35 a month. But more important, by staging the largest Chinese strike of the 19th century, the workers demonstrated to their current and future employers that if pushed hard enough, they could organize to protect themselves, even in the face of daunting odds.

Kirby came by to gloat. "You accomplished nothing," he told them.

Li Yu was not discouraged. He sensed a strength from what had happened that could sweep across America, if not all the way back to China, that could ensure his dreams, if he could only learn how to sustain it.

"Bring on the work, we're ready," Li Yu proudly said to his crew.

"That's right," they growled in unison, their spirit unbroken.

Kirby was speechless. Loyalty and trust were foreign concepts to him. "You Chink idiots belong together," he muttered and stalked away.

Everyone was relieved to get back to work. Perhaps something like the strike was needed to rally not only labor but also management and concentrate everyone's focus.

"Since the strike, the men are working hardy and steady," even the relentless Strobridge acknowledged.

For a while, the Irish foremen used clubs and the butts of their whips to strike the Chinese workers, but never hard enough to break any bones. Li Yu knew that they had realized that they couldn't afford to put men out of action. Eventually, the whippings of the Chinese workers by the white foremen ceased, but the Chinese were still not voluntarily allowed to leave the workforce.

For Li Yu and his crew, when they completed their eight-hour shifts in the tunnel and ten-hour shifts outside the tunnel, Li Yu told them, "Shift's over." With pride and defiance, they triumphantly headed back to camp.

"Awake and realize that you've got the power, you can move this mountain," Li Yu told the Chinese workers. "You're not accepted, but don't let anyone tell you, don't you ever, ever believe, that you are inferior to anyone else."

Li Yu's words meant a lot to them. Eventually, all the Chinese railroad crews of the Central Pacific followed Li Yu's lead — eight hour shifts in the tunnel and ten-hour shifts outside the tunnel.

"Brother, think of all the young men you have influenced," Li Chang said. "Li Yu, you've given them hope. More than that, you have given all of us the strength to stand on our own."

"When I was in China, I often dreamed of a far-off place where a hero's welcome would be waiting for me. Where the crowds would cheer when they saw my face, and a voice kept saying, 'This is where you are meant to be.' But I was mistaken, that dream was about you, my brother," Li Chang said.

One evening, Li Chang met Li Yu before he reached camp and said, "I remember when you were younger, you lived in my shadow. Now I live in your glow."

Li Yu smiled and shook his head at Li Chang.

The next day, Li Yu spoke to Kirby. "I am no better than you, and no worse," he said. "We are the same."

An agitated Kirby, with his whip hanging from his belt, said nothing. That day, in the late summer of 1867, the Chinese had finally finished the tunnel.

14

The Summit Tunnel Is Broken

"At last!" Li Yu cheered. On the day his crew broke through the tunnel, he threw his hat in the air, jumped up and down and screamed, "Yippee!" like a cowboy. They used picks and sledgehammers for the final breakthrough. Through the granite and then through the holes, they heard the poundings from the other direction and their shouts answered.

It was no longer the hard Sierra granite before them but fellow Chinese workers breaking through from the other side. They worked faster, forward, into the lantern light. They could smell the other side. They stuck their arms through the holes and shook hands with men on the other side.

Li Yu's crew worked on the western shaft of the Summit Tunnel. After the dust cleared, the rubble was pulled away. Suddenly, a fresh breeze of cool air came at them. The two shafts were linked together. Li Yu saw wondrous dirty faces. Li Yu looked into his crew's eyes. They had run blindly into the darkness, but had kept running.

The final breakthrough was heralded by a single light, and that not of the sun but a lantern. There was much broken rock still to be removed. The breakthrough had to be extended up, down, and sideways to complete the whole tunnel. The grade had to be built, the ties put down, the rails laid and spiked. But that light was exactly where it should have been, the engineers had achieved a triumph of the first magnitude. The facings were off by only two inches. The Summit Tunnel was 7,042 feet above the sea. It was the highest point reached by the Central Pacific.

A tremendous feeling of accomplishment set in on that day, August 28, 1867. Li Yu's crew ran and ran, their feet skipping from one end of the tunnel and to the other. The Chinese had done it with black powder, nitroglycerine and muscle power. Well over 95 percent of the work was done by the Chinese men. They, together with the foremen and the bosses, created one of the greatest moments in American history.

The Central Pacific already had track laid east of the tunnel, out along the Truckee River, but it couldn't connect the track—or collect the ample government subsidy for it, until the tunnel was finished.

When it was over, Crocker was the only one of the Big Four who praised and thanked the Chinese for what they had done. The Chinese meanwhile were called "Crocker's pets," and he was known to them as "Mistuh Clockee." Once fresh air blew through the length of the Summit Tunnel, Crocker decided he had had enough of nitroglycerin. He terminated use of the dangerous compound along the Central Pacific route.

In five years of construction, the Central Pacific had laid just over a hundred miles of track, while the Union Pacific had laid five times that. But with the Sierras finally conquered, Collis P. Huntington wired Crocker that he could supply him money and iron to lay 350 miles of track in 1868.

On November 30, 1867, the grading through the Summit Tunnel was finished, the track was laid, and the spikes were pounded in. On that date, the first scheduled train from Sacramento arrived on the eastern side of the Sierra Nevada.

Leland Stanford, Mark Hopkins and Crocker rose before dawn

in Sacramento and with their wives, the press, and some bleary-eyed legislators rode a single passenger car and locomotive on a ceremonial ride to the summit. They watched a squad of Chinese tracklayers working through the Summit Tunnel. All the onlookers cheered joyously as the beaming Chinese banged the last spikes into place on the eastern slope and a locomotive, its whistle screaming, eased its way into the darkness of the tunnel and out the other side.

In tears, Mark Hopkins said, "At last we have reached the summit, are on the downgrade and we rejoice. The operators and laborers all rejoice—all work freer and with more spirit— even the Chinamen partake of our joy. I believe they do five extra percent more work per day now that we are through the granite rock work."

On December 6, 1867, the investors arranged a Saturday junket to dwarf all previous excursions. Nearly 800 passengers, invited from the New Democratic Party-controlled state legislature, government officials, Sacramento power-brokers, and the press, squeezed into ten passenger cars and two baggage cars arranged as eating and drinking saloons. It was the first passenger train to cross the Sierra summit.

The festive train stopped only for wood and water until it reached Colfax, where a second locomotive was attached and they chugged up the steepening mountain grade. Abandoned mining cabins, some moss-covered, roofless and falling into decay, and others more recently built but now deserted and half torn-down, were scattered throughout the mountains.

Cape Horn and the yawning gulf above the American River, 1,600 feet below, caused many to gasp and hold on to each other. Those hardy enough to descend from the cars stood amidst the swirling snowflakes and wind and gaped at the majestic mass of rock known as Donner Peak on one side, and the dim, unfolding

CHINESE BROTHERS, AMERICAN SONS

Donner Lake valley on the other. Finally at 2:30 p.m. the Summit Tunnel was reached and entered to loud cheers.

The exhilaration of the Summit Tunnel breakthrough and the festivities of the excursion notwithstanding, the Central Pacific bosses and the mainly Chinese workforce still faced many problems.

The snow was the main one. Up to one-half the Central Pacific's labor force was assigned to shoveling to keep the tracks clear. Even the tops of the telegraph poles were sometimes buried by drifts. The storms cost the Central Pacific time and money, and which of the two was more valuable could not be said. One day after shoveling snow for twelve hours straight, with callouses bleeding through his gloves, Li Yu said to Strobridge. "Why don't you cover the tracks?"

Strobridge looked at him. "You're crazy," he said. "It would take longer to build than it did to grade and lay down track."

But Li Yu shook his head. "Every winter it will take hundreds, maybe thousands of workers to clear the tracks of snow. It will save the railroad time and money to build sheds to cover the tracks."

The directors made a costly but necessary decision. One day, over lunch with Crocker, Stanford took out his pencil and began estimating the cost of covering the track with snow sheds in its most vulnerable parts. It meant putting a roof over the track that led through the Snow Belt. Power snowplows, driven forward by twelve locomotives linked together, scarcely budged the densest of these snow drifts. On the harshest days, travel was almost impossible.

Winter was only one obstacle. Other conditions also affected the workers. Landslides rolled tons of soil across the completed track, blocking access and sometimes smothering workers. Melting snow mired wagons, carts, and stagecoaches in a sea of mud. And once through the mountains, the crews faced terrible extremes of weather in the Nevada and Utah deserts. There, the temperature could plummet to 50 degrees below zero—freezing the ground so hard it required blasting, as if it were bedrock—or soar above 120, causing heat stroke and dehydration.

The U.S. government pushed the railroad companies to complete the railroad project faster and faster. The two companies were paid by the number of miles and the bosses in turn demanded and pushed their workers to perform faster and faster. Over the winter, laborers raised trestles and shoveled the fills.

In 1867, the Union Pacific was progressing, a mile a day, two miles a day, sometimes three miles in a day, racking up miles, collecting the government bonds and selling its land grants. It was penetrating Utah with surveyors, its grading crews were well into Wyoming and its track layers past Cheyenne.

For all of 1867, the Central Pacific completed only 39 miles, but it was across the roughest, most challenging terrain of the entire transcontinental route, and they managed it without any federal mortgage bonds that whole year. Of course, there was the galling seven-mile gap east of the summit, but they eventually overcame that, and then the bonds flowed in.

Crocker promised his partners in the Central Pacific that he would build a mile per day in 1868. But Huntington thought Crocker should aim higher. "If I were in charge of construction, instead of purchasing materials and raising money, I would build the cheapest railroad that I could and have it accepted by the government commission so it moves ahead fast."

If the road washes out, Huntington advised, fix it later. But the Central Pacific needed five essentials: money, labor, ties, iron and rolling stock. The second and third they had, the first, the four and the fifth depended on Huntington.

CHINESE BROTHERS, AMERICAN SONS

The iron that was supposed to be coming wasn't coming fast enough. What was shipped after June 1st would not reach the terminus of the track in 1868.

"We need more iron, fast," E.B. Crocker, Charles' brother and manager of the Central Pacific's Sacramento office, told Huntington. "As far as paying for men to come here, that will not work. They leave us as soon as they get here and chuckle at the thought of having swindled us. No, the Chinese are our men. They cost only about half and we have plenty of men for foreman and to do the skilled work. You say the UP has men who will lay more track than any other men in the U.S. Perhaps so, but we will see next summer. You send the iron along fast and in time."

In the winter of 1866-67 and again in 1867-68, sometimes all of the labor force had to be used to shovel away the snow. Beyond the danger of the work, there was the constant threat of avalanches from snow drifts high on the mountain slopes above the cabins and the work sites.

"We have to get some dynamite up there to take the overhanging snow away," Strobridge said in the midst of yet another snowstorm. "I want volunteers."

Li Chang had volunteered many times for many tasks, but this time he asked: "Why should the Chinese take all the risks?"

"We could order you to go," Kirby snarled.

"You can whip me again, and I still won't go," Li Chang said.

Kirby still had no idea that Li Chang was the man he had whipped in the gold fields. Li Chang had never told Li Yu either.

"I'll go," said Li Yu.

"Count me in, too, then," called a friendly voice from the past and out of the snow. Li Yu looked over and saw Jimmy Smits. "We'll blow up that mountain together," Smits said.

"You don't have to do this, Li Yu," Li Chang said grabbing Li Yu's hand.

Li Yu shrugged off Li Chang's hand and with a fierce determination said, "The needs of the many outweigh the needs of the few. We'll get us through this. I promise to get you back to San Francisco." The pride burnt so strong in Li Yu; it almost could have warmed Li Chang's hands.

Li Yu received a spare shirt from one of his headman's crew. Another worker offered him his bowl of rice. "You'll need it for the climb."

Strobridge instructed them where to go to set the charge. "If you're successful, the snow will spill down harmlessly away from the camps," he said.

Strobridge and Kirby sent off Li Yu and Jimmy Smits with compass in hand, black-powder kegs strapped to their backs and ropes tied to their waists. They started climbing towards the huge threatening combs of compact snow leaning over the granite bluffs. Smits had brought two pick axes and handed one to Li Yu. Both carried tins of matches.

They headed out into the blizzard. The snow was falling too fast and thick to see them. The strong wind made the snow blow nearly horizontal so that they had a problem seeing more than about ten feet in front of them, even though it was daylight. Snow fell at a minimum of two inches per hour, usually six inches or more an hour. The wind blasted the snow so it fell in drifts that looked like waves made of snow.

There was no protection. Sounds were so muted, they had to holler from six feet apart and still couldn't hear each other. "I'll see you off this mountain and free of that devil Kirby," Smits said to Li Yu, yelling in his ear.

At that moment Li Yu felt close to Smits like a brother. Free of the dust and smoke of the tunnel, Li Yu drank in lungfuls of cold, fresh air as if it were plum wine.

They continued to hurry, slipping and sliding up through the snow. Smits became a shadow; there were no footprints to be seen. Li Yu staggered after him.

It was nearly impossible to tell how far they had gone, but Li Yu thought they had traveled perhaps a mile when the rope at his waist tightened so suddenly that he thought he was cut in two. His feet went out from under him and he landed on the snow, sliding across the surface. He heard a thud and crash in front of him.

Li Yu rolled back onto his side and thrust the pickax down hard into the snow. He held on. He knew Jimmy must be hanging just ahead and he looped the rope around the pickaxe, undid it from around his waist, shed his keg of powder and followed the rope into the whirling snow.

Smits had lost his pickax and was holding on to the rope for dear life on a steep slope. Li Yu pulled him up gradually, then grabbed his coat.

"I got you," Li Yu said.

They began their ascent again through wind blowing down the slope, lashing them with sharp-edged snowflakes, snatching warmth from their bodies, nipping at their ears, nose and hands. Snow fell into their boots. Their chilled feet were as stiff as wood. And the hill got steeper and steeper.

"Wrap your arms around yourself and tuck your hands into your armpits," Smits told Li Yu. "Your hands will warm up."

Another hundred yards.

"We're almost there, above the snow," Smits said. "I see the cloud layer. It looks like we could just walk right into heaven."

Li Yu felt his body was being dragged down with lead weights, his lungs ached as he pulled in the cold air. Numbed and frozen, he didn't know if he could go on.

"No more," Li Yu said, dropping to his knees.

"Try," Smits said. "My compass says we're on the right

course."

They made sure they were roped together securely, and they continued on. At times, Li Yu lost Smits in the mist and snow, but there was the omnipresent rope tug to remind him that he was not alone.

"I'll get you off this mountain," Smits reassured Li Yu.

Suddenly, they stumbled out above the clouds; it was like stepping into another world.

They had made the climb to the shoulder of the mountain— just beneath the summit— and the unaccustomed brightness blinded them. Below, the gray clouds stretched out endlessly like a dark, angry ocean.

"We're not done yet," said Smits, "We have to go back through that."

Above them, the snow hung on the peak like some heavy mane.

The sun warmed their bodies; they began to thaw. It was a cruel but beautiful wilderness, and that comforted them as well.

They sought a route to the top of the cliff between snow-covered icicles, looking for a place to detonate the dynamite. Here and there, the wind had whisked away the coating of snow to reveal glasslike stems and petals that caught the golden light of the sun and seemed to glow with a life of their own.

Li Yu, now inspired, started to climb again, the powder keg bobbing on his back, weaving his way through the garden of icicles.

"Stay close," Li Yu said to Jimmy Smits, as they looked at the snow. "It's ready to come down at any moment."

"Go ahead, I'm slowing you down," Smits said. "I won't go anywhere."

Li Yu then saw a bone protruding through Smit's frozen trousers. Smits had broken his leg during the fall.

"If there are no heroes to save us, then you be the hero," Smits said.

"I'll be back as soon as I can," Li Yu said.

Li Yu started back up the cliff, breathing heavily as oxygen deprivation began to set in. As he made his way through the ice, he couldn't help but think this was a strange, beautiful place to die. He couldn't stop grinning. Li Yu's thoughts turned to Wang Wei. "We still have a chance to find the sunshine, let's keep on looking for the light," he thought.

Finally, Li Yu reached the summit, up where the clear winds blew. Only spotless blue sky was between him and heaven. The wind whipped masks of snow into the air like ghosts whirling and dancing around him. Beneath him, the clouds looked like a dirty sea whose waves crashed upon huge castles.

Shielding his eyes, he squinted at the sun. Checking his compass, he faced in the right direction and while holding his breath, high-stepped through the snow until he reached the right spot. He dropped his keg of powder to the ground.

Li Yu pulled out the fuse. He breathed in. The first match didn't light, neither did the second. Praying for his brother's strength, he struck the next match.

Li Yu repeated to himself, "All you gotta do is light this fuse, then you got ten seconds to run like hell."

Thankfully, the wind died down for a second or two, and the flame burned strong. Carefully, he lowered it to the fuse. His teeth chattered while the fire sputtered. Li Yu resisted his first impulse to run; his hands encased the flame until he was sure the fuse would go on burning.

He high-stepped back along his tracks. Halfway down the cliff, the rock shook with a loud roar. The sound of the blast ricocheted off the snow above him and vomited heaps of snow spilling down around him.

Li Yu realized he had done it; he had started an avalanche. The noise of the explosion was quickly drowned out by a louder and then even louder sound, a huge roar as if from a giant throat full of great rage.

He started to slide along the ridge, desperately trying to latch onto a rock or an icicle while at the same time frantically searching for Jimmy Smits. Finally, he landed — alive, but breathless and bruised, his gloves shredded by the icicles.

Cupping his hands, Li Yu shouted, "Jimmy, we did it! Where are you?"

No response. Crawling, he searched through the whirling snowfall along the cliff face until he found the rocks where he had left Smits. He stumbled around blindly while the snow fell thicker and heavier. He found some drops of blood near Smits' abandoned powder keg leading away from the keg as if he had dragged himself away.

"Jimmy!" he called in vain.

Perhaps Smits had gone down on his own; maybe someone had rescued him. He no longer saw any of the marker stakes they had placed on the way up. He blundered on, hoping he was headed towards camp and not away from it.

Li Yu might have gone 100 yards or 500 — he couldn't tell — when he realized there was no way Smits could have made it to camp, even with help. "Jimmy knew that with the storm clouds closing in, I wouldn't leave him so he crawled away so that I would not have to stay."

Li Yu staggered on, sometimes crawling. He now saw a marker. Now he knew he was getting closer to camp, he felt the tears freeze on his cheeks.

"Thanks, Jimmy, you kept your promise. You got me off this mountain," Li Yu said.

The wicked and wild wind grew even stronger. He

miraculously kept moving. He laughed deliriously. But the cold had finally seeped deep into his bones; they had turned to ice. He wanted so badly to sit down. He was about to close his eyes. But somehow he trudged on to the next marker.

Now Li Yu felt peaceful. The extreme cold enchanted his brain. It didn't feel violent any more, even with the wind ripping past him. It was like certain parts of his body were saying "hush" like he was disappearing piece by piece.

Then, "Ding!" a message came from his brain to say, "Please, don't die. Just hold on. And there will be tomorrow. And in time, you'll find the way. We will find each other." In his confused state he was thinking of Wang Wei, his brother Li Chang, the hoped-for search party—all of them.

"Anyone there? Anyone there?" a familiar voice grew nearer amidst excited voices.

Li Yu saw Li Chang. A human chain was formed of his headman's crew and a couple of Americans. Li Yu was rescued.

"Is Jimmy here? If he isn't, he needs help," Li Yu implored through stiff lips.

Li Chang just stretched out his hand silently towards his brother.

Li Yu awakened to the fire crackling as it consumed the dry branches. "Jimmy?" he asked.

"No, he didn't come back," Li Chang mournfully said.

Sobbing, Li Yu struggled to sit up, "We've got to look for him."

"No search parties. We were told by Kirby. The Central Pacific doesn't want to lose any more men," Li Chang said. "The storm's over. Supply wagons have come in. The avalanche did the trick. We're safe. You're a hero. A hero's welcome awaits you at the camp. You will be cheered when they see your face."

"No. Jimmy's the hero," Li Yu said.

ED SHEW

"Ah, yes. Jimmy will be remembered as a hero and a legend, as you are my brother. He will never die. Follow your heart. You'll never go wrong. Now let's eat," Li Chang said.

By 1868, a total of 51 Central Pacific locomotives were pulling freight and passenger cars along the single track. The Central Pacific used a system known as the Timetable and Train Order of Operations. Conductors carried timetables, but they had to wait for telegraph orders at every station before they could proceed with their fifty-ton locomotives pulling hundreds of tons worth of iron. Racing up and down steep grades, often trying to make up lost time, engineers could never be sure what lay around the next curve. In one three-month span, there were four separate crashes on the Central Pacific line. These wrecks crippled new locomotives, wasted materials, crushed and burned engineers and brakemen.

On April 10, 1868 some four feet of snow fell on the summit and the east face of the Sierra, causing two large avalanches on the exposed line, recently graded and tracked, and on the stage road, delaying travelers for 18 hours and paralyzing the little work trains supplying graders and trackmen lower down on the Truckee. Crocker ordered an assault on the covering snow. With sun reflected off the mountainsides, clearing the tracks of the immense amount of snow took a cruel toll on the Chinese diggers. Watering and bloodshot eyes were the least of the symptoms. "The snow has blinded a good many and we have to buy up all the cheap goggles in the market. Only think of that. What an item in railroad building," Crocker remarked.

In June 1868, construction of the permanent snow sheds began. Every sawmill in the Sierra was busy. Workers were paid top rates, $4 per day for carpenters and $2.50 to $3 for common laborers. Li Chang was in heaven with this temporary pay raise.

CHINESE BROTHERS, AMERICAN SONS

By the end of 1868, about 55 miles of track had been covered. One section extended 28 miles without a break. For nine miles west of the summit and four miles east of it, the sheds ran almost continuously.

It cost a fearful amount, but there was no alternative.

The shed construction job was completely finished in 1869. The Central Pacific, at Li Yu's suggestion, was the first railroad to do it, and other railroads, most notably in the Swiss Alps, later copied it. It was an engineering feat of the first magnitude. In July 1870, Van Nostrand's *Engineering Magazine* said the men of the Central Pacific "just roofed in their road. They have conquered the snow."

The 1866 Railroad Act amendment authorized the Central Pacific to construct their route eastward until they met with the Union Pacific Railroad as fast as they could with compensation depending on miles for continuous track created. This set up a race that inspired everyone—the directors, surveyors, engineers, foremen and workers of both the Union Pacific and the Central Pacific to go as far and as fast as possible. And that led inevitably to corners being cut.

On June 16, Crocker sent a wire to Huntington in New York: "The track is connected across the mountains. We have 167 continuous miles laid."

Finally, the first passenger train from Sacramento heading across the Sierra Nevada rattled up to the summit on June 18, 1868 and halted at the mouth of the great tunnel for several hours while a swarm of Chinese cleared snow and boulders from a small avalanche just east of the far portal. Water poured down in torrents from numberless crevices and seams in the granite walls and roof of the long dark cavern. Once under way, the train was forced to halt again and again inside the tunnel to await the shovel brigades. But finally it rolled beyond the snow line and descended along the Truckee.

On July 7, 1868 Charles Crocker told Strobridge that the Central Pacific "would soon be out of spikes." Crocker wrote Huntington, "We supposed you were sending spikes with the iron. We are in a horrible fix." Only a few days before, Crocker complained that they were "lamentably short of locomotives as well as cars," fretting that they could not keep materials moving quickly out to the end of track. Now spikes—and then they found a shortage of fish joints, too.

They were moving quickly—the rails were ten miles beyond the Big Bend of the Truckee and Crocker was prepared to double the track-laying force to lay four miles per day. The graders were working seventy-five miles ahead.

Much to Li Yu's dismay, Crocker frequently ordered Strobridge to allow shoddy work along the line. Crocker decided that the "main thing is to lay track." He had the men spike seven out of every 13 ties, which saved a third of the spikes, and when they ran out of the joints he had a tie placed beneath the joint and a fistful of spikes hammered in around to keep it approximately in place. Of course, they could not run passenger trains over such improvisations, but they crept the work trains forward at a slow walk, hoping they would not derail.

Crocker moaned, "We have in California 183 miles of iron and only 89 miles of spikes, with 81 miles iron and 75 miles spikes to arrive in 60 days. It is very unsafe to half-spike the track at this season of the year."

Speed was never easy for the Central Pacific. Everything— from locomotives to rails to spikes—had to be built at iron works in the east and then ocean-shipped around the tip of South America or through the jungles of Central America to the San Francisco docks, loaded onto steamboats and shipped up the Sacramento River. Schedules rarely held.

CHINESE BROTHERS, AMERICAN SONS

The Central Pacific had transported all their materials thousands of miles, they had overcome lawsuits, opposition, ridicule, evil prophecies, monetary uncertainty, and losses. The Chinese railroad workers had drilled long tunnels, shoveled snow, set up sawmills, hauled locomotives and cars and uncounted tons of iron over the mountains. Nothing had come easy, most of all the tunnel at the summit of the Sierra Nevada. It was all work that changed the world.

As the first through passenger train swept down the eastern slopes of the Sierras towards Reno, Nevada, a total of 154 miles from Sacramento, Li Yu and his crew comprehended fully the importance of the event. The Chinese abandoned their natural impassiveness and apparent indifference and welcomed the iron horse with the swinging of their conical hats and loud, uncouth shouts.

"Now we have some reason to believe," Li Yu said.

But their joy and optimism was tempered by an enormous challenge of a different type which lay ahead — the completely dreadful, unfriendly terrain of the "Forty-Mile Desert."

15

The Forty-Mile Desert

For Li Yu's crew, the Forty-Mile Desert felt as if they had reached the end of the Earth. They couldn't believe the dust. Every night when they went to bed, they told themselves that this bleakness couldn't go on—that they would wake up to find a pretty green valley over the next hill. But each morning the same dead land stretched on—empty white sky, a bleak, gray horizon and ankle-deep alkali everywhere. The dust was as fine as flour, and it got between their teeth, and up their noses and in their ears.

"What a hell-hole! Alkali dust is choking every hole in my body," Li Chang said with a sly grin.

"I can't spit or swallow without tasting the bitterness," even Li Yu protested. "I hate the desert; it's got no pity."

The Forty-Mile Desert was named during the rush of overland immigrants seeking California's gold. It was the distance from the last good water of the Humboldt River, as the river evaporated and trickled into the sand, before the ox trains finally got to the Truckee River. The railroad would change that, but first it had to be built.

East of Reno, the desolation began to assume its most repulsive form—miles upon miles of black igneous rock and volcanic debris. Outcrops of fossilized lava, interspersed with volcanic grit were the main features. The country was so devoid of vegetable and animal life that even the wilderness howled for relief. There was no water. The desert was filled with the bones of thousands of animals that had not made it to California. The second route, to the north of the Humboldt River, was just as bad.

In a respite and as a reward for the successful completion of the Summit Tunnel, James Strobridge directed Li Chang and Li Yu to take a load of Chinese supplies and food to Chinese tracklayers before track was laid in the Forty-Mile Desert. They took a "mountain mud-wagon," pulled by horses, from the eastern summit, through a mixture of slush, mud, and ice. Everywhere they looked, there were Chinese at work. They had pigtails coiled around their heads and wore blue cotton blouses.

One night, Li Yu received a letter from China; he had not received a letter from his wife Sun Wei in over a year. This letter was from Li Wu, his never-seen son. Simply, it said:

> Mother has died. I am coming to America. I may even arrive before you receive this letter. The money you send is well spent. If you wish, please continue to send. The clan will be grateful. We have been well taken care of. Our family, because of you and Uncle Li Chang, will never go hungry again. Soon we will have a feast together. I know you are working on the Great Firewagon. Don't worry; I will know how to find you. I will say, 'Tell me where the two Chinese men are who wear cowboy hats.'
> Your son, Li Wu

Li Yu, digesting what he had just read, was overwhelmed by waves of guilt, guilt that he had felt many times since arriving in America. The truth was he hardly remembered Sun Wei. He had never loved her as a man should love his wife.

Closing his eyes, Li Yu did not cry; he was relieved. "There may come a time when I will see that I've been wrong," he said. But now he could think about Wang Wei without feeling guilty.

Looking at the moon that evening, he spoke to her. "If you need to be loved, here I am. I know I'll find you somehow," Li Yu said to Wang Wei.

Li Chang told Li Yu, "I think a miracle will happen. You'll get to her somehow."

Li Yu heard word that a woman was traveling up to his railroad camp. Some said she was a Chinese demoness. Was she Wang Wei? He pictured a nurse coming to bandage wounds and touch foreheads or a princess surveying her subjects, or a woman led on a leash as her owner sold lottery tickets for the use of her. Dreaming about Wang Wei, Li Yu's clothing and bedding were wet and sticky when he awoke in the morning.

To the east, out where the desert met the foothills of the Sierra Nevada, the Central Pacific engineers were planning the railroad onwards through Nevada. At Truckee Meadows, the wild grass grew up to three-feet high. The California pioneers would stay there to fatten their horses and cattle before pushing westwards over the Sierra Nevada barrier. When the track was open from Sacramento as far as the Meadows, Crocker sent fifty carloads of supplies to Strobridge each day, divided into five trains each hauled by two locomotives. They were the heaviest that ever went over the railroad, but they all made the trip safely. The track was good enough. As quickly as the supply trains were unloaded, they started back over the mountains for another load.

Li Chang and Li Yu were optimistic, and they said to their crew, "Isn't it heavenly to be out in the desert making a mile or more per day instead of in those accursed mountains making a foot or a yard per day?"

The Central Pacific was on the move. "Work on as though Heaven were before you and Hell behind you," Huntington said to Crocker.

After Wadsworth, where the crews said good-bye to the Truckee, and until the track got to the Humboldt Sink, the route was northeastward across the Great Desert, a vast waste of sand and sagebrush and white alkali deposits, with high mountain ranges to the south and bleak hills to the north. The desert ran nearly a hundred miles, without a tree, without water, without anything that could be used for construction. A popular saying was that "a jack rabbit had to carry a canteen and haversack" to get across it.

All needs were hauled over the Sierra Nevada Mountains. There was not a known coal bed on the whole Central line, there was not a tree that would make a board on over five hundred miles of the route.

There was some water but it was so strongly alkaline that it could mostly not be drunk. Li Chang tried putting molasses in it, but that helped it very little; he added a pickle, but the alkali remained the dominant taste, and it was unfit for drinking.

Li Yu chided Li Chang, "I thought you could make something out of nothing."

"Only food," responded the winking Li Chang.

To supply the daily water needs of more than 5,000 workers and 400 horses, and the requirements of every steam locomotive, the Central Pacific spent big money boring wells in the desert east of Wadsworth. But with eons of leached minerals souring it, most of the wells were worthless. Mostly the railroad used a fleet of flatcars with water tanks shaped like semi-conical vats that worked like spouts of water towers. Taking on water from the Truckee River, the water train ran constantly across the Forty-

Mile Desert and back again to Wadsworth. At the end of track, the water had to be transferred to barrels and sent ahead by wagons to the graders.

The Central Pacific then faced a most unusual but serious problem with some of its Chinese workforce. Late in May 1868, they got to the bottom of it. "Worthless white men have been stuffing them with stories," Crocker reported, "that east of Truckee the whole country were filled with Indians ten feet high who eat Chinamen and with big snakes 100 feet long who swallowed men whole."

To counteract this, they organized a junket for a couple of dozen Chinese men, to show them there was nothing to fear. "We sent good men along with them to show 100 or 200 miles of the country where the road was to be built," said Crocker. "The fact is there are no Indians on the line until we reach Winnemucca and then they are harmless like the Piutes on the Truckee, and the Chinese despise them. We have ticklish people to deal with, but manage them right and they are the best laborers in the world. The white men we get on our work here are the most worthless men I ever saw."

Nevertheless, the track layers were making great strides, while the graders ahead of them moved even faster. The thousands of men moved their residence each day. There were reverses, but somehow, even those became part of the greater forward momentum. Sunburned and dazzled shovelers released from snow removal in the Sierra began to concentrate and regroup into track laying crews for the push through the Forty-Mile Desert.

One good thing about the desert—it was flat. Wadsworth, where the Truckee River turned north, was a bit more than 4,000 feet in altitude. From there, the route moved up in about as gentle a grade as the Nebraska plains. For 275 miles, it gained only 1,000 feet of altitude, and in July and early August, the track layers put down and spiked forty-six miles of iron, or an average of one and a half miles per day.

From the beginning of the summer of 1868 to the end, Crocker kept in much closer personal touch with the men. He went up and down the road in his car, stopping along wherever there was anything going amiss, and remonstrating with the workers who were behind time. When he slept, which wasn't often, it was on the train. When he woke, he could tell from the movement of his car exactly where on the line the train was.

The summer of 1868 was the most brutal. Central Pacific tracklayers choked in the alkali desert. The heat was so intense; the ground was so dry. Some couldn't even remember their names in that desert. There were days when the sun was so cruel that the Li brothers just knew their eyes were drying up forever. Temperatures regularly rose to more than 100 degrees by day and fell below freezing at night. Mules died by the dozens, left to rot track-side as the crew moved on.

"Soon, these badlands will start treating us good," Li Yu said attempting to arouse his crew.

On August 19, Crocker wired Huntington that they had set a new record; they had laid six miles and 800 feet in one day. It was done, he proudly said "by no increase in men—but merely having a full supply of material all day and the boys putting in for glory even the Chinamen went in for a big day's work and to beat up the Union Pacific big day's work. We commenced at 4 a.m. and quit at 8 p.m., working 16 hours. I gave the boys a few kegs of lager after they got through. It was a terrible hot day and the gnats or sand flies were present and on duty by millions."

They were working at full capacity. "We have track laying reduced now to one of the exact sciences," Crocker boasted, "and can beat the world at it."

They were now regularly laying up to four miles of track per day, but it was still not fast enough. "The necessity for pushing ahead will compel us to sacrifice good alignment and easy grades for the sake of getting light work," ordered the chief engineer Samuel Montague. "Make temporary location by using sharp curves and heavy grades wherever you can make any materials savings on the work. The line we want now is the one we can build the soonest, even if we rebuild immediately."

Huntington hoped to get track laid to within 300 miles of Echo by December 10. Echo was 400 miles away. It would require more than three miles per day in a month of track laying, a record beyond any previous accomplishment of the Central Pacific. But it was a race they had to win.

"We have got to beat them," Crocker declared.

"Make it cheap," Huntington urged them from New York.

Mark Hopkins was of a similar mind. "We don't expect to build a road of the character we have been building through the mountain and deep snow line," he said.

In short, the Central Pacific was building as fast as possible a road that would be minimally acceptable to the inspectors.

On November 21, 1868, Crocker found out that a three-man team of special government commissioners would begin their inspection in three days. Crocker could not shake his anxiety, which was evident to the track layers and foremen. Some portions of the road beyond Wadsworth on the Forty-Mile Desert would not presently bear close scrutiny in ballast, culverts and trestle work.

Crocker's first move was to wear them out with a full timetable examining culverts, ballast and bridges. On November 24, Crocker escorted the inspection team out on the line in a special car fitted with beds, lounges, tables and chairs, and a kitchen. By the time the special train reached the shakiest stretch of road, Crocker used an old cardsharp sleight-of-hand trick to distract them.

"We are approaching the point where the *Sacramento Union* newspaper said it was unsafe to go over the road," he chortled to the commissioners. "Now gentlemen, here is a tumbler of water which I will set on the floor of the car. Take your watches. Note the time we leave this station and when we arrive at the other, so that you will know the rate of speed at which you have gone. I have instructed the conductor to tell the engineer I wish to go over that piece of the road at fifty miles per hour."

At the next station, the tumbler was still standing and little water was spilled.

"Now gentlemen, there is your lyin' *Sacramento Union*," Crocker said.

The inspectors laughed and said that was proof enough, and that they did not need to look at the culverts. They were satisfied that if the train could rush over the railroad at fifty miles an hour and not tip over a glass of water, it was pretty safe and well-built.

The inspectors had been snookered into staring at pocket watches and a water glass instead of looking at loose ballast, soft fill and cobbled culverts.

According to the inspectors' report of December 3, 1868, "The road is being constructed in good faith, in a substantial manner, without stint of labor, materials or equipment, and is worthy of its character as great national work."

Huntington sent Crocker his gleeful congratulations. "I think," he jokingly said, "you must have slept with them."

In 1868, the Central Pacific constructed 362 miles of railroad, virtually the mile per day that Charles Crocker had promised. The lines of both companies were about to enter Utah. There, they had completed as much as two-thirds of the grading, but still had track to lay and more grades to make. In Utah was by far the biggest city between Omaha and Sacramento, Salt Lake City. Up to that time, the westward-building Union Pacific and the eastward-building Central Pacific had been moving into a land almost devoid of people. The railroads were setting a precedent. Instead of building a railroad that connected one town or city with another, they were building into a void. They were not striving to take over trade routes, but rather to create trade routes and attract settlement.

Both railroads had a lot at stake in Utah — government bonds, land grants, the sale of their own stocks and bonds, future trade, and more. But what mattered most was winning. Far more so than even gamblers, the directors, superintendents, surveyors, engineers, foremen, grade makers, rail layers, ballast men, cooks, telegraph operators and builders — everyone connected to the railroad wanted to win. They were desperate to win and did whatever winning required. And the final act was played out in Utah.

No one in the Central Pacific — not even Huntington in his wildest fantasy — thought they could reach Monument Point by the middle of January in 1869. The tracklayers were lucky in those frustrating autumn weeks if they managed two miles per day.

The valley the tracklayers had reached had the dubious distinction of being one of the coldest spots in the nation. Frigid winter winds blasted down from Idaho, concentrating and intensifying before the walloping 11,000 foot Ruby Range and coming to a frozen standstill over their heads.

Even the optimistic Crocker became discouraged at the slow progress in track laying. Apart from the weather, they were plagued with mechanical difficulties with the locomotives and overly-green wood for fuel which reduced the power of the engines.

CHINESE BROTHERS, AMERICAN SONS

Huntington sent Crocker a telegram upbraiding him for delays and inefficiencies, writing, "If you fail it's your failure as you've had the means."

It arrived at the Humboldt camp at the worst time. A few laborers turned up with cases of smallpox, which sparked a panic. "The smallpox completely demoralized our track laying force," Crocker told Huntington, "and they could not have laid much more iron if they had it, as very nearly all the white man left the work and most of our best foremen, also. We are breaking in Chinamen and learning them as possible. They have much to learn but are apt."

Meanwhile, the seasons were passing. Li Chang and Li Yu had now worked for over four years in building the Transcontinental Railroad. At the end of an especially exhausting day, Li Chang met his brother Li Yu before his crew returned to their tent.

Li Chang said, "You have fought for the things that matter. The Transcontinental Railroad was the answer."

As they headed to their camp on the newly-leveled earth, Li Yu turned to admire a trestle the Chinese workers had just finished. "We cannot be satisfied with a great accomplishment. It's not the end of the road, just the starting point for the next leap."

Li Chang nodded with approval and said, "Someday our family will see our great accomplishment."

And sooner than Li Chang imagined.

16

THE ARRIVAL OF LI WU, SON OF LI YU

LI CHANG PREPARED a noonday meal for Li Yu and Li Yu's son, Li Wu.

A fairly normal, not an unusual, event for most fathers and sons—lunch together. But in the case of Li Yu and Li Wu, it was the first time they had ever met.

Here they were, strangers. Li Yu, at sixteen, had left China when Li Wu was still in his mother's womb. In the silence, a hundred questions stampeded through each of their minds.

Beneath the surface, Li Wu speculated whether Li Yu felt as terrified, as gripped by a knot in his stomach, as he did. When Li Chang arrived with the food—steamed rice, bitter melon with chicken in black bean sauce—Li Wu was feeling nauseous.

Li Wu was almost fifteen; Li Yu was thirty. Li Wu knew immediately that it was his father, even without the cowboy hat. But his father looked older than he had imagined. Li Wu was already six inches taller than his father, but not as fit and muscular. His father wore clean Western attire: a plaid shirt and denim jeans as did his Uncle Li Chang. His boots were well-worn but clean. He had a scar on his right cheek.

The silence was broken by the click of chopsticks and by both Li Yu and Li Wu furiously blowing on the boiling hot tea served by Li Chang.

"Does he hate me?" they both wondered.

"Why is Li Wu here? " Li Yu asked himself.

"Why am I here?" Li Wu wondered. "Was my father's absence a blessing or a curse?"

Finally, Li Wu declared, "I want to know you. I want you to know me."

"Enough," Li Chang said. "You have the rest of your lives to catch up. Now, you eat."

Li Yu and Li Wu smiled in agreement.

The unspoken words evaporated like steam from hot tea.

Li Wu showed his father the ring that Li Yu had sent his mother. After her death, Li Wu said, "I wear it with pride and honor."

Li Yu felt some guilt about having not returned to China to see his wife and son. But Li Wu, even at this young age, was aware that Li Chang and Li Yu had financially supported grandmother, mother and himself and the rest of the clan.

Li Wu was an only child, but always in the back of his mind there had been a distant, anonymous figure, his father. A man who was not there either in body and spirit but who nevertheless had an immeasurable impact in terms of the comfort his remittances of money provided.

As a boy, Li Wu had written his father Li Yu several times. The replies were guarded, unfeeling. But Li Wu, wise beyond his years, didn't blame his father, himself only a boy when he left for Gold Mountain.

Coming full circle, Li Wu found himself further examining Li Yu as if he were a piece of fruit in the Canton market. His father's hands were calloused. He was only thirty years old but there was quite a bit of graying hair. But the facial features and mannerisms were identical to his, especially the pug nose.

Li Yu had been unemotional as he looked at his son for the

first time. There was no surge of relief, no need for tears. The sadness and longing he had felt as a teenager was diluted with age.

"There are feelings I'll never find," Li Yu said. He knew he couldn't recapture something he had never had. To try was futile, if not self-destructive.

The closest they came to the big question of, why are you here, was when Li Yu said, "I dutifully sent you and your mother money. After several years, your mother didn't encourage me to return to China, nor did I want to."

They liked each other immediately, even Li Chang could tell that, as they looked into each other's eyes with hands folded. But beyond that, Li Wu knew he owed his father respect and obedience, the same as he did his Uncle Li Chang. It was the Chinese way. The father-son relationship was indisputable, and the most important one in the Chinese family, a superior-inferior relationship. Li Wu, as Li Yu's son, must please, support and be subordinate to his father.

Li Wu quickly became a man. With his large hands and with Li Chang's cooking now putting meat on his bones, he became a railroad worker. Meanwhile, the Central Pacific made its final push towards Promontory Summit.

Li Wu started as a water carrier but he found it was bad for two reasons: the water buckets were heavy; and men developed a powerful thirst in this dry country.

"I swear my arms are two inches longer," Li Wu said. "After a couple days of lugging the water buckets around, I ached so badly, but I now can say I can lift my hands above my waist."

A good thing about the job, Li Wu discovered, was that he got to see every part of the rail-laying operation. Tommy Merton was a black man and the wagon driver and together they delivered water to all the workers within five miles. At least once a day they took the wagon out to the grading crew, the men who leveled the roadbed for the ties.

His favorite part of the job was bringing water to the spikers, who were a special crew. Li Wu admired them. The talented spikers were cocky; they pounded a spike down in only three swings. Using special hammers with tapered heads called "spike mauls," their rhythm was steady, the same all day long. Over and over again, they went after a spike, the steel of their maul rang out clear twice, and then there was a final, flatter ping. The spike caught the rail and bit down hard into the wood. Someday Li Wu wanted to have that feeling.

Also, Li Wu liked his job because of Merton. He had fought for the Union army. Some of the Irish men who had fought with the Confederate army called him "Billy Yank," and others derisively called him, "Nigger." He only had one good arm, but he worked harder than anyone Li Wu had ever seen—well, except for his Uncle Li Chang. Merton's right arm had been shot off at the bicep in the Civil War's Battle of Gettysburg, so he had learned to do everything with his left hand. He drove a mule or a horse team like no other. At day's end, when the animals straggled to the barn, he just whistled and said, "Ain't much further, Honey Chile."

Li Wu had never seen a black man before. He angrily asked Merton, "Why whites call chink and laugh at talk?"

"My daddy was lynched," Merton said grabbing a rope and forming a noose. Li Wu understood; he didn't bring that subject up again.

Li Wu never stopped being amazed at the number of men working on the railroad, which was like a small city on wheels.

Li Wu saw the long lines of horses, mules, and wagons, and how at dawn the animals ate hay and barley as trains cleared the horizon and shunted in from the west with materials for the

ED SHEW

day's work.

The signal to begin rang out. Foremen galloped about on horseback shouting out their orders. Swarms of laborers—Chinese, a few Irish and Americans—hurried to their work. What at first seemed like confusion became orderly action. A train of some thirty cars were loaded with track-laying materials, ties, rails, spikes, bolts and more. The equipment and supplies were thrown off the train as near to the end of track as possible. The rails were loaded into low iron cars and hauled by horses and delivered along the route of the anticipated day's end of track, and then came the rail gang, placing the rails on the ties, while a man on each side distributed spikes, two to each tie. Another distributed splice bars, and a third the bolts and nuts for it. Behind them were the spikers, two to each side. Two more men followed to adjust and bolt the splice bars.

The next car contained a complete feed store and a fully-equipped saddle and harness shop with a movable blacksmith shop with a score of smiths repairing tools and shoeing horses. The third one was a carpenter's shop and wash house. The fourth held sleeping quarters for the mule skinners, the men who drove the teams. Next in line was a sleeping car that held 144 bunks. The sixth and seventh were dining halls, the larger one of which fed 200 men at once. Right after that came a combination kitchen car and telegraph office, followed by a store and eight more sleeping cars. A supply car and two water cars pulled up the rear. Five hundred head of beef trailed along beside the train to keep the Americans supplied with meat. The bunk cars, with complaints about the stink and bed bugs, smelled worse than a pig farm.

Simultaneously, wagons distributed telegraph poles along the grade. Men nailed cross-arms onto them while another gang dug holes for the poles and a third gang erected the poles, keeping

CHINESE BROTHERS, AMERICAN SONS

pace with the rail gang. Down the track, a line of telegraph poles "stretched back as far as the eye could reach," Li Wu said. The telegraph wire from the last pole was strung into the car that was the telegraph office. Its last message each evening was back to Sacramento to report on the progress made that day. To the east stretched the newly-graded earth for the ties and rails.

Twice a day, the camp train moved to the end of track—at noon, to give all white railroaders a hot meal, and at night, to give supper and to provide sleeping accommodations. At day's end, by the side of the grade were the campfires of the Chinese, blue-clad laborers who waited for the signal to begin the next day. Divided into gangs of thirty men each, they worked under American foremen. The Chinese had their own cooks and slept in tents which were cooler in hot weather.

Li Wu could see the Chinese were systematic workers, competent and wonderfully effective because of their tireless and unremitting industry.

"From dawn to the light of the moon, I carry water buckets to the work crews," Li Wu said, but the men just complained. "This water tastes like pond scum," they said. Not to the Chinese workers who drank boiled water with tea leaves.

Li Wu hoped to move up to a better job, but Li Yu said he needed "seasoning" and that being a "bucket boy" was a good start. Also, Li Yu told him, "I want you to become independent; I can't always look out for you."

Feeling the effects of their weekend whiskey, the white workers were the meanest on Mondays. And it was true that it was a wonder the white workers didn't get sick from the water. By the time the water was hauled from the main tank at the rear of the train, it was a little muddy, and after a few tobacco-chewing fellows had slobbered their spit into the bucket, the stuff could choke a horse.

ED SHEW

Li Wu stared at the tracklayers. There was a graceful rhythm, almost like a dance. Ahead of everyone were the "joint-tie men." Working in twos, they bedded a tie every 14 feet. "Fillers" then set the rest of the ties for the eight "iron men," who slid out the 560-pound rails and, at the command of "down," dropped them into place. Next came the "spikers," who gauged the distance between the rails and pounded down the spikes. Once the fishplates were bolted tight at the rail seams, the "track liners" used crowbars to make the final adjustment to the alignment of the rails.

As the spikers drove their last spikes, "back iron men" pulled the next load of rails forward on a horse cart. As soon as the rails were slid off the rollers, they dumped the empty cart to the side and hustled back to reload. The whole process started just past sun-up and went on all day—the rails thunked down, the spike mauls pinged on steel, and the dusty wheels of the supply wagons creaked up and down the right-of-way.

As the rails went down, Li Wu was close at hand with his water pail and tin dipper. If he was more than two steps behind, a big man named Mick Dooley growled, "Is that damned water boy napping again?" Then he laughed if Li Wu tripped on a rail as he scurried about.

Li Wu picked up a new maul with a smooth hickory handle and shiny steel head that lay beside the tracks. The red-haired Sean Kennedy said, "Give it a swing if you like." He must have looked unsure. Kennedy said, "Go ahead. There's nothing to it." He even walked over and started a spike for Li Wu with two quick taps.

Hefting the maul, Li Wu got up on his toes and swung as hard as he could. Grazing the head of the spike, the maul flew sideways down the tracks. To make matters worse, the handle of the maul smacked across the rail and broke clean off. With his mouth open, he stared at the severely splintered hickory in his hands. He expected Mick Dooley to step forward and hit him upside his head. Instead, the whole spiking crew burst out laughing.

"I'm glad my father isn't around," Li Wu said.

The grinning Sean Kennedy was the only one who showed any kindness. Kennedy explained his mistake, saying, "You've got to keep your eye on the target and swing smooth. Otherwise you'll be sending a maul to the carpentry shop every time you miss."

Tail between his legs, Li Wu picked up his buckets and headed back to the wagon amidst the chuckling.

But Li Wu was stepping up; he was promoted to the position of "dish swabber." He thought the new job was a lot worse than being a "water carrier," a job reserved for the youngest and greenest. Now he was stuck in the kitchen and dining room. The work train moved so often that the tin plates and cups often fell out of the cupboards, so to make things simple, they nailed the plates right down to the tables. Just one nail in the middle, that's all it took.

So instead of bringing the plates to the dishwasher, he brought himself to the plates. They gave him a bucket of water and a rag, and he hustled up and down the line, wiping each plate quickly as he could. He worked fast, because the dining car sat 200 workers. They ate in shifts. When a new group was ready to sit down, the workers didn't want to wait, and he heard about it if they did.

He rolled out of bed at 4 a.m. to get breakfast started. He couldn't get used to being up when it was still near pitch dark outside. Everyone else got up at 5:30 a.m.

First, he got out big buckets of coffee—the men served themselves by dipping their tin cups in—and then they laid out platters piled up with bread and huge plates of meat. The workers stuck their forks or their hands into whatever happened to be close by, so he kept his hands clear. The amounts of food and the appetites of the men were enormous, like trying to feed a herd of cattle. Manners, forget it! Some stepped right across the table and headed out the door.

Li Wu liked the Chinese way much better. Li Chang cooked for twelve to twenty men under sanitary conditions.

Li Wu made $18 a month and he sent most of it home. He felt it was the least he could do, since both his father and uncle had done the same.

Working in the kitchen, Li Wu was amazed that somebody didn't die of an awful disease. Nothing, not even the plates he was swabbing, was clean. No one seemed to care, but he did the best he could. By the time he got to the end of the table, chunks of food were still on the plates after his cleaning. Some of the men wiped their plates off with their sleeves or hands before they piled them high, but most of them dug right in.

What could he do? With 200 hungry track men hollering at him, he couldn't clean any better. The dirtiest spot on every plate was right there in the middle, because his rag always caught on those nails.

"With all the slimy stuff oozing from my rag, who knows what could be growing under those nail heads?" Li Wu wondered.

One day several white railroad workers stopped Li Wu and said they wouldn't tease him anymore. They apologized for "messin" with him.

"No pull Chinaboy's pigtail anymore. We're going to treat you right, from now on."

They then pulled down his pants in the dining car to ear-ringing laughter.

"Velly good. Chinaboy no piss in your coffee no more," Li Wu shot back, as he scurried into the arms of Tommy Merton.

To get out of that filthy dish washing, he volunteered to help with the meat cutting. And he honestly said that hacking up steers was more appealing than wiping crusty food off those plates.

Every job had a bad side, no matter how good. He could have guessed the bad side of butchering, blood and guts. But he didn't see this coming; Danny Glynn was his name.

Li Wu's hands cramped up pretty bad. Pulling the hides off those big beef cattle, even when fresh, really wore him out. Glynn was not a clean person. He was a pig of the pig-on-a-manure-pile variety. His apron was dirty, stained black with blood. Who knew what else? He refused to take it off. Li Wu was told he slept in that apron. And Li Yu never saw Glynn wash his hands and rinse himself off even once. But he handled a blade with a silver blur, like no one else, when he slabbed out steaks or chopped up stew meat. He talked the whole time, never looking down at his work. Li Wu expected him to take his fingers off, but he never slipped. "A man can still hope, though," Li Wu said.

Li Wu longed to work with the Chinese workers. But his father Li Yu told him it was good for him to see both good and bad Americans. In this case, they were all Irish and they now numbered about 500 of the 10,000 workers on the Central Pacific Railroad. The rest were Chinese.

One day, Danny Glynn joked about all the Chinese who had lost their lives at Donner Pass, on the other side of the Sierra Mountains. "How stupid, hanging over a mountainside in wicker baskets to set black powder charges! That'll teach 'em. Nitro blew those heathens all the way back to China where they belong."

That afternoon, Li Wu cut himself. Danny Glynn yelled, "Those boys will be in here chewing on you, Chink, if you don't

ED SHEW

get some steaks ready pronto." Hurrying, his knife slipped. Blood dripped onto the floor. The railroad doctor was out tending to a man on the grading crew, so Li Yu took him by wagon to Dry Dirt.

No real doctor was in town, but they stopped at the saloon where a sign read, M. Welby, Physician, and peeked through the swinging doors. A white-smocked lady called out, "If you want the boy's bleeding to stop, bring him inside. I only see gunshot wounds in the street." She took his good hand, looked down at the bloody bandage and asked, "A gunfight or bear huntin'?"

Her joking relaxed Li Wu and she did a fine job of sewing him back together. Finished, she gave him a big hug and made him promise to be more careful. The hug made him lonesome for his mother.

Tommy Merton stopped by to tease Li Wu. "You'll end up workin' as a one-armed mule skinner if you can't tell the difference between a hand and a beefsteak."

It felt good to laugh.

"Where's uncle?" Li Wu asked.

"Your Uncle Li Chang went to a place called 'Hell on Wheels,'" Li Yu said. "Some never come back from there, but he will."

Li Yu hoped Li Chang would not lose all his money again this time.

Hell on Wheels was a collection of two dozen saloons, five dance halls and 3,000 people. Some were ragged tents, but there were now a lot of wooden store fronts, quite a few painted with brick patterns that look almost like the real thing. Hell on Wheels offered a quartet of vices for Chinese men: gambling, opium, alcohol and brothels. It was a town made to carry as the workers moved down the line. The entire town was packed onto flatbed cars or wagons and hauled to the next appropriate spot, reconstituted and renamed. Li Yu said six men with hammers and screwdrivers could put up a city block in a single day.

One frame tent was 100 feet long and had a mirror-backed bar, cut-glass goblets, gilt-framed pictures, and a band playing day and night. Li Yu joked that the paint hadn't even dried on the joint before they were serving up "road poison." Sometimes, there was a singer smelling of cheap perfume and of the cheap whiskey they passed off on the Central Pacific workers, and the workers passed off their hard-earned wages to the proprietors— lost in gambling.

Many of the gambling halls and the saloons operated 24 hours a day. It was very noisy, very crowded and very rough. Most of the women were prostitutes who were there to make quick money and lots of it. And so they located themselves wherever there was a fluid population of men with money to spend. It cost about $10 an hour to trip the light fantastic with those soiled doves, and if the railroad worker had anything left, they drugged him and stripped him of everything of any value before kicking him out into the street.

Bull's big tent was a full-service establishment. They had almost every kind of gambling game that anyone could desire to play. And in the back, there were cubicles partitioned with canvas for the women to transact business with their customers. And then a Dr. Rufus announced that he had established offices in the rear of Bull's Big Tent and specialized in the treatment of sexually transmitted diseases. So actually they could go to the big tent, spend an afternoon or evening's diversion, catch things they really did not want, and hopefully have them taken care of before they headed back to the railroad.

Li Wu was promoted to the grading crew who worked out ahead of the track men. There was a call for volunteers, and he had jumped at the chance. He didn't waste a lot of time saying good-bye to Danny Glynn.

ED SHEW

When he told his father, Li Yu said, "Pretty soon you'll be a foreman," he joked, "and bossing me around." Li Wu was almost on full wages now, $30 a month.

Their job was to cut away the high spots, shovel the fill into wagons, and dump it in the low places. Teams pulled scraper blades behind them for the final leveling of the grade. When the digging was rough, they used their picks. If that didn't work, they blasted. It was actually fun watching a charge go off. Not only did they get a little break from their work, but they got to watch some nifty fireworks.

The fatherly Li Yu swung by once in a while; he tried to pretend that he wasn't checking up on him but Li Wu knew better. He preached to Li Wu for two nights about how to protect himself during the blast. The trick was, "Fight the urge to duck your head at the powder flash. Look straight up to dodge the material that rains down; it's anybody's guess where it's going to land," Li Yu said. Li Wu was glad his father had coached him.

The managers and foremen pushed them ever harder. The land was desolate, the air was so thin that they got nosebleeds. But come what may, in the end the Central Pacific railroad would be built. Li Chang shook his head at the shoddy track-laying which had become the norm. All they did to prepare the grade these days was to scrape away the snow and blast a chunk of rock here and there. Sometimes it felt like the tie setters chased them right down the mountain. Much of the track would have to be repaired before the first train could make it through. It gave Li Wu chills to know that they were going to drive their work station over the trestles and sections and line they were creating.

The Wilson River Bridge was ready for a test run. To Li Wu, it looked like a 600-foot long crisscross of toothpicks. Li Yu said they weren't going to let a train go any faster than four miles per hour.

"But if I choose, I'd rather climb down one side of the gorge and hike back up the other hill rather than ride over that flimsy trestle," Li Wu said.

Li Wu never thought they'd make it, the train inching its way across the bridge. The bridge crew left their guy ropes in place, and they pulled as tight as a set of guitar strings as the steel wheels of their flatcar creaked out onto the trestle. The bridge timbers flexed under the load, and he waited for the ropes to pop.

"Should I jump or just close my eyes and hang on tight?" Li Wu thought. He had no answer but fear. When they reached the other side, Li Wu thought about what would have happened if the trestle had given out. He bet the Central Pacific would have used them all for fill and carted in some extra dirt to level things off.

The grading work was getting boring, so Li Wu volunteered for what Strobridge called a new morning "detail." He figured wrongly that any job would be a welcome change of pace from dirt work. When he stepped forward, Strobridge pulled out a rusty old navy six-shooter and a box of cartridges from his knapsack.

"Go hunt down some snakes, get to it on now," he said.

Apparently, rattlesnakes were spooking the animals. Strobridge wanted someone to walk ahead of the crew and clear them out. Li Wu's first thought was, "That'll teach me not to volunteer without knowing what I'm in for. But I guess I could still be working for Danny Glynn."

He was a lousy shot with that six shooter, but he told no one. Li Wu told his father's friends there were 60-foot snakes out there, and that he had killed them all. Some even believed him. At least his daily snake hunting duties were short. He checked the grade each morning. Most of the time there was only a rattler or two, and they slinked off before he even lifted his gun. He crept real close and squeezed the trigger as soon as he heard the first rattle. But he had some sympathy for the snakes. They had had this country to themselves for so long. Now just because a railroad was coming through, the Central Pacific expected them to clear out of their way.

Li Wu appreciated his pick and shovel work now. Dry and dusty, when he tossed a shovelful of dirt into the air, he ended up eating half of it. But though it was hot and dirty, it was relaxing compared to snake patrol. To the east, the land was totally flat without a hint of a hill as far as could be seen. Had God taken a giant rolling pin to this landscape? Li Wu yearned to go fishing in the woods far behind them, near the mountains.

More than 10,000 draft animals and 10,000 workmen were now working along the Central Pacific roadbed with a constant cloud of dust hanging over them. Six mules died on one day. They dropped in their tracks and the mule skinners just cut their lines and rolled the bodies off to the side for the buzzards. Quite a few Chinese died from heatstroke, too. The difference was that the Central Pacific gave the Chinese shallow graves. Sometimes the white foremen stuck a board in the ground for a marker. Some of the Irish asked to be laid out under the roadbed. Life was cheap in the desert and luck could run out at any second.

Li Wu hadn't seen a tree or a shrub or a blade of grass for two weeks. His hands were so rough and calloused from all the picking and shoveling that they felt like sandpaper. All their water was now being hauled fifty miles. It took a full-time crew to keep the big tanks on the flatcars filled.

A fight broke out between the graders and tracklayers. The track men had been pushing the grading crew, and bad feelings built up. Laying rails on flat land was easy so the graders had trouble staying ahead of them. When a muleskinner didn't pull his scraper ahead fast enough to suit Mick Dooley, he bellowed, "Clear those nags out of the way so we men can get to work!"

That really set the all-Chinese graders off. They wheeled around and a tough fellow called Wang Chung spit in the dirt and cursed Dooley. Next thing Li Wu knew, both groups charged each other with their fists clenched. Conical hats went flying, and mules jerked white-eyed at their bits. An unbraked wagon rattled off on its own. A fist cracking into the jaw of a man next to Li Wu got his attention, and he barely ducked a punch thrown at his own head.

The foreman restored order by cracking his bullwhip over their heads and finally emptying his six-shooter into the air. Though they grumbled for the rest of the day, there were no more fisticuffs among them.

After dinner, Li Yu bartered a truce between the Chinese and Irish workers. They all shared a drink of whiskey with one another. Dooley was still unwilling to acknowledge the role of the Chinese railroad workers, but admitted, "There is no bad whiskey. There are only some whiskeys that aren't as good as others."

Li Yu offered this toast: "Tonight, I'd much rather have your shot of whiskey than my cup of tea."

Crocker was now getting his one to two miles a day and then some. They laid 55 miles of track in one month, but Strobridge pushed for more. Spies said the Union Pacific was going even faster than they were. The sun was setting earlier, but Strobridge wasn't letting a little thing like darkness slow them down. They worked by moonlight. With that setting, Li Yu couldn't help but think about Wang Wei. He knew he should be happy; his son Li Wu was now with him.

"What is wrong, father? How can I help you?" Li Wu said.

Li Chang pulled Li Wu aside, "If your father is trying to hide his tears, it may be wise to pretend you do not notice. Sometimes, the best way to comfort someone is just to be near them. Now get back to work, before I charge you for my counsel."

When the moon wasn't out, they strung lamps along the grade. Sometimes piles of sagebrush were burnt to help them see the way. Li Wu's eyes burnt, and it was hard to breathe when the wind blew the wrong way.

Li Yu heard that the Union Pacific crews had laid down 6-1/2 miles of track in one day, working from dawn to dusk. The Central Pacific's mainly Chinese crews then laid down seven miles in only fourteen hours. The race was getting tight. The Central Pacific built their grade alongside a stagecoach line. They were going faster than ever, but every traveler confirmed that the Union Pacific was doing the same or better. The race was going to be tight for sure.

One morning, Li Yu's crew found a wooden grave marker in the middle of the right-of-way. Carved out of a buckboard set, it looked fifty years old, it was so weathered and gray. But the date scratched across the top read 1855-1863. The rest of the words, which Li Yu could only partly read, said something about NEW YORK and a girl named MARY LOU. Dying young was the saddest thing in this whole world.

Though it had been heart-wrenching when his mother died, Li Wu thought there was something much crueler in the death of a child. Why her and what might she have become? Even on a hot day, seeing that grave of the little girl, sent a chill up his spine. Their crew wondered what to do with the marker when Dooley came along. "Let's get on with it, boys," he said, and wrenched that board out of the dust and tossed it off to the side without even breaking his stride.

When Li Wu talked to his father at supper and told him what Dooley had done, Li Yu just shook his head and said, "Americans do not have the reverence for the dead as we do. But remember not all Americans are like him."

Though he knew the railroad would not be steered around a little girl's grave, Li Wu wished that at least someone had paused to say a few words to honor her soul. He said he hoped the travelers had laid her deep enough so she won't be disturbed by the men and machines. Li Yu was thankful to the wife for raising Li Wu well.

They returned to the gravesite, and Li Wu and Li Yu placed a new marker nearby which said, "There is no footprint too small to leave an imprint on this world."

All hell broke loose one day, and it was a reminder that the Chinese were still not accepted. Newtown, as the locals called the place, had sprung up just beyond the end of the track. The gamblers and fancy ladies and saloon keepers were all there, but for a change they weren't the cause of the trouble.

The instigators were two brothers named Chester and Leonard O'Donnell, who followed the roadbuilders toting a one-ton printing press (which the Central Pacific carried for free on its train) and published a newspaper called the *RR Gazette*. The newspaper was a good public relations tool for the Central Pacific Railroad and informed the public back west of its progress and expectations.

But the newspaper started vehemently criticizing the Central Pacific's use of Chinese laborers. Irish workers were irate that the Chinese suppressed their wages, and the O'Donnells published rants about how the Chinese were subhuman and should be treated like slaves. Li Yu now wished that he couldn't read English.

One day, the O'Donnells printed an editorial saying that:

The Chinese are not only an inferior and undesirable population, but they are an actual threat to American culture, American government, and even the Caucasian race. How can the Chinese work so hard for such low wages? They must possess some superhuman power, perhaps a result of their mysterious religion, their strange and isolated culture, or induced by smoking opium which allows them to accept their situation and continue to work hard.

Beware, the Chinese are outwardly quiet and submissive but are inwardly sinister and cunning. We're sure the Chinese railroad workers are part of a secret plan to invade and take over the government of the United States replacing American culture with that of the Chinese.

We call upon the Central Pacific's leaders Charles Crocker and James Strobridge and the Irish foremen to be diligent and once the work is completed to ship these Chinamen back to China where they belong. The United States must not allow the Chinese to contaminate our society and must enact exclusionary immigration policies to keep these yellow people out.

As mean-spirited as those words were, if the Chinese railroad workers had stayed sober and if they'd been paid on time that month, everything might have turned out okay. But Crocker was a full month behind in their wages, and instead of smoking opium, the men got drunk; it was cheaper. There was no stopping them.

When the trouble started, Li Yu and Li Wu were walking past a little shack that called itself the J.R. House restaurant. They heard some yelling and looked up the street. There must have been fifty

CHINESE BROTHERS, AMERICAN SONS

Chinese with their queues swaying back and forth as they ran towards the O'Donnells' print shop. They were a fearsome sight, swinging ax handles and spike mauls and yelling in Chinese at people to clear out of their way.

Li Wu wanted to follow along and see what happened, but Li Yu wisely got him out of there quick. A few minutes later, they weren't halfway back to their camp when they heard the first shots, a couple of flat cracks that sounded like a Colt .44. He didn't think much of it because gunfire wasn't unusual in a Hell on Wheels town. Then all of a sudden, it sounded like a whole army was letting loose. Six-shooters and shotguns and rifles popped off so fast that it sounded like a Gatling gun.

Later that Sunday evening, Li Yu found out where the shooting had come from. According to Chen Ming, who took a bullet in the arm, the Chinese workers stormed onto the O'Donnell's print shop railcar and smashed it up. But when they stepped back off the car, a bunch of Irish vigilantes opened up on them. Twenty-five Chinese were killed; a dozen were wounded.

The killers set fire to the Hell on Wheels Newtown. They threw Chinese bodies into the flames of the burning buildings. Some held Chinese bodies to the fire, burning their lower limbs to a crisp and leaving the upper trunks untouched.

The attack at Hell on Wheels was extraordinarily violent, revealing a long-held, almost wild beast-like hatred of the Chinese. Besides those who were burned alive, Chinese railroad workers were scalped, mutilated, branded, decapitated, dismembered and hung from signage. One of the Chinese railroad workers had his penis and testicles cut off and toasted in one of the remaining saloons as a "trophy."

The Central Pacific just dug a big hole and buried most of the Chinese together. There was no service. There were no markers. Nothing. The remaining bodies were left in the open, mangled, charred and decomposed to be partially eaten by dogs. The railroad wanted to keep it quiet. As for the O'Donnells, someone tipped them off before the Chinese men got there, and they sneaked off.

Li Wu sat down and cried. He questioned why the world was the way it was. "Why can't we live together? It's enough to make me ashamed of the human race," he said.

Li Wu couldn't believe that the railroad got away with piling a bunch of shot-up bodies into an open grave. Just one day before, these Chinese brothers had been pounding spikes and sipping tea, yet today they were dead. One of them, Shen Wang, was the finest singer that he had ever heard. His voice was so pure, that he made people smile by just saying, "Hello, how are you?" He sent money home to his wife and five children. No more. It was hard to find words to describe the sadness and anger that Li Wu felt. Li Yu told his son to reject the notion of revenge. If Chinese killed the Irish fellows in retaliation, every newspaper in the country would be scrambling to print the story with a fat headline.

No arrests were made. The massacre was defended, because the Chinese were said to be the aggressors. While disapproving of the torturous acts of the massacre, the newspaper supported the self-defense justification of the whites.

Li Wu celebrated Thanksgiving on the railroad. They got part of the afternoon off. That gave them time to eat a special meal of abalone and water cress soup that Li Chang prepared for his work crew, now at sixteen men. In addition, Li Yu and Li Wu went to a pie shop that a lady had set up in a tent, and they shared a big piece of pumpkin pie. It wasn't a moon cake, but Li Wu wasn't complaining.

An American holiday, so only a half day of work, not that

either the Chinese or the Irish railroad workers could do much as it was so cold. The ground was frozen. They should have quit for the winter, but the Union Pacific was still racing along, and they had to keep up.

Whether they loaded rails on the cars or dropped them in place for the spikers, they had to be careful of their footing. It was easy to tip a load of iron over on a man in this weather. It was worse, too, because the animals got skittish in the snow. Sometimes their fingers were so stiff and cold from hanging on to the rail tongs that they couldn't even straighten them out when quitting time came. The boys Li Wu really felt sorry for, though, were the scouts and couriers. He watched an Army scout come into the Wasatch Depot one evening who was frosted up so bad that he looked like he was frozen to his saddle; his horse didn't seem very happy, either.

Li Yu took Li Wu to the hotel for Christmas Eve dinner, another American holiday so they got another half-day off. It was so cold in the lobby that they saw their breath. The manager tried to convince them to stay, but they went down the street to a little dining hall instead. Though it wasn't Chinese food, the change was good. The only thing on the menu was steak and potatoes; at least it was warm inside. The meat was supposed to be beef, but it was so stringy and gamy that Li Yu figured it was really bull elk. Even if the food took some extra chewing, he enjoyed getting away from camp.

Since it was an American tradition, Li Yu gave Li Wu a Christmas present, a new fur-lined pair of mittens. Li Wu felt bad about not having a present for his father. But Li Yu said, "Having you here is present enough; I wish your uncle was here, but he said we needed to spend more time together the two of us. He's right."

A few weeks later, the Chinese workers celebrated Chinese

New Year with a very fancy meal. Li Chang outdid himself. Cantonese like their fish steamed, so the flavor was savored, rather than deep fried. It took six minutes to steam the fish — the meat was smooth, and easily removed from the bone.

"Fish, too, can be overcooked, and one of the first things cooks learn in China is how to properly steam fish," Li Chang told them.

The Americans had not invited the Chinese to celebrate their New Year, but still Li Chang invited Strobridge, Crocker and the American foremen to his Chinese New Year dinner and later shared the leftover food with the other white railroad workers in the camp next to Li Yu's crew.

Strobridge looked at the chicken dish and said, "Your chicken isn't done."

Li Chang didn't get angry. "It's not undercooked," he said. "Cantonese people love white meat chicken, but it has to be cooked just right, so the meat is silky and the inside of the bone still hints of blood."

Strobridge tasted the tender chicken. "It tastes better than it looks," he said.

He and Crocker, and in fact all of the other white railroad workers, passed on the chicken feet and steamed chicken blood.

Li Chang also served shrimp with lobster sauce. The shrimp were large and fresh, and he made one batch for his Western guests in a bland white sauce, while for the Chinese he made it with black bean sauce and ginger. To his surprise, his guests preferred the dish the Chinese way.

"Pretty good," Strobridge said. But he turned his nose up at the Chinese broccoli.

"And fish cooked with the head on — disgusting," Crocker said.

"Chinese New Year is the most important of Chinese

holidays," Li Chang explained to the gathering. "It is a time to be reconciled, to forget all grudges and sincerely wish peace and happiness for everyone." He was content; his food had again brought people together.

The day after, there was an accident. The construction train was creeping down a small grade as it had to when the rails were slick. Li Yu and Li Wu were riding on the flat car at the end of the train, when someone shouted, "Runaway!"

Li Wu looked up the hill and saw four loaded flatcars hurtling toward them. When cars uncoupled on the flat stretches, a little slack in the linkage was all it took and the coupling pin could fall out, leaving half of the train behind. But cars getting away on a steep grade was serious business. The fellow who had lost the cars whistled, and the engineer opened up the throttle and lay on his whistle to clear the tracks. They picked up speed, but Li Yu saw the cars were closing fast.

Li Yu and Li Wu got up to jump clear, but a trestle at the bottom of the canyon was getting close. He shook his head and pulled Li Wu back down.

"Hold me, I don't want to die alone!" Li Wu cried out.

They crouched down tight and watched those tons of iron flying toward them. Hitting the trestle full steam ahead, the engineer blasted his whistle all the way across. Li Wu's eardrums almost split as the whistle echoed up and down the rock cut and mixed in with the chatter of the wheels and the squeaking of the bridge timbers.

When they hit the other side of the bridge, the cars were closing so fast that it looked like they were dead meat. Then Li Yu noticed the loose ties on the end of their flatcar and yelled, "Let's derail it!"

Li Wu assumed his father was talking about derailing their own train, but then he realized he meant knocking the oncoming cars off the track. They each slid a tie off the back of their flatcar. As the ties hit between the rails, they flipped over once and then rolled sideways. For a minute, Li Wu thought the flatcar was just going to knock the ties out of the way, but the left wheel suddenly hopped up in the air as they had hoped.

What they didn't expect was the speed of the airborne car shooting straight towards them. Li Yu grabbed Li Wu's arm and realized it was too late to jump. Suddenly, the flatcar rose and then fell. With a terrible grinding sound, the wheels crashed down between the rails, the rear cars jackknifed, tipped on the side and skidded to a halt in a heap of wood and iron.

"I guess we picked the wrong train today," Li Yu said.

Crocker might have congratulated them on saving the work train, but instead they and other Chinese workers—no Irish— had to shovel and pry through the wreckage until way past supper time, clearing the line for traffic.

Li Yu said, "Son, don't worry, remember we only worked a half day on Thanksgiving and Christmas."

Li Wu longed to be a spiker. Sean Kennedy had showed him last time how to bend down to start the spike. Standing up, he almost tripped, his heel caught on the crown of the rail. The Irish men behind him chuckled, even the Chinese spikers did too. His hands turned hot and sweaty.

He swung the maul back. He then tried to drop it down smooth as the spikers did all day long. He surprisingly hit the spike flush. At that instant, he understood that swinging a pick on the grading crew all those days had made him stronger and his aim truer. Why, this was easy! Hitting a fat spike head was nothing versus nailing a tiny crack and hollow with a sharp end of pick for days on end. On his fifth swing, he hammered the spike flush; the rail rang out with a loud ping. With practice he could get it down to three strokes like the best spikers, like his father Li Yu.

A few of the fellows cheered, and even Dooley let out a "humpf" that indicated he'd done a passable job. Off to the side, Strobridge, who was standing next to Li Yu, said, "Looks like we've found ourselves another spiker."

Strobridge promoted Li Wu to the spiking crew. Possibly, Strobridge had also heard people talk about how he had saved the work train with his fast thinking on the back of the flatcar.

Li Wu said to his father, "That was your idea, not mine."

"Well, you helped, and besides you're big and strong," Li Yu said. "I know you can do the job. I saw you."

Li Wu's eyes moistened. "All the money you sent home to China allowed me to eat and grow more," he said. Li Wu was six inches taller than his father at 5-10, and 30 pounds heavier at 170 pounds.

The spikers, whether Irish or Chinese, were always skeptical about trying to fit a new man into the crew, but they had seen enough to give Li Wu a chance. Though it still took him five hits to get a spike down, he hadn't broken a single maul yet.

Li Wu was excited to finally be a part of their crew after envying the spikers for months. He felt the strength in the heft of his hickory-handled maul and in the ring of steel. He learned to swing with the same motion all day long. There was variety on the grading crew, as he switched off between picking and shoveling, and hauling fill. But on the spiking crew, it was pound, pound, pound all day long. He stuck out his chest as he hit those spikes home. He didn't even mind the cold. Ping, ping, ping, ping was his sound.

Ping, ping, ping was the perfect sound. The spike bit into the wood, and he stepped forward again. He didn't always finish in three hits, but he kept trying. Li Yu claimed he needed to swing smoother and just let the weight of his maul do the work, but he loved to let loose with all his strength.

Li Yu told him of building tunnels through mountains of granite in tight quarters and no margin of error, and how Uncle Li Chang had held those spikes and he pounded incessantly on them with no breaks for hours at a time.

Spiking these rails gave Li Wu the feeling that he was playing a direct part in tying America together. To prove it, he only had to glance back and see the new rails leading all the way back to the mountains and Sacramento.

But Li Chang was still upset about the shoddy work that they had them do on the track to push construction forward faster. He said the grades were too steep and the curves were too sharp for safe travel.

"Every mile is money in their pockets," Li Chang said today. "But what good is track that can't hold a train?"

The weather was cold. The Central Pacific spent as much time fixing derailments as laying track. Nothing was worse than trying to jack a heavy locomotive back onto the rails when it was bitterly cold. Half the time, Li Yu had no feeling in his fingers. He skinned his knuckles so bad on some days that the back of his hand got crusted up with blood and stuck inside his glove, but he was so cold that he never felt a thing. He swore a fellow could cut his fingers off in this weather and hardly know it.

Li Wu's spiking got better all the time, but he still fought the urge to over-swing. His father told him again and again to let the maul do the work and not worry if he couldn't put every spike down in three hits. He didn't always listen, though, because he loved to swing hard. If his rhythm was good, and he was knocking down a spike in four blows, he couldn't help but try to do it in three. That's when he fouled up and dinged the rail or sent a spike flying down the tracks.

CHINESE BROTHERS, AMERICAN SONS

Li Yu bit his lower lip and mumbled, "Take it easy, son."

Li Wu knew his father would be talking to him after supper. His worst fear was that he'd mess up so bad that Strobridge would send him back to work with Danny Glynn.

As the weather warmed, he liked his job as a spiker more and more. The pace was so hectic that he barely had time to catch his breath, but there was something in the rhythm of the work that made the days fly by. He learned to be more patient, too. It seemed like the only time he messed up was when Li Yu was looking. Maybe he was trying too hard to impress his father.

Li Yu knew his son had come a long way from his water-carrying and snake-hunting days. When things went well, he wished that his mother were still alive to share his feelings. Li Wu missed his mother too.

Li Chang comforted Li Wu. "Death steals your mother, but it doesn't steal the word," he said.

Li Wu read the letter that his mother had given him on her deathbed: "Remember everything I taught you. All those words can help you face what lies ahead."

"I feel guilty for not appreciating all that she did for me over the years," Li Wu admitted.

"You are sure to miss her advice and love," Li Chang replied. "She worried when you were sick. I bet she even told you bedtime stories. You're feeling vulnerable and you're in a strange country, but you can heal. Talk to your father and me about your loss. We are here for you, no matter where you go. You know you are not alone."

"I remember she used to hold me until I fell asleep. I knew for sure I was loved. Other times, I'd hear her crying for my father. If I could only get another chance …" Li Wu said.

Li Yu entered the tent. He had eavesdropped on their conversation.

"Already, you have made your mother proud, and me too," he said to his son. "I am so happy you are here with me and your uncle. We're together and now a family."

Li Yu playfully tugged on Li Wu's queue.

"Father, why is it always the best people who die?" Li Wu asked.

"I understand, you wonder why she was taken away from you. But you can be grateful that she was given to you, and you to her. Remember when your mother held your hand, and remember that she holds your heart forever. Think about the smiles and laughter. You were blessed to have such a beautiful soul in your life. In the end, how your mother lived is more important than how long she lived."

"Father, I never thought you and I would be together," Li Wu said. "I guess I misjudged everything."

"The hidden truth is no longer haunting us," Li Yu said. "Today, we have touched on the things that were never spoken. That kind of understanding sets us free," Li Yu said.

Feeling reassured, Li Wu said, "I want to be the kind of man you are."

"No, I want to be the kind of man you want me to be," Li Yu responded.

17

THE CHINESE STRIKE BACK

ON THE DRY FLATS of the alkali deserts of Utah, the Chinese crews of the Central Pacific, coming from the West, and the Irish crews of the Union Pacific, coming from the East, met head on, and even passed each other. Working within a stone's throw of each other, blasting was twice as dangerous. They literally blew each other up.

In the race of the railroads to lay the most track (the government subsidized each mile at $16,000 to $48,000, plus hundreds of millions of acres of right-of-way), the rivals ordered their crews to lay parallel roadbeds for hundreds of miles.

On January 15, 1869 the Central Pacific had got as far as Ogden, 625 miles east of the Sierras and 744 miles east of Sacramento. Going west from Ogden to Bear River, the grading lines of the two companies were generally 500 feet to a quarter of a mile apart, but at one point they were probably within 200 feet. Between Bear River and Promontory, the Union Pacific was close to the Central Pacific and the two lines actually crossed twice.

When the two companies came within a 100 feet of each other, the Union Pacific Irish taunted the Chinese with catcalls and threw clods of manure. When the Chinese ignored them the Irish swung their picks at them, and to the astonishment of the whites, the Chinese fought back.

They all worked fast and hard all day long, even though it was obvious to them all that one side or the other was wasting time, labor and supplies.

Knowing how well the Union Pacific was doing, the Central Pacific put its entire effort in January into laying track from Elko toward Humboldt Wells. On the 28th of that month, the tracks were 150 miles east of Elko. After getting to the Wells, the track would run northeastward to the state line, then on towards Promontory. But Humboldt Wells was still 224 miles from Ogden, and the Central Pacific had not yet reached it.

Charles Crocker came and threatened the Chinese crews. According to one foreman who was there, "He stirred up the track layers with a stick; told them they must do better or leave the road." That got them working even faster.

Accidents became the norm on the railroad. In addition, the level of antagonism continued to rise. Whenever the Irish workers of the Union Pacific got a chance, they hooted and hollered at the Chinese workers. Not surprisingly, some of the Central Pacific co-workers were not much different, and the Chinese outnumbered the Irish more than ten to one. The Chinese always waved to let the Irish know when they were about to set off a charge so the Irish could clear out of the way. In contrast, the Union Pacific's Irishmen were in the habit of purposely firing their blasts without giving warning to the Chinese workers of the Central Pacific.

Li Wu couldn't figure out why the Irish resented the Chinese so much. "I just can't comprehend what all this fighting is for," he said.

Were the Irish jealous of the work the Chinese got done? The Irish made a lot of noise, but Li Wu could see that the Chinese accomplished more. While the spiking crew waited for the rails to be brought forward, he watched the Central Pacific crew fill a ravine. At first he thought they were moving at a snail's pace. But the more he watched, the more he realized that it wasn't slow, it was just smooth and steady. Looking at them, he saw what his father Li Yu meant about keeping an even pace when he worked.

The Chinese two-wheeled dump carts never stopped rolling. As three carts were dumped into the ravine, three more were being shoveled full. The draft animals plodded along at the same pace as the workers, and they never seemed to need any lashing or prodding. If they were short of mules or horses, Chinese didn't hesitate to pull the carts themselves. Li Wu never saw an Irishman doing that.

Li Wu told his father that another Chinese worker had died in a blasting "accident."

"I swear, if Patrick O'Connor makes one more joke about 'burying rice-eaters under rock piles where they belong,' I will go after him with a pick handle," he said.

But Li Yu told his son, "There's no right, no wrong in this. We will strike back at the right time and place."

Li Yu said he had heard that President Grant would be at the site when the rails met. If Grant talked to all the bosses, Li Wu wished he would tell them to stop blowing up innocent people. That was something both Irish and Chinese workers of both the Union Pacific and Central Pacific could agree upon. Another was that they couldn't believe the greed of the two railroads. Since both companies were paid by the mile; they kept preparing two separate grades side by side. The workers swore that if the government didn't stop them, these rascals would build two sets of tracks all the way from Omaha to Sacramento.

Li Yu said Li Chang called the railroads "the lowest sort of thieves. Call it a contract or a subsidy or whatever name you like, it is stealing pure and simple."

By February 28, 1869, the Central Pacific had made another 20 miles in 13 days, which for the Central Pacific was disappointing. The line was 40 miles east of Humboldt Wells, almost into Utah, but it was still 144 miles from Promontory. The Union Pacific on that date had track up to Devil's Gate Bridge on the Weber River and was thus but six miles from the mouth of Weber Canyon and 66 miles from Promontory. But the Central Pacific was closing the gap.

The Union Pacific got its bridge built first, and on April 7, 1869 its first locomotive steamed over the Bear River to enter Corinne. The Central Pacific was still almost 15 miles west of Monument Point. Not until April 10, 1869 did Congress step in to halt the overlapping grade-work.The race was exciting, but Congress was now querying the railroads in earnest. In particular, there was the cozy relationship between some leading members of Congress, who were recipients of enormous dividends, and the company formed to finance the Union Pacific, the Credit Mobilier. In addition, the Big Four of the Central Pacific were also founders of the Contract and Finance Company which was set up to fund the Central Pacific.

President U.S. Grant ordered officials of both the Central Pacific and Union Pacific to meet and settle this nonsense about where the railroads were going to join. After some haggling, they agreed on Promontory, Utah Territory. All the workers agreed that when the president had all these crooks in one room, he should have hauled them off to jail.

Li Chang was dying. He had survived a severe, bloody whipping while he and his brother Li Yu were mining the Gold Mountain, homemade whiskey and lynch mobs in Hangtown, the Summit Tunnel, the Forty-Mile Desert and, yes, Western cooking. But he couldn't dodge the boulders and stones that rained down on him from the intentional blasts from the Irish workers of the Union Pacific, as both railroads worked often side-by-side, in the rush to finish the Transcontinental Railroad and make fortunes for their deceitful owners.

Two more Chinese workers were not so lucky. They were buried beside the grade along with their wax-sealed bottles: Wang An, July 1, 1849, from the province of Kwangtung, China and Zhou Bo, September 15, 1839, also from the province of Kwangtung, China.

It was late afternoon, and there was a shattering explosion, a roaring, crashing sound as the boulders and rocks came rolling down on them. Panicked, Li Wu peered through the wind and dust.

"Uncle, where are you?" Li Wu shouted. There was no sign of his uncle anywhere. Li Wu shouted to the other workers, "Uncle is buried in the rocks! Please help find him! He'll be crushed to death!"

The Union Pacific Irish workers on the side were standing back, sniggering. The Central Pacific Irish foreman ran up and grabbed Li Wu's arm. "Back to work, you coolie, enough! Back to work!"

Li Wu pulled himself free and dug frantically through the rocks with his bare hands. He thought of his uncle's words that their family would never be separated again. Finally, Li Wu saw the tip of Li Chang's s boot protruding above the pile of rocks.

"Help me!" Li Wu shouted.

The Chinese workers dug Li Chang out of the rubble. They found him still clinging to his water pails, and still alive. Normally, Li Chang stayed at the camp-site kitchen. But on this day, he had shoo-ed away the bucket boy and delivered the aromatic oolong tea to his gang himself.

Li Wu took off his brown smock and wrapped it around his uncle's broken body. As the workers carried Li Chang over to a bamboo mat in a nearby tent, Li Wu ran to him with a cup of hot tea. In his arms, Li Wu cradled Li Chang and massaged his uncle's quivering body. "Drink tea, my uncle."

Li Chang said, "I will get better," as he felt his organs being stabbed by his broken ribs.

"You must," Li Wu muttered back.

As the days passed, Li Chang did improve, or so he said. He went back to his kitchen, straining to prepare his work gang's meals — slicing and cutting chicken, bok choy, black mushrooms and Chinese sausages; stir-frying everything in a wonderful pungent sauce with ginger and garlic and green onions that permeated the Chinese camps and wafted over to the railroad cars of the envious white Central Pacific workers, tired of their boiled beef and potatoes and beans. He was obviously in great pain.

Li Yu knew what had happened and something inside him snapped. "Justice is revenge," he said. "I must do something. These men understand only violence."

It finally happened. The Chinese decided that they had had enough, and they planted a grave — a charge that was meant to kill — above a rock cut where a Union Pacific Irish gang was working. The "mysterious" blast, a dynamite charge, killed an Irishman and buried several Irishmen alive.

From then on, the Union Pacific's Irish laborers showed more respect for the Chinese. The Irish agreed to a truce. They promised to give fair warning of all their blasting if the Chinese did the same.

"Why does it take someone dying to knock some sense into their heads?" Li Wu asked.

The Union Pacific's tracks were only fifty miles east of them now. That ended the war. The grading crews, however, went on scraping furiously in parallel lines beside each other but in

CHINESE BROTHERS, AMERICAN SONS

opposite directions.

"I am dying," Li Chang said as he lay on a bamboo mat, with a comforting smile to Li Yu, his brother. Li Wu, his nephew, stood silently by with tears glistening on his sunburnt cheeks. Li Yu was making a meal.

"Why didn't you tell me you could cook?" Li Chang asked Li Yu. "I knew you were a gold miner and a builder of our new country, America, but you surprise me and make me more proud than ever."

The aroma of ginger and the taste of the rice congee, congee without the ingredients or toppings, that Li Yu so lovingly prepared, were offered by Li Wu in teaspoonfuls to Li Chang, lying between them.

"No need for tears," Li Chang said in a whisper, as he firmly grasped the calloused and bruised hands of the kneeling Li Yu and the standing Li Wu.

"My brother, I was afraid I'd made a mistake when I asked you to come to America with me," Li Chang said. "Then I remembered I was so ashamed when I was a miner and tortured, and my queue was cut off. I knew then I could never go back to China."

He coughed and blood came out of his mouth. "America is our country, your country now," he said. "Therefore, I wish to give you a new name, Li Kin-Kwok, which means 'build the country.' This is what you have accomplished. Remember always that we built this nation's railroads. This country broke the boy in you, but it couldn't break the man that you have become."

"I became strong being on your shoulders; you raise me up more than I could be without you," said Li Kin-Kwok, formerly Li Yu. He could not find any more words. His mind was racing. He recalled the times Li Chang had held him in the darkness, calmed his restlessness, and relieved his sadness.

Li Chang stretched out his other hand. Sensing that the newly-named Li Kin-Kwok needed reassurance, Li Chang said, "I have been and always will be your brother."

Li Kin-Kwok now kneeled and grabbed Li Chang's butcher's knife off the chopping block, then cut off his own queue. "You've brought me too far, I can't turn back now," he said.

Li Wu asked for the knife to do the same. Li Kin-Kwok hesitated. "If you do it, China is no longer your country," he said.

"I'm never going back; the past is the past," Li Wu said. "I am home now; my place is with you. My father, please cut it off for me."

As Li Kin-Kwok took the butcher knife to his son's hair, Li Wu felt as if he was on the guillotine. A chill stoled over him. "Am I still Chinese?" Li Wu asked himself.

Unbeknownst to his brother Li Kin-Kwok, Li Chang had searched the Sierras for gold, breaking away from camp every chance he got. He had hoarded the nuggets he found in a leather saddlebag, waiting for this day. He gave it to his brother.

"Use the money to help build this country," Li Chang said. "Also, the two railroads will soon be joined. Seek out James Strobridge. Promise me. He has something for you."

Li Kin-Kwok held back his tears and massaged Li Chang's hand. "Brother, you taught me that life is either a daring adventure or nothing. You were right."

Li Chang winked and said to Li Kin-Kwok, "Now I know my life has had meaning. Life is about creating yourself and you have done it."

Li Chang seemed ever nearer to death and out of breath. Still, he waved Li Kin-Kwok closer. He pulled him by the arm to get closer, as he leaned forward.

"I see the three-inch scars on your head and face from the beatings you received searching for Gold Mountain," he whispered fiercely. "I know the lines are there on your back from the whipping you received while seeking justice on the Transcontinental Railroad." His voice grew stronger. He tightened his grip on Li Kin-Kwok's arm and looked at him intensely.

Li Kin-Kwok noticed his brother's eyes were wet with tears. "But they aren't scars, cuts and bruises," Li Chang added. "These are your badges of honor."

He slumped backwards.

With a lump in his throat, Li Kin-Kwok looked directly into Li Chang's almost-shut eyes. "You taught me that one's dignity may be assaulted and vandalized, but it can never be taken away unless it is surrendered. I am not ashamed of my scars. I know that we belong here."

He thought for a moment, and then added, "I will set up a newspaper, in English and Chinese. Words are powerful, and I have much to say. I can become a voice for people of all races, for those unheard and without justice. I now know there are two ways of exerting one's strength: one is pushing down, the other is pulling up."

"And talk to Strobridge," Li Chang said.

"And, yes, I will see Strobridge," Li Kin-Kwok replied. "I have learned much from you, my brother. As Confucius said, 'A man of humanity is one who, in seeking to establish himself, finds footholds for others and who, in desiring attainment for himself, helps others to attain.' This I promise to continue to do."

"Are you alright, uncle?" Li Wu asked. "How do you feel?"

"My heart holds my memories," Li Chang said. He looked again at his brother. "Promise to give me a kiss on my forehead when I am gone—I will feel it."

Now Li Chang rested and was silent, but his eyes and those of Li Wu and Li Kin-Kwok spoke words of comfort to each other. Li

Chang grew weaker. He motioned Li Kin-Kwok to come closer.

"Not enough ginger," Li Chang whispered in his brother's ear.

Li Chang felt free. He closed his eyes for the last time. Li Kin-Kwok kissed his brother on his brow.

18

THE TEN-MILE DAY

AFTER MONTHS OF increased tension, closed-door Washington lobbying, Congressional pressure and aborted meetings between the Central Pacific and Union Pacific, on April 8, 1869 the railroads settled upon Promontory Summit, the most God-forsaken place one could imagine, as the meeting point for the two lines.

The Union Pacific and Central Pacific lines ran through some of the grandest scenery in the world, but the spot where the two were joined together was improbable and undistinguished. No one had ever lived there, and after the ceremony no one would ever again. The summit was just over 5,000 feet above sea level. It was a flat, circular valley, bare except for sagebrush and a few scrub cedars, perhaps three miles in diameter. The only structures were a half-dozen wall tents and a few rough-board shacks, set up by merchants selling whiskey.

To signify that the graders and track layers had accepted what their bosses and Washington had decided upon, on April 10 the Union Pacific stopped grading west of Promontory, and on April 15 the Central Pacific stopped grading east of the summit. The companies pulled back their men, their tents, their cooking facilities, their equipment, their wagons, horses and mules, everything to one side or the other.

The race was over. Who had won? It didn't matter anymore.

Generally, the men involved breathed a sigh of relief that it was over. Charles Crocker spoke for most of them. He had suffered from insomnia for months, and he said, "When Huntington telegraphed me that he had fixed matters with the Union Pacific, and that we were to meet on the summit of Promontory, I went to bed that night and slept like a child."

The Central Pacific moved ahead briskly. On April 9, 1869, it laid 4.2 miles of track. The next day, it set down 3.1 miles, and the day after that, 4.6. By April 17, it had reached Monument Point. There the Central Pacific established three sprawling grading camps. Hustle and bustle were the words that came to people's lips when they saw this hive of activity. As one example, on April 18 a train came from Sacramento that was 32 cars in length. While the Chinese workers unloaded each car of its rails and ties, others were putting intermediate ties under the rails already spiked into place, and still others were putting in additional ballast and tamping it down.

On April 22, 1869, the Central Pacific was eighteen miles from Promontory Summit, the Union Pacific twelve.

The tracks were not yet joined, but increasingly immigrants were moving west by rail rather than wagon trains. Immigrants who traveled from Omaha to beyond Ogden on the Union Pacific hired stagecoaches at the terminus which took them to Monument Point, then got on a Central Pacific train, and they were in California only a little over a week after leaving Omaha.

There were constant reminders of the changes that the Transcontinental Railroad had already wrought. Freight wagons carrying supplies to the end of track from Sacramento and Omaha rolled constantly past the construction crews. Wells Fargo stagecoaches, which had once spanned the continent, still provided service between railroad heads but their run became shorter with each passing day.

CHINESE BROTHERS, AMERICAN SONS

Li Kin-Kwok explained to Li Wu that Jack Casement's men of the Union Pacific laid four and a half miles of track in a single day and then six miles. Crocker told Strobridge that the Central Pacific must beat this record, and Strobridge got the materials together and laid seven miles and a few feet. So on Oct. 26, 1868, Casement got his Union Pacific men up at 3 a.m. and put them to work by lantern light until dawn and kept them at it until almost midnight, and laid eight miles. Not to be outdone, Crocker boasted that his men could lay ten miles. Dr. Thomas C. Durant, vice president of the Union Pacific, wagered $10,000 that it could not be done.

Most people believed that laying ten miles of track in one day was impossible. But the Central Pacific had already done the impossible many times. In the first years of construction, Chinese laborers had dug sixteen tunnels through the solid granite of the high Sierras, overcoming fierce winter blizzards, snowdrifts over 100 feet high and avalanches that swept away whole crews. Charles Crocker decided he had one last thing to show the Union Pacific — and the world.

The Union Pacific had neither enough time or track to top Crocker's men, he cunningly made sure of that. They waited until April 27, 1869, when the Central Pacific had only fourteen miles to go, the Union Pacific nine — and that up the eastern approach to Promontory Summit, heavy work at best. Spies were everywhere telling each railroad how each one was doing, but Crocker's army stood ready for its final battle, the Ten-Mile Day.

On the evening of April 27, 1869, Crocker and James Strobridge, his right-hand man, called for volunteers for the difficult task ahead. Each crew was promised four times its normal wages if it could meet the challenge.

Nearly all the team leaders stepped forward. Fourteen hundred of the Central Pacific's best laborers (foremen not included), all Chinese except eight Irish, were selected out of the almost 5,000 volunteers. Li Kin-Kwok volunteered and was chosen, and Li Wu brought hot tea to his father and the other Chinese workers.

In a circus-like atmosphere, there were photographers and newspaper reporters everywhere and gangs of spectators from back west. Frilly-dressed ladies held parasols to keep off the sun while men dressed in suits and stovepipe hats strutted about. As daylight spread, workers from rival construction camps jostled for the best view. Nearly 5,000 people were camped out near the northeast shore of Utah's Great Salt Lake, making a lively and colorful crowd. Businessmen and workers, a military band, and army officers from the nearby garrisons had come to this desolate valley to see the last great push in the building of the first Transcontinental Railroad.

A skinny fellow puffing on a big cigar tapped Li Wu on the shoulder and asked, "What's your job, coolie?"

Li Wu was tongue-tied as he tried to explain in broken English. Li Kin-Kwok saved him by saying, "He's my assistant, sir."

Bill O'Reilly, a Central Pacific railroad worker, was standing nearby. Li Kin-Kwok looked over at the crowd of well-dressed visitors and said to him, "I'm itching to hand those fellows a shovel, and tell them to make themselves useful."

Li Wu grinned, and Bill O'Reilly said, "I wouldn't advise it, Li. They'd probably just hurt themselves, or worse, damage good equipment."

They all had a good laugh at that.

Later, Li Kin-Kwok was smoking a pipe outside their tent, watching the light fade in the west.

"Father, what do you think?" asked Li Wu. "Will we win the bet for Crocker tomorrow? They call us Crocker's Pets because of our fast work."

CHINESE BROTHERS, AMERICAN SONS

"Son, we're not his pets," said Li Kin-Kwok. "Pets are animals. We'll lay the track faster to prove we're the best workers, not to help him win."

"The Irish workers won't like being beaten by Chinese workers. They say we're weak," Li Wu said.

"Son, you know we are not," Li Kin-Kwok said.

A mile away in an elegant railroad car sat the boss, Charles Crocker. He checked final preparations for the next day's race with Strobridge. "Winning this race will be easy compared to what we did in the high mountains," Crocker said.

"Yeah, that work was so tough," Strobridge said. "When we win tomorrow, it will be because of the Chinese workers. They are steady. They keep working, even when it seems impossible. We couldn't have built it without them."

They all had breakfast at 4 a.m. Li Kin-Kwok told his son to stand ready to replace anyone who was too exhausted to continue. Li Wu was excited to watch the show.

At 7 a.m. all eyes rested on Charles Crocker as he steadied his horse beside the grade. The crews knew it would take 1,600 railroad flatcars to carry everything they needed to lay two miles of track. Five trains, each made up of an engine and sixteen flatcars, were already waiting, some at the end of the rails and others in the sidings beside the main railroad. Wooden ties had already been placed in piles along the entire ten-mile route. Everything was set to go.

With a sharp shouted command, Crocker's arm rose and fell. The engineer on the first train pulled hard on the whistle cord and a shrill blast pierced the cold, damp morning air. The race had begun.

Li Wu had never seen the Chinese work so fast. Before the dust settled on the newly-set ties, the tenders clamped their tongs down to the rails and rolled them off the beds of the horse carts. And no sooner were the rails clanged down than the spike mauls rang out.

Five men to a rail, three blows to a spike, 30 spikes to a rail, and 400 rails to the mile. The rails weighed 560 pounds each—that was nearly a quarter of a million pounds of lifting for every single mile they put down.

The teamsters worked their horses so hard bringing the rails forward that they hitched fresh animals to their supply carts twice during the morning.

Before sunrise, a wagonload of Union Pacific officials had arrived on the scene. They had come to watch Crocker's humiliation and to laugh at him, but there was no laughter. A train arrived, and Chinese laborers leaped onto the flatcars. The noise was deafening as sledgehammers knocked out the side stakes and rails tumbled to the ground. The clanging of falling iron continued for eight minutes, until the first sixteen flatcars were empty.

As each supply train was unloaded, three Chinese men rushed to the end of the rails, what they called the end of track. The trio scrambled ahead to the first loose ties. Then they began lifting, prying, and shoving to center the bare ties on the grade.

The emptied train then steamed back to the siding, and men hurried to load iron cars with exactly 16 rails and 32 rail joiners each. A crew of six Chinese workers and an Irish boss hopped aboard.

To the right of the track, two horses were hitched by a long rope to an iron car. With a yell from the boss, the horses lurched against their harnesses, and the cars rolled forward on the track. When the iron car reached the end of track, a wooden keg was smashed over the rails. The iron car rambled ahead as new track was laid, spilling spikes through the open bottom and onto the ground where they could be used. Dust clouds choked the air.

CHINESE BROTHERS, AMERICAN SONS

With the iron car moving steadily along, eight Irishmen laid rails just ahead of its rolling wheels. These "ironmen" were Michael Shay, Thomas Daley, George Elliot, Michael Sullivan, Edward Killeen, Patrick Joice, Michael Kennedy, and Fred McNamare. The four forward men seized the 560-pound, 30-foot long rails, while the four rear men slid the rails to the rollers on each side of the iron car. The lead ironmen ran forward.

"Down!" shouted George Cooley, the foreman. With a loud thud the iron hit the ties within inches of the previous rail. Without a moment's rest, the eight ironmen went back for more. On average, a pair of rails was laid every twenty seconds.

While rails clanked to the ground, the Chinese crew from the iron car loaded fishplates, nuts and bolts into baskets attached to poles slung over their shoulders. Then they jogged up the line, tossing out ironware every ten yards. Where rail ends met, another team fastened the fishplates loosely with nuts and thrusting bolts.

When each handcar was unloaded, the horses were detached from the front and hitched to the back. At a gallop, they hauled the empty iron car back to the supply dump. If a returning car got in the way of a full iron car, the empty one was flipped off the track until the full car passed. Nothing slowed the flow of supplies to the end of track.

A track-gauge team measured the rails to insure they were exactly four feet, eight and one-half inches apart, the new American and British standard, and the rail ends were loosely fastened with fishplates.

Next came the spike setters. Each man picked up one of the spikes lying scattered beside the roadbed, and quickly set it in position with two hits. Another gang of Chinese followed. With three blows from the maul, each spike was driven home, securing the rails and the ties.

ED SHEW

Some crews had marvelous names. "Fishplate men" tightened the nuts on the thrusting bolts with long-handled wrenches. "Gandy dancers," or "track liners," aligned the rails to the ties using massive track bars. A foreman would sing out a simple tune with a strong beat. Like the crew on a rowboat, the gandy dancers would all push together on the final beat, aligning the rails.

Following close on their heels, a surveyor directed a rail gang who lifted the ties and shoveled dirt under them to keep the track level.

The last and largest special work team included 400 tampers and shovelers. They used crowbars, shovels, and tamping bars to pack the ground around the nails. The crew formed three long lines, one on each side of the track and one down the middle. Each tamper gave two crunching tamps to the gravel, or ballast, before moving on, while shovelers filled in where needed.

From the first pioneer to the last tamper ran a line of men nearly two miles long. Like a mammoth machine with hundreds of well-oiled parts, Crocker's men moved rhythmically forward. The ribbon of track rose across the plain at the pace of a walking man. Tired workers were pulled from the line and replaced. But most, including the eight ironmen, showed no signs of quitting.

Alongside the grade, the telegraph construction party worked frantically to keep pace with the track layers. They set poles; hammered on the crossbars; and hauled out, hung, and insulated the wire.

The track boss Strobridge stalked up and down the line, barking out commands and encouragement. The steady hammering of spikes, the rhythmic thud of iron rails, and even the men's labored breathing beat like a drum across the barren plain.

A reporter pulled out his pocket watch and counted the rails as they were laid down. To everyone's amazement, 240 feet of iron were placed in one minute and twenty seconds. By 9 a.m. almost two miles of track had been spiked and tamped. Even the Union Pacific men had to admit it was quality work.

Water, food, and tool wagons creaked up and down the line as the heat rose with the morning sun. Chinese men, including Li Wu, wove in between the crews, delivering water and tea to quench their thirst.

With the completion of another two miles of track, the second supply train pulled back to a siding and the third train steamed forward, belching thick clouds of black smoke. Next in line, ready to serve the midday meal, was the so-called Pioneer Train—the boarding house for some of the workers, and the office and living quarters of James Strobridge and his wife. At 1:30 p.m. the whistle sounded, calling a halt for lunch. Whirlwind No. 62, the locomotive on the Pioneer Train, pushed the kitchen cars up, and the boss served hot boiled beef to the workers. Chinese cooks pitched in, but alas no longer was Li Chang among them, to feed the hungry and joyous Chinese a feast worthy of their efforts. It was clear that they would set a new record, so the fellows wasted little time laughing and bragging.

On this particular lunchtime, a strange thing happened. Usually when the lunch whistle blew, a line was drawn in the sand between the two groups, Chinese and whites. This time Li Kin-Kwok and four other Chinese foremen and the more numerous white foremen mingled with each other's camp and their crews ate and shared the time together. It helped that everyone was in good spirits.

Li Kin-Kwok cracked to Sean Kennedy, "If you ate dried cuttlefish you'd be able to work as hard as we do."

"If you ate more beef and potatoes, you'd be bigger," countered Kennedy.

ED SHEW

Some of the Irish were even seen drinking tea instead of their usual coffee. And the minute lunch was over, they all went back to work with a bit of the camaraderie that had been missing until now. Perhaps something good had begun.

A quick measurement showed that six miles of track had already been laid, spiked, and bolted that morning. Whoops and hollers went up as the news spread among the men. They were now confident they could reach their goal of ten miles in one day, and they named their rest stop Camp Victory.

At 2:30 p.m. work began again, but a special crew had to be called in. The tracks were now climbing the western slope of the Promontory Mountains. The climb was steep and full of curves, and the rails had to be bent. Lacking measuring instruments, this new crew judged the curves by sight. They jammed the rails between blocks and slowly and carefully hammered them into the right shapes. Every rail took extra time to mold and fit.

As the afternoon wore on, the foremen continued to ride the line, encouraging the men. The horses pulling the iron cars were changed every two hours, but they could no longer run up the steep grade. Now they had to walk slowly up the steep hillside. The rail gang was dripping with sweat, and their muscles were burning from overuse, but not one man stopped to rest. With each hour, another mile of track was laid in the direction of Promontory Summit.

The commander of a detachment of soldiers came out to watch. "It was just like an army marching over the ground and having a track built behind them," he later wrote. The progress, he said, was "just about as fast as a hard walk...a good day's march for an army."

By 7 p.m. the sun was dipping behind Monument Point. Strobridge signaled for a final blast from the train whistle. The exhausted men cast down their tools, and the day's work came to an abrupt end.

How much rail had the men of the Central Pacific laid? Two Union Pacific engineers took out their surveying chains and began to measure. Everyone waited for the final count. Then it came. The railhead was ten miles, 56-feet farther east than it had been the previous evening.

The crews flung their hats into the air, cheering and shaking hands all around. They had done the impossible again. The Union Pacific's record was destroyed, and Thomas Durant had lost his bet. A total of 25,800 ties, 3,520 rails averaging 560 pounds each, twice that number of fishplates, 28,160 spikes, and 14,080 nuts and bolts had been placed to complete the job.

The eight Irish track layers were declared heroes and were featured in later histories. Each had lifted over 125 tons of iron. No single crew has ever beaten their record. But the Chinese workers had also once again proven themselves to their rivals, just without the accompanying accolades.

Crocker called for one of his locomotives to test the track. The train roared over the line up to 40 miles an hour, setting the rails and proving the job well done.

Other Central Pacific workers had kept the telegraph wire unreeling during the day, stringing it up on freshly-planted poles, and when they were finished, the news was flashed to Sacramento and around the world.

"We got our forces together and laid ten miles and 56 feet in one day," Crocker later said, "and that did not leave them room enough to beat us on; they could not have done it anyhow, because when they laid eight miles they had lanterns, and we did not use them, we laid out ten miles by daylight."

What the Central Pacific did that day will be remembered as long as this Republic exists. White men born in America were there, along with former slaves whose ancestors had come from

Africa, plus immigrants from all across Europe, and more than 3,000 Chinese. There were some Mexicans, as well as French Indians and at least a few Native Americans. Everyone was excited, ready to work, if called upon, eager to show what he could do. Even the Chinese, usually methodical and a bit scornful of the American way of doing things, were stirred to a fever pitch.

Li Kin-Kwok lead them in cheering, "CP, CP, CP, CP!" Everyone joined in. They had come together at this desolate place in the middle of western North America to do what had never been done before.

Finally, the last of the five construction trains backed down the long grade past Victory to the construction camp just north of the lake. There were 1,000 men piled onto sixteen flatcars for the ride, cheering, laughing, chattering, kicking their feet, swinging their arms, breaking into song, congratulating one another. It was a peace train, and for a moment they were a team, Chinese and Irish alike.

Li Kin-Kwok squeezed Li Wu's hands and looked him in the eye. "People say that it can't be done, yellow and white together. Well, here today we made it work. We have our disagreements, of course, but before we reach for hate, always, always make sure to remember the day when it didn't matter what the color of our skin was. We can work together. We can dream of a better land. There can be peace and understanding when we make our enemies our friends," Li Kin-Kwok said. "Son, I wish Li Chang was here to witness this."

The Union Pacific construction chief Jack Casement was not a good loser. He said his men could do better if they had enough room to do so, and he begged for permission to tear up several miles of track in order to prove it. Durant said no.

On the Central Pacific side of the tracks, it was Huntington who was disgruntled. "I notice by the papers," he wired Crocker, "that there was ten miles of track laid in one day on the Central Pacific. Which was really a great feat, the more particularly when we consider that it was done after the necessity for its being done have passed."

"I'll bet that fellow Huntington doesn't know how to do much more than carry his money bags to the bank," barked Strobridge.

19

The Golden Spike

THE WORK SLOWED to a snail's pace. Beginning on May 3, both the Central Pacific and the Union Pacific began discharging large numbers of men and sending others to the rear to work on parts of track that had been hastily laid.

"The two opposing armies are melting away," reported the *Alta California*, "and the camps which dotted every brown hillside and every shady glen...are being broken up and abandoned. The Central Pacific force is nearly all gone already, and that of the Union is going fast."

However, many of the men, especially the Chinese, stuck around to watch the final ceremony. "Besides," Li Kin-Kwok said, "I'm curious what Strobridge has for me."

Li Kin-Kwok said the railroad officials had gotten two solid gold spikes ready for the occasion.

"Boy would I like to take a swing at them," Li Wu exclaimed.

All that was left could be seen from Promontory Summit. Along the line of the railroad were the white-tented camps of the Chinese laborers. From every one of them, the Chinese were advancing, advancing. The Central Pacific's end of track was now only four miles from Promontory Summit. The Union Pacific had nine and a half miles of track left to lay. The Central Pacific's Chinese had to grade just four more miles and lay track

CHINESE BROTHERS, AMERICAN SONS

over the ties and spike down before reaching the summit.

By May 9, all of the remaining rails were in place except two. The momentous joining of the Transcontinental Railroad would take place 1,086 miles west of the Missouri River and 690 miles east of Sacramento.

Meanwhile, Hell on Wheels closed with a flourish. With nothing else to do, there was lots of drinking and fighting going on. The whiskey sellers, gamblers, and prostitutes continued to do business right up to the end.

One reporter wrote, "The loose population that has followed the railroaders is turbulent and rascally. Nobody knows what will become of this riff-raff when the tracks meet, but they are lively enough now and carry off their share of the plunder from the working men."

The Central Pacific's regular passenger train packed with excursionists headed for the Summit. Leland Stanford's special train followed. It was made in the early Pullman style, with a kitchen, dining room, and sleeping accommodation for ten. Aboard were Stanford, Mark Hopkins, the chief justice of California, the governor of Arizona, and other guests. Also on board was the last spike made of gold, the last tie, made of laurel, and a silver-headed hammer. The spike was six inches long, had a rough gold nugget attached to its point and weighed 18 ounces. It was valued at $350.

The locomotive pulling the passenger train was named Jupiter. It was the Central Pacific's Engine No. 60, built in Schenectady, NY and now headed for a permanent place in railroad history.

On Friday afternoon, May 7, 1869, the train arrived in Promontory. The telegraph operators for each line were present and set up to send and receive wires, but there was no official from the Union Pacific present. Stanford sent a message to the Union Pacific's Ogden office, demanding to know where the hell the Union Pacific delegation was. Jack Casement, construction boss, replied that very heavy rains had sent gushers through West Canyon and damaged the Devil's Gate Bridge. The Union Pacific couldn't get its trains to the summit before Monday, May 10.

The dawn on May 10, 1869 was cold, near freezing, but the rising sun heralded a bright, clear day, with temperatures rising into the seventies. Spring in Utah that year was as glorious as it could be. A group of Central Pacific and Union Pacific workers gathered, but there were not many of them left, and the best estimates put the crowd at 500 or 600 people, far fewer than the predictions. During the morning, two trains from the Central Pacific and two from the Union Pacific arrived at the site, bearing officials, their guests, and some spectators.

When the big moment arrived, two bands struck up a march, and a double-file procession of soldiers aligned themselves along the tracks.

A small group of Chinese clad in neat blue smocks and wearing "coolie" hats watched from afar, Li Kin-Kwok in his usual cowboy hat and the hatless Li Wu included. The Chinese were not asked to be a part of the ceremony as white Central Pacific workers set a rail in place on their side and white Union Pacific workers picked up another rail and stepped toward the open place on their side.

As a seething Li Wu stood and watched, both Central and Union Irish railroad crews drove spikes down the length of the last two rails. They saved the gold and silver ones for that special laurel tie. The Union Pacific just hammered the last spike down on their side. Before the dignitaries took their turn, the Central Pacific's Mick Dooley bent over that last spike and lifted his maul to strike the last spike—ping, ping ....

At the bandstand, Li Kin-Kwok saw Strobridge calmly waving

him forward. "Does he have something for me?" He wondered, "What secret had Li Chang kept from me?"

Li Kin-Kwok scanned the dignitaries on the large platform. To Strobridge's right was the impassive Stanford who as governor had called the Chinese "a degraded people." As president of the Central Pacific Railroad, he called the Chinese "workers without equal."

To Strobridge's left was the frugal and earnest Mark Hopkins, treasurer of the Central Pacific Railroad. Hopkins advocated deals, legal or otherwise, that made fiscal sense, and reacted in horror when his associates made promises beyond the pale of reason.

To Hopkins' left was a woman. As Li Kin-Kwok strode closer, he could see she was a Chinese woman, about his height, with long black hair—tied in back, large eyes and an oval face with high cheekbones and silky white skin wearing a purple and black cheongsam, a loose jacket and trousers that covered most of her body, revealing only the head, hands, and the tips of the toes. The baggy nature of the clothing also served to conceal the figure of the wearer regardless of age. Her feet were not tiny; they had not been bound. This probably meant she was born into a poor family from Canton.

Li Kin-Kwok tearfully closed his eyes.

Time stood still. He recalled a young girl on a makeshift platform fifteen years before. Perhaps it was a mirage, caused by being too long in the desert. Loneliness and empty days were no longer his friends. It couldn't be, but now they were here—face-to-face. They had met again. Some people wait a lifetime for a moment like this.

"What is the worst that can happen? She may want nothing to do with me. But she's here," Li Kin-Kwok said.

He saw the truth in her eyes—just like in San Francisco—all

those years ago. But now there was a smile on her face; her gaze was one of joy and hope and expectation, not of despair. She was looking for him. He walked forward, as his heart cried.

Back at the line, Dooley took the maul and with the third measured, confident, smooth backswing he let the maul follow through and ping, the spike was in. Then he hollered for all to hear, "We did it!"

Li Kin-Kwok looked into her eyes. He felt so alive. She locked his arms in hers.

The eyes of Wang Wei and Li Kin-Kwok met. "I've waited all my life for that look in your eyes," Li Kin-Kwok softly said.

"How long I have waited," Wang Wei whispered.

He lifted her up in his arms. They were complete; their destinies were one. The world stood still.

Finally, Li Kin-Kwok said to Strobridge, "How can this be? What miracle has happened?"

"Your brother Li Chang did it," Strobridge said. "He bought her back from Mark Hopkins. He used to be a grocer and he bought her as a maid. Now look at the bastard! Your brother's been paying him before you even joined the railroad. She cost Li Chang $3,000. He thought you'd forget about her. You never did. She must be quite a woman."

Now Li Kin-Kwok remembered the records found by Jimmy Lin. "Wang Wei was sold to a wholesale grocer with the initials 'M.H.' from Placerville. Oh my, that was Mark Hopkins."

"From his grave, my brother Li Chang's generous heart has helped make our lives whole. He was strong enough to carry us," Li Kin-Kwok said to Wang Wei.

The officials stepped forward for the final show. The railroad bigwigs gave speeches. "The greatest feat of the 19th century," Stanford said.

"The greatest feat in the history of mankind; only Americans could have done it," Hopkins added, thereby dismissing the Central Pacific's Chinese workers.

"This is true," Li Kin-Kwok added. "They now call me Li Kin-Kwok; we are the Americans who built this railroad and helped build this country."

A telegraph wire was attached to the Golden Spike, with another to the sledgehammer. When the Golden Spike was tapped in, the telegraph lines would send the message all around the country. The spike was placed in a hole already drilled, so that it only had to be tapped down and then be easily extracted.

Photographers were free to roam; they took whatever pictures they liked, ordering men to get into this pose or that and to stand still, and doing all the other things that modern man were accustomed to doing for photographers. Because of that arrangement, some of the most famous photographs in American history were taken, but none of them show any of the Chinese.

Grenville Dodge, Durant and Stanford had argued for nearly an hour before the scheduled time to begin, which was at noon, over who had the honor of placing the Golden Spike. The Central Pacific officials declared that, since Stanford had tossed the first shovelful of earth in the construction of the road, and since the Central Pacific was incorporated earlier than the Union Pacific, Stanford was the man to drive the last spike. Dodge said Durant should do it, because the Union Pacific was the longer railroad. Just a few minutes before noon, Stanford and Durant settled the controversy.

Strobridge and Samuel B. Reed, construction engineer, put the last tie, the laurel tie, in place. Durant tapped in his spike. Stanford swung the silver-headed maul and missed, striking only the rail. It made no difference. The telegraph operator closed the circuit and the wire went out, "Done!" Stanford then tapped the

ED SHEW

Golden Spike in.

The two engines, the Central Pacific's Jupiter and the Union Pacific's No. 119, were unhooked and moved ever so slowly toward each other until their pilots touched over the last rail. Whistles shrieked and a roar exploded from the crowd. Champagne bottles were smashed against each engine.

Above the din, Durant shook Stanford's hand, declaring, "There is henceforth but one Pacific Railroad of the United States." The dream of a Transcontinental Railroad was now a reality.

The Chinese cheered like madmen when the engine from the West and the one from the East rolled toward one another and touched.

"Get back, coolies!" shouted the crowd. But the Chinese firmly stood their ground. Today, the Chinese laborers had no shame. They had burst through the barricades. They were warriors.

"If you are passive in situations of injustice, you have chosen the side of the tyrant," Li Kin-Kwok said to Li Wu, his son.

"I know, I understand," Li Wu said to his father.

"Are you sure? We are tied to one another. If we allow people to think that it is alright to act unjustly towards some people, this attitude can spread until eventually people might act unjustly in more and more places," Li Kin-Kwok said. "Furthermore, if you choose to do nothing when faced with an obvious wrong, you empower the wrongdoer. If your friend is being picked-on by a bully and you just stand there and do nothing, you may as well stand with the bully because you didn't help your friend."

"Call us what you will, but it is our hands that helped build the railroad!" Li Wu shouted back at the crowd.

Across the nation, bells pealed. Even the venerable Liberty Bell in Philadelphia was rung. Then came the boom of cannons, 220 of them in San Francisco at Fort Point, 100 in Washington

CHINESE BROTHERS, AMERICAN SONS

D.C., countless fired off elsewhere. It was said that more cannons were fired in celebration of the railroad than were fired in the Battle of Gettysburg. Everywhere there was the shriek of fire whistles, firecrackers and fireworks, singing and prayers in churches. The Tabernacle in Salt Lake City was packed to capacity. In New Orleans, Richmond, and Atlanta and throughout the old Confederacy, there were celebrations. Chicago had a parade that was its biggest in the century—seven miles long, with tens of thousands of people participating and cheering.

The "Golden Spike" was hammered down to hold the last length of track and the iron rails spanned a continent. But of the hundreds of people in that memorable photograph taken at Promontory Point in Utah on May 10, 1869, there was one group who were wholly invisible—the Chinese. Nowhere to be seen were the 12,000 railroad men from China who had dug the tunnels, built the roadbeds, and laid the track for half of the transcontinental line crossing the most precipitous mountains and torturous deserts of the West. These Chinese were faceless. They didn't exist.

And they now dispersed. It was too dangerous to stay. The driving-out had begun.

The Promontory Summit was again deserted except for a few canvas tents flapping in the wind, the whispers of wind through the sagebrush and rabbit grass, vibrating telegraph wires and perhaps the call of a coyote, while the railroad went past west and east, into the future.

Epilogue 1

The Time Machine

YEARS LATER, some of the Chinese railroad workers journeyed back to the Sierra Nevada to search for the remains of their loved ones to return them to China. On these expeditions, known in Cantonese as *jup seen yau* ("retrieving deceased friends"), they hunted for old grave sites, usually a heap of stones near the tracks marked by a wooden stake.

The excursion began at 6 a.m., May 10, 1873. Li Kin-Kwok wistfully thought back on how his adopted country had changed. All those years ago, as he and his brother Li Chang trekked through California in search of Gold Mountain, they saw six grizzly bears in one day. As late as the mid-1850s, antelope and elk were abundant. Deer used to graze quietly with cattle, and venison was a common dish on miners' tables. Before the discovery of gold, trappers caught beaver and otter on the Sacramento and Yuba Rivers, but they, of course, disappeared with the elk. All changed in less than two decades.

Li Kin-Kwok with Li Wu, his son and Wang Wei, now his wife, took the rails across the Sacramento plain, over Arcade Creek, to the Sierra Nevada range, through the deep Newcastle Cut, up the miraculous continuous divide toward Dutch Flat and passed cliffs jutting out of Cape Horn. This is where Li Chang, his brother, and risk-taking peasant boys from Kwangtung province had woven reed baskets and swung out into the chilly air.

CHINESE BROTHERS, AMERICAN SONS

Along the road-side, Li Kin-Kwok saw long flumes of wooden channels bearing water for the miners below. At Gold Run, he saw the results of hydraulic-mining carried on in the deep valley below the railroad. The acres that had been washed away had to go somewhere, and they filled up the rivers and creeks. What were once swift and clear mountain torrents were now turbid and not so rapid streams, whose beds had been raised by the washings of the miners. They once contained trout, but he imagined a catfish would now die in them.

Out on the edge of darkness, their locomotive pulled them up through forests of solitude toward the snowy peaks, every cut challenged by the cold-hearted, hard granite, and the marked and unmarked graves still visible along the roadbed. The train plunged into the bow of the mountains, tested by nitroglycerine and out into the sunlight, then through the snow sheds. A tree-lined lake flashed out from its emerald setting among the mountains.

The mountain air streaming into the car was cold and damp like wintertime, and smelling like pine. They went past the sparkling town of Truckee, where every board on every dwelling looked as if it had just come from the saw mills, fresh and bright. The streets were crowded with U.S. Grant lookalikes, healthy, bearded men. Then the train plunged down into the Truckee Canyon. The track ran between the frothy green river and threatening slopes past Reno to Wadsworth. The sun went down behind the mountains as they set out again across the Forty-Mile Desert.

Li Kin-Kwok pointed out where, one by one, horses had died, wagons were abandoned and where they had desperately struggled for water. The accelerating train sped off across the darkening Nevada desert, never out of sight of snow-capped peaks, rousing a cloud of ash-colored alkali dust to settle over old animal bones, wagon parts, mile markers, and occasional gravestones out in the sagebrush.

The train carrying Li Kin-Kwok, his wife and his son, rolled eastward along the Humboldt through the night, stopping at Elko to let off the silver miners. It labored through the day toward and past Humboldt Wells and the eastern ranges, steaming across the Utah border in the darkness, the gloomy desert crossing thankfully obscured for most of them by sleep.

At dawn Li Kin-Kwok woke Li Wu.

"Stand up," he said. "We're passing your Uncle Li Chang's grave."

Later, they went back to the spot. Digging under the stones, Li Kin-Kwok, Wang Wei and Li Wu found a skeleton next to a wax-sealed bottle, holding a strip of cloth inscribed with "Li Chang, born June 1, 1828, Canton, province of Kwangtung, China—died March 1, 1869."

Li Chang's bones were not returned to China. Li Kin-Kwok simply printed an addendum on the strip of cloth: "An American, A Man of Humanity."

Li Kin-Kwok saw again the acres of white tents and the smoky cook fires, and he could smell the stir-fried dishes prepared by Li Chang with their comforting aroma of ginger. He dreamed of the thousands of his fellow Cantonese workers, shortening curves and ballasting the track—perfecting the road. They were almost all young, and their faces looked individually quick and intelligent.

A full moon was out. Li Kin-Kwok stood looking at Wang Wei for a moment, and then turned to the moon. They had been meant to find each other. For Li Kin-Kwok, it was no surprise to see the softness of the moon and the gentle sparkle of the stars in her eyes. A Chinese custom is that when viewing the moon one makes a wish. Silence took over, saying all they needed to say.

CHINESE BROTHERS, AMERICAN SONS

They both smiled.

At Promontory, Li Kin-Kwok remembered fondly how the Chinese and Irish had forgotten their differences and shared the joy of the Ten-Mile Day and the relief and anticipation in the joining of the railroads.

"We did not do it alone," Li Kin-Kwok reminded Li Wu. "Together we did so much."

But the Central Pacific Railroad cheated the Chinese workers of everything they could. They tried to write the Chinese out of history altogether. They were not only excluded from the ceremonies, but from the famous photograph. But at least one man remembered.

At the celebration at Promontory Summit, James Strobridge spoke to the press and other guests about the great enterprise.

"When the other guests arose from the table," the *Chicago Tribune* correspondent noted, "Mr. Strobridge introduced his Chinese foreman and laborers, who had been with him so long, took the head of the table, making some excellent remarks, and inviting them to the banquet. This manly and honorable proceeding was hailed with three rousing cheers by the Caucasian guests, military and civilian, who crowded around Strobridge to congratulate and assure him of their sympathy."

Then the party broke up for good. The Chinese withdrew to their camp on the western slope of the Promontory Summit, the Irish to the east. There was an enormous amount of corrective work to do on the tracks, but the Central Pacific immediately laid off most Chinese workers, refusing to give them even their promised return passage to California. Only a few hundred Chinese were retained for maintenance work, some of whom spent their remaining days in isolated small towns along the way, a few living in converted boxcars.

The rest of the Chinese dispersed. Left to fend for themselves, some straggled by foot through the remotest lands of America, looking for subsistence work and survival, a journey that scattered them throughout the nation. Some took their skills to other railroad enterprises. They built railroads in every part of the country—the Alabama and Chattanooga Railroad, the Houston and Texas Railroad, the Southern Pacific, the railroads in Louisiana and Boston, the Pacific Northwest, and Alaska. After the Civil War, it was Chinese men who banded the nation north and south, east and west, with crisscrossing steel. But for the most part, as individuals, the Chinese were lost to history.

As the train sped along, Li Wu talked to his father about riding the rails eastwards in search of opportunity. And indeed, in the end, he became an adventurer like his uncle and father, and an officer with Teddy Roosevelt's Rough Riders. Li Wu died on July 1, 1898 in the Battle of San Juan Hill, the decisive battle of the Spanish-American War.

Li Kin-Kwok's wife Wang Wei became an outspoken critic of the Chinese Six Companies' lucrative trafficking in Chinese girls as prostitutes or household servants. Li Kin-Kwok never asked her about that life. But according to the 1870 U.S. Census, sixty-one per cent of 3,536 Chinese women in California were classified by occupation as prostitutes. Wang Wei rescued many young Chinese women and girls. She was a matchmaker, finding them Chinese men to marry, or she reunited them with their families back in China.

"At times our own light goes out and is rekindled by a spark from another person," Li Kin-Kwok said to his son, Li Wu. "Each of us has cause to think with deep gratitude of those who have lit the flame within us."

The two coasts were now welded together. Before the Transcontinental Railroad, trekking across the country took four to six months and cost about $1,000. On the Transcontinental

CHINESE BROTHERS, AMERICAN SONS

Railroad it took six days and cost $150. Intracontinental trade was transformed. Just as the railroad opened the markets of the west coast and Asia to the east coast of America, it brought products of eastern industry to the growing population west of the Mississippi. A production boom ensued as the railroad transported the vast resources of the middle and west of the continent for use elsewhere. The railroad was America's first technology corridor.

While encouraging the growth of American business, the railroad also promoted the evolution of the nation's public conversation and intellectual life. Americans traveled the length of the continent in a matter of days, and they gazed, studied and analyzed their entire country from the windows of their train cars. Conversations begun in New York ended in San Francisco. Books authored in San Francisco found homes on New York streets a week after their publication. The rails carried more than goods; they provided a connector for concepts, an avenue for an exchange of ideas.

Not everyone benefited from the transformation. The railroad was an irreversible benchmark of encroaching white society, that unstoppable force which forced Native Americans onto reservations. Settlers branched out from the iron road into Native American land, the buffalo herds upon which the Indians had depended vanished, as they were easy prey for sports-hunters brought to the plains by the railcar-load to slaughter the animals.

The Transcontinental Railroad through America's center spider-webbed outward to the north and south. Settlers coming west consumed millions of acres of land. By 1900, a number of routes ran parallel, the Northern Pacific and Southern Pacific among them, reaching westwards from Mississippi to the Pacific. It all created fortunes for the moguls of the Gilded Age, but the construction of the iron network also exacted a monumental sacrifice. On average, three laborers perished for every two miles of track laid. The *Sacramento Reporter* of June 30, 1870 reported that a train bearing the accumulated bones of 1,200 Chinese workers on the Central Pacific passed through Sacramento. But many others lie to this day in unmarked graves.

"They are not forgotten," Li Kin-Kwok said.

On his tour of America in 1879, the Scottish novelist Robert Louis Stevenson traveled to California in a third-class "immigrant" car on the Union Pacific Railroad. He grew troubled by the segregation of the Chinese railroad men in a separate car, but even more disturbing to him was the attitude of the white passengers toward those who had helped build the railroad they were traveling upon—"the stupid ill-feeling," he called it. Of these white Americans' conceptions of the Chinese railroad men, Stevenson wrote: "They never seemed to have looked at them, listened to them, or thought of them, but hated them a priori."

The work of the Chinese can still be seen. The Central Pacific prided itself on its workmanship. One can go up to the Sierras even today and look at the retaining walls and culverts that were built by hand by the Chinese, still doing their job and still objects of beauty.

Hundreds of miles of the track are still in service today, especially through the Sierra Nevada Mountains and canyons in Utah and Wyoming. While the original rail has long since been replaced because of age and wear, and the roadbed upgraded and repaired, the lines generally run on top of the original, handmade grade. It is the current Union Pacific Railroad from Omaha, Nebraska through Ogden, Utah to Sacramento, California and beyond. The eastern part of the route was the 19th century Union Pacific Railroad. The Central Pacific Railroad—the western part of the route—became part of the Southern Pacific Railroad which later merged with the Union Pacific.

CHINESE BROTHERS, AMERICAN SONS

The tracks over the Promontory Summit were torn up in World War II to use as scrap iron. Today people can drive—cautiously—through high fills and long, deep cuts which trace the Central Pacific's lines. These are stark mementos of both human failure and achievement, monuments to government stupor and creativity, to the competitive instincts and organizing ability of the railroad's owners and managers and, most of all, to the men who built them.

"Son, someday you'll be riding in a plush car amongst the fancy gents and ladies, but don't forget that the backbone of this railroad, this country, are the men that we left buried back along the line, men like your Uncle Li Chang," Li Kin-Kwok said.

"Father, I now understand," Liu Wu replied. "The things I do for myself are gone when I'm gone, but the things I do for others remain. They are my legacy, and yours too."

"Yes, strive to make the best of what you have and make an impact on those around you. Help others to attain, and you will live on forever," Li Kin-Kwok said. "Build bridges and get to know others better, and deny the racial stereotypes that ultimately endanger us all. When we value others for their uniqueness and differences, we enhance the possibilities for our children and ourselves."

"I believe we have two lives—the one we live with, and the one after that based on what we contribute. Think of all the young men you have influenced," Li Wu said. "Now, I'm starting to sound like you and Uncle Li Chang."

"Don't be me, son. Be better than me," Li Kin-Kwok said.

For the Chinese involved in the railroad's making, the results were not always happy ones. The thanks of a grateful nation included a series of vicious laws that blocked the Chinese from citizenship. Ignoring the crucial role that Chinese immigrants played in constructing the Transcontinental Railroad and

California infrastructure, Chinese immigrants became targets for white workers who blamed them for driving down wages. Riots against Chinese in California were commonplace in the 1870s and 1880s.

Los Angeles witnessed its own brand of racially-motivated mob violence. After suspected Chinese gangsters killed a white cop in an October 1871 shootout, 500 agitated white and Hispanic Angelenos gathered in the city's Chinatown and began rounding up Chinese residents. The mob stabbed and shot them, dragged them to a makeshift gallows to be hanged and mutilated, making the event the largest mass lynching in American history. When the dust had settled, eighteen mangled Chinese bodies lay in the streets, amounting to a full ten percent of the city's Chinese population. The largest mass lynching in U.S. history was not African Americans but of Chinese. None of the victims – including a respected doctor and a twelve-year old boy – had participated in the initial shootout. All perpetrators were released on technicalities after serving brief sentences.

A total of 300,000 Chinese arrived in the United States between 1854 and 1882, drawn to the California gold rush and to jobs in mining and railroad construction. As Chinese American historian L. Ling-chi Wang has pointed out, "Up until 1882 America was open to everybody who wanted to come. We welcomed everybody. The only people that we excluded by law, at that time, were prostitutes, lepers and morons. And in 1882 we added the Chinese to that list."

In 1882, the U.S. Congress passed the Chinese Exclusion Act, the first anti-immigrant act in U.S. history. The law ended Chinese immigration and prevented Chinese, and later other Asian immigrants from becoming naturalized citizens, thus disenfranchising that population. Congress extended this Act in 1892 and again indefinitely in 1904.

CHINESE BROTHERS, AMERICAN SONS

Children of Chinese born in the United States were also excluded from citizenship until an 1896 law established their rights as citizens. Not until 1926 would California's suffrage provision, allowing "no native of China" to vote be overturned by the U.S. Supreme Court. The Chinese Exclusion Act would remain in effect until 1943, when the United States lifted the immigration ban, because China was then its ally in World War II against Japan.

Fifteen years after the Li brothers and Wang Wei arrived in San Francisco on November 9, 1869. Li Yu indeed set up a newspaper in Chinatown and dedicated it to mutual understanding. He was much influenced by a Unitarian song he had come across:

> Fear not, out of our dreams comes a new prophetic voice
> We shall demand a deeper justice by our courageous choice
> Commitment sets our heart and soul ablaze
> When our hunger and our passion call us on our way
> We are sure that the flame burns within
> Then we are fulfilled and our future can begin...

By the early 1870s the United States was in a deep recession. Many men were unemployed. In San Francisco, Denis Kearney, an Irish immigrant, helped form the Workingmen's Party, which focused its anger on the Chinese, who often worked for lower wages than the whites. Kearney started every speech with the ringing phrase, "The Chinese Must Go!"

The Wasp, a San Francisco newspaper, carried the anti-Chinese rhetoric to an extreme. In its edition of November 11, 1881, it published a drawing entitled "A Statue for Our Harbor." Immigrants to San Francisco's harbor were to be welcomed by a menacing Chinese effigy, his clothes in tatters, his long queue wafting in the breeze.

Starting in 2010, the 1882 Project, a non-partisan coalition of Chinese American and Asian American leaders and their supporters, pushed for a formal apology from Congress for the Chinese Exclusion Act. With the passage of Senate Resolution 201 in October 2011 and House Resolution 683 in June 2012, the 112th Congress provided that formal apology. It was only the fifth time ever that Congress had made a formal apology to a specific group of people, the others being African Americans for slavery, Japanese Americans for internment camps, Native Americans for violence, neglect and mistreatment, and Hawaiians for the overthrow of their monarchy.

The House expression of regret came in a resolution sponsored by Representative Judy Chu (D-California), who was the first Chinese American woman elected to Congress. For Chu, the apology was deeply personal.

"It is for my grandfather and for all Chinese Americans that we must pass this resolution, for those who were told for six decades by the U.S. government that the land of the free wasn't open to them," Chu said on the House floor. "We must finally and formally acknowledge these ugly laws that were incompatible with America's founding principles."

She told her fellow lawmakers how her grandfather did not have the legal right to become a citizen, how he was forced to register and carry a certificate of residence at all times for almost forty years, or else face deportation. He could be saved only if a white person vouched for him.

The Chinese came to America, as do all immigrants, searching for a better life. "Their blood, sweat and tears built the first transcontinental railroad, connecting the people of our nation," Chu said. "They opened our mines, constructed the levees and became the backbone of farm production." But as the economy soured in the 1870s, she added, the Chinese were made scapegoats. "They were called racial slurs, were spat upon in the streets and even brutally murdered."

It was only in the 1940s, as anti-Asian political sentiments shifted from America's ally, China, to its enemy, Japan, that Franklin D. Roosevelt maneuvered legislation through Congress repealing the exclusion laws, but their effect would continue to be felt for generations to come. It was not until 1965, when the Hart-Cellar Act prioritized the reunification of families and the immigration of professionals, that Chinese were able to legally immigrate and be naturalized in larger numbers.

"Today is historic," Chu said. "This is a very significant day in the Chinese American community. It is an expression that discrimination has no place in our society and that the promise of equality is available to all."

Epilogue 2

Back to the Future

In a case of history repeating itself, at the Golden Spike centennial celebration of the completion of the Transcontinental Railroad in May 1969, the 12,000 Chinese workers of the Central Pacific Railroad were ignored. Only once during the three-hour program were the Chinese mentioned, and then only in passing, along with the roles played by the Indians, Irish, Mormons and blacks.

The main speaker, U.S. Transportation Secretary John A. Volpe asked, "Who else but Americans could drill ten tunnels in mountains thirty feet deep in snow? Who else but Americans could chisel through miles of solid granite? Who else but Americans could have laid ten miles of track in 12 hours?"

Volpe had no clue of the history. The irony of Volpe's speech was that these 'Americans' were in fact, foreign-born Chinese barred for years from becoming citizens.

However, on May 9, 2014, U.S. Secretary of Labor Thomas Perez participated in a public ceremony inducting into the Department of Labor Hall of Fame the Chinese railroad workers whose work had been crucial to the completion in 1869 of the nation's first Transcontinental Railroad. Deputy Secretary and Chinese American Christopher Lu and descendants of the railroad workers also took part in the ceremony at the Department of Labor headquarters in Washington, D.C.

CHINESE BROTHERS, AMERICAN SONS

A glass plaque commemorating their efforts now hangs alongside well-known figures in American labor history such as Cesar Chavez, Samuel Gompers and Bayard Rustin. Lu said the United States was beginning to "right an old wrong. These were immigrants who came to this country seeking a better life, and they had a chance to work on something really extraordinary. And then you had a nation that not only did not appreciate their efforts, but then led to exclusion after that."

Lisa Hsiao, a sixth-generation Chinese American, said the recognition had been long overdue. "Maybe implicitly [it's] a little bit of recognition of the injustice," she said. "The Chinese railroad workers were widely discriminated against. They were hired because nobody else would do the work."

Susan Yu said she took comfort in seeing her great-grandfather's efforts remembered in the halls of the U.S. government. "To me, that's quite meaningful in that it's a final acceptance."

Author's Note
regarding Cape Horn

WERE CHINESE WORKERS lowered in baskets to place explosive charges at Cape Horn? Debate has been furious among railroad enthusiasts and historians for decades. Many accounts, starting in the early twentieth century, told of Chinese workers hanging over sheer precipices in straw baskets to chip away holes for explosives. Once the fuse was lit, they signaled to be hastily drawn up to avoid the blast, and many would lose their lives when the basket was not drawn up fast enough. The idea of Chinese workers hanging from baskets to do such hazardous work created a powerful image and many drawings have been done depicting workers in such baskets. But there are no reports from engineers and no photographs of baskets being used during construction at Cape Horn.

However, a report from an unidentified traveling correspondent was published in a Massachusetts newspaper, the *Pittsfield Eagle,* on December 14, 1868. "The most thrilling scene that came under my observation was in the Sierra Nevada on the Central Pacific. Here on the side of a precipice 2,400 feet above the base, and the slope is steep that the Chinamen who did the work were let down in baskets, and in this position drilled holes and charged them in the side of the mountains. At one time there 460 of these charges connected by a fuse, exploded at one time. Masses of rock weighing many tons, fell to the bottom with terrific fury. When the debris had ceased to fall, the echoes were still reporting among the distant hills. So stunning was the shock that I would never willingly witness the like again."

In an 1869 tour book, a traveler reportedly was told, "When the roadbed was constructed around this point, the Chinese laborers who broke the first standing ground were held by ropes until firm footholds could be excavated in the rocky sides of the precipitous bluffs."

An 1869 article in *The Overland Monthly* based on witnesses described how workers "were suspended by ropes from above, the chain-bearers signaling to those holding the ropes, up and down, forward or back." One account described how workers sat on boson's chairs, flat seats of woven ropes like swings, and were let down the slope to prepare for drilling and blasting.

Gordon H. Chang, author of *Ghosts of Gold Mountain, The Epic Story of the Chinese Who Built the Transcontinental Railroad*, published in 2019, concludes that "though there are still questions about exactly where and when the baskets were used, the use of them by Chinese laborers in constructing the rail line at a perilous location in the Sierra cannot be dismissed as myth."

Afterword

I AM A seventy-year-old American of Chinese ancestry, and while I haven't often felt Chinese, in my life I have been reminded many times that I am Chinese, that I was, that I am different and that I and my family, painfully, did not "fit in." Perhaps, this was because of cultural differences or external forces or my own personality or my own lack of self-esteem or who knows what. Once, I viewed the discrimination of the Chinese and my experiences as not being equivalent to the discrimination of African Americans or other minorities in the United States. But I have learned from my research for this book, from my own unique life experiences, and from my own self-realization that the fundamental elements of fear, ignorance and arrogance are common to all such racial tragedies. No one is better than anyone else. To rank historical struggles by one's race is not purposeful, but respect is an absolute requirement.

In 2011, when I had the good fortune to retire early from a twenty-five-year human resources position at a local college, I decided to write a book about the Chinese experience in America. I understood that race had to be an integral part of the story of where we have been as a country, and where we need to go. I discovered that the Chinese of Kwangtung Province, the home of our father, had built the western, most treacherous part of the first Transcontinental Railroad. I further learned during my research that twenty percent of the miners during the California gold rush days were Chinese. I decided to write a story of two brothers, Li Chang and Li Yu, who could mirror somewhat my relationship with my older and only brother, John. I also wanted to showcase the importance of food, because few other cultures are as food-oriented as the Chinese, my family included. Another element to the book is a homage to my wife Jo Ann in the form of the never-ending love story between Li Yu and Wang Wei.

Let me start by declaring, I am the offspring of a "paper son," as are my brother and my three sisters. In the late 1920s, our father, Jimmy Lee Shew, born in Kwangtung Province in southern China and fleeing poverty, purchased (I suppose) someone else's identity papers. Those documents indicated he was a blood relative to Chinese Americans who had already received U.S. citizenship. This explained why our mother always told us that our last name was Lee instead of Shew. From the Chinese Exclusion Act of 1882, the first anti-immigrant act in U.S. history, all the way up to 1943, Congress enacted a series of exclusion laws that all-but ended Chinese immigration, the only ethnic group in the history of the United States to ever have been specifically denied entrance into the country.

I grew up in the 1950s in midtown St. Louis. There were few Chinese in St. Louis back then. Those we knew ran Chinese hand-laundries — six of them within a one-mile radius of our house. Our mother Rose was raised and worked at a downtown, Chinatown laundry run by her parents. In the mid-1960s, Chinatown, known as Hop Alley, was leveled and replaced by a baseball stadium. Our mother, one of whose sisters was sold by her parents, toiled long hours in the stifling heat, wielding a heavy 8-½ pound iron and pressing white shirts for white customers. She was so tired she often missed school.

Our mother was bright, intelligent and had a quick sense of humor. She never forgot a name or a birthday. She could remember the names of all of my wife's ten brothers and sisters, and their children's names, too. An articulate person, no one could tell that she had been forced to quit school after the ninth grade. She was married at fifteen. Her escape from the sweatshop conditions of her family's laundry was an arranged, loveless marriage with our father fifteen years older than she. Five children quickly followed in eight years. I was the youngest. Mother was a proud woman. I recall her saying, "I don't stand behind my husband; I walk side-by-side."

At the same time, mother knew her place. Since we didn't own a car, we headed downtown on the street car to obediently pay a fine at city hall for not having a lid on our garbage can.

"Say nothing," she told us. "This is a white man's world."

Kindergarten for me was a half-day morning at the public school. Starting first grade at a strict private school, the students could not go out for recess after lunch until they had finished their meal. The food was foreign to me, so the food that I could not trade or give away, I stuffed under my shirt or into my pants pockets and threw out in the alley adjoining the playground. Of course, later on I grew to enjoy chili, spaghetti and toasted cheese sandwiches, but never the beets served to us almost daily.

A not-so-humorous but poignant story was when in second or third grade, we were invited to a potluck at the school. We typically did not eat meat except when father cooked us grand meals on Sunday. In any case, we all wanted to "fit in," and mother decided to participate. She made a Cantonese dish of tomato, green pepper and beef in a black bean sauce. This particular food was usually reserved for Sunday's special meal. The families began eating a variety of cooked and cold foods on offer. Some time elapsed and not one person had even sampled the food which our mother had specially prepared. I can still recall the sadness in her face. She did not "fit in." When she turned her back, I quickly scooped up several servings of the tasty dish and gobbled them down. When she came back, she was delighted to see that some of her food had been eaten, and that made me happy too. As a plus, we later had a small platter of wonderful leftovers that evening.

Father worked as a waiter in a Chinese restaurant, which meant he was off work 1-½ days every two weeks. In those days, there was only a handful of sit-down Chinese restaurants. The one full day he was off, he cooked for the family. That was the only day of the week we had meat. Preparing that Sunday meal was how he showed his love for the family. Our enjoyment of that meal made him so very happy. To this day, the greatest compliment I can give to a Chinese restaurant we visit (Cantonese, please) is that "the food almost tastes as good as dad's."

Those were glorious meals of roast duck, roast pork, barbecued pork, Cantonese whole chicken, ground fish patties, yu-choy and bok choy, celery cabbage, bitter melon, Chinese okra, winter melon, seaweed and water cress soups, black mushrooms, Chinese sausage, jook, bean curd, shrimp in lobster/black bean sauce, etc. Sometimes he made luscious steamed barbecued pork buns (*char siu bao*). Fresh out of the steamer, he packed a dozen or so, wrapped them in a paper bag and he sent me off with them to two elderly Chinese men who owned the oldest laundry in the city. These "gentle" men would give me a couple dollars and a cold orange soda. Like Chinatown, their laundry, too, fell victim to urban renewal.

In college, I stayed up late, waiting for father to come home from work. Still smelling of chop suey, he'd cook a meal. Like Li Chang, father could make something out of nothing—and it was oh so tasty. We ate; we said nothing to each other. Later when mother and father moved into a government-subsidized senior housing community, he would prepare sweet and sour pork and chicken sub gum (two Americanized Chinese dishes) for the residents. Preparing a meal was father's way to "fit in" with his fellow seniors.

In my teen years, I was the only Asian in my high school. At a robust 5-foot-3 and weighing 108 pounds as I turned fourteen in late September of my freshman year, I tried out for the football team. I loved sports, but as I reflect upon those days, probably an equally important reason for doing so was an attempt to "fit in." It worked; I developed into a football player talented enough to receive a couple of partial athletic scholarships in football and another in soccer.

High school was a generally lonely experience. I was invited to only one party in high school — on the night of graduation. I didn't go. Still, I was able to "fit in" by being an athlete. Whether it was the in-crowd, the brainiacs, the nerds or whomever, I was accepted because of that. I was not invisible, not shunned, not demeaned because of sports. Martial arts and Bruce Lee movies were all the rage then, and that helped me "fit in" too, a bit. Well, maybe not. A senior high school yearbook photo had me in the school lunchroom, with the caption, "Why don't they ever have chop suey?"

When I was growing up, my brother John, now a retired graphic designer, was my rock. He would spend his whole weekly earnings from his newspaper route to take me to baseball games. We played endless games of baseball, basketball, football and even built a miniature 18-hole golf course in our backyard. Consequently, this book is dedicated to both my wife and to my brother. My three sisters are now retired: two as retired registered nurses (RNs), the oldest from service jobs. The brothers in the story are somewhat based upon my brother and me. In the beginning, Li Yu looks up to Li Chang; by the end of the book, Li Chang now looks up to his younger brother Li Yu. I still look up to my brother; perhaps, he looks up to me, also.

CHINESE BROTHERS, AMERICAN SONS

My wife Jo Ann tells me that in writing this book, as the Chinese brothers, Li Chang and Li Yu evolved into American sons, I have evolved into a new person. But it's not so simple. The work I did as a caseworker in family services, as an investigator enforcing state anti-discrimination laws, twenty-five years in human resources, and several years as a retail grocery manager and most importantly growing up Chinese (born in 1949) when there were very few Chinese in St. Louis, have shaped who I am. Whether it's being spat at a couple times during the Vietnam War, to the constant questions and comments to this day, "Where are you from? Your English is so good!" Or seeing a noose in someone's locker while investigating a racial discrimination charge. Or attempting to counsel a fourteen-year-old who had three children from separate fathers—I've seen a lot.

Growing up in a Chinese household, I was conditioned to be obedient, loyal and, at times, non-confrontational. It is common in the Chinese culture to not question authority, to not be problematic or opinionated. A defining moment while in human resources was when I heard an employee grievance on behalf of a new HR director. The director told me to remember that I was part of management and to make my decision accordingly, and I responded that my recommendation would be based on an objective investigation, board policies and administrative procedures. I was never asked to hear another grievance at the college. I did not "fit in" to the stereotype.

In 2016, I personally met thousands of voters running for state representative in a district not aligned with my political beliefs. I had frank discussions regarding healthcare, education, campaign ethics, labor issues, gun reform, reproductive rights, seniors, etc. My greatest anxiety was when speaking with labor union members in the trades—generally an all-white, male audience. They didn't think I was "one of them." I didn't "fit

ED SHEW

in." A retired union pipe-fitter confirmed my suspicions that many turned a deaf ear when I spoke. Nevertheless, what a rewarding experience! I gave voice to those unheard. Literally, two voters cried tears of joy. They told me that no one from my party affiliation had ever knocked on their doors.

In 1993, our dad died of heart complications at eighty-two (his papers said eighty). He had provided for us throughout, but I don't ever recall having even one conversation with him. He could barely speak English anyway. But he knew enough to proudly parade me through the kitchen of the Chinese restaurant he worked at, telling all who could hear, in his broken English, "My son plays football."

Our mother died one year later (only 69) of pancreatic cancer. At the end, all of her demons had vanished; she was full of good humor. She talked for hours with my wife of her childhood and her love for her children. Her loveless life with father was but a distant memory. My wife and I cared for mother for two months; she died in our home. She was not always there for her children—swept away by the demons she battled and the stomach-churning life experiences she withstood. But she was, at the end of her life, free.

I am very lucky to have a supportive wife. She is a retired Advanced Practice Nurse. In other words, she was like a doctor (assessing patients, prescribing medicine, going on hospital rounds, etc.), but she didn't get paid like a doctor. When we married in 1977, an interracial marriage, we constantly received stares when we walked hand-in-hand. We have two adult sons and three grandchildren (10, 7 and 4); all are healthy and sports-minded. Our oldest son has a PhD and is employed as a conservation program manager at a non-profit, the youngest is a lab supervisor at a university medical school.

In 2013, we had a change in ministers at our church who

emphasized social justice. Now being retired and working on this book, I became more active in social causes, thanks to Beth Griffin and Tim Gardner. I recall the first time I was at the state capitol, a TV crew was filming the health care rally. I was afraid I might be on the evening news with these "rabble-rousers." A month later, I was blocking a street and the exit from the legislators' garage urging them to pass health care reform. In addition, four times a year, I'm now engaged in lobbying activities in our state capitol, mainly about health care. Initially, when I was part of a group visiting a legislator, I was silent and just nodded approvingly. Now, I'm a team leader when meeting legislators. I found my niche; I grew to "fit in."

My wife and I have done some work with an environmental group to protect our natural landscape from development. My wife is active in environmental causes at both church and the region.

Recently, I was asked, "Don't you think you've been helped by being Asian?" I guess, if that means being denied employment and housing and being stopped seven times for traffic violations in my life—and not once being given a warning, always given a ticket. Well, I just smiled.

In the 1970s, our country had just gotten out of the Vietnam War. There was no cable TV back then, but on the evening news—every day—we were bombarded with reports of war atrocities with the death toll of U.S. soldiers rising every day.

My brother, just discharged from the Army, and I began looking for an apartment. We weren't picky. We saw a sign, "vacancy, apartment available." We inquired. The apartment manager told us nothing was available. Suspicious, yes, but we shrugged our shoulders and went to the next apartment complex about 100 feet away. We got an apartment there. And guess who had the apartment next door? My current wife Jo Ann. And so

I can say, "Because of housing discrimination based on being Chinese, I met my future wife." So, yes, I can say, at least one time, I was helped by being Chinese. We've been happily married over 42 years. I "fit in." We "fit in."

How fitting that 2019 was the 150th anniversary of the completion of the first Transcontinental Railroad. With this book, I hope to help people understand the racism and the demonization that the Chinese went through, all the hardships and struggles they endured when searching for gold and building the railroad. While not America's finest moment in the treatment of the Chinese, it was a defining moment in American history. This railroad laid the foundation for the extraordinary economic prosperity enjoyed by the United States in the years that followed.

The sacrifices of the Chinese railroad workers helped to link this country together in a way that has allowed generations of Americans to dream of even greater achievements and lay down their own tracks toward the future.

Like the Li brothers, I am proud to be of Chinese heritage and to be an American.

BIBLIOGRAPHY

Books/Videos for Research

Ambrose, Stephen E.; **Nothing Like It in the World: The Men Who Built the Transcontinental Railroad 1863-1869**; © 2000; Ambrose-Tubbs, Inc.; Simon & Schuster paperbacks edition 2005, New York, NY

Asian Americans: Gold Rush Era to 1890s, University of California, 2005, part of the California Cultures project

Author Unknown; (The Chinese Peasant's Lament, my title); **With a Single Step: Stories in the Making of America**; an exhibition at the Museum of Chinese Americans (MOCA); September 1, 2009-December 31, 2020, New York City Chinatown

Bain, David Howard; **Empire Express: Building the First Transcontinental Railroad**; © 1999; Viking Press, a member of Penguin Putnam, Inc., New York, NY

Boessenecker, John; **Gold Dust & Gunsmoke: Tales of Gold Rush Outlaws, Gunfighters, Lawmen, and Vigilantes**; © 1999; John Wiley & Sons, Inc.

Chang, Gordon; **Ghosts of Gold Mountain**; © 2019; Houghton, Mifflin, Harcourt, Boston & New York

Chang, Iris; **The Chinese in America**; © 2003; Penguin Group, New York, NY

Durbin, William; **The Journal of Sean Sullivan: A Transcontinental Railroad Worker**; © 1999; Scholastic Inc., New York, NY

Fraser, Mary Ann; **Ten Mile Day and the Building of the Transcontinental Railroad**; © 1993; Henry Holt and Company, LLC, New York, NY

Helgeland, Brian; (Video) **42**; © 2013

Hill, Michael; Duty; Honor and Amends; **St. Louis Post-Dispatch**; May 11, 2015; p. A12.

Kingston, Maxine Hong; **China Men**; © 1980; Random House, Inc.

Kowalewski, Michael (editor); **Gold Rush: A Literary Exloration**; © 1997; California Council for the Humanities; Heyday Books, Berkeley, CA

Ling, Huping; **Surviving on the Gold Mountain: A History of Chinese American Women and Their Lives**; © 1998; State University of New York Press, Albany, N.Y.

McClain, Charles J.; **In Search of Equality: The Chinese Struggle against Discrimination in Nineteenth-Century America**; © 1994; University of California Press

Mones, Nicole; **The Last Chinese Chef**; © 2007; Houghton Mifflin Company, New York, NY

Morn, Mary Katherine; Shelton, Jason; (a song) **The Fire of Commitment**; © 2001

Perl, Lila; **To the Golden Mountain: The Story of the Chinese Who Built the Transcontinental Railroad**; © 2003; Benchmark Books Marshall Cavenish, Tarrytown, NY

PBS Home Video; **Transcontinental Railroad**; © 2003; WGBH Educational Foundation; A Hidden Hill Productions film for American Experience, written and produced by Mark Zwonitzer; directed by Mark Zwonitzer and Michael Chin; © 2003; http://www.pbs.org/wgbh/amex/tcrr/peopleevents/p_cprr.html

PBS Home Video; **Becoming American: The Chinese Experience**; http://www.pbs.org/becomingamerican/ap_prog1.html

See, Lisa; **Dreams of Joy**; © 2011 by Lisa See; Random House, Inc., New York

See, Lisa; **Shanghai Girls**; © 2009 by Lisa See and 2010; Random House, Inc., New York

Steiner, Stan; **Fusang: The Chinese Who Built America**; © 1979; Harper & Row, Publishers, Inc., New York, NY

Stevenson, Bryan; **Just Mercy**; © 2014; Spiegel & Grau, an imprint of Random House, a division of Penguin Random House LLC, New York, NY

Twain, Mark; **The Adventures of Huckleberry Finn**; © 1884

Winokur, W. William; (Video) **The Perfect Game**; © 2009

Wong, Ken; **Gold Spike Rites Snub Chinese Rail Workers**; The Chinese American Journal; Volume 3, Number 20, May 14, 1969

Yep, Laurence; **The Journal of Wong Ming-Chung: A Chinese Miner**; © 2000; Scholastic Inc., New York, NY

Yep, Lawrence; **Dragon's Gate**; © 1993; HarperCollins Children's Books, a division of HarperCollins Publishers, New York, NY

Yin; **Brothers**; © 2006; Philomel Books, a division of Penguin Putnam Books for Young Readers, New York, NY

Yin; **Coolies**; © 2001; Philomel Books, a division of Penguin Putnam Books for Young Readers, New York, NY

Web Sites for Additional Research

Abraham, Terry; **No Tickee, No Washee: Sympathetic Representation of the Chinese in Humor**; July 2003; http://webpages.uidaho.edu/special-collections/papers/notickee.htm

Basu, Moni; **In Rare Apology, House Regrets Exclusionary Laws Targeting Chinese**; http://inamerica.blogs.cnn.com/2012/06/19/in-rare-apology-house-regrets-exclusionary-laws-targeting-chinese/

Chinese Traditions and Culture; http://www.chinese-traditions-and-culture.com/shopping-in-china.html

Fuchs, Chris; **150 Years Ago, Chinese Railroad Workers Staged the Era's Largest Labor Strike;** June 21, 2017; http://www.nbcnews.com/news/asian-america/150-years-ago-chinese-railroad-workers-staged-era-s-largest-n774901

Guangdong Province; http://www.chinatoday.com/city/guangdong.htm

Jia, Elizabeth; **Congress Makes Formal Apology for Chinese Exclusion Act;** http://www.wusa9.com/news/article/222217/187/Congress-Makes-Formal-Apology-For-Chinese-Exclusion-Act

Kaiser, Kathy; **Sweet Be Thy Slumber: Historic Cemeteries Provide Contemplation and Beauty;** http://www.frontrangeliving.com/escapes/cemeteries.htm

Lalire, Gregory; **Baseball in the West;** http://www.historynet.com/baseball-in-the-west-2.htm

Lincoln and the Railroad; http://www.uprr.com/aboutup/history/lincoln/lincoln_rr/index.shtml

Pierre, M.D., Joe; **When Racism Motivates Violence;** https://www.psychologytoday.com/blog/psych-unseen/201506/when-racism-motivates-violence

Rock Springs Massacre, https://en.wikipedia.org/?title=Rock_Springs_massacre

Sherrard-Smith, Gavin; **Daily Mail;** http://www.dailymail.co.uk/news/article-496844/My-felt-like-As-British-teacher-faces-40-lashes-man-speaks-out.html

Sierra Nevada Geotourism Mapguide (300 Chinese deaths at Cape Horn); **Cape Horn and the Transcontinental Railroad;** https://www.sierranevadageotourism.org/content/cape-horn-and-the-transcontinental-railroad/sie3CF4CAC0C3AA88FF9

Stanford University; **Chinese Railroad Workers in North America Project,** http://web.stanford.edu/group/chineserailroad/cgi-bin/wordpress/

Sullivan, Andrew; **The Strange Hush of Freezing to Death,** The Dish, April 29, 2013

The Chinese Exclusion Act; https://www.broadwayworld.com/bwwtv/article/PBS-American-Experience-Special-THE-CHINESE-EXCLUSION-ACT-to-Have-National-PBS-Broadcast-Debut-May-29-20180508

The First Transcontinental Railroad; http://www.tcrr.com/

The History Place; **Irish Potato Famine;** © 2000; http://www.historyplace.com/worldhistory/famine/america.htm

Voting Rights and Citizenship; http://www1.cuny.edu/portal_ur/content/voting_cal/americans_chinese.html

Waite, Kevin; **Here's the Shameful History of California's KKK You Probably Didn't Know;** http://www.rawstory.com/2015/10/heres-the-shameful-history-of-californias-kkk-you-probably-didnt-know/

Walkerson, James; **The Life of a 49er in the California Gold Rush;** http://www.shiftins.com/content/california_gold_rush.aspx

Wang, Han Si Lo; **Descendants of Chinese Laborers Reclaim Railroad's History,** http://www.npr.org/blogs/codeswitch/2014/05/10/311157404/descendants-of-chinese-laborers-reclaim-railroads-history

Wise, Tim; **Racism, Violence and the Irony of Stereotypes;** http://www.timwise.org/2011/08/racism-violence-and-the-irony-of-stereotypes/

About The Author

Ed Shew was born in 1949 in St. Louis, Missouri (USA), the son of Chinese parents. His peasant father immigrated from Guangdong province in southern China. His mother, whose parents ran a Chinese hand laundry, was born in St. Louis' Chinatown (also known as Hop Alley), which was leveled in the mid-1960s for construction of the St. Louis Cardinals baseball stadium. Ed grew up in the city of St. Louis and is married with two sons. Moving to be closer to some of their grandchildren, he and his wife Jo Ann now live just west of St. Louis in St. Charles County, Missouri.

They visited China in 2012. Ed's lasting memory is from rural southern China, witnessing the breathtaking natural scenery of the mountain-side, jade- and emerald-colored, terraced rice fields. They have been farmed for centuries and many still with plow-pulling water buffalo.

In his spare time, Ed is engaged in social justice activities for his church and the community. In addition, he's a devoted fan of the St. Louis Cardinals baseball team.